THREADING THE NEEDLE

ROMA SERIES BOOK THREE

GABRIEL VALJAN

Winter Goose
Publishing

Winter Goose Publishing
2701 Del Paso Road, 130-92
Sacramento, CA 95835

www.wintergoosepublishing.com
Contact Information: info@wintergoosepublishing.com

Threading the Needle

First Edition, October 2013
ISBN: 978-0-9894792-1-9

Cover Art by Winter Goose Publishing
Typeset by Michelle Lovi

Published in the United States of America

ROMA SERIES

By Gabriel Valjan

Book 1 – Roma, Underground (2/2012)
Book 2 – Wasp's Nest (11/2012)
Book 3 – Threading the Needle (10/2013)

For Claudio Ferrara & Dean Hunt

*La vita va vissuta e non guardata—viene a volte da alcuni
rimuginata, riflettuta, scritta*

L'Italia è l'antica terra del dubbio.

Italy is the ancient homeland of doubt.

—*Massimo D'Azeglio*

1

This was a bad idea from the start.

Isidore Farrugia sat in a car, watching Bianca from across Via Manzoni. He was off-duty, out of his jurisdiction, and doing the best and worst of all possible things: doing a favor for a friend.

But his gut was telling him this was a bad, bad idea.

She said that she had to meet someone with information, someone who wanted to meet her in person. Not good. Bianca had explained that in the past her drop-offs were anonymous and in public places. A postal box. A newsstand. Never face to face. The ideal was through the computer. Remote and anonymous.

None of them could forget Loki. None of them had forgotten Rendition.

Bianca wouldn't say what the information was and when Farrugia asked, all she said was that her contact was a man. He didn't ask her how she knew. Farrugia knew better than to expect a straight answer from a woman. The female brain was wired differently, processing nuances below masculine capability, and the female heart was attuned to the unknown frequency of feminine intuition.

She ordered something from her table outside.

Nobody seemed suspicious.

The waiter delivered her drink. She had ordered something sweet. Rabarbaro? Women and their sweet drinks.

Two university-age kids were sizing her up for flirtation.

Her contact, she said, did not know what she looked like. If this someone was expecting an American in jeans or some gaudy ensemble that American women thought was fashion, then he would be in for a surprise. Bianca fit into Milan with her Aspesi turtleneck, Alessandra

Colombo leather jacket with the rose-accent, ruffle fringe, and a pair of Tod's. He saw that she sensed the two amateur Casanovas, turned her head and dismissed them. Quite remarkable, since she was wearing sunglasses.

That must be him.

Definitely an American. Down the block, about to turn the corner onto Via Manzoni.

He was walking fast, hands in pockets. No messenger bag, no bag at all, so maybe this wasn't him, despite what Farrugia's gut was saying. A few meters behind him, two other men followed. Matching camel jackets, matching haircuts. The man in front peered over his shoulder.

This must be him. Farrugia knew that worried expression.

Bianca hadn't seen him yet. No time to call her cell. Her contact was early-twenties, handsome with a nice navy jacket, although from the looks of him he'd had little sleep for a few nights. He glanced again over his shoulder.

The other two behind him picked up their pace. It was definitely him.

This was a bad idea from the start.

Farrugia opened up the car door. The car was a small rental and climbing in was like putting a sardine back into the metal tin. No typical American could fit in that automobile, and he knew the stubborn strip of fat around his midsection was what made his extraction an act for Houdini or Chaplin. The next risk was crossing the street and not getting killed by a real car or grazed by an angry Vespa.

The two tails on Bianca's man had that experienced stalking gait. Several notches up from street vermin. Farrugia was thinking contract killers, possibly with a military background. Hair was short and they weren't neo-Nazis. They were lean, looked foreign, and moved with precision. A career soldier's walk was never erased from neurological memory. Their jackets were relatively short, so that might mean no shotgun, unless one of them had a sawed-off for the maximum amount of spray while his partner had the handgun for the final shot, usually to the head.

Farrugia thought all of this in the seconds it took to negotiate one car horn and one silent obscenity from behind fast-moving glass.

He was on the divider in the middle of Via Manzoni when Bianca saw him.

She stood up and both their eyes drifted to the fast-walking man. Farrugia had hoped she wouldn't do that. That is, stand up. Everybody knew everybody now.

The two men were almost there. His Beretta Raffica was ready.

The contact walked up to her, turned her shoulders so her back was to his two trackers. Air-kiss to her right cheek, air-kiss to her left. Pause. His hands slid down her hips. He said something to her, kissed her on the lips, then ran inside Bar Gadda.

What the . . .

The two in pursuit graduated from walk to run. They got into the bar before the door closed. Farrugia unzipped his jacket and withdrew his gun. Instinct. He didn't think about the traffic after the divider. He ran. There was a squeal of rubber. Farrugia realized that he still had functional legs when he reached the pavement's gray flagstones. Horns blared behind him, but he focused on the commotion inside the bar in front of him.

He slid through the door, eyes searching, and out of reflex said, "Stay calm. I am Commissario Isidore Farrugia." The customers couldn't have cared less once they saw the Beretta. Their eyes and a few of their arms pointed the way out back. With his adrenaline flowing as it was, he wouldn't remember much of what he saw, but would always remember the old lady crossing herself and calling upon the saints and the Virgin. He did the same in his mind.

A restaurant kitchen was always a well-lit trap for a confrontation. Cops and bad guys. Rats or roaches and the health inspector. Illegals and Immigration Services. The Albanians and the Romanians made way for him and pointed. The broken plates crinkled as he stepped on the shards. The chef looked scared with a huge knife in his hand. Farrugia was trying not to look frightened with the pistol in his. Almost thirty years as a cop, pension calculations and the whisper of mortality moved through his head. The Beretta had two settings: three-round burst or single fire. His was set to single fire, and each round would count.

Ahead he spotted the streak of navy blue and then camel. Hunted and hunter. Then the metallic slam of the back door flung open to crash against a hard wall. There was some indistinct yelling. Farrugia's eyes took it all in while he calmed his heart down with deep belly breaths and moved through the kitchen. His belt was tight. He promised himself that he would lose the stomach if he lived through the day.

The busboy on Farrugia's right said, *"Vicolo cieco."*

Dead end. That door would make him an easy target for two potentially armed men on the other side. He approached the door. He peeked through the sliver of light, since the door had returned home on its hinges. The busboy was right. A wall a few meters to the left, a large, fragrant metal dumpster against it, left you with no choice but a hard right turn and a fast run down an indeterminate alley out to Via Manzoni.

The American didn't know that. He had turned left. Arms and legs appeared and Farrugia heard pleading.

The saints might not help him, but the Virgin had always been kind. He gripped the gun, breathed in, and trusted his eyes and trigger finger to think for him. In through the door and outside.

Too late.

Man One fired a single shot into the American's chest. Man Two fired the headshot. Farrugia faced two automatics now turned on him, and the only thing he could do was resort to his lame academy training.

"Police. Put your weapons down."

In this two-against-one dialogue their likely reply is to shoot him, knowing that at his fastest he could wound only one of them.

A choked siren, the screech of one blue-and-white cop car, its silent blue twirling lights now blocked the alley from Via Manzoni. Farrugia saw the first man's eyes look leftward again. No weapons had gone down.

No concession. Farrugia was the apex of the triangle with his gun, and these two were the base angles pointing theirs at him. Unequal . . . unlikely he'd survive if they shoot.

The car doors down the alley opened and closed. There was a squelch of walkie-talkie exchange. The siren lights played like a rave-party color on the walls.

Farrugia repeated himself. "Weapons down."

Another leftward look. The second man lowered his gun. Farrugia almost breathed.

The gun went off.

The first man had shot the second in the head and, as Farrugia was about to step forward and pull his trigger, put the barrel into his own mouth.

The two cops walking down the alley stopped when the shot went off.

Four gunshots can have a way of ruining a drink. Four.

The orange zest, the hypnotic cardamom and the other curatives in Bianca's drink suddenly turned sour. Two shots might be a matter of syntax, like a judicious comma and then the full-stop period. Or they could be a call-and-response exchange. But the second set of shots, Farrugia, her contact, and two suspects made four men.

One of those shots may have been for Farrugia.

She had to know before the other cops came. There were already sirens in the distance, she couldn't tell whose. Here in Milan, ambulances and police cars sounded the same to her, like the European starling with their *nee-nah nee-nah* through the ancient streets. But within minutes Via Manzoni would be covered with screaming sirens, the smell of rubber, bright lights, a cacophony of voices, a multitude of colors, and every type of police, from authoritative uniform to the suited support staff to process the crime. There would be tape to cordon off the bodies, tape to section off each part of the bar and the path to the denouement in the alley, and tape to identify the section where the witnesses had been herded off for questioning.

She was worried about witnesses recalling the American embracing a woman. She was worried whether any surveillance cameras in the shops or on top of the traffic lights might have recorded Farrugia's transit across the street, his momentary interest in the future victim. She was worried whether any surveillance cameras had captured her.

But she was most worried about Farrugia.

Down the street, a man in an eco-fluorescent uniform and ear protection was spray-cleaning the sidewalk with pressurized water from his *l'agevolatore*, a moveable, jointed steel arm on top of a truck. A policeman ran down the street and asked him to stop his work. The streets can remain dirty for a few more hours for the sake of preserving the crime scene. The imposing *l'agevolatore* stopped. The water stopped. Everything stopped.

She had to move.

Navy-blue cars with red pinstripes—the *carabinieri*—began to arrive as she cut through the crowd. She expected to see women making the sign of the cross and men bypassing the five wounds of Christ to simply kiss their thumbs as a way of kissing the Cross of Christ and acknowledging death. She had seen Italian-Americans do that thousands of times back home. Not here in Milan. She heard murmurs of inquiry, exchanges of speculation, and the confident assertion from someone that three men were dead. She flowed with the crowd to the open mouth of the alley, her head bowed in respect.

She saw Farrugia.

He was speaking to someone from the *Omicidi*, the Homicide Squad. He was visibly unnerved, but unharmed. She surprised herself by saying, "Thank God."

There's was a smaller crowd moving out of an old-style *carrelli* on Line One, a street tram like the ones in San Francisco. The street was blocked off at both ends.

She needed to call Dante.

She decided on the nearby metro, the Montenapoleone stop. That would lead her anywhere that was away from the noise, away from detection. She would have a chance to think, collect, and determine what was on the jump-key he had slipped into her pocket during that surprise kiss.

She would never forget that—not so much for the kiss, or that he was handsome and kissed well. But that he was young, terribly young, and now dead.

2

"Yes, she is here," Dante said into his cell phone, eyeing her as he spoke. "Gennaro, how can I know what she knows if I just got in? Give me a chance. Let me get lunch, talk to her, and I'll tell you what I know after I know it."

Dante was infusing his Italian with broad, reassuring vowels to soothe Gennaro. He was always polite enough not to let himself or the other party get too excited. He had already heard reports of the shooting before Bianca called him, but he hadn't known Farrugia was involved until she told him he was uninjured. He had dropped a quick note on Gennaro's desk, and then dashed back to his apartment. Bianca was already there when he arrived.

The apartment on the third floor was worth the steep rent. Bianca's decision in décor was simple soothing colors of white, some slate gray and bamboo brown, and occasional forest green. The Zen elegance and simplicity was their sanctuary and antidote to the city's frenetic energy.

Gennaro was still venting in his ear. He put his hand over the receiver and switched to English. "How are you doing?"

"I'm fine," she answered, putting some ice cubes into a glass of water.

He had to admit she did look fine, though she had never worn her emotions on the outside.

Gennaro took a momentary pause, and he slipped in, "Farrugia? Is he okay?"

"I told you, Dante," she said, "he's fine."

Dante winced and held up his index finger to let her know that he'd be one minute more.

Gennaro did not believe Farrugia was fine. "We are calling it the Manzoni disaster. It was a disaster for Farrugia since his weapon is now with Ballistics and his dust jacket, his entire career, will go to the Ministry of Internal Affairs. You know the Viminale are experts at cracking nuts. Alessandro is out of the office calling in whatever favors he can."

Before Gennaro could build up momentum, Dante said, "Thanks. I'll see you later," and snapped his cell shut.

"So," he said, "how are you doing?"

"Already told you. I'm fine." She sipped from her glass of cold water. His eyes followed her hands and the glass. There was no sign of a tremor. He knew that she noticed—she noticed everything. Her hands placed the glass down softly onto a coaster on the tiny table against the wall of the tiny kitchen. "I'm fine," she repeated, but preferred to remain standing.

"You must be. Three people are dead and your hands aren't even shaking. Care to tell me what happened?"

"Dante, don't start. Are you suggesting I'm cold as the ice in the glass?"

"Clinical, not cold, there's a difference." He'd much rather play good cop than bad, but he needed to know what happened. He also needed her to open up about it, both for his sake and for hers.

"Fine. I'm a clinical bitch then. You don't seem to think I'm clinical in bed."

"What does sex have to do with it? And I didn't call you a bitch. Stop dodging the issue. I want to know what happened."

"You didn't call me a bitch, but it was implied. Besides, you just talked to Gennaro. You know what happened."

"And now I'm talking to you. Please tell me what happened. You were there. Gennaro wasn't."

"What is there to tell you, Dante?"

"What would there be to tell? Let's try . . . a young kid is dead, two other men are dead, and Farrugia is up to his neck in shit. I'm worried for him."

"I see, you're more worried about Farrugia than your girlfriend? I told

Farrugia not to get involved, but he insisted." She took another sip, ice clinking. "He'll manage."

Dante threw up his hands, and then yanked the chair out from the table. The legs shuddered across the floor.

He glared at her. "Let me remind you that if it wasn't for Farrugia, you would've been dead in Boston. Let me add to that simple fact another: had Farrugia not been there today . . . it's what, one forty-five now?" He tapped the face of his watch. "Correction, it is one forty-six . . . you would be inside a body bag at the morgue right now with that kid and his two killers."

"Stop being dramatic."

"Dramatic? I'm being clinical."

"Fuck you, Dante."

Dante was silent. The echoes of his own voice still rang in his ears. They sounded more like an interrogation. Bianca was not one to open up in the best of times. Confrontation would only close her down more. His hand swept the worry lines from his forehead and he clapped his hands. "Let's start over. I'm sorry. Let us sit down and talk this through."

She took her chair slowly. He remained standing. Dominant and submissive.

"First, how do you expect me not to be upset? You go off and rendez-vous with this kid and you don't tell me. Not a word. I'm at work when I get all this shit dumped on me. That's how I find out. My girlfriend is on the other side of the city where there are gunshots, three dead bodies with a friend of mine who is now looking at his career possibly going down the toilet."

Her face registered nothing. "You're repeating yourself. You already said Farrugia was in trouble. It's not like I was having an affair. You don't seem too mad at Farrugia."

"No, you aren't having an affair but why is it that I still feel like some-one got fucked? Why is it I feel like it was me—first by you and then by him? You're wrong, I am mad at him. But you're my priority. I'll deal with him later."

"You'll deal with Farrugia?" she said with a smirk.

He ignored the insult for the attempt to change the subject that it was. "Don't think I won't. But this isn't about him right now. This is about you. This is about us."

She made an abrupt sound in her throat. "You came because I called you. I didn't ask you to. I'm just fine."

"You're kidding me, right? Yeah, I came because you called me. Think I'm mad now? Imagine me if I had found out all of this after the fact. You know what? Next time I'll forward your call to my voicemail. See how you like that."

He had moved his hands to the top of his chair. They were white knuckled from wringing the wood. He then sat down, giving up the dominant position. "Let's start over again. You went and met this kid. Who is he?"

She pushed her chair back some. He slid both the glass of water and the coaster across the table. A habit from years of doing interrogations. At least now he was good cop.

Dante Allegretti, forensic accountant, was used to questioning asshole accountants who thought they were clever, used to the supremely arrogant corporate douche bags with combo JD and MBA degrees. But this was Bianca Nerini, and she was a better forensic expert than he'd ever be in several lifetimes. She was also the woman he loved.

"He is . . . he *was* a kid from Bicocca with information," she said.

"University of Milan?" The new campus in the old Pirelli district was known for its research facilities. "What kind of information?"

"I don't know." She took another sip. The ice made a gnawing sound.

"I don't get it. Something had to entice you, Bianca. How did the two of you meet? I mean . . . how did the two of you find each other?"

"I found him." She paused. "Remember, recently the Guardia di Finanza received some helicopters?"

"Yeah, that was a few months ago. So what? The Aviation Service uses them for border control, and they're supposed to be our brand of homeland security. So what?"

Bianca seemed to weigh her words. "I was looking at the company who manufactured the helicopters, the contracts and—"

His hand went up. "Please, tell me none of that has anything to do with Rendition."

"It doesn't," she replied, lips tight. "It doesn't."

"No Loki, no phantom messages, or game-show clues?"

"Nothing. Will you listen to me? As I was saying, I started looking at the contracts and started exploring and found a name. I went elsewhere and started researching and found the same name, but this time this same person was disguising company-confidential information and publishing it on his blog under an assumed name."

"I see. When you say the 'same name,' you're talking about your dead friend, and when you say 'researching' you really mean that you hacked into the manufacturer's computers and reviewed their financials. And, when you say, 'assumed name' you mean like the name 'Bianca Nerini.'"

She glared at him. *Bastard* was on her face.

He knew that he had crossed the line. But, dammit, he had to get her to open up.

"Do you want me to explain, or not?" she said.

"I'm sorry, Bianca. My bad. So, this kid . . . was he an employee, possibly an intern at the helicopter company? Gennaro said that he was twenty-three. That's tragically young. How would he get access to sensitive information? And if he were blogging this information somehow, why would he want to meet with you?"

She cleared her throat. "You're right. Whoever wanted to stop him probably could've found him by tracking his ISP address. But they didn't right away."

"What did they do?"

"His blog disappeared. Literally. Completely gone. I didn't have time to determine who shut it down. I hacked back into the company's computer system and saw that he was there too, hacked in and still downloading files. He was doing it remotely, like I do, probably from a cyber café. Kid had a natural aptitude. He was smarter this time and I think he left less of a footprint, so whoever shut him down thought he had stopped. They must've thought they spooked him enough."

"What was he doing this second time you went into the system?"

"Duplicating files, collecting data. When his blog got shut off I could sense he knew somebody was onto him and it was a matter of time."

"Sensed? A matter of time? You sensed he was in trouble, I see. Maybe he didn't pay his service provider?"

"I checked that. He paid his bills on time."

"Of course. ISP address or not, you know who he is. Who he was."

"Yes."

"You just told me at the beginning you didn't know if he was an intern or an employee."

"He was an intern."

His hands were on the table in a way that asked for her hands. He took them, his hands stroking hers. Dante was looking down at their hands together and then his eyes looked up into her eyes.

"You know I love you, but please . . . be straight with me. If I ask you a question then please answer it. Don't give me half-truths, shaded statements, or some bizarre slanted interpretation of what you think I'm asking you. Don't string me along. I'm on your side. We've been through too much already to be playing these kinds of games. Okay?"

"Okay." She pulled her hands away.

"Good. First, who was this kid? What is his name?"

"You know his name, Dante. You just talked to Gennaro."

"A phone conversation and nearly a full glass of water later and I still know less from you than I do from Gennaro. I want to hear it from you."

"Charles Brooks. He's an American, studying law and economics at Bicocca, interdisciplinary studies. He comes from a military family. His father was in the Armored Division. Charlie was working on a minor in natural sciences. Atmospheric science. As an intern, he was working on an ethics committee for the manufacturer, Adastra, and doing their project estimates and reviewing proposals."

"And what did he say to you when you two met?"

"Not much. It happened so fast, Dante. He must've known he'd been followed. I stood up to say hello. He might've said hello, but then he went inside the bar and then . . . well, you know the rest."

"I know the rest from there. Let's back up a little. How did you two come to meet? Who contacted whom? Who decided the place?"

"I called him. The place came later. My idea."

"You called him?"

"Why is that so hard to believe?"

Dante decided to play a hunch. "Oh, I don't know. My blog disappears. I think someone is onto me. Weird noises in the night start making me paranoid, and then a strange woman phones me up and suggests we meet. It's not the first thing I would do."

She closed her eyes and her hands made a mask around her nose. She rubbed her face. She wasn't wiping away any tears. Dante knew she was thinking.

"I had to prove myself to him. So I hacked his computer while he was on it. I showed him projects I had worked on with Rendition without telling him about Rendition. My purpose was to show him I had forensic skills and that he could trust me to help him take his data to the next level. After giving him a visual of my work, I directed him to a payphone where I called him. I asked him to go to that payphone only if he trusted me. He did. We arranged the meet."

"The Bar Gadda on Via Manzoni?"

"Yeah, the Bar Gadda."

"What about the kiss?"

She tried not to look surprised. "I don't know. It threw me off. Are you going to ask me if I enjoyed it?"

"Not at all, but I'll ask if he said anything to you. Did he?"

"No, I don't think so. How could he? He must've seen that he'd been followed. He might've said hello before he ducked into the bar and then . . ."

Consistent answers without much deviation.

"He gets killed," Dante said, "I know the rest from there, but here is what I think. You are sitting outside of Gadda. Nice day, nice weather. You start enjoying a drink. Maybe you look at the watch, wondering why he is late because women are allowed to be late but men usually aren't, especially American men, who aren't hampered by a Mediterranean loose sense of time. You look up, see Farrugia and think, 'Oh, shit. Something is wrong. Farrugia is coming. What the hell could this mean?' You look or Farrugia looks down the street . . . doesn't matter which of you looked first, because you see the boy and you know he has company. Your boy walks up to you. Maybe he says, 'I've been followed. Sorry,' or maybe he says, 'I'm scared. I've got to use the bathroom. Be right back,' but he knows he isn't coming back. Your boy gets killed out back by two experienced killers. I say 'experienced' because they killed him with a one-two tap." Dante pointed to his chest then his head.

Then he stopped and let her feel his stare a moment. "As for that kiss . . . I'm not jealous, not at all, Bianca. I'm thinking two things. One, a kiss is a nice distraction. Two, if I was a boy and I knew I was about to die, I'd kiss a beautiful woman, too."

Pause and stare.

"Why do you keep calling him 'boy'?"

Dante stood up, looked about for his suit jacket. He stretched out his legs and then leaned over and said into her ear. "I should be more respectful. He wasn't a boy. Young though he was, he was quite a man."

Her head flinched back. "What the hell is that supposed to mean?"

"He saved your life, Bianca. Your man made sure to turn your back to his killers so that they wouldn't recognize you. You were facing the street. Only the wait staff would've been able to identify you later, but you left quickly, so that's unlikely. None of them could've gotten a good look at you since they were inside. Your server only saw you twice, once to get your order and then again to serve you. The only thing he probably knows about you is the glass of Zucca and those sunglasses of yours. They helped you, too, but the kid's rushing inside distracted the killers from you: that saved your life. They went inside because they had to. And . . . and, if he had sat down to enjoy a drink, the nice weather, and the beautiful woman, you would be in a body bag right now. They would've killed you but they didn't kill you. They killed him. He was cornered in the alley and killed next to the garbage."

Dante kissed her on the cheek. "I owe him a lot, and at least I can give him the respect of calling him a man."

Dante walked away, stopped at the rack and put on his jacket. He knew that he was an asshole for getting the last word, but so was she. While buttoning his jacket, he said, "I'm going back to the office. I'll see how Farrugia is. He'll get a piece of my mind *after* I hear what he has to say."

Polite pause.

"You know I can't help but think that if I were him, Bianca, and I came out of hiding, because I trusted you with my life, I'd say something, bring that very special person that you are something . . . something besides 'Hello' and a kiss."

Bianca had her arms across her chest and she stared at him. "Why do you say that? Gennaro say something?"

"No, Gennaro just let me know what ballistics and forensics have up to now. The kid's name hasn't even been confirmed yet. Farrugia's report isn't even typed up yet, but I got the gist of that from the conversation. Gennaro didn't say a thing, but you did."

"What do you mean?" she asked like a petulant teenager with an attitude.

"That you don't trust me enough to tell me the complete truth. I need to go. I'll find a quick lunch on my way back. I'll be home later.

You know that you and Farrugia should talk at some point. I suggest you go to him before he comes to you."

A good five minutes after Dante left, Bianca threw the glass against the wall and watched the dwindling ice cubes skitter across the kitchen tiles. She started to cry with simple tears and then with heavy and jagged sobs.

Gunned down next to garbage.

She got a kid killed and she knew that she hadn't told Dante what Brooks had said or what he had given her. And he let her know that he knew, too.

Dante was right, damn him.

She still hadn't learned to trust him. Or trust anyone.

3

Alessandro looked sideways at him. Gennaro was sitting in Dante's chair at Dante's desk, finishing off his lunch, the white paper splayed open, with the grease of the departed sandwich shiny under the light.

Alessandro fed another pencil into the electric sharpener.

"Must you do that?" asked Gennaro in a paternal voice.

"Sorry, Chief. Habit, you know."

"So is picking your nose and adjusting yourself, but would you do it in front of a bishop? How many pencils do you really need? You preparing to stab someone?"

"Sorry, Chief." The old man was in a foul mood.

Gennaro had to admit that Alessadnro's latest set of pencils, beautiful Navas, did not deserve the electric indignity. Alessandro opened his middle desk drawer and located the metallic cube, a KUM wedge-sharpener, made of perfect German steel and with a fresh razor blade. He started twirling the pencil and watched the curling peel of dark wood.

Gennaro was watching him. He stopped.

Gennaro crumpled the lunch paper and wiped his hands on a napkin. "I'm sorry. I'm a little on edge. I'm waiting for Dante and I haven't heard from Farrugia."

"I understand, Chief." Alessandro agreed that this was a bad situation. First, it was the way Pinolo, their former boss, had packed them off to Milan from Rome. Did it by e-mail to Gennaro while he was on vacation. Asshole. Dante had been the first sent into exile. No doubt it was all payback for their exposing the Roma Underground scandal. Jealous bastard. Only Silvio in the Rome office had been spared. Now this fiasco with Farrugia would not help the situation.

"Boss?" said Alessandro.

"What?"

"I don't get it. Why was Farrugia there? I overheard you asking Dante if Bianca was okay. He was with her, huh?"

"Farrugia was with Bianca, and the kid, the one who got killed, was meeting with Bianca about something. What it was I don't know, but it all obviously went to shit."

"And Bianca . . . is she okay?"

"Dante says she is, but I guess we'll know more when he gets back into the office."

"And Farrugia? How is he?"

"Shaken up last we spoke. It was the shooting. He told me he'd never seen anything quite like it."

"What was it? What about it?"

Gennaro walked over and closed the door completely. He stood in front of Alessandro's desk. "None of this is in the reports yet. Only you and Dante know this, but Farrugia told me that the one gunman shot the other one in the head and then killed himself after they killed the kid."

Alessandro held the fresh Nava in his hand. "Shit."

"Shit is right. Farrugia was really spooked. Sure, we've had contract killers before, but they usually kill themselves once they get into custody. Not these two." Gennaro stopped. "That looks interesting there?"

"What?"

"The pencil. May I see it?"

"Here you go, Chief. Italian-made, nice lacquer, and beautiful to handle, dyed cedar wood, black Moleskin body and 2B graphite. So Farrugia was convinced that these two were professionals?"

Gennaro admired the Nava, rolled the pencil between his hands like a cigar. "He is. Don't take this the wrong way, Alessandro, but I think you need a woman in your life instead of pencils." He tossed it to Alessandro who caught it. "Definitely contract killers. Question is, why this young kid? Mother of God, the kid is but a child, twenty-three years old. University of Milan-Bicocca student."

"I heard that through the vine, and an American, too. As for women, well, you know my luck there. Bianca should be—hey, there's Dante."

Outside, Dante stepped out of the elevator and scanned the room. Gennaro cracked the door open and beckoned him to come quickly.

"What's with you?" Dante asked with a smile. His voice was fresh, but his face was tired. Must be Bianca.

"How is she?" asked Gennaro.

"She says she's fine, but I can tell she is shaken up." Dante unshouldered his jacket and hung it up.

"Good to hear she is well," Gennaro said. "Now what the fuck happened?"

Dante summarized the conversation.

Alessandro twirled his pencil in the silent aftermath. "So, basically you interrogated her."

Gennaro's silence indicated that he agreed.

"What? She was drip-feeding me information, drop by drop. I get an answer only if I ask exactly the right question. I can't believe the two of you are busting my balls for this. How is Farrugia?"

Dante sat down. He said nothing about the state of his desk. A grease stain and the lingering smell of a *Cotoletta alla Milanese* sandwich. Breaded veal.

Gennaro, hands in pockets, sauntered slowly up to the side of Dante's desk, the epitome of an old-school cop. "Drip-feed? Your wife isn't a coffee machine."

"She's not my wife. She's my girlfriend."

"You live together, so what does it matter. Fine, I'm old-fashioned. If you can pee in front of a woman the two of you ought to be married. As for Farrugia . . . I haven't heard a word. He's worried about the Viminale breaking his balls and his career. Didn't I tell you his weapon is over at Ballistics and his dossier is under review?"

Dante looked perplexed. "I know it's procedure and all, but why should his weapon be at Ballistics? Yeah, you had told me. He didn't discharge it. These guys kill the kid and then one shooter shoots the other and then kills himself. Four rounds for the Coroner. Four casings for the crime-scene technicians. None of them Farrugia's. End of story."

Gennaro said nothing. He looked over at Alessandro, who also said nothing. Gennaro leaned closer to Dante. "And you're absolutely certain that none of this mess has anything to do with Rendition? I'm talking about why Bianca was there in the first place with this kid."

"Bianca says it doesn't."

Gennaro was shaking his head, still looking at Dante sitting in his chair. "So we have two contract killers who destroy the evidence, even when the evidence is themselves. But Rendition's hands are clean? They weren't even aware of this?"

More silence.

"She told me about this company," Dante said. "Adastra. This kid had seen something. He disseminated it on the Net, she said, and then somebody shut his blog down. She said that this kid went back in after his blog had been shut down. He broke into their system to do more snooping and—"

"Excuse me, Chief. " Alessandro cleared his throat as if he had to make his best impression in front of the class. "Dante just said she said that this kid's blog had been shut down. The kid is still going into Adastra after the fact, which means that someone had to know, since they'd found him in the first place. Which means he must have found something really irresistible in this company. But here is what I don't get . . . they—whoever they are—had shut off his blog. Fine. That's one thing. Killing him, quite another."

Dante looked around first at Gennaro and then back at Alessandro. "So what's your point?"

"Shutting down the blog seems like a warning, like saying, 'We are onto you. Cut it out.' Which suggests that this kid wasn't that big of a threat. Nuisance, yeah, but then you send a couple of high-end professionals after him? It doesn't make sense. I mean, this kid was killed execution-style with one bullet to the chest and another bullet to the head. That was the scenario, right?"

Gennaro turned to Dante and said, "He has a point. This kid must have been blogging for some time. His television show gets canceled, so to speak, and the next thing we know he's dead in an alley. If he was such a big threat then kill him first and then get rid of the blog later. You said yourself that Bianca told you he was doing this blog under another name. Perfect. Kill the author and let the alias simply fade. Mission accomplished."

"And another thing," Alessandro said. "If this kid had seen something, doesn't it seem reasonable that Bianca had probably seen something? She was in the company computers after him, and she has a lot more experience than he ever had."

Gennaro was smiling. "You know something, Alessandro, I think sharpening those pencils is improving your brain."

"Thanks, Chief."

Gennaro's cell phone rang and continued to ring. His eyes surveyed the terrain of the desk.

"It's on your belt, Boss," Dante said.

"Hate this damn thing . . . *Pronto* . . . Isidò. Are you . . . Hold on." Gennaro wrapped one hand around the receiver, since there was a knock on the door and a head peeking through, inviting all of them out to the main area. Something about "You gotta see this."

"Stay quiet and stay on the line," Gennaro said to Farrugia.

The three of them, Alessandro, Dante, and Gennaro, walked out single-file over to the main floor, where the rest of the office was crowded around a television. It was the large, annoying head of Giancarlo Ragonese on the Free Channel about to speak to the public. The banner under his chin was racing towards the left side of the screen. *Murdered American student sparks international outcry. What will Italy do?*

"Are you there, Isidò?" Gennaro said. "It looks like Ragonese is about to say something about Manzoni, and you know that I don't mean the author. Just listen." Gennaro looked down at the receiver. "Yeah, I know Ragonese is an ass, who doesn't. But he must have something—what?" Gennaro listened. "You know as well as I do that these mannequins can't have real information this fast. They're just out to stoke the flames. It's almost an election year. Just stay quiet. Stay on the line and enjoy the bullshit."

Alessandro could hear Farrugia uttering Calabrian curses that only a linguist would know and appreciate. One of the experts in Receivables clicked the volume up a few more bars.

"This is Giancarlo Ragonese with the Free Channel reporting. Behind me, as you can see, is the Bar Gadda, where hours ago a bright light was snuffed out." The camera zoomed in on the alley. "It is here in a dark alley next to a garbage dumpster that Charles Brooks met his grisly end. Execution-style. Charlie, to his friends, was pursuing law and economics at Bicocca. He is remembered as a quiet young man, a hard-working student with a promising future, bright but humble. He was twenty-three years old."

Ragonese did his signature finger in his ear when the other talking head in the studio with her cramped face and Teflon hair said, "How tragic, Giancarlo. Are there any preliminaries on the investigation?" The camera cut to a university ID photo of Charles Brooks. There was a pause. No doubt Giancarlo wanted the camera back on him.

"Details are hush-hush, as is to be expected. Brooks was highly esteemed by his peers and his teachers. He comes from a typical American family, who most certainly will demand a thorough investigation, as they should, since this is a most despicable and senseless act. America and Italy have been trying to heal their past. Italy remembers the Cermis Incident, remembers the Amanda Knox case, and now we have this incident. Elections are but months away and—"

A voice in the room yelled, "That no good son of a bitch. Why did he have to pull out the 'Cermis Incident'? What the hell do those American pilots have to do with Amanda?" Somebody else said, "Sssh. Shut up."

Ragonese's furry lips continued to move. The beard was not flattering, but neither was his journalism. "What we do know is that Charlie Brooks was murdered in this alley by two men. Two shots were fired into him. We don't know why. Another two shots were fired. The assassins were fatally wounded by Commissario Isidore Farrugia and—"

Epithets streamed out of Gennaro's cell phone. A few heads turned. Gennaro said "Sssh!" into his cell.

"The heroic Commissario Farrugia is not available for comment. It remains a mystery as to how and why Commissario Farrugia happened to be here on the scene, but he couldn't save the young man. I'm told by reliable sources that Isidore Farrugia is a distinguished officer of the law, but he has been known to be quick-tempered. I've also been informed that there will be an investigation into whether these two assailants could have been taken alive. The investigation will also determine whether Commissario Farrugia had any information or could've done anything to save the young student. The Brooks family will want to have these answers. Did these two men have to die? Did Charlie Brooks have to die? Was Commissario Farrugia too quick to pull the trigger? The Brooks family is flying in from Virginia Beach as I speak."

Inflammatory Ragonese and his damn clichés.

The woman mannequin had that worried look again, as she waited to interrupt Ragonese. "Such a sad affair," she said. "As a mother I can only imagine what his mother must be going through. And Giancarlo . . . wait . . . we seem to have a connectivity issue . . . ah, there you are Giancarlo. Please keep us informed of any other developments."

Ragonese was not looking up at the camera. He was reading a piece of paper in his hand. "Wait! I've just received some disconcerting news. A shocking revelation."

Somebody in the office said, "He should have been an actor."

Farrugia was boiling over again, Gennaro was trying to calm him with a 'ssh' lullaby.

Ragonese looked up into the camera. The man's face was genuinely pained and horrified by whatever he had just read.

"I . . . I don't know exactly how to say this," Ragonese said. "I am speechless and I hesitate to say this on the air without verifying this."

Another heckler in the office: "Hasn't stopped you before."

A reinforcing *ssh* was heard followed by a "Shut the fuck up."

"Ladies and gentlemen, it truly saddens me to read this, but in my hands I have a declaration from G9—Gruppo 9—accepting full responsibility for this terrible act and . . . I'm speechless."

There was a silent, collective feeling of "Oh, shit" in the room. The G9, the ultra-extremist, ultra-violent anarchist party was claiming responsibility. The group came into existence in 2001 after the demonstrations in Genoa took an ugly turn for the worse. The joke was that the group was one step ahead of the G8.

"I read this declaration with great sadness to you. Quote. Gruppo 9 accepts full responsibility for the death of Charles Brooks. The late student is but a symbol of American interference in Italian politics. He was old enough and intelligent enough to know better. He made his choice and we made ours. Unquote." Ragonese's voice cracked. Even those who hated the newscaster felt some pity.

Someone shut off the television. Silence.

The water cooler broke the dead air when it made an ominous gurgle and the unexpected bubble floated to the top and burst.

4

With Farrugia still talking into his ear, Gennaro led the procession back into Dante's office. Alessandro disappeared, off elsewhere, leaving Dante alone with his former boss. Gennaro had his head tucked down, listening to Farrugia, and then snapped the cell phone shut, and clipped it onto his belt.

"This is bullshit," Dante said. "We know Farrugia didn't shoot those two men."

"You and I know that, but the rest of Italy doesn't. Of course, Ballistics will know. Unless, of course, some phony report comes out saying he did."

"You don't think that, do you?"

"Nothing surprises me at this age, Dante. Nobody expected G9 to take responsibility for this kid's death. It's a political year. That young man's family will fly into Malpensa, and everyone from the Pope to the politicians will be on them. The Americans have an election in November and we'll have ours in April and this 'international incident' is fodder for both sides. Politics."

"You think Gruppo 9 will shift opinion that dramatically?"

Gennaro sat down. "History shows that in times of discord people want security. Voters go conservative or to the far right." Gennaro shifted his weight around, looking for the soft spot in Dante's chair. "Sorry about taking over your desk. I was waiting for you here because I wanted to see you when you returned from talking with Bianca. I'm glad that she's okay. Life is about to get ugly for Farrugia, even if and when Ballistics clears him. Then it'll be, 'What did he know and why was he there?' You know Farrugia will do his best to protect Bianca."

Dante was thinking, trying to get all the facts into some pattern. "If Ballistics clears him then it's a Homicide investigation. If it goes the other way, I'd think if anything, Gennaro, people would consider Farrugia a hero. You and I both know he didn't kill those two, and even if some bullshit report comes out saying that he did, sympathy should be on his side. The two guys were killers. The G9 implied that these two had been carrying out their orders."

Gennaro picked up one of Alessandro's pencils that had somehow wound up on his desk and started twirling it. Soothing. "Of course Farrugia might look like a hero. At first."

"I don't follow. You just said 'law and order.' That fits."

The pencil was bobbing up and down in front of Dante. "I did say that. 'Law and order,' but as the elections come around there is sure to be some criticism from the moderates and from the left, saying that the police should be more circumspect. Those who commended and supported Farrugia will start thinking out loud that maybe Commissario Isidore Farrugia had taken the law into his own hands and that he had acted as judge, jury, and executioner. Next thing you know his entire career is under review: his anti-mafia cases, his unorthodox methods, and who knows, there might even be some details around what happened in Boston. Before you know it, some politician'll be turning this into North versus South."

"C'mon, that's ridiculous. Escalation and speculation."

Gennaro's face was stoical. "You think so? Politics is all about the calculated irrational. Telling the lie that is most likely to be believed. Whether I walk up to the right side of the cross or to the left side, I don't want Isidore Farrugia crucified in the middle."

There was a knock on the door. It was the Chief's Chief, Lino Perego. "DiBello?"

"Yes, *Dottore*. What can I do for you?"

"Thought I might find you in your office." Perego smiled. "I know you and Dante and Alessandro all worked together in Rome, but you should try and wear out the carpet in your *own* office."

"I'm visiting old friends."

Perego had a piece of paper in his hand that he wasn't sharing. "I know Isidore Farrugia is also an old friend. Word of advice?"

"Sure," said Gennaro.

"Proceed cautiously and be discreet. That goes for you, too, Allegretti. There is a shit storm on the horizon. Be sure to tell Monotti."

"I'll tell Alessandro," Dante said.

"You came for something?" Gennaro asked.

"I did." Lino closed the door behind him. "That shit storm I mentioned? Here's the first shower. I was asked to have you investigate the Manzoni Affair. Top priority. In fact, it is your only priority as of now; and the same goes for you, too, Allegretti. Add Monotti to your team, if you believe he can help you."

"With all due respect," Gennaro said, "we're not Homicide."

Lino Perego had been named after the actor Lino Ventura; the name had turned out to be prophetic. He had that nose, the parted hair to the side, those dark eyes, and, when necessary, the iconic arched eyebrow when he needed to make a point. The eyebrow now lifted, and then came that disarming smile.

"I know you're not Homicide, but Farrugia is a friend, is he not? You're his friend, too, Allegretti, right?"

Dante nodded and deferred to Gennaro. Too many damn rhetorical questions with that smile.

"Yes, we're his friends." Gennaro asked, "What are your orders?"

"They're not *my* orders, DiBello. This comes from above my head. From Rome—you know, where the pigeons live."

"Rome?" Dante said, stunned.

"Yes, Rome. From Maximo Cassagio's office."

"Pinolo?" Gennaro said, unable to hide his surprise.

Lino smirked, "Little 'Pine Nuts' himself. I know that there is no love lost between the three of you—the four of you, if I include Farrugia—and Pinolo, as you call him."

Dante was thinking five, if he were to add Bianca. Maximo Cassagio was nicknamed Pine Nuts for the supposed side effect of taking steroids: diminishing testicles. In reality, Pinolo was a big prick and not very intelligent, which made him a big, dangerous prick.

"No, there is no love between us. He had initiated my transfer while I was on vacation."

Lino's face switched to cinematic coldness. "I know all about that; if it's any consolation, this is not directly from Pinolo, but from an attorney named Michael Farese. The attorney contacted Pinolo."

"U.S. Attorney Farese," Dante asked. "Organized-crime Farese?"

Gennaro gave Dante his shut up-and-let-Perego-talk look.

"One and the same. It seems the American Justice Department is taking an interest in the Brooks murder, and I guess when Farese heard Farrugia's name he pulled strings to get himself on the plane tonight to Malpensa with the Brooks family. Not uncommon for U.S. attorneys to have political aspirations, you know."

"I know," Gennaro said. "Rudy Giuliani made a name for himself working with Falcone and Borsellino before leveraging it into a political career. Not uncommon at all."

Perego turned to leave. "Oh, I forgot. Pinolo is sending another present. It seems thoughtful enough of him to provide a translator, since Farese doesn't speak Italian."

Gennaro's eyebrow arched now. "Translator? They're a dime a dozen."

"I know. He is sending someone from the Rome office."

"Who?" Dante asked, though he was already beginning to suspect.

Lino was opening the door unaware that Alessandro was trying to enter the office. "I didn't catch the last name. Someone named Silvio. I've got to go." He pointed with his sheet of paper. "Keep me informed, DiBello."

Alessandro was all grins. Dante and Gennaro looked like undertakers in front of a *commedia all'italiana* performance done by Berlusconi.

"So," Alessandro said, "Silvio is coming to Milan?"

"Long story, Alessandro," Gennaro said, pencil still in hand. "It has to do with Pinolo and Farese. Poor Farrugia."

Alessandro looked to both Dante and Gennaro. "Pinolo? Farese? What does Farese have to do with Farrugia? Anyway, I was talking to this girl I know in Ballistics, and I've got something interesting."

Alessandro moved to Dante's desk. Dante convened with them there to hear the news.

"What is it?" Dante said.

"She is beautiful and . . ." Alessandro started explaining her figure with his hands.

"Alessandro!" Gennaro said. "The bullets, please."

"Right, Chief. The bullets, the ones from the two gunmen, they're Gévelots."

Gennaro slapped his forehead and dropped his head between two hands. This meant something that Dante was not aware of.

"What is it, Chief?" asked Alessandro. "Something wrong?"

"He asks me if something is wrong. I feel like the Gévelots showed up *come l'ombra di Banco a Macbeth*."

Not Hamlet seeing his father's ghost, but Macbeth seeing Banquo's.

5

She swept up all the broken glass, all that she could find.

The apartment felt hollow. This was the worst argument she had ever had with Dante. Defensive from his interrogation, still recovering from what had happened—trying to understand what had happened—and then there was the finality of what had happened. A young kid was dead.

Dismissive as it might sound, Charlie Brooks was just a kid, no matter how intelligent, how precocious he was in his studies or with his hacking skills. Twenty-three years old was nothing. She thought back to when she was twenty-three, when she had thought she knew all the answers to life, or thought she had a better idea than everyone else. The difference was that she had made it to twenty-four. This kid was dead and would be forever twenty-three.

This kid was dead.

The Melchiorre Gioia apartment was to be her joyless tomb, not unlike the subterranean chambers that the Roma Underground used to explore in Rome, though with better plumbing. Dante suggested it, and Gennaro reinforced its necessity—she had to stay inside, out of sight. She recognized the necessity since she had been there on Via Manzoni at Bar Gadda. So she would stay, sequestered in her own sarcophagus above ground, with fresh food in her refrigerator, fresh laundry in her closet, her computer as her only access to the outside world. No walks with Dante along the Naviglio Martesana, which started at the northern end of Via Melchiorre Gioia and wound through nineteenth-century factories and railroad arches, working-class houses, little parks, old boroughs, and aristocratic villas. No irate near-collisions with bikers or joggers in the bike lane. No observing couples kissing or holding hands as they walked along the waterway. The canals required the force of water, locks, stone, and time. Like the little dam at the southern end of her street, her life was now nothing but dry time.

But there was the jump drive. She still hadn't looked at it. Whatever was on it got Charlie Brooks killed.

Damn, why couldn't this kid have been preoccupied with football, with porn, with dating girls and getting his heart broken, with hanging out with his friends, doing all those normal, foolish things of youth?

No. She understood Charlie, because like her, he had lived for the data thrill, lived for analysis adrenaline.

She was different, just as he had been, and in the same way. As a young girl there were no superheroes who used their brains only, their savvy skills, to stop bad guys. Well, there *was* Wonder Woman. Big whoop. Sexy costume, breasts that she'd never have, or want for that matter. And that Lasso of Truth? C'mon! Lame, lame, lame. Invisible plane and bullet deflecting bracelets? Why couldn't there be a cerebral version of Cat Woman?

She looked over the apartment. Dante had found it. It was a nice place, located on Via Melchiorre Gioia not too far from the Central Railway Station. It was also not far from the Bicocca campus.

Clean, airy, and safe; third floor and accessible by elevator. It had two bedrooms, with a shower in between the rooms. She and Dante had made one room the master bedroom and the other a workplace, which they shared. She used it more than he did. There were his books, his furniture, his espresso machine, everything he had when they had first met in Rome.

An archway separated the living room from the dining room. Dante seemed happy with his kitchen. She was happy with the dishwasher and microwave. The laundry room was also a plus. The dining table in the living room was pleasant, though she preferred the counter and stools to the dining room. A French window opened out onto a small balcony. It was all very nice and very domestic.

He had tamed her.

She had resisted at first, but in the end had conceded. Dante had domesticated her. She liked it, at first, but now she had the stirrings of resentment. The fight today made her question everything, all of this.

She had money, though she never recouped what she had plunked down to finance hoodwinking Alan Ancona and Lorenzo Bevilacqua. She still had plenty left over from Robert Strand's bearer bonds in Lucerne.

She could start over yet again. There was the packed carry-bag and her laptop, the disposable cell phones and SIM cards. She was already thinking of looking into a reliable source for another passport. New name, new place, no worries.

Yet she knew that she had to stay. She had to do it for Charlie. She had to make good with Farrugia despite Dante and his relentless Q&A. Can't leave without an act of betrayal. Damned domestication.

Still, she wanted to run, wanted to be Alabaster Black again, wanted to be somewhere else, be someone else with another name.

He needed to collect his thoughts with some caffeine. The waiter in the oyster-white shirt and black slacks had just asked him if he wanted more while a cold breeze came in from the street in a fast stride.

Farrugia sat in a dark, anonymous corner of a café. He was from Calabria, San Luca, to be exact, where breakfast was the traditional two Cs: caffè latte or plain caffè. His mother loved black coffee with home-made biscuits. The kitchen always smelled of hazelnut. He recalled the day that he found her body on the kitchen floor, apron bunched up around her waist, violated twice, first sexually, and then by the blast of a *lupara*, the mafia sawed-off shotgun. The *'Ndrangheta* had hired free-lance thugs, because the Calabrian mafia neither used that particular shotgun, nor raped, nor killed women.

From that day forward, he avoided hazelnuts. He also had become an enemy of the *'Ndrangheta*, the Calabrian mafia; the *Camorra*, the mafia in Naples; *Cosa Nostra*, the Sicilians. All mafia. It didn't matter.

Vendetta. From the Latin, *vindicta*. Vengeance.

This was why he and Gennaro understood each other so well. They had empathy for each other. *Empatia*. Gennaro lost his wife, also to the mafia.

He had decided to read all the newspapers after Giancarlo Ragonese had decided to declaim his name, Farrugia, to all of Italy on the Free Channel. He looked at the picture of Ragonese on the front page. On the *Corriere della Sera*. With his beard, he looked like the god Pan.

Goat-fucker.

He had read all the coverage on the Brooks murder and the G9 declaration. All the papers were doing some form of exposé on the terrorist organization. Gruppo 9 was nothing but another bunch of murderous barbarians.

Farrugia bought copies of all the major newspapers: *Repubblica* and *Il Fatto Quotidiano* for the left, *Il Giornale* and *Libero* for the right; and *Il Sole 24 Ore* for the position of the financial elite, increasingly a world unto themselves. That covered everyone except the Lega Nord who did not care about international politics unless it was immigrants and how to stop them.

Milan was not endearing itself to him—he thought of the city symbol, the *Bissa*, a coiled serpent swallowing a child, and felt chilled. He remembered his history primer, and the importance of the mercantile north. Every child in southern Italy was reminded of Milan, before and after Garibaldi.

At least, before this fiasco, he had taken some delight in the *Duomo di Milano*, the only Gothic à la International-style cathedral in Italy. A little overdone for his taste, but still admirable.

Milan was gray. Gray concrete, gray pavement, gray people, gray skies, and more gray. Even the pigeons were gray.

Self-pity accomplished nothing. Time to keep his vow.

He opened up a city magazine, *Urban*. This periodical was not unlike *The Improper Bostonian*, which he had read in Boston while working with Gennaro on the Ancona and Bevilacqua case. It was a magazine infused with humor—raucous interviews, cinema and theatre reviews, as well as pictures of fashion-wear for people with perfect bodies and disposable incomes. It also had extensive listings of gyms for people who wanted perfection, or at least to lose a pinch of belly fat. He was thinking of joining a gym.

He decided against the place named Manzoni because that was bad luck. The other places were too, too fancy and rich. Finally he picked the place on Via Falcone, named after the bird and not the famous judge. They had a membership special. One month free.

It was time to hit the gym, as the American sitcom characters said.

Her Mac was out, screen open, powered up. The jump drive waited. She contemplated what secrets were hidden there, what the zeroes and ones said about Charlie's death. There had to be Adastra documents that she hadn't seen in her spelunking through the company servers.

Adastra was a very different adventure from anything she'd handled before: military specifications and standards. She knew she could learn fast. She had learned the ins-and-outs of import-export scams for the antiquities market, learned a thing or two about molecular biology and wasp genetics to investigate Cyril Sargent and Nasonia Pharmaceutical. That project did have an element of military contracts and hardware, but that had been an unintentional discovery.

Whatever Adastra was doing was verboten, dangerous, and secretive enough that Charlie was murdered for it. Not scared off, not bought off, but literally silenced. Murdered.

She seeded the jump drive into the USB port.

Hiring not one but two killers, exporting them from their country of origin and then importing them into the mission country to neutralize a target, all that took considerable resources—fake passports, black-market weapons, money. And it took a certain amount of sleeper activity to observe the target's routines and form a plan, unless an analyst had mapped all that out for the two contractors in advance. Resources were also needed for extraction, the exit strategy. All that was expensive. A mission that turns suicidal was a complete loss of investment and resources.

Charlie was a college kid, so he had to be an easier mark than usual. Yet, they had to have had contingency plans; Farrugia and Gennaro had told her that all professional killers do, except the lower-level mafia drive-by-shooting grunts. These two were not grunts, so they had to have contingencies. Backup weapons contingency for a malfunctioning weapon; interference contingency for foot-patrol police; communications contingency for an unexpected witness; telecom contingency for failed traffic lights, delayed trains, and inclement weather. They might have underestimated Charlie. Charlie could not have come up with Farrugia.

She'd done that.

The image of the two men following Charlie flashed through her mind. They'd simply seemed foreign to Farrugia, but they were American to her. Two men, the one-two shots that Dante had described. All that fit into one adjective: agile. The adjective used in only one context: military. U.S. military. Active or ex-Spec Ops.

She thought of Robert Stone in Boston. Of Tirso from Bulgaria.

Moving the mouse over the files she noted file types and weight. Mere kilobytes. Most of the files were generic documents—memos, reports, and an occasional spreadsheet. And one file with an odd extension. That file was several megabytes. Probably an image file or drawing of some kind; and since Adastra dealt with hardware, like helicopters, this file was likely a schematic.

Her cell rang. She saw that it was Gennaro, actually using his cell phone. She answered.

"Bianca?"

"Yes."

"Gennaro."

"I know."

"Catch you at a bad time?"

"What do you want, Gennaro?"

"Um, I don't want to be imprudent, but I want to invite myself to dinner. It'll be me, Alessandro, and Dante, of course."

"Just inviting yourself, of course. Why didn't Dante call me?"

"He thinks that you're mad at him."

"He's right. What about Farrugia? Shouldn't he join us? I imagine he wants to keep a low profile since Ragonese sprayed his name all over the Free Channel."

Gennaro sighed. "A few of the newspapers are running his picture with 'Commissario Isidore Farrugia' in nice bold, black letters under a glamorous headshot. I do need to contact him and confirm about dinner. He has been lying low."

"I can understand why. I know about the picture. It's on the internet, too."

"Shit. It just keeps getting better. Technology." Another sigh. "The Americans will make a movie of the week about him. Somebody is likely to fictionalize his existence. I can read it now: Commissario Brunetti, Commissario Montalbano, and our own Commissario Isidore Farrugia. He was not made for this."

She smiled but didn't betray it with her voice. "Don't forget the disclaimer 'no resemblance to persons either living or dead . . . all events are from the author's imagination.'"

He laughed. "Glad you are in better spirits. This is going to get difficult, yes?"

She paused. She had thought of herself working alone on this, as she always had with Rendition. No backup, no fallback, no contingency plans. But she realized with a start that Gennaro's conversation was based on an assumed *we*, and she had only now noticed it. She had become domesticated.

"Bianca? You there?" he asked.

"I heard you. Let me know if Farrugia is coming. I'll assume dinner is the usual time, about seven thirty or eight o'clock. And yes, I think this situation is shit. We need to do something about it."

Gennaro chuckled. "I'll call him and get back to you. And yes, you're right about 'shit,' but you know what they say about shit, don't you?"

"What do they say, Gennaro?" she said, clicking and using image-viewer software to open up the drawing, already moving on to the next thing.

His reply came over the line as the image opened up. "You can't polish shit."

She pressed the button to end the call and looked at the graphic on her screen.

It was a schematic for an armored tank.

Farrugia signed up for a one-month membership. He purchased on the premises some athletic clothes as well as a practical carry bag for his clothes and gear. He got the tour of the facilities, a fast walk through the frightening machines for reshaping the human body, and noticed that this modern fitness emporium dedicated to physical culture had not a trace of body odor.

He was shown the showers, escorted around the pool area, shown the food bar where he could get healthy, organic food as part of a menu designed by a certified dietician. He read the handouts that the young man with the flawless body and posture had given him.

There was a "group exercise" schedule and a "mind-body" schedule. The first listed the numerous masochistic ways to groan and sweat en masse. The other schedule was daily departures to Nirvana. While the young Adonis in his perfect shirt, snug slacks, and RAI accent—*lingua toscana in bocca romana*—was returning with Farrugia's locker key, Farrugia decided on a group class. *Tabata.*

He read the description again, "A one-hour class of twenty seconds of full-out effort followed by ten seconds of recovery, repeated eight times in four-minute sets." This class, he read, will "maximize fat-burning, increase athletic performance, and improve cardiovascular capacity."

He informed his tour guide of his decision. The young man gave him that alarmed lift of the eyebrows. "Could I, perhaps, recommend something a bit . . . milder?"

"Thank you. This is the class I want."

Professional and undoubtedly as courteous as Charon at the helm of his boat on the river Styx, the young man wished him well, but asked before Farrugia left, "Are you *the* Isidore Farrugia?"

Farrugia replied, "We'll see whether I am after this class."

Bianca picked up the phone, saying, "Hi, Gennaro," in English, since she was so engrossed in the open documents on the Mac. She did not listen to what he said.

"I'm sorry, what was that?" she asked him, in Italian this time.

"Farrugia is coming to dinner. He texted 'must eat healthy.' His exact words."

"Must eat healthy?"

"That's what he texted. He says that there are 'too many eggs, too much meat, too much cheese, and heavy cream in the food here.' I told him to bring a stalk of celery. Also told him that just because *he* had come close to getting shot doesn't mean that *I* have to starve to death. You know how hard it is to type all of that on this stupid phone?"

"You texted all that? You've come a long way, baby. I'll cook something healthy, but you're responsible for dessert. Go wild."

"Least I can do. Baby?"

"American advertising. Sorry."

"You know, Farrugia sounds different."

"Different? How?"

"Winded, out of breath, but there was this really soothing music playing in the background. I think he was about to take a nap."

She clicked the phone off. Her eyes caught a sparkle of truant glass and a small column of ants on the kitchen tiles.

6

With Dante's temper flickering on low, and Farrugia's new *eat healthy* motto, and dinner in a few hours, the stress was mounting. The task for her was to determine a course . . . for food. This was tricky since Dante was the one who actually knew how to cook it, and she wasn't sure how cooperative he would be. She was the one who had to make good with Farrugia, not Dante. She remembered the saying "the way to a man's heart is through his stomach." Other women might beg to differ on that point. She wasn't forgetting that dinner also included Alessandro and Gennaro.

Poor in technique as she was, Bianca decided to fall back on that staple of northern Italy cuisine: polenta. It was to her advantage that she was an American. Polenta in other parts of Italy was coarse-ground. Polenta in America, in Milan, and in Calabria was fine ground. Cornmeal. It was relatively healthy. The stomach that concerned her most was Farrugia's.

The next decision-point was either *minestra* or *zuppa*. One was, for consistency's sake, somewhere between a soup and stew with vegetables, while the other, *zuppa*, was more elegant, more refined. Next up was to consult the web and work with the items in Dante's cupboard and pantry. This, she noted, was starting to feel like one of those popular chef challenges on American television. Make a gourmet meal out of a potato, six sardines, and a breath mint.

No polenta in the house.

She had decided: *Zuppa di Bianca alla Casa Dante*. It was ingratiating, but between Dante and Farrugia and her lack of cooking experience she had to try her best.

Follow the soup with grilled fennel sausage. *Si è deciso.* It is final.

Farrugia would have to concede his moratorium on meat. He had to. Both dishes were Calabrese and yet secretly American. Creamy red-onion soup might remind Farrugia of the beach town Tropea with its sweet red onions, and every American knew how to grill. Perfect for the balcony, with minimal cleanup.

Now that Gennaro had advanced to texting, she could request some nice bread and a slightly sweet red wine. She had already asked him to bring dessert.

And through all this, the back of her mind was chewing on, *Why a tank? Adastra did copters and planes.*

Gennaro's bread, after she had toasted it, went well with the *zuppa*. A touch of flour made the soup creamy. Pre-made vegetable broth from the pantry—all right, she cheated—complemented the onions. The grill came out of storage and the sausage was grilled on the balcony. Alessandro and Gennaro ate with enthusiasm, with occasional bursts of *complimenti.*

Dante was like a sullen teenager stealing looks and averting his eyes. Farrugia was more brazen; he stared. She stared back but didn't dare smile. He ate in silence. She knew that they had to talk, but, for now, let him be Salvo Montalbano and eat his meal in respectful silence. It had been *zuppa* to sausage with no discernible or immediate fatalities.

There would be time for talk after dessert: carrot-yogurt tart.

When Gennaro had announced the tart for dessert, Alessandro and Dante tried not to look like kids receiving clothes for Christmas, while Farrugia's eyes looked up like the puppy dog questioning his owner's sanity.

"Healthy," said Gennaro. It was also shockingly good.

After Alessandro and Gennaro had returned from the kitchen with the after-dinner drinks, and seeing Dante and Farrugia still entrenched in their adolescent moodiness, she put it on the table.

They all stared at the jump drive.

She allowed them a round of silence for Charlie Brooks. Twenty-three years old, bright, and killed for what?

It was time to talk.

Dante was first. "What did you find on it?"

"Files, some financial and mostly internal communications. The gist of the communication is clearly around some top-secret project. The way the screws are bolted down, this project is a real priority, really hush-hush."

Gennaro sipped Sambuca with no *mosca*. "That's all well and good, Bianca, but most companies, especially in Adastra's business sector, would have projects of that nature. We know that whatever Brooks stumbled over got him killed. Financially speaking, was there anything irregular? Anything suspicious?"

"Not at all, and that's what bothers me."

Alessandro piped up. "What do you mean?"

"Every project, particularly defense-industry projects have irregularities. Small blips. Nothing is *that* smooth. This is big money, government money, and that means stifling regulatory compliance, so every company usually has a slush fund for when projects run over, and when unexpected expenses arise, like—"

"Hiring two assassins," said Dante.

Alessandro was not amused. "Not funny, Dante. Okay, you couldn't find their slush fund, Bianca, or see queer transactions. Things are *that* squeaky clean, like you said, but here is what I don't get. I've said some of this before with Dante and Gennaro, but . . . this guy had to have known what he was looking at because he is publishing it on his blog. Not quite a Wiki-leak, but he's publishing it. I wish we could've looked at his blog because maybe that was the incriminating material." He sat back into his chair to collect his thoughts. "I still don't get it. They shut off his blog and then kill him. You'd think they would shut it down, he gets the message and stops, or he doesn't stop and then they kill him. It doesn't add up."

"He didn't stop, Alessandro. He went back into the Adastra computer system. If it was a message, it didn't work."

"How much time passed between the blog shutdown and his death?" Dante asked.

"Less than forty-eight hours."

Gennaro finished a sip. "That's almost immediate, given that maybe the killers were in transit. Or maybe they had logistical issues and were working them out. Or maybe they were queuing up for tickets to La Scala or waiting in line to see *The Last Supper*. Who the hell knows?"

"He is right," Dante said. "I mean Alessandro is right. It doesn't make sense. We talked about this. Shut the blog down and then kill the kid? My thought would be kill the kid first and let the blog wither on the vine because nobody is posting. Much easier for the blog to go offline, fade away. This kid was doing this blog under a different name, some alias, right? Even easier."

Bianca nodded.

"That works. His blog goes offline. The web has millions of neglected pages. Nobody would know or associate that blog with a dead college kid."

Alessandro was shaking his head. "The only other thing that bothers me is the way this kid was killed. When I think of defense-industry *contract*—no pun intended—I think Karen Silkwood. I think accident. This was violent and attention getting; execution-style murder and then the two killers don't allow themselves to be arrested. Doesn't make sense. It should have been simpler. Brooks could've fallen down drunk somewhere and died. Car accident. Run in with drunken hooligans. But not gunned down in an alley."

Silence.

"Maybe they had no choice?" Gennaro said. They all looked at him.

"I mean maybe they had no choice. Farrugia showed up and—"

"Don't," Bianca said. "Don't even suggest that Isidò got this kid killed. No, it can't be that."

"A message then?" Dante said. "They kill him to send a message."

Alessandro's hands went out, Christ-like. "A message to whom? This is a college kid, Dante. This isn't an American conspiracy show."

Dante took his first sip of his Sambuca. "Bloggers have followers. He could have been made an example of . . . a warning. We don't know who else knows about this blog or what they were doing with the information." He looked over at Bianca.

"I'd need to look at my cache to see if there is anything that suggests he had followers. You know, some kind of metrics, an image with a counter, assuming it wasn't done in Flash, or some other dynamic language."

Blank stares.

"I thought you said his blog was gone," Alessandro said. "How would you do that?"

"You can save web pages offline. I saved some of his. The blog is gone, yes, but I have some pages locally—on my computer. The problem is, they're dead html, which means they're static and there's no interactivity, no navigation or coherence to the web pages, because the content is dead, no longer existing in cyberspace. I might be able to see if he had followers, but I don't think that is our problem. We know who killed Charlie Brooks. Literally. But we don't know why."

Dante's eyes were watching her over his next sip. She couldn't tell if he was still mad. He shouldn't be. She'd never opened up this easily about her work before. Though, all right, she had hidden the jump drive from him earlier.

He put down his small glass of Sambuca. "You mean who ordered it." He paused. "At least you can review his posts. That might give us something. Like Alessandro said, his posts have to have the incriminating material on them. Somehow. You said he was disguising things on his post."

"He was," she said. "His posts had the look and feel of top secret documents. You know, black-outs over text that is considered sensitive.

You could read between the lines though and develop a context for the information. But I have another idea. It's been bothering me all day."

"What?" Alessandro asked.

Bianca paused. "There was a recent image on the jump key. It was a fairly large file. The image turned out to be an armored tank. All I remember about tanks is from World War II movies with my grandfather, but let's assume this tank is the modern souped-up incarnation."

"Souped-up?" said Gennaro, seeking help in understanding Bianca's American slang thrown in with her Italian.

Alessandro put his hand on Gennaro's arm. "She means all the greatest technology. The other slang is 'latest bells and whistles.'"

Gennaro's mouth opened. "Ah, 'latest bells and whistles.'" He looked perplexed. "How is a bell late?"

Dante leaned forward. "You two can ask Silvio when he comes. Tell us more, Bianca. Something special about this image file?"

"Yes. It had been downloaded two days ago. Same day as when his blog was shut down. Now, the other thing is . . . and I'm not certain about this. Like I said, I traversed the same pathways on the Adastra servers as Charlie did, so I looked at the exact same data, same communications, the same financial spreadsheets that he did. I would've remembered seeing a tank."

Alessandro twirled his drink—also Sambuca—on the table's surface. She had forgotten coasters. "Adastra does helicopters, don't they? We got some helicopters from them a few months ago, didn't we? Some nonsense about border patrols."

Dante snapped his fingers. "That's right, but Adastra is working on a tank."

Gennaro gave Dante a sour look.

"What?" Dante asked.

"Like the kids on the television say, 'Like, duh.' Are you soft in the head? Of course they are working on a tank."

"Yes, a tank," Bianca said, "a special tank of some kind, but that's not my point. Charlie had stored this image on his jump key two days before he was murdered and it's an image that I had never seen while I was exploring Adastra. There is something else though."

"What?" Alessandro said.

"The file size. I said it was a large file size."

"So what?" Dante said.

Farrugia cleared his throat, speaking for the first time. "It means he took the picture of the schematic with a digital camera. He didn't resize the image. The image was never on their server. It was in-house and on paper. Somebody else knew about him taking that picture and had him killed. Those two who chased him? Their orders were to kill him. That was the plan from the start."

The room became silent. The other men collected the dishes and started the cleanup in the kitchen, leaving Bianca and Farrugia alone at the table.

"We should talk," she said.

"In the morning," he said. "Right now, my body aches."

7

The next morning Alessandro, Dante, and Gennaro were ascending together in the office elevator.

This was Gennaro's favorite part of the day, the coming and going on the mechanical transport, because this lift was a modern marvel, a true engineering accomplishment. What a contrast to the office elevator in Rome, which even Il Duce couldn't make run on time! Alessandro and Dante shared his silent awe.

They entered. He pressed the button as the ground-floor doors closed.

That Piranesi carriage from hell that they had in Rome was a metaphor for Italian bureaucracy. Baroque and ostentatious on the outside with burnished brass doors. Inept on the inside—slow, hot, humid, and inhumane. *Carceri d'Invenzione.*

"So have Farrugia and Bianca made up?" asked Alessandro.

"How should I know?" Dante said. "She doesn't talk much to me."

"So you should talk to her, Dante," Gennaro said.

"He's right, Dante," Alessandro added, "and besides, make-up sex is hot."

Gennaro, holding his briefcase like a kettlebell, turned to Alessandro. "What is it with you and the sex, Sandro? Couples talk. They should talk. You should talk to her, Dante. It's like confession: good for the soul, good for the relationship." He faced front, looked up at the climbing light overhead. "Then you have hot sex."

"Why me? I didn't do anything wrong? Besides, I doubt there will be any make-up sex—not with Farrugia staying overnight."

Both Alessandro and Gennaro turned to Dante, silent question marks on their faces.

Dante pressed the button for their floor again.

"What? He stayed over. It was late. His place is across town. She said that she and Farrugia should talk. I thought it was a good idea. That okay with you two therapists?"

Gennaro's face wrinkled. "She's talking to him before you. Are you sure you can leave those two alone together?"

"What is it with you, Gennaro?" Dante shouted. "Are you like this one over here with the sex?"

Gennaro's hand came up. "*Aspetta* . . . wait, will you. What I mean is those two are stubborn. Mules or jackasses, take your pick. I meant, leave them alone without a referee, and anything can happen. Farrugia has a temper. You saw him last night. He was quiet as marble. Not a word until dessert. You and I know, even this pencil sharpener over here knows, a quiet Farrugia is not a good thing. He has a temper. She has a temper."

"Every woman has a temperature," Alessandro said. "It's only a matter of degree, hot or cold."

Dante and Gennaro gave him a silent *shut up* look.

Two more floors.

Gennaro said under his breath, "Don't forget, Attorney Farese is likely to be here. Not a word about Bianca being at Manzoni, you hear? Let these Northerners think us Southerners are slow. It buys us time."

"But Farese is an American," Alessandro said. "Doesn't seem like a bad guy. He was with us in Rome and you knew him in Boston, Chief. What was he like?"

"What was he like? A shadow, he was like a shadow. I'm having a hard time understanding why he's on this case. This isn't a RICO or mafia case."

The light with their floor number blinked on and the elevator doors opened.

Farese and Perego in their nice suits happened to be in front of them. They said their hellos and shook hands. Heads around the office glanced up at the elevator chime like a flock of sheep. They returned to their work. Gennaro headed for his office.

The office was all stark lighting and simplistic décor. The desk had been full but now it was empty. Perego's orders. Everything had to go to make room for the Manzoni case files, which would arrive soon.

He was the lead investigator now. Perego's orders, again. A new crop of file folders, hard accordion-case files, ballistic reports, witness statements, and grisly photos would seed, grow, and overrun the clean mahogany surface.

There was a crucifix on the wall with a small section of palm leaf from Palm Sunday last year, desiccated and brittle, a gift from the wife of an office colleague, now retired. Gennaro still hoped to retire at the end of the year with a full pension. Farrugia was in Milan using his own vacation time to help plan the retirement party. He'd insisted.

He hung his coat up, walked over to his far office window, the one away from the office hallway, and tilted the blinds for more light. He faced his desk and saw a shadow on the desk blotter.

U.S. Attorney Michael Farese. There were official smiles and professional handshakes, again.

"How do you feel about leading this investigation, Mr. DiBello?" The charismatic lawyer wore a fresh-pressed white shirt, French cuffs, dark navy suit, thin pinstripe, and red tie with small gray dots. Never had a human being survived the flight into Malpensa airport looking more refreshed.

"How should I feel, Mr. Farese?"

"Please, after the Bevilacqua case, it's Michael." Another smile.

"Is that because of the way the Bevilacqua case turned out? Some would say Boston was a fiasco, for you and the U.S. Justice Department."

The man shrugged. This switch to first names accorded with Machiavelli's dictum: "Keep your friends close, and your enemies closer." Or was that Sun Tzu?

"That was an unfortunate outcome. But no, I'm simply asking you how you feel about leading this case. Some might think there is a conflict of interest because Detective Farrugia is a personal friend."

"I didn't ask to be the lead investigator, and I'm in no position to refuse. May I be frank, Michael?"

Farese doled out an affirmative shrug and assumed the chair opposite him. Good, he wasn't standing. It was a dangerous sign when any lawyer chose to stand and place his hands into his pockets, trying to look like one of the boys. It was cheap affectation. This was a bullshit case with Farrugia's career in the balance. Factor in a cultural divide; factor in two capricious governments he didn't understand very well—the U.S. and that of Northern Italy. Also factor in people like him, a curmudgeon, Bianca, a former covert operative, and civil servants like Alessandro and Dante, none of whom meant a thing to brokers, like Farese and Perego.

Enough pontificating.

"Here is what I think, Michael. This is a murder case. I'm a financial forensic expert . . . sorta equivalent to your IRS agent, but with a better reputation, I hope. Well, you already knew that from when we met in the Roma Underground case. As you can see I'm now in Milan. You can say I'm out of my element and—"

Farese lifted his hand. "I understand. I really do."

"Do you? I might be an old warhorse accountant, and maybe I should be taken out back and turned into glue, but I'm still a cop. My cop instinct tells me that I'm being set up. If I find something in the case, there are no proper channels for me to pursue it, since I'm Finance working Homicide, and if I should go to Homicide or Forensics or the Coroner and so on . . . what do you think they are going to say to me? You fill in your own expletives."

Farese crossed his one leg over the other. That was corporate, political, and meant to convey empathy.

"I'm from Campania, a work transfer from Rome. That makes me the country bumpkin in oversized overalls. Now I get this case? Now what does that make me look like? It makes everyone think the country rustic is trying to give a university lecture. And don't think life will get any better for you with me in this position."

"How's that?"

"Whatever I find in this *investigation* still has to bear legal scrutiny, whether in your country or in mine—if there is even cause for it to enter your legal system."

Farese still wore the unmovable mask. "Do you see any reason for it to go to the American courts?"

"This criminal matter might well turn into a civil matter after the international fallout. Civil suit against the University of Milan, against the Bar Gadda, against me, against the Pope—you tell me."

Farese tapped his knee and smiled, either amused with the paranoia or confident in his pre-prepared statement. "I assure you, Gennaro, that'll never happen. This is strictly a matter of justice."

"With no politics? My understanding is that the Brooks family came over with you."

"They did. They are resting at a hotel, arranged for them by the Embassy."

"Arranged by the Embassy, huh? So, it's already fast-tracked political. You already know how sensitive this country is about the Amanda Knox case and especially the Cermis incident. I'll assume that the Brooks family will be briefed about Cermis. They might not know it since that happened over a decade ago. I wish I could say that we have forgotten, but Italians have a long memory. You know that from your mafia cases."

That perfect smile shone again. "They will be briefed. This is a sensitive situation."

"Sensitive? The Italian people already know that this boy's father was in the American military. The man lost a son, and the Italian people are horrified about that. I'm sure you saw or read about the memorial on Via Manzoni. But, as I was saying, people will picture the boy's father in his uniform the minute they see him on television or in the news. Far as we know, the satirists right now are drawing cartoons of him in his battle fatigues. And then, there is the matter of . . ."

Farese got up without a sound and closed the office door. He returned and leaned over the desk.

"I know that jackass Giancarlo Ragonese shot off his mouth about the Cermis affair," he said. "We both know he did it for his own gain. He's an ass and—"

Gennaro put his hand up. "My turn to interrupt, counselor. We're agreed on one point: Ragonese is irritating as a hemorrhoid, but you see my predicament, don't you? You understand my point about Cermis? It shouldn't be taken lightly. That matter offended all of Europe, not just us Italians."

"I understand that. First, Brooks's father is career Army. He drove tanks for over twenty years. Cermis involved Marine pilots who clipped that gondola car and those unfortunate people who fell to their deaths."

Gennaro realized he was tapping a pencil. Alesssandro's habits are catching.

"Fell to their deaths, yes, but the media in your country initially presented it as an accident. The American people were never told about the jets, the bet, and the gondola line. Mind you, Italians love the American people but dislike and distrust your government. When those irresponsible boobs walked out of the courtroom smiling like . . . what is the word . . . Jack o'lanterns, it was ghoulish. A travesty. Call it the Cavalese cable disaster or the Cermis massacre, my point is Ragonese stirred up the hornet's nest and this case can't just be a fucking PR opportunity for you, the Brooks family, or the U.S. government. Understand?"

Farese's face was serious. "As I said, it is sensitive. Everyone is aware, from Justice to State, how quickly people remember the past. This will get handled properly. This is a legitimate investigation."

Gennaro lowered his voice. "Convenient that this is an election year, isn't it?"

Both of Farese's palms were now facing Gennaro. "I sympathize. I really do. Do your best. Your chain of command is your superior Perego and me. You will get the cooperation you need. On another matter, I understand Detective Farrugia has to speak with Internal Affairs, and that he'll have his union rep there."

"He will. He speaks to the union rep soon. I don't know exactly when."

"Good. I can say a few needed words at the appropriate time and place about how cooperative all the agencies should be during this difficult time, and I will make sure everyone understands this is a team effort. We genuinely want to solve this murder."

Gennaro stood up, still holding Alessandro's pencil. "That is appreciated."

Farese buttoned his blazer, the cue for his closing statement. "I'm certain Detective Farrugia will be vindicated. Attention should be focused on that terrorist organization since they claimed responsibility. Let's start there, okay?"

"Okay."

Farese smiled again and left. The door closed.

The phone rang.

"DiBello here."

"Chief, it's us, Alessandro and Dante."

"What do the two of you want?"

"We saw everything. Lot of talking between you and Farese in the office."

"What the hell . . ." He glanced up and saw the two of them peeking through their office blinds. Alessandro was sharing the phone with Dante.

"You two are incorrigible."

"Thanks, Chief. What did U.S. Attorney Farese say?"

"What did he say? I'll tell you what he said so listen very closely." Gennaro glanced up. The blinds parted further. "He said, 'Don't count your money in front of poor people.'"

8

Farrugia had never had French toast. It looked like he might not yet.

He sat at the counter, on the stool, watching Bianca frittering about the kitchen. There she was, with her long legs, her hair tied up, an egg in hand and eyes consulting Dante's iPad, either for a French toast recipe or instructions on how to crack an egg.

"I could just go to the corner and get us pastries," he said. "It'll just take a moment. Honest."

She had that hurt look.

"Never mind," he said. The hard stool was uncomfortable. The squat-pulses in the group exercise class did not help. His glutes did not concern him since he always possessed something of a pancake ass. It was his gut. He pinched an inch, or was it more? Still there. He wondered whether these French toasts would be of any help.

"You know that you have a problem with ants. You might want to put some cinnamon down."

She looked over to the troublesome spot. "Cinnamon, huh?" She turned to him. "You really need to be careful, you know."

"Tell me about it. I've never had French toasts."

"It's French *toast*, and I'm talking about being careful going out and about. You might have to contend with the media and photo snoops."

"Let me enjoy my coffee, please. I know. That bearded goat Ragonese had to mention my name. Bad enough that he had to get elegiac about the slaughter of an innocent—which it was, no disagreement there—but mention the Knox and Cermis affairs in the same breath? Asshole."

Breakfast was served. He looked down at his plate. A slice of stale bread, partly soaked in a couple of whisked eggs then slightly burned in a pan. He could see places where the bread remained dry. Perhaps he needn't have worried about his weight.

She added a bottle of maple syrup to the counter.

"Did the French really invent this?"

"Eat, Isidò. You've died nearly a thousand times. I doubt that my breakfast will kill you."

He followed her lead, placing syrup on the golden-brown bread. It soaked into the dry spots. "Or dinner."

"Was dinner that bad?"

"No. It was delicious. Though the conversation didn't improve my appetite. This whole thing is under my skin like a tick. The alley still bothers me."

"I can imagine. Two killers. One shooting his partner and then—"

"That and seeing the kid. He pleaded, Bianca. He begged for his life and they killed him anyway. I mean, I've seen some brutal things in my life, but most of the time it was after the fact, and one mafia scum killing another doesn't bother me. It's when they kill innocent people to get at one of their own that I get very upset, or when they kill witnesses before trials. Even then, I'm usually there after the fact. This time, I saw it, and this kid was an innocent. Ragonese was correct about that. He was just a kid. An ordinary goofy-looking kid."

"Sorry. We shouldn't talk about this over breakfast."

Farrugia's appetite was healthy despite the conversation. The knife and fork cut toast and mopped syrup. It was . . . passable, though that might say more about his hunger. He took another slurp of very hot coffee. She had made it American-style to match breakfast. French roast and French toast. Bianca was consistent.

"No," he said. "We should talk. Like you, I didn't put all my cards on the table last night."

"What do you mean? I don't understand."

Farrugia paused over his choice of words. "You know that you're dear to me, Bianca. I might be an old friend of Gennaro, and he and I have that bond of death and anti-mafia work, and I'm sincerely fond of the gang, but it's professional with Alessandro and Dante. You're a woman and it's different. I'm not trying to sound chauvinistic or the typical protective Italian here, because it's not that. You and I are alike in many ways. We both don't trust. We both kept our secrets last night."

She sipped her coffee and examined him with the eyes of a chess master.

"We both know that's the truth," he said.

"How so?"

"Trying to draw me out? Okay, I can play. First, you didn't tell Dante about this kid. You came to me instead, and even when you did, you didn't tell me everything. I went with you because I had a bad feeling. At first you said no and I had to twist your arm, so to speak, and good thing I did because you would've been killed. What?"

"I don't want to hear this from you. I heard the same thing from Dante. Farrugia saved your life in Boston, Farrugia saved your life on Via Manzoni, Farrugia this, Farrugia that."

"Calm down, Bianca. That's not my point. And yes, I *am* telling you that those two would've killed you. I saw them. I know killers. You have to believe me that they would've killed you. What I'm getting at is that you need to trust."

She stopped eating. "Like you do? Who do you trust? You trust Gennaro? You trust me?"

"I trust Gennaro, yes."

He saw a tear forming. He heard: "And me? You don't trust me?"

He was silent.

"You bastard. I can't believe you."

She put her coffee down. She glared at him. A tear rolled down from her right eye.

"Let me ask you this, Bianca," he said. "Nobody except me knows that the kid said something to you before he ducked into the bar, right? You certainly didn't mention it last night. I didn't ask. I didn't even mention the kiss."

"Dante knows about the kiss. He found that out from Gennaro, through you. So what?"

"Dante should have found out about the kiss from you. That's exactly my point. Did he say something?"

"Charlie? Yes, he did."

His eyebrows went up. He stopped his knife and fork.

She said nothing.

"You know something, Bianca, even amongst friends and even with the man with whom you share your bed, you still keep secrets." He took a last sip of coffee. "I won't ask you what the young man said. I won't ask because you have some reason for not telling me or anyone else for that matter."

"Off to meet Internal Affairs?" She wiped her wet cheek.

"Yep. I'm supposed to have a union rep there." He checked his watch. "No need for you to worry. I won't mention you at all to them, or about whatever the last words were from Charlie, or the kiss. Nothing." He walked over to the peg on the wall and took his jacket.

"What will you say then?"

"I don't know, but I'll be consistent. I might say that I was going to see the poet Carlo Gadda's birthplace on Via Manzoni, or that I wanted to do window shopping, and it took me time to find parking when I noticed Charlie Brooks and two suspicious men following him. Instinct kicked in. I could say that."

"Thank you."

He put first one arm in the sleeve, then the other, and with a shrug made his shoulders comfortable. "Only thing is, all that goes to hell if someone identifies you and says you looked across the street and saw me, or if anyone saw you period. Then you become a material witness."

"You're a material witness, too. You saw Charlie die and you confronted the killers. Do you think anyone saw me? Dante seems to think I left the scene fast enough. I hacked the surveillance cameras. The traffic lights were too far apart to be of any use."

"Don't forget, the shops on Manzoni might have surveillance cameras. I'm not worried about them."

"You're not?"

He nodded. He knew he could use a shave, and he wished that he could stay, but he couldn't. He did take a quick shower and they had an unused toothbrush. His more immediate concern was IA.

"Shop cameras are usually cheap crap and limited. You say that the traffic surveillance doesn't say much, and I'll take your word for it. I'm more concerned about the two college kids who wanted to try their moves on you. They're the only ones who had a good look at you. They were studying you. The issue is if they made a statement to the police about the lady with the leather jacket and the unique fringe. The fringe on that jacket stood out. No disrespect to the rest of the ensemble, but the fringe was memorable."

"Fuck." She stamped "No good fashion statement goes unpunished."

"I really need to go," he said.

As he walked away, she called out his name.

"Yes?"

She walked over to him and hugged him. "I'm sorry."

He didn't know what to do with the embrace. He stroked the back of her head and wished he could promise everything would be okay.

Gennaro was perusing a witness statement when he heard the double rapping knock against his open door. He slid his glasses down the bridge of his nose, looked up over the frame and found Alessandro and Dante standing there, like eager schoolboys reporting to their headmaster.

"Ah, one for each testicle. Come in."

Alessandro, paper in hand, looked over to Dante and led the way as the worried pupil of the two. "Chief, it's official. You remember when I said I had an in at Ballistics."

"Yes. A potential girlfriend. When you say you had an 'in' I presume that wasn't premature." He smiled. Alessandro and his love life, real or imagined.

"Funny, Chief, but you might not find this so funny. It's there on paper."

He handed him the paper. The report provided the narrative and Alessandro, the commentary. "Ballistics confirms the casings are Gévelots. The bullets from the autopsies . . . same findings, of course, and, from what I'm hearing, the guns found with the two assassins are Hungarian-made. Real pro stuff. The weapons are cold. Serial numbers are gone and they don't match to any other crimes in the databases, including Interpol's."

Gennaro took off his glasses. "Of course not. Dante, please close the door. You two need to sit down."

Dante returned and pulled up a chair to join Alessandro.

"Autopsies give us anything else?" Gennaro asked. "Any drugs, distinguishing tattoos on the killers, that kind of thing?"

Alessandro shook his head.

"With all due respect, Boss," Dante, said, "why aren't we asking who these killers are, their names, that kind of thing?"

"Because they don't exist. They both might as well be named Mario Rossi. *Il Signore Rossi* one and two."

Alessandro glanced over to Dante. "John Doe? I'm not sure I understand, Chief."

Gennaro tossed the paper onto the desk. It landed softly on top of the witness reports. "The two of you ever hear of Mino Pecorelli?" From their blank looks, he continued. "He was a journalist in the seventies. From Isernia, and he worked in Rome. Pecorelli had phenomenal contacts. They gave him real credibility, but they were also very scary people. He founded the *Osservatorio Politico*, which specialized in political scandals. Really hard-hitting stuff, and not this bullshit we see in gossip magazines. Mino had balls and a sense of humor. He kicked it up into high gear after Aldo Moro was kidnapped and killed. Please tell me you know who Moro was?" They nodded this time. "Pecorelli had his own theories about complicity in Moro's death. When I heard about the Gévelots I thought of Mino."

"You thought of this journalist because of the bullets?" Dante said. "Why?"

Gennaro turned his chair sideways and talked to the crucifix on his wall, as if he was confessing to Christ.

"Pecorelli called out names, but it was his publication of Moro's letters that got him killed. He was gunned down in the Prati district. Four gunshots. Bullets? Gévelots. Did your girlfriend in Ballistics tell you that they are rare?"

Alessandro said nothing.

"She's probably too young, like you, to remember the Years of Lead. You have heard of *gli anni di piombo*, haven't you?"

Alessandro shifted uncomfortably, not liking the implication that he was young and ignorant. While that implication was sinking in, Gennaro's eyes searched Dante.

"I've heard of the Years of Lead," he said, "but I could never keep track of the conspiracy theories. The seventies were full of conspiracy theories."

The leg of Gennaro's eyeglasses did a metronomic dance in his right hand. "I'm not talking about UFOs. The Gévelots from the Pecorelli assassination were traced to a basement beneath the Ministry of Health, to a stockpile belonging to a terrorist organization, the *Banda della Magliana*. Anyway it became a who's who list of criminals and associations—not just with Pecorelli but also with other journalists—and the blood ran uphill into the top levels of finance, government, and industry. I'm surprised you didn't know about this, Dante. You're older than Sandro. It went all the way up Andreotti's ass."

"I knew some of the history," Dante said. "I didn't know the specifics about Pecorelli or the bullets used to kill him. Everybody knows about Moro and the *Brigate Rosse*."

Gennaro's eyes examined Alessandro for any knowledge of the things everyone knew.

"Of course I remember Andreotti," Alessandro said, "but not so much in connection with Pecorelli and Moro. I know him for *Tangentopoli*, the bribery scandals, and the Achille Lauro and the Craxi feud. I was a kid then, Chief. I was a teen when the Berlin disco bombing happened."

"Sorry, Sandro, I forget how young you are sometimes; although I wish history was better taught in our schools. Today, history is being revised, and not so much for objectivity. Andreotti has had a long career, but that's not the point of my focus. It's these damn bullets. This gets out to the public and people hear *Gévelots*, and we have a problem on our hands because old-timers like me remember. A pimple like Ragonese explains *Gévelot* and the pot gets stirred again." Gennaro looked out to the hallway. "Oh, shit. Here comes Perego."

Alessandro and Dante stood up and buttoned their suit jackets.

Perego knocked, stuck his head in the door and said, "All of you should listen to this. The Free Channel is running an update."

Gennaro put on his glasses. "Isidò was right."

"Right about what, Boss?"

"Ragoneses is a goat fucker."

Alessandro and Dante both left, smiling. As Gennaro buttoned his jacket, he looked at the crucifix.

"What did I do to you to deserve this?"

9

A listless gray hallway of meaningless cinderblock in the bowels of the building led Farrugia to a square room where two men waited for him. They sat on opposites sides of a rectangular table, with a single light overhead and one oblong panel of two-way glass on one wall. The other wall was more of the same, anonymous gray.

Farrugia knew his place was on the side of the table, the one with his back to the door so he couldn't see who might enter the room. That was the rule, the standard layout for an interrogation. The man opposite him was allowed to see who entered because he was the director, while the everyman to Farrugia's right, the union rep, was his advocate and defender, his prompter feeding him forgotten lines.

Impartiality was not the guiding principle here. Interdepartmental politics were—and that was the other rule, the unspoken but well-known rule that went back decades. Nobody liked Internal Affairs. They had a job to do, but as the joke about the Italian civil service went: "All paychecks come from the same place, the road to Rome."

A round of introductions, a tepid glass of water for tepid hospitality, and yellow-lined memo pads were distributed to both sides of the table. The expectation was that one side of the table would draw a canary in a cage while the other side drew the cage, all the pretty bars, and the open door, seen from the point of the view of that bird.

Both cops and the mafia, as Farrugia learned, hate the same thing: the snitch.

"Thank you for coming, Commissario Farrugia," the IA tool said. "You have your union representative with you. I wish to say outright that this is a formality and we hope to resolve this rather quickly since you did not discharge your weapon. This is merely a formality but one that my department and other departments, namely those that deal with the public, have to indulge in because of the sensitive nature of this particular case. By no means is this meeting meant to impugn your reputation, malign your years of service, or be misconstrued as a criminal investigation. Please note that there is no stenographer. This is not a deposition."

Farrugia knew that there was a camera watching, perhaps five people behind the two-way analyzing how he spoke, how many times he blinked, swallowed, or moved in his chair. And they would replay that tape from every conceivable angle more times than the sports experts replayed the questionable game-winning play or the penalty-losing foul.

"Please state your name and the date of the event."

"Isidore Farrugia, and it happened May eighth."

"I'm sorry, I mean your full name, rank, and date of the incident."

"Commissario Isidore no middle name Farrugia, and the incident took place on May eighth."

"Please explain why you are in Milan?"

"A colleague of mine is retiring. I decided to take some vacation time, travel north and help him arrange his party."

"Your colleague's name."

"Gennaro DiBello."

"Is he a friend also?"

"Yes."

"Length of either professional or personal relationship?"

"Twenty-five years in both capacities, friend and colleague."

"Please explain why you were there on the Via Manzoni."

"To kill time. I'm sorry, bad choice of words. I guess I was there to do touristy things. Gadda's birthplace and home, the fashion stores, relax and see the sights."

Some scribble of notes. Stick to simple statements, Farrugia.

"And how exactly did the events arise from there?"

"I was in my car, and upon leaving the car, which was parked across from Bar Gadda, I had, out of reflex, looked both ways and crossed the street. Before crossing I noticed the young man who—"

"You mean the deceased. Charles Brooks, Jr."

"Yes, him. Shall I continue?"

"Please do."

"I saw that this young man appeared distressed. He kept looking over his shoulder, and that called attention to the two men behind him. They seemed to be following him, and when Mr. Brooks looked again I concluded that he was indeed being followed and I proceeded to cross the street."

"To accomplish what?"

"To help him."

"So you weren't just crossing the street? You decided to help him because you happened to see him and thought that he was in trouble with the two men following him? How did you plan to help him?"

"Yes, I thought that. I didn't know how I could help him. I thought perhaps if I joined him, then maybe his followers would be discouraged. One of him and two of them, so I thought that if I approached Mr. Brooks, it would even it out to two against two."

"I see. You crossed the street and . . ."

"I was delayed crossing the street by traffic, and when I reached the other side, Mr. Brooks had already decided to run into Bar Gadda. Seeing that the other two men were in pursuit, and through the front door of Bar Gadda, I followed in after them . . ."

"At what point did you identify yourself?"

"Once I was inside Gadda, and then as I proceeded out back."

"You identified yourself while in pursuit, and as you reached the rear section of the kitchen where there was a door that opens out to the alley, correct?"

Farrugia nodded and saw numerous scratches of pen against yellow.

"And then what happened?"

"I tried to determine my strategy since the door was partially closed.

I didn't know the alley or exactly where the two perpetrators were. It happened very quickly. Two shots were fired. I went through the door and it was a stalemate. Mr. Brooks was already dead on the ground, and I had two weapons pointed at me. I identified myself again, a squad car arrived, and I assume that the leader of the two made the decision to—"

"To shoot his accomplice and then himself?"

"Yes."

"How have you passed your time since all this has happened?"

"I joined a gym."

"Constructive. Admirable. Any nightmares? Any vivid recollections?"

Psych-eval question. Nobody admitted to flashbacks.

"No. None."

"Have you gone out?"

"Gone out? Yes."

"Tell us about last night."

"I had dinner with friends."

"Name them, please."

"Gennaro DiBello, Alessandro Monotti, and Dante Allegretti."

The man's writing was too slow and precise writing down the last names. Dramatic since he already knew the names from surveillance.

"And Bianca Nerini. She's Allegretti's girlfriend."

Might as well admit it since he already knew that she was on the surveillance list.

"And then?"

"We ate and we talked. I can describe each course if you wish."

"Not necessary. Did you talk about the case?"

"No."

"Not at all?" The man put his hands together and interlocked them. This meant he had something. "You do know that DiBello was appointed lead investigator?"

"No, I didn't know." No need to lie there.

"In fact, he was appointed head of the investigation by his superior

Lino Perego in a joint investigation with the U.S. Attorney Michael Farese. You didn't know any of that?"

"I didn't." Same question twice meant he thought the first answer was a lie.

"What did you talk about all evening?"

"How much we dislike Giancarlo Ragonese and some idle chitchat, like the weather, and other mundane matters."

"Nothing about the case, nothing about ballistics?"

Another nod.

"And how would you characterize Mr. Allegretti?"

"A good guy. Everyone there is someone I like. I wouldn't break bread with them if I didn't."

"And Monotti? And, um, Ms. Nerini—how do you feel about her?"

"Already answered you."

"Like her enough to stay overnight? Are you and Ms. Nerini more than acquaintances?"

The union representative put his arms across Farrugia's chest. "He's been cooperative. Relevance?"

"I find it strange that he spent the night. This is the same group of individuals who worked the Roma Underground case, and it's peculiar that they didn't speak about the Brooks case. Rather odd, when one considers that Commissario Farrugia traveled to Boston. Ms. Nerini lived in Boston last year."

The union rep looked at Farrugia. "I'll allow it."

"I went to Boston to see her, and I also saw Farese. I helped him with a case."

"And where was Mr. Allegretti when you were in Boston?"

"Here, in Milan."

"You and Ms. Nerini together in Boston. You stay overnight? Where did you sleep?"

"What is it to you?"

"All about character, Commissario. You departed three hours after

Mr. Allegretti left for work. That's a very long breakfast."

"I stayed because it was getting late, I was tired, and my place was across town."

"You were tired? But not too tired to join a gym and take an advanced exercise class. You could've taken a taxi. One of the other guests could've given you a lift—Mr. DiBello, perhaps. You were tired from staying up late talking about nothing?"

Farrugia stared at the man. It seemed they were done being polite.

The union rep agreed. "I think we are through here."

"No. I have one question," Farrugia said. "I would like to know whether I could have my weapon back. It wasn't part of the crime."

The man folded his hands again. "I'm afraid I can't do that. You're not cleared yet. There are some questions that remain unanswered."

"Like what? What questions?"

"Perhaps you can answer this one: a surveillance camera down the street from Bar Gadda has a view of you in your car. It seems that you were sitting in your car for quite some time. Did you need to consult a map to find the fashion houses, perhaps La Scala, or where Verdi died? One might think that you were staking out Bar Gadda, waiting for something to go down."

"We're definitely done," said the union rep. "If G9 killed the student then Commissario Farrugia has the expectation to protect himself, as an officer of the law."

"And as an officer of the court he should understand that he is also a material witness against Gruppo 9. We can offer him protection."

"From them or you?" said Farrugia. "Nothing like not feeling safe in your own house."

"I'm not an unreasonable man, Commissario Farrugia. Tell you what—I'm sure you can get a temporary sidearm. Besides, your Beretta is really passé. You should have one of the new Beretta eight thousands. DiBello's boss can probably get you the Beretta Cougar, but there's the problem of yet another regulation . . ."

"Another regulation? Which one?"

"You'd have to qualify the weapon. A regulation, you know."

"I know. Mere formality. Like this meeting."

10

If it rolls like a tank and shoots like a tank, it is a tank.

Early the following morning, Bianca was back in front of her computer, staring at the schematic of the damned tank in her private workspace. She was doing battle with Adastra's tank on her screen, on her white Google desk, its aerodynamic Venlet design from Italian office manufacturer Babini in contrast to this brutish creature with rolling treads and a mobile platform for a head. She sat in her Citterio chair and stared at this child of Mars.

Nothing seemed to distinguish this tank from the archival specifications for modern armored warfare she found online. Everything from the history of the 1st Cavalry Division to the evolution of the M1 Abrams in the Iraq Conflict and a fascinating digression on Rommel's desert tactics added up to a massive zero for her. There was not one iota of insight as to why this Adastra tank was so special, so interesting to Charlie, or so lethal for him.

Was he poaching information to show off to his Dad, who had served in the 1st Cavalry? But if Farrugia was correct and the schematic existed only on paper, and Charlie's photo snap was somehow witnessed, reported, and communicated up some chain of command that ordered his death, then that should bring her back to investigating Adastra executives. But which one? As for the military contract, the supply-chain management and the expenses—it was like reading an Escher drawing, the spreadsheet equivalent of the hand drawing the hand that draws the picture.

"You should take a break," he said.

Dante. She hadn't heard him come in.

"I will later; it's early and I'll get out on the balcony later. Off to work soon?"

Dante didn't say another word as he worked his tie. There was always pleasure in watching him dress in the morning. Unlike most men, Dante did not eschew the suit and tie. He took pride, like most Italian men, in subtle touches of rebellion. No tight tie in geometrical conformity for him. He was no Brit, nor like an unimaginative American with his standard four-in-hand knot. No. Dante was subversive as only an Italian could be subversive. He wound the thick material of his tie not once but twice around for that asymmetrical, elegant yet disheveled knot. Effortless nonchalance. He is an heir to Castiglione's courtier. *Sprezzatura.*

"You're a hermit, Bianca. It's not healthy."

"You forget that Charlie isn't dead a week, and that there actually might be someone out there who can identify me. It's best I don't go out."

Dante sighed. "You're right, but still you should get out even if only for some air. Do something with sunglasses and a scarf. I need to go." He looked guilty. "I know we haven't gone out much, but once this gets settled I'd like for you and I, maybe the group, to go out and enjoy a nice evening in a restaurant. I miss that." He leaned down and kissed her on the cheek. "I've got to go."

"I miss it, too" she said as he walked away. And she did. Much as she liked his home-cooked meals, she missed the social atmosphere of a restaurant, seeing other people enjoying life, conversing, falling in love and enjoying the simplicity of human contact. It was intimate.

If only intimacy were so simple. They'd been civil since Dante's interrogation, but the undercurrent was at a low riptide, and their conversations were as surreal as a Buñuel dialog. What was real was said but also imagined, known only from knowing each other so well. Their sentences should mean one thing but were instead italicized.

Her coffee next to her was dark, even cruel, and the cherry jam on her toast looked like dried blood. Time to get back to work.

The analysis of the Adastra financials was going nowhere; there was no discernible pattern in the dates, figures, or account numbers. There was no slush fund, or if there were one Adastra had done a damn good job of hiding it. When in doubt, think Occam, she told herself. What was it about the Adastra product line that made the company unique?

Time to look at Adastra helicopters.

Nothing too out of the ordinary, she thought as she clicked through the specifications: twin-turbine, five-bladed rotor, respectable cruise speed, admirable power-to-weight ratio, and excellent safety evaluations for "hot and high" operating conditions. Their birds could certainly carry a respectable number of commandos for paramilitary ops. The Italian taxpayer should be happy: value for the Euro.

More clicks: EU compliance certificate for ergonomics, a Green certificate for environmental emissions, some more lingo on integrated avionics, and other bafflegab jargon dreamt up by the Prosperos in Adastra Marketing. Nothing. It seemed that the selling point for this bird of prey of the Italian borders was its unique power reserve. That might mean something.

She closed out that window. Was there anything unique about the power reserve for the tank? Did tanks have a power reserve?

Nothing.

She opened up the browser cache. Time to look through the chaos of html pages, sort them by date, and parse for logic to forensically resurrect Charlie's website. This was not a very promising adventure, since the pages would come up like zombies with dead hyperlinks and gouged-out whitespaces where images should be. Viewing these pages would be like a color-blind dyslexic trying to make sense of Track Changes on a Word document by multiple authors.

The coffee was cold. This was frustrating.

There was another obvious avenue to pursue, but after this fiasco with Farrugia, she knew that Dante wouldn't like it. She wasn't sure that she liked it.

Still, it was a thought.

Dante walked out of the elevator. The flat-screen was on and the office bodies were gathered around for another vigil.

Not again.

The Free Channel and Giancarlo Ragonese were hard humping for the *Premio Cutuli*, the journalism prize; and if he converted his experiences to literature, the *Premio Strega*, the prestigious literary award. And if all that went international with movie rights, the Academy Award. The Oscar for Best Nonentity.

"What is he saying now?" Dante asked.

Gennaro's hands sprinkled imaginary fairy dust to indicate his *I don't know*.

The bearded one and a young man were on the screen. Dante recognized the other man as one of the political candidates. This man was handsome, with a blend of intriguing features: broad alpine forehead, chestnut hair, soft blue eyes, opaque skin, a leptorrhine nose, a solid jaw, and full lips. He was wearing a wool suit, gray pinstripe on black, French blue dress shirt, no tie, and open collar.

Cut to a commercial.

Dante scanned the crowd. Alessandro remained engrossed with the commercial, which featured a nice RAI talking head, although he doubted that Alessandro was admiring her for her enunciation. Perego was tense and anxious.

The last time the office had convened around the flickering altar of Giancarlo's magic realism, he had given a brief history of Gruppo 9, which had amounted to nothing more than postcard photos of former leaders, all of them dead, and a string of gruesome post-mortem photographs so pornographic for their violence that viewers sent in letters of protest to the studio and to the local newspapers. It was exactly the effect that Ragonese had wanted to have with his viewers. Ratings went through the roof. Ragonese had taken his lessons from American shock journalists. As for content and leads on Brooks and G9, he had said nothing of substance that wasn't already known.

Dante let out an impatient sigh. He hated the news.

"He's coming on," somebody in the room yelled. The office grew quiet.

"Good morning, my fellow citizens. Thank you for joining me once again in my series of investigations. We last discussed the G9, and today I'm privileged to have with me in the studio the leading candidate from the newly formed Communist Party, the L and S, the *Libertà e Solidarietà*."

Two men on a dais, a distant camera shot zoomed in. Canned applause.

"I welcome to the studio today L and S's own Raffaele Palmisano who, as you all know, is affectionately called 'Lele.' But before we conduct our interview, I'd like to address a viewer who has called in on the studio line, asking why I've grown this beard. 'Why has Giancarlo changed his look?' the loyal viewer has asked. I can assure you that this new look was not my stylist's idea—"

The goat had a stylist?

"I grow my beard as a sign of personal distress," the goat said. "Until there is a change in our Italy, a change from corruption to virtue, crime to safety, terrorism to peace, and—"

Someone in the room yelled, "Anybody believe this donkey?"

"Sssh," replied a chorus. Gennaro's eyes stared at the screen, his fingers against his lips.

"I will shave this beard after the next election," Ragonese said. "Let me now welcome Candidate Palmisano. But before we discuss your opinion on the recent events at Via Manzoni and the G9's declaration of responsibility, please tell us about yourself."

"Thank you. I—"

"As the unlikely candidate from Catania you've managed some remarkable feats in a short period of time," Ragonese said, interrupting his own guest. "Your popularity is in the ascendancy and your political platform straddles the delicate balance on issues dear to both conservatives and liberals alike."

"Let the man talk, you jackass," someone yelled.

"Thank you for having me here today." Palmisano stroked his own chin. "I admire your statement with your beard. It is very much like the Holy Father Julius II, who grew his beard as a sign of mourning for losing Bologna."

Ragonese seemed to take the flattery and lofty comparison like a kitten to cream. Why shouldn't he be compared to the Pope, after all?

Palmisano shifted in his chair and seemed ready to talk politics.

"Yes, I'm proud to say that my party has managed to negotiate some difficult obstacles. We have a blend of conservatives, liberals, moderates, and even some Greens. We believe that Italy must move forward. We believe that Italy can be as economically successful as the Germans. Viewers at home can go to my website and read the party's proposals for nationwide educational reform, for healthcare, immigration, and technology. I'm particularly proud of the technology initiative. I believe every home in Italy should have a computer and the latest in connectivity."

The website address ran on a banner below the man's face.

The bearded Ragonese was smiling. "Thank you. By the way, I love your party's slogan, '*Bene commune.*' It is simple but absolute elegance, given the diversity of your party. Bravo."

The music cue signaled that the conversation should get serious.

"Candidate Palmisano, I spoke to our viewers about G9 recently and about its statement, claiming full responsibility for the senseless murder. As you know, the Brooks family is here in Milan, awaiting developments on the case. What can you say on the matter?"

"There is no indication that the law-enforcement agencies are not being diligent. A family grieves and a nation here is hopeful that justice can be found and served. We must simply wait. Be patient. Have faith in law enforcement. I've tried to speak with the Brooks family but, because I'm a Communist, they've refused to meet with me. I respect their wishes, but I extend my condolences nonetheless. It is unfortunate, these political differences, but the L and S and myself have every faith that G9 will be brought to justice."

"That is truly unfortunate," Ragonese said. The camera did a fast cut to a quivering flame inside a votive and bundles of flowers at Via Manzoni. Makeshift cards and posters were not litter but declarations of sadness while viewers heard Ragonese speaking. "Grief is human and politics should step aside, indeed. I know that you went this morning to Via Manzoni and paid your respects. What are your plans while in Milan?"

Palmisano said, "I did visit Via Manzoni to lay flowers where the young man died. After I'm done speaking with you, I plan to meet with local representatives within my party, and tomorrow I'll leave for Rome to discuss anti-terrorist legislation and—"

Ragonese's face dropped along with his hand holding his index cards. His surprise didn't look feigned. "You, a Communist, are proposing an anti-terrorism law? Please elaborate."

"The measures were already drafted, but they've been revised in light of recent events. While the G9 is a terrorist organization, they are but one type of terrorist. Our anti-terrorist legislation broadens the definition of 'act of terrorism' and I plan to define 'terrorist' to include economic and politically coercive actions, whether it is done by an individual or a group. We've redefined 'group' as well. For example, a bank that drives food prices up through speculation or a corporation that provides untrained private security personnel to kill civilians can be as much of a terrorist as a Bin Laden or a Carlos the Jackal."

Ragonese gave his scholarly look. "As much as you've offered support to the Brooks family and the American people in these tragic times, you've also been critical of some U.S. policies."

"I have. Friends should disagree. America and Italy have a long-standing friendship. Italian-Americans have made great contributions to their new homeland and to the world. We also share a political heritage. We're both republics, although our developmental history and point of view are different."

Ragonese did his Rodin, hand to chin. "But you remain critical."

"I do. I'm critical of American corporations, their efforts and policies on globalization, and I believe that if they are to function here in Italy they should pay taxes and hire Italians. Italy will not repeat the failure of American corporations in Ireland or tolerate that kind of abandonment. That was a fiscal disaster, and the Irish people suffered emotionally and financially. It will not happen in Italy."

"Strong words," Ragonese said.

"In light of the loans debacle, I feel U.S. financial instruments in our banks should be scrutinized. I'm also advocating for a reduction, a de-escalation policy, of U.S. and NATO installations and offices throughout Italy. I'm particularly vocal about U.S. military personnel who've committed crimes and escaped prosecution. That unfortunate history goes back to the second world war. Unfortunate but true and seldom discussed."

"So true," Ragonese said. "But still, you take a particularly strong, I would daresay, radical position."

"I disagree. I'm not against the U.N. or NATO. Italy's membership in NATO is not up for discussion. But if I'm elected prime minister I will block the addition of the NATO base in Vicenza and the construction of the new radar installations in Sardinia. And I will revoke the order for new fighter planes and helicopters. The people of Vicenza and Sardinia have spoken and I must honor their voice. The construction of these bases in Sardinia would also be an environmental disaster. On this point I'm proud to say even my political opponents are in agreement with the L and S. I can't say that I've convinced them about the fighter planes and helicopters, but it is remarkable progress that there is even agreement amongst the parties. Again, this is too brief a forum to discuss all my policies on behalf of my party, so again I direct viewers to the L and S website."

The guy in Receivables holding the remote, said, "Palmisano has some serious balls."

Ragonese read off the website URL and added, "One last thing, Lele, if I may call you that."

Palmisano smiled. "Please ask, Giancarlo."

"You know that the Americans, especially their conservatives, will criticize your policies. They'll certainly criticize your lifestyle, since you're an openly gay man."

The guest practiced his politician's laugh. "Giancarlo, thank you for the levity. I find that subject quite funny, but I know I should be serious. Even the liberals in America are conservative, and I understand full well that many U.S. conservatives are aligned with fundamentalist Christian groups who will disapprove of me. Again, our historical and cultural developments are different. I accept the fact that the American president ends his speech invoking God's blessings, whereas I would never do such a thing as a European, not because I'm a Communist, but rather because it's inappropriate. Cultural difference aside, the U.S. should respect our political differences, and not impose their beliefs and—"

"I admit it. The American government has been moralistic."

There was more canned applause. Behind the two men there appeared a montage of Palmisano sunning himself on the Letojanni beach of Taormina with his partner at his side.

"The religious elements in American society will attack your personal preference," said Ragonese with the serious tone of an American talk-show host.

Somebody yelled, "I can't believe Ragonese said that. 'Personal preference.' Look at those pictures. Disgusting."

Dante was uncertain if *disgusting* referred to the fact that Ragonese ran the pictures or to the pictures themselves. Palmisano did not look the least perturbed.

"I will say it on the air, because I'm not ashamed of it. I'm a '*cattocomunista*,' a Catholic, openly gay, and a Communist. And, if that seems like a contradiction of collectivistic terms for an American or an Italian then so be it, but Italy seems to have accepted me. My popularity is proof, and my candidacy is a statement that the Italian people are ready for change. You might be shaving that beard soon, my friend, if I am elected prime minister."

The applause spiked to higher decibels.

"Thank you, Raffaele Palmisano, and if elected you bring the shaving cream."

Both men shared smiles and a laugh together.

The flat screen flashed off.

Gennaro hadn't said a word. Perego was now standing next to him.

Then, perhaps the last thing Dante expected, happened. The elevator chimed, the doors opened, and out walked Silvio, paper in hand.

He looked rested but confused. He must be utterly disoriented by the fast elevator and the new office, the bright lights, the crowd of faces around the television, because he didn't recognize him or Gennaro.

He held out his paper in front of him, like a tourist, and said, "This is the latest I'm early. Where can I find Signore Prego?"

11

Farrugia listened to his voicemail. The union rep said something about a second IA interview tomorrow; this time about "going over the timeline." The union rep tried not to sound worried, but he wasn't very successful at it. The rep could pretend not to be worried but Farrugia himself was. His job and career and pension were on the line.

Both he and the rep shared that sailor's trepidation of being out in open water, with neither of them knowing how to swim, the both of them hanging onto one stick of wood, while the sharks circled.

Damn. Almost time for yoga class. He had switched his allegiance away from the intense exercise class earlier in the week, needing soothing escapism rather than proof he was not too old. He could afford the indignity of being less flexible. Men were allowed to be physically inflexible.

At his first class, the instructor welcomed his presence. He was, after all, the only man in the class, and she did say something about him being *the* Isidore Farrugia, which drew some discreet but interested looks that he didn't seem to mind. Far better to enjoy the appreciative glances of attractive women, some with Cirque du Soleil flexibility, rather than endure a Paleolithic muscle-bound hominid in the weight-room who *had to prove* that he could lift heavier weights, bench press more than *the* Isidore Farrugia. How tedious, and too much of a reminder of Pinolo.

Besides, yoga helped him sleep better, deal with stress better. He felt better, even after just one class, his first experience with yoga ever.

Today's class was to be something different, called yin yoga. Noelle would guide the contortions of the body and liberate the mind for forty-five minutes.

He tossed his cell phone into the locker, closed it and wrapped the key's elastic thingy around his wrist. Towel and water bottle in hand, with enough time for him to get his props: two blocks, a mat, a bolster, and one of those soft, lovely blankets for shavasana at the end of class.

Yin yoga, she explained as he entered the room, is only five poses. Five sounded reasonable as he established his personal space. Her calming voice said that the challenge was "you must hold each pose for five minutes. Challenge is in the mind and not the body." That did sound challenging.

Still, this had to be easier than the vinyasa yoga he did with her in the heated room that left him feeling overcooked. He remembered welcoming the death pose, shavasana, and he remembered calling Gennaro when he had stepped out of the class to use the restroom. He was shivering from the cold air outside the studio, perspiring and having to pee. Shavasana, not child's pose, became his sanctuary. If only death were so kind.

Today there was another man in the class. He looked familiar. He kept looking. Yes, at him, checking out *the* Isidore Farrugia.

Farrugia confirmed that he didn't know him. What he'd recognized was that formulaic look: close-cropped hair, southern face . . . familiar somehow. Good, he was as flexible as the wood that made Pinocchio. The instructor was touching him. She always asked if it was okay to touch—what she called "an adjustment."

Throughout the class they continued to exchange looks.

Kapotasana. Pigeon pose. The instructor demonstrated, modifications included, and the advanced version made Farrugia contemplate chaotic thoughts that embarrassed him. All this lascivious flexibility, how could he not. He looked around the room at all the shapely, toned female bodies. Perfection.

Their eyes met again. Him.

Good . . . he looks as if pigeon pose pecked at his sciatic nerve and sent a message to his brain by way of his ass.

Then Farrugia realized it. His cop instinct, the one that told him,

"This is fucked." He knew the man's type now.

IA tail. The man was IA. He had told them he'd joined a gym.

A cop knew when he saw another cop.

Shavasna couldn't come soon enough.

Power reserve. Power supply. She clicked the mouse.

This was beyond frustrating. It was a dead-end brick wall. The M1-series of tanks used a gas turbine engine and JP8 jet fuel. That was a lot of power. She crosschecked her notes on supply-line management. The fuel, Jet Propellant 8, was a kerosene-based fuel replacement for diesel, mandated in MIL-DTL-83133. The Brits use it, too. And NATO. Code F-34. The fuel dates to the late seventies and is considered less prone to freezing and, apparently, lacks the odiferous qualities of diesel.

Too old and too traditional. It wasn't the damned fuel.

Power supply and avionics; power reserve for avionics.

She clicked open one of Charlie's documents. Now, there was a nice military word: "cognitive workload." She read about the electronic system. The design principle was to "reduce the number of logistical variables for the pilot and reduce reaction time." Translation: less time fiddling with the controls means more time to destroy targets with the weaponry. She ran her index finger down the list of the helicopter's payload. Scary shit.

She scanned a hundred pages of "interactive and integrated functional capabilities" and lost track of the acronyms. There was another document, called the GFD, the Glossary for Definitions, which was the military's way of obfuscating language at all sorts of levels. Redundant redundancy. The military was the one human enterprise on the planet that could be symbolized by the dragon eating its own tail, the Ouroboros.

No power reserve or supply for the Adastra helicopter's avionics.

No power reserve or supply for the Adastra tank's electronic system.

The common denominator between the two was Adastra and, with all the sub-contracting, it was difficult to tell what Adastra did that was proprietary. This was starting to look like any standard defense contract, where multiple companies bid against each other to obtain first-line status on the contract and then formed partnerships with their competitors to divide the spoils. This wasn't raping the taxpayer. It was corporate incest.

Dante would be upset. Gennaro would be upset. Farrugia would be incandescent.

She hated the idea; it was desperation, an admission of weakness, what the military called "a lack of mental fortitude," but she was tired of the brick wall, the dead-end.

"What the hell . . . everybody needs a consultant these days," she said to her screen.

She was contacting Loki.

12

Gennaro had his cell to his ear, the voice of Isidore Farrugia pounding his eardrum with profanities. He listened and waited for his chance. Alessandro entered the office, waited for a while, eager to say something, and then turned to leave. Gennaro motioned to him to stay and that he should sit down.

"Will you please calm down, Isidò?" The colorful and updated vocabulary was expanding his linguistic register in ways he wouldn't have imagined.

Farrugia paused for breath, and Gennaro saw it as an opportunity. "How can you accuse me of not listening? This is the most I've spoken after I said hello. I know you're upset. Just because I don't see you in front of me doesn't mean I'm both blind and deaf."

"What the hell am I supposed to do? I've got IA everywhere I go. I'm in a yoga class and there is IA" came blaring through the phone.

"Now listen to me . . . just because there was a man in the yoga class doesn't mean Internal Affairs is after you."

"You think I'm paranoid. You think—"

"No, I'm not saying you're paranoid. Okay, maybe you are a little bit. For all you know, Farrugia, this man could have been admiring you."

More expletives.

Gennaro listened, rolled his eyes, and picked the thread of thought out of the linguistic barrage. "I was not implying that you're not comfortable with your sexuality. For all you know the man could've been looking at the wall behind you and you just got in the way."

The office phone rang.

"Hold on. My other phone is ringing." He picked up the office phone, said hello. It was Perego, telling him about a meeting in twenty minutes. "A meeting? I didn't get an e-mail about any meeting." He used both shoulders to keep the phones in place to click the mouse and check e-mail. "My calendar says nothing about a meeting with you, Dottore Perego. What? I understand. Please hold one second."

He relaxed his shoulders and took the cell. He was about to say something to Farrugia, but Farrugia was questioning the personal integrity of Gennaro's ancestors in Campania.

Alessandro was wearing a subtle smirk.

"DiBello," Perego said into the right ear, "what is that noise?"

He lowered his cell phone. "That? I must apologize. Telemarketer. I will meet with you in fifteen minutes, yes?" He hung up the office phone with Perego, shot a look over to Alessandro, who had not moved. It was back to the cell phone and the crazy Calabrian.

Farrugia had lapsed into the *grecanico* of his grandparents on his father's side, a dialect Gennaro couldn't penetrate, so he placed his hand over the receiver and asked, "What is it, Sandro?"

Alessandro had his confused-boy look. "Farrugia is taking yoga?"

"What is it you want, Alessandro!" Then he held his index finger up. "Wait, Sandro," and returned to Farrugia on the line. "Farrugia, you need to pick your battles carefully, my friend. No cop on any police force in the world screws with Internal Affairs and gets away with it. It's in every academy handbook for cadets. Where? In the back on the blank page. Now just play along and stall them. And stop breaking my balls. You have your union rep. What? I don't care if he's useless."

Farrugia was still profanely insistent.

"Would you just listen to me, Isidò; you don't seem to get it: we are in Milan now, not in Rome. We are out of our territories. Do you understand that? I want to retire. I do not want to be carried out. Naples is not outside my window and the Aspromonte is not outside yours so please focus on that second interview with IA so the rest of my hair doesn't turn white today. I've got Perego and Farese to contend with and a shitload of paperwork all over my desk straight out of Kafka's imagination and I've got Sandro in front of me," at which Sandro smiled and nodded, "and I have no idea where the hell Dante is," to which Sandro began to explain, but Gennaro shooed the answer away with his free hand and pointed at his office door. "And Silvio just showed up. What?"

Silvio was exchanging pleasantries with Dante in the hallway.

"What are you whining about?" Farrugia said, apparently too shocked to be profane. "Silvio is there?"

"I'm not whining. Farrugia, you make sure you go to that second interview. Call me later. I so look forward to hearing from you again."

"Yes. Thank you for listening."

"Is that sarcasm?"

"Ask Silvio."

"Go and think about it and goodbye, Farrugia."

He closed the cell and threw it down like something dirty he had fished out of a sewer. He stared at Sandro.

"Sorry. What is it that you need, Sandro?"

"I was wondering when all of us are planning to have dinner?"

"I don't know. Food is not on my mind. Why?"

"I wanted all of you to meet my new girlfriend, Paola."

"Another one?" On saying it, he realized from Alessandro's face that he had hurt the man's feelings. "Sorry. I don't know what's come over me. Yes, we should all have dinner. I'd like to meet this woman. From Ballistics, right?"

Alessandro nodded as Gennaro started escorting him to the door, outside of which Silvio was waiting in the hallway. "I'll talk to Dante and we'll make the arrangements. Thank you. Come in, Silvio. Sorry to keep you waiting."

Alessandro left, and now Silvio presented himself. Mother of God, what a morning. He needed more patience. Silvio looked far too good-natured and bubbly, like a teacher's pet with a new adventure about frogs and snakes.

"Nice to see you, Silvio. Welcome to Milan. What can I do for you?"

"It's nice to see you, Dottore DiBello. I was having a malfunctioning experience with the automatic emulator and I was contemplating your assistance." Gennaro forgot that Silvio tried to speak English at all times.

He didn't bother to translate English back into Italian, because he understood him. "Sure, Silvio I'll help you with the copier. Just let me turn my voicemail on." And he walked to his desk and pressed a button on his phone's console. "That should do it. Are you ready?"

"Always already."

"That's nice, Silvio, that's nice."

Farrugia saw the union rep up ahead. The man was roly-poly, with a full face, pink with a creamy white babyish complexion and a distended belly from too much time behind the desk. Although he could tell that the man was well educated and well intentioned from when they had last met. But he was too soft-spoken for certain police work: too soft for the neighborhood patrol, impossible for undercover work, and not quite convincing for management. He was a competent bureaucrat with the roly-poly wife, roly-poly children, and house in the QT8 District.

They waved to each other. His conversation with Gennaro had rattled him. The meeting was set for early morning, so no Noelle and no yogic harem. This second meeting to "discuss the timeline" felt like a mousetrap set to break the backbone of the narrative he had set down in the last interview. He did not plan to lie. He would be like any author of fiction and simply be selective with the details. Shade the truth. It was simply an *espediente narrativo*, a narrative device, a little incoherence.

They went together down the great gray way to meet the same IA inquisitor, who waited for them with his canary pad and sharpened cat's claws.

"I meant to ask this the last time," he said. "Is this room out of the *Guantanamo Bay Architectural Digest*?"

The man at the table turned a page from his pad over. "I appreciate the humor. Please have a seat." He pointed to the chairs opposite him.

Farrugia pushed his preemptive strategy forward. "Look, it is our friend from the *Agenzia Informazioni e Sicurezza Esterna*. I heard his great-grandfather was also a member of the *OVRA*."

The man across the table looked up shocked and pale. The union rep turned egg white. Maybe a little too preemptive.

"I am *not* with the Secret Service and I resent the implication my great-grandfather was part of the Fascist Secret Police."

Farrugia smiled. "We all have Fascists in the family tree, but you know that for some of us, it never quite left the blood."

"I don't like your tone today," the man replied and the union rep put his hand on Farrugia's arm.

"And I don't like you," he said. "I don't like your questions and I don't like that you have one of your IA details following me. You knew I went out to dinner. You suggested that I was sleeping with my friend's girlfriend because I stayed overnight, and now I'm sharing a yoga class with one of your operatives. If you are not Secret Service, you are following their guidebook."

"Operative? Are you crazy?" the man said, looking at the union rep for some kind of explanation. Getting nothing, he turned to Farrugia. "And I don't give a damn whether you like my questions or not because you'll answer them. Sure, you have your union rep and you can invoke your rights, but one way or another you will answer my questions. If you don't like me or the questions, then file a formal complaint."

Farrugia's fingers did a little percussive ditty on the table. The union rep looked as if he was about to have a coronary.

"File a formal complaint?" Farrugia said. "Are you the one who is crazy? I do that and you know damn well that complaint goes into my jacket and my next boss will have me as the *commissariato* in some remote corner of Sardinia helping old ladies find their lost poodles. Nobody likes working with a complainer. And do you think I'm like one of those street snitches in the American movies?"

"You . . . a snitch? You haven't given me a thing. Why, do you have anything?"

"No."

"Well, then you're not a snitch. And as far as I'm concerned, I'm interested in your timeline for the day of the Manzoni incident and not what you do for exercise. It is a murder investigation and it involves a detective outside of his jurisdiction. Milan is not the American Wild West. I told you the last time that nobody questions your integrity."

Farrugia leaned forward, his index finger tapping the table. "Being here questions my integrity. Your questions question my integrity. And whatever you put in that file folder questions my integrity. It's all about appearances and insinuation. You know how the rest of us feel about IA policing the police."

The man leaned forward and stared back at Farrugia. "'Rest of us?' I'm a cop just like you. *You* put yourself here. Did you hear me? I didn't. IA wouldn't exist if cops . . . never mind," he said, his voice descending in scale.

The bastard was right. He had put himself here. Isidore Farrugia had fucked himself. He sat back and assessed the man.

Young guy, mid-thirties, clean-shaven and in a dark suit, white dress shirt, and dark tie. The shirt was like the man's mind, revealing nothing beneath the surface. Minus the sunglasses that could be in his jacket pocket, minus the weapon that could be in the room behind the two-way mirror, the man still looked like Secret Service.

"Now, will you cooperate and not make this difficult?"

Farrugia made a face, looked the other way, and his fingers did another percussive flourish on the table. The union rep was sweating.

"Tell me why I should?" he said. "I mean, the public thinks I killed those two men in the alley. Thanks to the Free Channel, the nation thinks I'm a hero. I might've not saved the kid, but I supposedly killed the two G9 bastards—you know, terrorists, the bad guys. What stops me from going on Ragonese's show and making a living doing the celebrity circuit?"

The suit put up his hands. "Absolutely nothing."

"I could do that, but does that mean I have IA following me? Your man was in my yoga class. My instructor touched him. Would you prefer I hand him a towel before we take our showers or confer with him about our next group exercise class?"

Farrugia could hear the union rep swallow. The suit did a patient percussion of his own with his fingers. Farrugia looked down at the fingers.

"Tell you what," the man said, "let me enlighten you as to your options, Commissario Farrugia. You could cooperate. You could tell me to *vaffanculo* and walk right out that door behind you. Feel free. You could have your union rep file a formal complaint. It is your right. You could make a guest appearance on television and let everyone in Italy think you're a hero. In fact, you could even go back to San Luca and have a ticker-tape parade in your honor. I don't give a shit. You can stay in Milan and take more yoga classes and run off with your instructor and your mystery man and start an ashram for tantric sex. I don't care. But let me lay out two scenarios for you. You could go on television and tell Italy that you didn't kill those two. People will think you are being modest. You may persist, tell people that you're not a hero, and get people to believe you, create a scandal. You don't want that."

Silence. Farrugia's hand did the *let's hear the rest of it* roll.

"For now, everyone thinks you killed the two G9 terrorists. We have your weapon, and after you enjoy your moment in the sun and have the entire world lavish their praise upon you, it could conveniently come out that the bullets from your weapon and those from the two bodies don't match. You'll look like a liar. Nobody will remember that you never said you didn't kill them."

"That's blackmail," the union rep bleated out.

Farrugia's hand covered the pudgy man's hand as if to tell him to shut up. "No, it's leverage. It means: stays put and obey. What do you want from me?"

"I want to know why you were there. I want a timeline and what you knew. Now if you'll—"

The door opened and the man across from Farrugia turned pale.

It was U.S. Attorney Farese and Perego. Farrugia spotted Gennaro and Silvio in the hallway.

Perego walked over, tapped on the glass of the two-way mirror, made the sign of the slit throat and pointed to the hallway. Farrugia could hear that door open and Silvio talking to the unknown spectators from the observation room. Perego went out to the hallway.

Farese yelled, "Out," in English, his thumb hitchhiking to the door behind him. "You—both of you—outside now!"

Confused, the IA man looked to Farrugia who translated. "I think he means you," and turning to the union rep, "you too."

The IA man stood up slowly. "By whose authority?"

Perego returned and handed him an official-looking letter. Farrugia saw the echo of a seal through the back of the page, but the stock of the paper was too heavy for him to discern the symbol. IA looked down, made a face, and collected his things.

As the union rep was about to pass him, Farrugia caught his sleeve, looked up from the chair and said, "Thank you for everything."

Perego returned and handed the cassette of the recording from the other room to Farese.

Farrugia was quiet. Gennaro stood next to him without saying a word.

Perego came over to Farrugia. "I'm Lino Perego. You've met U.S. Attorney Farese."

Farrugia nodded. No handshakes, just straight Lombard efficiency this Perego.

"As you know," Perego said, "until now DiBello has been the lead on the Manzoni matter."

"Until now?" The seated Farrugia glanced up at Gennaro. Silence.

"Now you are," Perego said. "DiBello will assist you and share his findings with you. Monotti and Allegretti are on your team, plus whatever resources you need."

"I thought I was just being investigated by Internal Affairs."

Perego tried to look casual. He smiled and lowered that eyebrow. "That's been suspended indefinitely. You're the new lead investigator. This IA nonsense is not your priority."

"I'm the new lead?" asked Farrugia.

Perego looked over at Farese and said nothing. Gennaro remained mute as a statue.

"Fine. Brooks is the priority, I get it," Farrugia said.

Farese replied, "Not Brooks. There's another priority."

Farrugia shot a confused look at Gennaro, then to Farese. "What then?"

"Another murder," Perego said.

13

Her cursor beat to the rhythm of the Cole Porter song on the internet-radio channel. She was waiting for Loki. They had agreed on a time, and Bianca had made sure that it was when Dante was not around. It felt like emotional cheating, an act of infidelity, but there was no alternative in her mind to getting at the crux of Charlie's murder. Any crumb from Loki would be sufficient. Anything.

The IM sound announced that Loki was online and typing a message. The avatar sat idle.

Loki was using a different avatar this time. Usual Norse trickster, yes, with the majestic green cape and fearsome bladed instrument, but that faded before Bianca's eyes into a female form, with that green cape melting like shrink-wrap around slender hips and subdued breasts. The androgynous face remained unchanged. Bianca could do without the outrageous antelope-horned helmet.

Bianca's own avatar remained the same. She clicked the tab closed to kill the music. Loki required her full attention.

"Hi," said her old friend from Rendition.

"Hi, yourself." Bianca enjoyed the ambiguous tone.

"Manners these days? U asked 4 my help."

Sarcasm, in turn, was typical Loki. "Not help. Asked 4 input." She didn't like the reminder. "Reached impasse."

"Broadening the vocabulary, I see."

Okay, the sarcasm was worse when it was deserved. "Less text, more content. B serious. Have something?"

"4 u always, but . . ."

"But what?" Evidently she was in for another one of Loki's teaser sessions.

Long pause.

"But . . . what?"

The IM windowpane indicated that Loki was typing a response. Bianca was both anxious and impatient.

"My advice is . . . drop this & STAY AWAY."

"?" Bianca typed her shorthand for *why?*

"Pandora's Box."

A fast response. Not typical of Loki, who usually deliberated. "Mixing ur mythology now?"

It wasn't as if she and Loki hadn't had to deal with challenges before. Loki was the one who contacted her in Rome and who led her to Boston. True, Loki was connected to Rendition, whom Bianca didn't trust and with good reason after the Robert Strand business. But Loki and she had reached an unspoken agreement. Bianca had worked the Nasonia investigation in Boston partly for the challenge and partly to help Loki—not Rendition. Free-lance. Rendition did deposit money into an account in Rome afterwards, but she hadn't touched it, since that would flag her location for certain. Bianca had helped Loki and Loki helped her. In fact, it was Loki who had contacted Farrugia, without Bianca knowing it, or Farrugia realizing it, and that act alone saved her life in Boston.

Loki was typing.

"Scary people. STAY AWAY."

This was getting disconcerting. "Any scarier than the big R?"

"Y-E-S." Slowly, for emphasis.

"What did U find?"

"Enuf."

"Damn it," Bianca yelled at her screen. She began to pace the workroom. Let Loki wait a few more seconds. Bianca wondered again why they'd never just Skyped and dropped these ridiculous, adolescent games, but she knew the answer to that question. Games were what Loki did.

The espresso wasn't helping the nerves.

Bianca finally dropped in front of her screen. "Y shld I B scared?"

"Want a clue?"

Loki's answer made Bianca smack the side of the screen. "You bitch . . . you bastard. Whatever the hell you are!" After two years of working together remotely, Bianca still didn't know whether Loki was a man or a woman. Farrugia said "woman" but his reasons weren't particularly convincing.

"Fine. Throw a clue. How many?"

"# of clues all depends on how smart U R 2day."

Bitch . . . Bastard. "Throw ur 1st clue."

Intentional pause. "Look @ company name."

Bianca thought of the name, Adastra. Okay. Adastra . . . Adastra. Adastra.

"'To the stars in Latin."

"Quarter of one gold star 4 U, but not done. Rest of the phrase?"

Bianca opened another tab in the browser and did a quick web search, got the result and typed it out for Loki. "Per aspera ad astra = To the stars through hardships."

"1/2 gold star."

Bianca was tempted to type "WTF" but she refrained. Loki could be a tease but not without a reason: something vital, something nuanced was missing here. Loki was typing.

"Ad astra per aspera = To the stars through hardships = Through hardships to the stars. Nice example of zeugma or chiasmus, if that's ur sorta thing."

"Thanks, not my kink, but ur point IS?"

Loki's avatar stayed male and the bladed instruments sparkled. "Pain = Pain. STAY AWAY."

Bianca's fingers were furious on the keyboard. "Done playing games W/U. Tell me what U found. I've hit the wall. Nothing in financials; 2 many CEOs & 2 little time; subcontracting hell; & tank is only thing I've got that doesn't fit."

She waited and let that message go before Loki's eyes.

"Tank, yes, but not the answer Y CB ↓."

Bianca translated the line. A down-arrow was a nice, neat way of saying someone is dead, but it sure didn't tell the whole story about why a kid was gunned down in an alley. And that was something she really needed to know.

"WTF does that mean?"

Another Loki message hit her screen within seconds. "Right start, but wrong assumption. Tank = Yes/No. Missing crucial detail."

That was insulting. Bianca knew that she'd walked over the Adastra data on the servers and on Charlie's jump key dozens of times, and she'd scoured what she had locally on her computer a half-dozen times. This was bullshit.

"WTF!"

Another dramatic pause. "The tank is the means, yes; but the real issue is how to enable the tank to do what it does."

Bianca took this apart in her mind. Tanks did what? They blew things up, right? How did you blow things up? Ammunition and—she pulled out her notes. But this didn't make sense. The weaponry was standard for the M1 tanks; no new technology there, so what the hell was Loki talking about?

Cryptic bitch.

"Don't understand. Payload = std 4 armored infantry. The usual boy toys. As 4 enabling, I looked at pwr supplies & pwr reserves, but U know that."

Loki's avatar hadn't changed. Bastard.

"True. Pwr reserves/supplies = non-issue BUT concept of enabling is not. 1 enables a weapons systm, but the ? 4 U is how M1 discerns target."

Bianca read and reread the typed challenge. Tanks used sabots, a high-velocity explosive round that acted like a projectile. For close-quarters, tanks used machine-guns mounted to cupolas. She thumbed through her notes on Desert Storm and spotted a line about how infrared was used for night battles. The enemy thought they were clever and had buried their own tanks in the sand, but the U.S. . . . well, shot fish in the barrel, using infrared.

Bianca looked up at the screen to confirm that Loki was still with her. Bianca was almost certain that the cursor was smiling.

Bianca typed, "Infrared? But that's 4 nights & nothing in the contracts about infrared or night vision equipment."

"Now on right trail but not quite infrared. Almost. Think AI."

Artificial intelligence. Bianca flicked the pages of her notes up and opened another tab to view documents. Software specifications for the tank were hundreds of pages deep. She did a keyword search on "infrared" that yielded nothing and another keyword search on "artificial" . . . nothing. This was frustrating and Loki's guessing games weren't as fun as they once were.

"Just did searches: artificial & artificial intelligence = NOTHING. But wait, I have another idea."

Bianca remembered something about word searches. She had been doing "Find whole words only" searches. She deselected that as the default option and did a partial word search on the one word likely to have a stem change: intelligence. She typed it and hit the return key.

Voilà. Next thing to do was to consult the GFD, and find the definition. She opened the Glossary for Definition document. Bingo.

"A.I.D. or A.I.D.S. Cynical bastards."

Loki's avatar changed back into a woman, and then the message, "Full gold star."

A gold star appeared, burst into dust, and faded into cyberspace. Loki was gone.

Bianca smiled for a second. Loki was pleased. She had found the answer.

Sort of. She still didn't know how the tanks used it. Only that it had gotten young Charlie Brooks killed.

Anthropomorphic Intelligent Design or A.I.D.

Anthropomorphic Intelligent Design System or A.I.D.S.
Cynical bastards.

14

Their car was on the highway, heading southeast of Milan. Gennaro was driving and hadn't said a word for about five minutes. His eyes were fixed on the road ahead.

Farrugia counted the number of clouds in the sky. It was a sunny day to be in such a foul mood. Presently, he began whistling a tune, the one from the movie *The Bridge on the River Kwai*.

Gennaro's eyes stayed fixed on the road, hands on the wheel. Not one word, though his knuckles grew whiter.

Farrugia gave the car, an Alfa 159, the once-over. Nice mouse-gray interior. Clean. He peeked at the back seat; it was roomier than his ten-year-old Volkswagen Golf in Rome and palatial, compared to his car in Milan. No clutter. It wasn't the Gallardo the State Police ran, but the car pool provided some nice cars.

He whistled another chorus. Gennaro eyed him. Peripheral vision.

Farrugia pulled down the visor, swung it around to the passenger window, and then back to its origin. He clicked it in place and verified that it was flush with the roof with a tap. He looked out the window again. He changed his mind and pulled the visor down. He looked at himself in the mirror, pawed his chin. The razor was dull this morning, and besides, he was thinking that the hot yoga class would have done wonders for his skin. He worried that missing a day at the gym might compromise his progress. He pinched his belly.

Gennaro looked down at Farrugia's waist and then back to the road. Farrugia kept whistling the tune and craned his head to read the sign, the one that announced Lodi, until they passed it and his whistling elongated to a sustained note. They were moving southeast of Lodi.

Gennaro stared at him.

"What? What did I do?" asked Farrugia, his hands mea culpa in front of him.

Gennaro reverted to his intent-driver pose.

Farrugia restarted his musical solo.

"Stop it!"

"What! Why do you want me to stop? You haven't said a word since we left the Grand Inquisitor. You stood there and didn't say a word. Are you mad at me about this lead-investigator nonsense?"

"It's not nonsense. What could I say back there? I spent my entire morning getting apprised of the situation and prepared for the transition." A long moment passed. "What could I say, Isidò? Huh? What? You tell me!" Gennaro cut some driver off as he swung into another lane, stepping on the accelerator. A car horn blared.

"We don't talk anymore," Gennaro said.

"What? We don't what anymore?"

Gennaro stared ahead and said, "We don't talk anymore. None of us talk to each other."

"Are we an old married couple now? What's this bullshit about nobody talking to anybody?" Farrugia shifted around in his seat. "Fine. You want to air your grievances. I have one. How come you never told me that you were the head investigator on this Brooks murder? You could've told me the night we were having dinner at Dante's."

Gennaro glanced at him before turning his eyes back to the road. "What would have been the point? You were in one of your moods. Everyone was trying not to make you angry, Isidò. We all figured that with the shooting . . . you had your own set of problems. Why would I add to your headaches by telling you that I was feeling like I was being set up? As for grievances, you didn't tell me why you were with Bianca on Via Manzoni. I hear that from Dante. Who the hell knows where Dante is on all this because he sure as hell was the one who should know anything about it."

"What headaches? I was angry with Bianca. We were talking. I heard what she said and I said to her, 'This doesn't sound good. Let me go with you. I'll sit across the street. If I'm wrong, I'm wrong, but if I'm right then I'm there for you.'"

"Well, you were right. You were dead right about three times. And did she tell you what it was that this dead kid had on him that was so important?"

Farrugia looked out the window. "No."

Gennaro tapped the wheel. Another distance indicator passed.

"She's another one," Gennaro said.

Farrugia twisted in the seat to look at him. "What is that supposed to mean?"

"You go to help her. She doesn't even tell Dante. The kid gets killed for something, or over something, but we don't know what because she didn't tell you or tell Dante. I get promoted and then I'm demoted. You get IA interrogations and a yoga partner. What's with the yoga?"

With the hands again Farrugia said, "It makes me feel good. I sleep better at night. As for Bianca—maybe she didn't know. I'm not responsible for what she says or doesn't say to Dante." He paused. "Are you angry with me about the demotion? I really don't need this shit."

Gennaro put on his signal. He preferred another lane.

"'You *really* don't need this shit'? Excuse me, but I'm the one who is about to retire. I'm the one with has his pension dangling in the wind, and I'm the one with the dark cloud over my head."

"While we're comparing our miseries like old ladies, I have IA."

Gennaro glared at him. "Don't tell me that Bianca didn't know. She had to have known that this kid was in some kind of trouble and that he couldn't go to the police. She's better at casing a scene than either of us, or the two of us put together. And who can blame the kid for not going to the police? Look at us."

"She hadn't cased this scene right, I'll tell—Wait a second. 'Look at us.' What the hell does that mean?"

Gennaro indicated himself with his own thumb. "Our superiors are playing us. Look at me, for example: I'm financial police, member of the great Guardia di Finanza, and I'm appointed the lead on a murder with international consequences? What's the logic? About as logical as a walrus in the tropics. And then there's you?"

"What about me?"

"Organized Crime Bureau expert on vacation. You've got your IA interviews, the yoga partner and Ragonese singing your praises like you are Aeneas founding Rome."

Farrugia gave him a cold stare.

It didn't stop Gennaro. "You and I know that you didn't kill those two, and the people above us know that you didn't, and the people in Ballistics have to know that you didn't kill them, but nobody in that entire menagerie of fools will issue a statement. Why? The emperor has no clothes. It's a damn Pirandello play and we're the leads."

The whooshing sound of the air passed as the car continued at high speed.

"Are you upset about being demoted? Because if you are, let me tell you I didn't ask for this case. I came here to Milan to help you with your retirement party."

"What? I thought you were in Milan to help Bianca."

"I was. I did."

"A surprise party?"

"Surprise!" Farrugia said, hand next to face, elbow on the door as he stared out the window.

Gennaro weaved and bypassed cars. The sounds of their horns receded.

"Jesus, drive like a normal person," Farrugia said.

"I told them. I told Farese and Perego that this was all a conflict of interest. You and I are friends. Did they listen? No. They said that it was 'mere formality.'"

"IA had said the same thing: 'mere formality.'"

"Farese is leading the investigation and Perego acts like second in charge. Strange, isn't it? I just watched Perego hand over to Farese the IA tapes of your interrogations. Does any of that make any sense to you? Farese comes into Perego's house and he walks out with the furniture. Does it make any sense to you?"

Gennaro goosed the accelerator again. The driving was growing frightening. Farrugia checked his seatbelt strap.

"Makes no sense, Gennaro, but what does? Look at me. I'm a cop with no gun. I'm the hero who never fired a shot. I tell them to check ballistics and they tell me it won't matter because if I deny it I'm a liar and if I say yes, the ballistics make me a liar. And now I'm driving to a crime scene with a madman. Each day my life gets better."

The madman slowed down as they approached the exit. Farrugia looked around. Unfamiliar territory. The GPS said southeast of Milan and southeast of Lodi.

Gennaro's voice lowered. "I've got a few things to tell you."

"Like I said, my days get better by the moment. What is it?"

"Your weapon is in the glove compartment. Farese and Perego authorized it. And about those bullets from Via Manzoni? They're Gévelots."

Farrugia was silent. He didn't open the glove compartment. He was too busy taking in the disclosure.

Gennaro sighed. "And the crime scene we're going to?"

"I'm not going to like this, am I?"

"No. Raffaele Palmisano is dead."

15

"So Lele is dead," Farrugia said as the two of them sat in the parked car. The crime scene unit was up ahead of them on the inclined embankment. He had now taken his Beretta out of the glove compartment.

Gennaro said nothing. He stared ahead through a beautiful and seemingly peaceful stand of trees. Had the killers also found the trees, the entire area, beautiful and restorative, or just a convenient place to murder another human being? For him it had already been a long day, first dealing with Farese and Perego back in the office, then whisking Farrugia away from his interrogator and the useless union rep. Now this.

Raffaele Palmisano, the promising L&S candidate, was dead.

"Know any preliminary details?"

Gennaro heard the question but he was chasing a memory. Farrugia snapped his fingers, an annoying habit of his that he hated, as it reminded him of his childhood, when he would see British tourists summoning waiters for service with the obnoxious snap of their pudgy Anglo-Saxon fingers. He had wandered back to his personal *anni di piombo*, his Years of Lead, memories of which were now pressing down on him: the death of his wife, Lucia, the death of other beloved friends, too many to name. Whether natural or not, death was death.

Farrugia snapped his fingers again.

"Stop that! No . . . no details."

"I'm sorry. This is getting to you, isn't it?"

"What do you think, Isidò? Ever wonder, no matter how old you get or how much you've endured in this life that there might be that one last thing that breaks your spirit? The best candidate that this county has seen in decades is dead. Agree with him or not on what he stood for, no one can deny that he was standing up for this country. This is not how

I had imagined it at my age. This is probably my last investigation, and instead of a nice, clean auditing job, I get a homicide and this one of all homicides."

"You're getting nostalgic on me?"

"I was thinking of my childhood. As a child, we understand everything and nothing."

Farrugia tried again with humor. "Christ, don't go to pieces on me now. You sound like a Foscolo poem. I'll take you to the beach and you can play with the stones, I promise. But please stop—the next thing I know we'll be crying and you'll quote that old line from catechism class, 'We are in exile from the Truth, the eternal life until we are again in the House of Our Father.' I'll bless myself, but only to remind myself that I'm still alive. Lele isn't and we have a job to do. C'mon." Gennaro had parked.

Farrugia went to open the door. Gennaro grabbed his arm. "Don't you ever think of your mortality?"

Farrugia let go of the door handle. "Now is not the time. Yes, I think of my bones. I'm not as spry as I once was. Don't get me wrong, my mind is limber, but the corpse is starting to show. I'm getting liver spots. I'm darker under the eyes. I hesitate before I do things that I once would never have thought twice about doing. I understand fear. It takes me longer to feel fit, longer to recover, emotionally and physically. I eat a little too much and my body punishes me harder. Are we done now?"

A tap on the glass from a policeman interrupted their conversation. It was time for them to go up the hill to the scene.

Gennaro and Farrugia ascended the steep path from their parked car. This was an obscure spot on the famous Via Francigena, the pilgrim's path from Canterbury to Rome. For whatever reason the path of St. James to Compostella was the pilgrim's path everyone seemed to know well. Tuscany and Lombardy were working with the Vatican's ORP, *Opera Romana Pellegrinaggi*, to restore this ancient road and encourage visitors. Francigena, once the great Lombard Way, was undergoing a revival.

This exact spot, the crime scene, was a section of the path that was under construction. Farrugia observed lush greenery, a view of Corte S. Andrea in the distance, a view of the Lambro River, romantic and secluded and a perfect place for a dead body.

A young man in boots, wearing a uniform poncho with the initials of his official rank, came over to Gennaro and Farrugia.

"Hikers found the body this morning. Coroner will rule on time of death later, but we estimate between midnight and four a.m. The hikers who found the body were a couple on their honeymoon. They had decided to take a nice early-morning walk before their breakfast. They ignored the signs about renovations, came into this area, and found him around seven a.m. We have their statements. They're staying at a local bed and breakfast."

Farrugia asked, "Before I look at the body, did you find anything in the vicinity, like a weapon or something else that suggests foul play? Are there any footprints around the car other than our hikers'? Any tire marks?"

The man shook his head.

"No footprints? Nothing? The Holy Ghost didn't float in here and float away."

"Commissario, with all due respect, I don't think you understand."

"What is there not for me to understand? I'm here, and you have a dead body. This is a high profile case and we need to rule out homicide."

The young man started to stammer. Gennaro could sense that he was awed, and perhaps intimidated, by Farrugia's reputation. He had wanted to impress, and it wasn't going well. Gennaro decided to save the young man from Farrugia. "Please explain to us what it is that we don't understand."

"With all due respect—"

"Enough with the respect already—you respect me and I respect you. I need facts not respect."

The young man swallowed hard. "It's that we're not sure that it was homicide."

Farrugia and Gennaro looked at each other and both responded almost simultaneously, "What?"

"Follow me."

The vehicle, a mint-green Fiat Punto, was not the car either Gennaro or Farrugia had expected Palmisano to be driving. Nice car but conservative, a family car with a hatchback and a lot of glass. A lot of glass.

The car might've been a good choice for a man of the suburbs, but for a politician? Maybe if the man liked the paparazzi, since there was no place to hide with all that glass. On the other hand, it was a decidedly terrible choice for a man whose politics might invite the occasional rock. Palmisano, like every politician, had the paparazzi pack following him, but aside from his sunbathing on the beach he was never persecuted like his peers. The paparazzi and Palmisano were almost like Gennaro's nostalgia: a relic of the past in that the photographers respected him as a public figure. In fact, Palmisano was quite congenial with the paparazzi parasites and their cameras. He indulged them but didn't spoil them.

And though Palmisano had no need to stage sympathy like Berlusconi and have an attacker bop him on the nose with a small statue of the cathedral, he did have his detractors, such as the homophobes. But even that was mild—a few shouts once, and a poorly aimed egg. Lele was too widely regarded as a man of the people. Affable, charismatic, and classy.

Time to view the body.

Farrugia was at the rear of the car. He could see the man's tilted head through the glass of the hatchback. The CSU staff confirmed that he could approach the body. Farrugia donned the purple nitrile gloves, started from the back, and idled down the side of the car until he was next to the victim. The driver's side window was up. Palmisano's eyes were motionless, mouth agape, head back in ecstasy. Farrugia looked down and understood why. Palmisano was naked from the waist down, his trousers bunched down to his knees. Farrugia looked at the rest of the man: the hand, the stain, and the passenger seat. Other than the stain, the car was immaculate.

He looked up when he heard a stifled laugh. One of the CSU team with a woman next to him was on the other side of the car.

Farrugia walked over to the man. "Something funny?"

"No, Commissario."

"Then why were you laughing? I like to laugh. Tell me what was so funny."

The man turned red.

"What is your role on the CSU team?"

"Fingerprint expert, Commissario."

"I see. Any fingerprints?"

"Numerous prints on the outside. My guess is half of Milan has touched this car, as if it were the Popemobile."

Farrugia looked at the car and back to the man. "How about the inside?"

"Numerous prints on the steering wheel, on the console for the heat and the radio, but nothing else."

"I imagine you haven't processed those fingerprints?"

The man nodded.

Farrugia wanted to indulge another way of thinking. "What do you think happened here? Walk me through the scene through your eyes."

The two CSU team members remained quiet.

Farrugia arched his eyebrow. "Well, I'm listening. I won't bite."

The man cleared his throat. "Isn't it obvious?"

"No, please enlighten me."

"A . . . romantic tryst."

"Ah. What a delicate choice of words." Farrugia smiled. This young man had been reading his grandmother's Victorian romances. Nobody said *tryst* these days, but *tryst* implied two partners.

"What's romantic about it? And you, Miss, do you consider this romantic? Would you take your boyfriend out here and . . . tryst him?"

The woman blushed. "The trees and the view are nice. Yes, it is romantic, Commissario."

Farrugia looked at her, read her identification tag. Ballistics.

"Was there any evidence that a gun was fired? GSR, casings?"

"No, none."

"An easy day for you, then. And you, Mr. Fingerprints, you said 'tryst,' huh? Please spell it out for me."

"Yes, Commissario," he answered, with head erect and shoulders back.

"This isn't the military. I'm not expecting a salute. Let's assume there was another person. Any fingerprints on the passenger side, like on the seat?"

"On the seat, sir?"

"That's what I said."

"No. I found no prints on the passenger side."

"How about the backseat? Amorous couples use the backseat."

"No, Commissario. No prints there, either."

"Thank you."

Farrugia saw a CSU member behind the car, who called him. "Commissario, please come over and take a look at this."

"Please excuse me," he told Mr. Fingerprints and Miss Ballistics.

Farrugia went to the rear of the car where the trunk was now open. A flap compartment had been opened and inside was the spare tire, all the requisite equipment for changing a tire, and some pornographic magazines: hardcore pornography with young boys alone, young boys with other young boys, and burly, rather large men, exceedingly hirsute men, in leather. The magazines were shiny and glossy, printed on high quality paper. None of the magazines were wrinkled or creased.

Farrugia's face was expressionless. Gennaro and the rest of the team peered down at the trunk's contents. Farrugia thanked them and reminded them to photograph it all.

He glanced out at the view in front of the car: romantic, indeed. He surveyed the car, dense wooded area and lots of foliage. Not a damn thing in the car. No pebbles or so much as a leaf on the mats; nothing on the front or back seats, or on the driver's side.

He made his way over to Gennaro. "We should go. I've had enough."

Gennaro agreed just as his cell phone rang. "I'll meet you in the car. Let me take this call."

Farrugia strode over to the congregation of the uniformed CSU. He told the fingerprint analyst to contact him if there were any database matches on the fingerprints worth knowing, and that he didn't care whether it was half of Milan or the Pope. Farrugia requested that the team leader let him know when the coroner's team has collected the body and started the autopsy. Even without toxicology he wanted something soon. Above all, he instructed the team to cordon off the area and allow no paparazzi in, especially from the woods.

"It's a zero-tolerance policy for all non-authorized personnel," he told them before he left, hoping that particular instruction would stick.

Farrugia motioned to the ballistics expert to join him for a brief talk. She followed him to a spot a little ways away from the crowd.

"I want to apologize about what I'd said before," Farrugia said.

"About what, sir?"

"I didn't mean to embarrass you like that in front of your colleague. That question, you know, about whether you considered this place romantic or not? The intention was to get your professional opinion, and I'm afraid that it might've come across as a cheap thrill comment about sex."

"No need to apologize. But thank you." She had a nice attractive smile and good teeth.

Farrugia started to walk away, but turned around. "Your name is Paola, right?"

That smile again. "Paola Mazzoleni. Ballistics."

Nice Bergamese name. It was time to join Gennaro for the ride back to Milan.

Farrugia closed the car door and immediately started talking.

"This doesn't feel right, Gennaro."

Gennaro put the car in reverse and did a K-turn, waved to the other policemen. They were extending the crime scene and blocking the future paparazzi off with crime-scene tape. Gennaro drove the car down to the turn for the highway. Then it would be another fast ride to Milan. He would tell Farrugia why soon.

"If it isn't right, then tell me why."

"You go through the trouble of locating a perfect spot like this for sex and you don't use the woods?"

Gennaro understood what Farrugia was doing. This was like a game of chess for him. He needed a counterargument to his logic. "It could've been cold last night. CSU approximates death between midnight and early dawn. Besides, the car is warmer. More intimate, I guess. You saw the man. He was behind the wheel."

"That's right; it might have been cold out."

Gennaro didn't buy the easy defeat. His role as chess-partner to Farrugia had been too brief. "I guess that unless we're told otherwise it looks like natural causes. A rather undignified way but—"

"This location is perfect for sex. You don't go alone to a place like this. A place like this takes some thought and planning. It takes familiarity to find a place like this—and to know it was restricted and under renovation. It suggests a rendezvous, or so we are led to think."

"Don't go thinking conspiracy theory, Farrugia, just because he's a popular politician. It's unfortunate, but these things do happen. This will be a scandal. What makes you think there was a second party? There were no footprints, except for our hikers'. There were no tire marks except for when Palmisano's car had entered the location. Where's your evidence?"

Farrugia slapped his stomach. "It's my gut."

"Wonderful."

Farrugia shifted in his seat to talk to Gennaro. "Doesn't it bother you that the car was so clean? Doesn't it bother you that there are no footprints and no tire marks? None? You expect gum wrappers or something. It's like the scene has been policed."

"The area was under renovation, Isidò."

Farrugia counted out on his fingers. "One: A couple knew enough to go hiking there. They said they were taking a walk, but do honeymooners just stroll? I mean they could have checked out the place thinking they could have a quickie but they got a surprise. Two: There is nothing on the passenger side. Not so much as a palm print on the passenger seat or on the driver's side."

"Why are you so focused on a palm print? Why isn't a fingerprint good enough for you, Isidò? Explain it to me."

"That's what doesn't make sense, Gennaro. You park the car at night in a secluded place. You have a beautiful view in front of you, which you can't see because it is pitch-black."

Gennaro had the car at a steady speed in a comfortable niche in the fast lane. He was chess-companion again. "Maybe the moon and stars were nice enough; they'd provide just enough lighting to look out across the plain and see Corte S. Andrea and the insinuation of the Lambro."

"'The insinuation of the Lambro'? Are you writing romances now? My point is that there is no palm print."

"Farrugia, you and the damn palm print!"

"Don't you get it?"

"Obviously, I don't."

"Palmisano is sitting on the driver side. He has his pants down, his thing out, and he's facing this beautiful vista with not a soul in sight. He didn't go into the woods—all right, it's cold out. He shuts off the car lights but leaves the engine on, possibly turns on the heat and the radio. He leaves his fingerprints everywhere. But his partner—"

"What partner? I thought we proved that there was no partner. No prints on the passenger side and no footprints on that side of the car. No other car was there."

"Exactly the case, unless the prints on the passenger side were wiped clean."

"Think so?"

"Imagine that he has a partner in the car on the passenger side with him. There had to have been prints getting into the car. You can't tell me that if the person on the passenger side was to go over and pleasure him that they wouldn't leave a palm print. Physically impossible not to do if you are about to lean over and—"

"Okay, no oral sex," said Gennaro, "but what if the man was alone and—"

"Masturbating? Go all that way, to all that trouble for privacy, drive up that steep hill, to play with yourself?"

Then it hit Gennaro. "Palmisano said in the Ragonese interview that he was meeting with party members or something that evening. He might have known the area if he had met with them before. We don't know who they are or where they live, but we will. They'll have to be interviewed. That's plausible. Palmisano meets with them and he leaves their house late at night. He is a little excited and he parks and does himself. Yes, that's plausible."

Farrugia listened and their eyes met.

"Plausible, yes?" Gennaro asked.

"What guy would leave his inspiration in the trunk of the car if he's going to masturbate? There are no footprints indicating that Palmisano had gotten out of the car to go and fetch his magazines."

Gennaro slapped the wheel. "Ah for God's sake, Farrugia. Maybe the man couldn't wait. Men, gay or straight, are impulsive. He pulls over, forgets his magazines, gets busy, and for all we know he had a heart attack."

Farrugia was quiet.

"So, what do you think? Is it plausible?"

"No."

"Why not?"

"Even the magazines don't seem right."

"What? Are you a purveyor of gay erotica, too? I knew that you were a man of many hidden talents, but this would make you a true renaissance man."

"Twinks and bears."

"What?"

"That's rather an odd combination, don't you think?" Farrugia asked. "The magazines were brand new, hardly used, and they featured boyish men, twinks, young but presumably not underage. Palmisano was no pedophile."

"Thank God for that."

Farrugia wasn't finished. "Solo twinks, and twinks with twinks. And then there were magazines with the heavy-set furry men, the bears and cubs, with their leather hats and large bellies. Isn't that extreme, these magazines, from one end of the spectrum to the other?"

Gennaro thought. "Gay men like different things, too. Who are we to know what he liked?"

"We saw a photo of his partner on the Ragonese show. He isn't a twink or a bear. None of his gay friends in the picture was a twink, bear, or a cub."

"What is it with you and this vocabulary? I get it that a twink is a young man but not underage. What is a cub? The only cub I know is that polar cub in Germany, Knut, who passed away."

But Gennaro may as well have been speaking to himself. "It seems too staged. The magazines are glossy and new, the kind of mix that someone who knew nothing of gay life might pick. Palmisano is in the car but never got out of the car. No fingerprints exist on the passenger side and the car is clean. I'll be very curious to hear what Palmisano died of."

Gennaro absorbed Farrugia's inferences. He had to admit, they were plausible.

Gennaro said, "Sandro called me on my cell while you were poking around the scene. Ragonese is going to be making some kind of statement on the Free Channel."

"Ragonese? What the hell does he have to say now? He couldn't have known about Palmisano's death. Tell me he doesn't know."

"I don't think he knows, not that he won't, soon. It's something else."
Gennaro was now thinking that his day kept improving.

16

A very quiet room.

A paperclip turned over in anonymous office hands, the overhead light was a bleaching obscenity until the flat-screen television was turned on and the grossly large head of Giancarlo Ragonese, bearded and with microphone, filled the screen's abyss with an unexpected zoom-in before the cameraman realized it and retracted his camera because they're, "Live, in Milan."

Farese and Perego stood near Farrugia and Gennaro. Gennaro saw Silvio through the glass window and open blinds of the copier room, arguing, it seemed, with the copy machine. Silvio did not understand the copier and the copier, in turn, did not understand him. Translator and his text.

"My fellow countrymen," Ragonese intoned, "I speak to you today with unexpected news. Sad, tragic news. As you know, this week, these last few days, have been difficult for our country; but today, in these trying times when we might have had a glimmer of hope, the few hopes we have been entertaining are being dashed, lifted like balloons and pierced, leaving us, like children, sad and on the verge of tears with history as our cruel parent and—"

"Get on with it you verbose windbag!"

"Ssh!"

"And you wonder why our forefathers killed Cicero."

Only Perego's crossed arms and stern face silenced the hecklers. Gennaro noticed Farese looking about for his missing translator.

"I have news that will weigh down your hearts as it does mine. I have been informed of a most disturbing contradiction about the unfortunate event on Via Manzoni, an event that—"

Gennaro sighed and Farrugia and Perego seemed impatient. This sound byte—whatever it was—was Ragonese typical gnawing at a bone. Or was it? Farrugia did not look relieved. Farese continued to look lost. Silvio continued to abuse the copier.

Ragonese was still marching toward the point. ". . . an unfortunate death of a young man, so full of promise, whose tragic demise unites two old friends, Italy and the United States, like two parents in search of justice for one child. The troubling news that comes to me concerns the role, the details, the truth about Commissario Isidore Farrugia and that fateful day at Via Manzoni in Bar Gadda and . . ."

The entire office turned their heads in unison and stared at Farrugia.

"I hold up to you a bullet. This is not the bullet that killed Charles Brooks, Jr., but it's the same type of bullet that ended his life and the lives of his assassins. Many of you watching this are asking, 'What's the significance, Giancarlo? The heroic Commissario was there, the heroic Isidore Farrugia delivered justice for us?' And I will answer you with my own question: How is it that the victim and his assailants were shot and killed with the same type of bullet, the rare Gévelot?"

"The bastard!" Farrugia said.

Ragonese looked off camera so that his rhetorical question could sink in. He even looked misty-eyed. Farrugia was right. The bastard.

"I feel compelled to point out the significance of Gévelot to those viewers out there too young to remember those years of unrest and uncertainty, *gli anni di piombo*, the Years of Lead, that hung over our great peninsula for two decades. I came of age in the seventies, a time of stark cynicism and darkness. It was a time when our politicians and other authorities could not be trusted. It was a time of proscriptions, Sulla and Caesar, the deaths of Antonio Annarumma and the Piazza Fontana bombing, with blood in the streets. I ask each of you to go and research the name of the late journalist, Carmine Pecorelli, and you will understand the ominous significance of Gévelot. Until then, I seek the truth, as all journalists should. Who is the terrorist, G9 or Isidore

Farrugia, or are they one and the same? We can only hope that in the next election justice will be done."

"*Pezzo di merda!*" Ragonese was a piece of shit.

The guy from Receivables began clicking the volume down, bar by bar, until someone yelled, "Stop! The beard is saying something."

Ragonese, looking Oscar-worthy, said, "I will return soon with an examination of Commissario Isidore Farrugia's career; but to those of you of my generation who do remember, I quote to you prophetic words from my studies at the Liceo Classico and University: '*Quo usque tandem abutere, Farrugia, patientia nostra? Quam diu etiam furor iste tuus nos eludet? Quem ad finem sese effrenata iactabit audacia?*'" And with an exaggerated sigh, also award-worthy, he concluded with, "*O tempora, O mores!*"

One of the hecklers, a young man in his early twenties, asked, "What the hell was that?"

The man in Receivables stood up and cleared his throat. "How long, O Farrugia, will you abuse our patience? And for how long will that madness of yours mock us? To what end will your unbridled audacity hurl itself?" A long pause, a bowed head, which he then lifted to declaim, "Oh the times! Oh the customs!"

"Oh the crap," Farrugia said and stomped off to Gennaro's office. The audience heard a door slam, followed by Silvio kicking the copier machine.

Minutes later Alessandro, Dante, Farese, Gennaro, and Perego entered Gennaro's office. Perego closed the door on Silvio, who managed nonetheless to enter the room to translate for Farese.

Farrugia was at the window, silent. Three times in his life he had felt a dark, murderous rage. When he found his mother dead. When he found Gennaro's wife dead. And now.

Gennaro stood in front of Farese and Perego as a shield between Farrugia and them. Farrugia wasn't sure whom Gennaro was protecting.

"Now what?" asked Gennaro in English, staring at Farese and Perego. "And don't tell me that I'm the lead on the other murder because—"

"What other murder?" asked Alessandro.

"Shut up, Sandro," Gennaro said without shifting his fiery stare from the other two men.

Alessandro sank back with "Right, Chief."

"I won't accept it," Gennaro said. "I would rather resign. You two need to come clean about what the hell is going on, because no matter how I turn or how he turns—" Gennaro pointed at Farrugia behind him "—we've been screwed. We've been loyal and we've served, but we will not be sacrificial lambs in some kind of political game here in Milan for you, the politicians, or the multinational interests in the next election. While we're on the theme of classical authors, I want to make it clear to the both of you that neither of us is going to the steam baths to willingly open up our veins for you. The two of you owe us an explanation. Alessandro and Dante are on my team and they stay in the room while one of you explains. Now start talking."

Perego cleared his throat, his hands again in his pockets. "Please believe me. Farese and I had no idea that Ragonese was going to pull this stunt. Honest."

"Only a small number of people knew about the Gévelot bullets," Dante said. "Just the people in this room and Ballistics."

"Then, for the time being, unless we discover otherwise, we have to assume we have a leak in Ballistics," Perego said. "We certainly didn't want the public to know about the Gévelots for exactly the reasons we just saw on television with Ragonese because—"

"We? You know all of this stinks. It foments suspicion."

Gennaro looked over at Dante and then returned his gaze to Perego. "Suspicion has been cast and it points at him."

Again, he pointed in the direction of Farrugia at the blinds. He was looking down at the piazza below. A crowd was forming outside the building. Farrugia moved one of the slats for a better look. People were gathering with signs that he couldn't decipher because of the high floor they were on.

"I understand you," Perego said. "Farrugia remains the lead on the Palmisano murder and—"

"Lele has been murdered?" Alessandro said.

"And I'll try and see what I can find out about Ballistics. Continue working together. Keep a low profile."

Farrugia let go of the slat with a loud snap. "Low profile? You have a mob outside of this building. Whether those people down there know I'm here or not, I don't know, but it doesn't matter because you'll probably have a mob outside every police station in Milan. You're feeding Ragonese his dinner, and if you call out the riot police the Free Channel will start running footage of riots from the last thirty years."

Farrugia felt his skin flush and, turning to Perego, slipped into Italian. "And if so much as one protestor gets injured or killed, people will start invoking the name of Carlo Giuliani and calling for someone's head."

Silvio, who had been translating, stopped before completing what Farrugia had said when he had heard the name Giuliani.

Farrugia went back to English then. "You might as well be writing Ragonese's script on the documentary and call it, 'The Year of Bullets, Part Two.' He took the short steps over to Farese and stood in front of him. *"Mi sta seguendo, avvocato Farese?"* When Silvio, white-faced, was about to translate the phrase, Farrugia put his hand on Silvio's chest and said, "I'll translate! Are you following my English, Attorney Farese?"

Farese looked down at Gennaro's desk. "I understand."

"Good, because since you're here and the Brooks family are here, the people out there, and viewers around the world, will start associating riot police with protest, the murder, and Gévelot bullets with terrorists and, by the way, me. And just wait until they hear about Palmisano, then . . . well, then you have, as you Americans say, 'a situation on your hands.'"

Perego stepped forward. "For now, it is in *our* hands, and that includes yours, Farrugia."

"Really? How is that possible? I'm surprised Internal Affairs isn't here yet." Farrugia looked at his watch for effect. "I've got to imagine that my friend is anxious to resume our conversation and my union rep is renewing his prescription for Xanax."

"Farese and I will take care of IA. Focus on the Palmisano murder," said Perego as he opened the door and motioned for Farese that they should leave.

"Ready, Silvio?" Farese asked.

Silvio snapped to attention. "Presently present." His smile did no good.

"Perego?" said Farrugia.

"Yes?"

"Who ever said it was murder?"

The door closed.

A few minutes later, after the tension eased . . .

"So much for my idea of a nice dinner," Alessandro said.

"What dinner?" Farrugia asked.

"Alessandro suggested that we all have dinner at Bianca's and Dante's," Gennaro said. "He wanted us to meet his new girlfriend. With this happening, I don't think it's such a good idea."

Farrugia grinned. "No, I disagree. It's a perfect time. And besides, I'd like to meet Alessandro's girlfriend, Paola."

"How did you know her name?"

"I'm a detective," said Farrugia, tapping Alessandro's shoulder. "I think it should be interesting sharing a conversation and dinner with ballistics since Ballistics is sharing so much more."

17

The agreed-upon time was still a couple of hours away. Gennaro had also agreed to do the cooking, if Bianca would do the shopping and prepping for the meal.

Perego had given the team the next day off as a meek gesture of psychological compensation for their aggravation and stress, since they all knew it was only a matter of time before the news on Palmisano would break out over the web, the Milanese papers and pavements. Alessandro had also managed to persuade his girlfriend to call out sick. It was not to be a dinner but rather a late lunch that could pass for dinner if the portions were right. And with Gennaro's cooking that much could be assured, but Dante had his doubts beyond that.

Bianca shopped with Gennaro's food list. She had decided that this would be the day she'd break her self-imposed seclusion. Dante didn't like it, but he approved of the sunglasses and the wig. He never understood why women would want a wig, but he was grateful for their existence this once.

Dante had found an errant book in the apartment, the latest installment of the Inspector Montalbano series, which reminded him that he had bought a book by another author in the same genre. It should be on the shelf in the workroom. He had been thinking about trying someone new, so had taken that next logical step at a local bookstore, taken it home with the best of intentions, then shelved and forgot the volume. Ah, the fickle heart of the book lover.

Montalbano was enjoyable though. The author, Camilleri, created a language in his literature that mixed up everyday Italian, cultured Italian, and Sicilian forms. The result was sometimes very effective and sometimes quite quixotic.

Dante returned the Camilleri to the shelf, and confirmed he had the author he wanted. Salvatore Niffoi. The book was next to a volume of Claudio Magris—another author on the I-must-read-someday list.

He smiled. Nice day off, a good meal ahead, possibly an enjoyable conversation, although he had no idea what to expect between Farrugia and this Paola.

Dante examined the Niffoi. He did an admirable job with Sardinian in his books—an even harder task since Sardinian is not an Italian dialect like Sicilian, rather a minority language. Language was central to mastering reality. Heidegger's phrase.

Dante turned to leave the room but found, like his errant book, that one of Bianca's pages, one torn out of her pad, had become truant and taken flight, landing on the floor.

He was returning it to her desk when he saw the horrific letters "A.I.D.S."

He knew he shouldn't, but how could he not? He stuck the page back into the pad, fanned the pages and started randomly reading her various words.

"Tank," "CB," "M1," "ammo" with a big X through it. "Ad astra per aspera = To the stars through hardships = Through hardships to the stars." All in her fast hand, with the equal signs emphatic in black ink. None of it made sense, other than this was Bianca investigating Charlie Brooks. He continued reading, this time slowly going through the pages, until he returned to the Latin phrase. He had had enough of the language of his ancestors after Ragonese's melodramatic news delivery.

"Zeugma or Chiasmus ≠ my kink, U Bitch!"

Dante blinked. He reread her phrase, itself an example of zeugma or chiasmus, almost a palindrome, though a twisted, jagged example of one.

U Bitch, my kink ≠ Chiasmus or Zeugma.

It wasn't the rhetorical terms that disturbed him. It was not the heavily inked Z or C or the not-equal sign that bothered him. It was "U Bitch."

To whom was she talking? Who was the bitch?

He heard Bianca come in the door with the bags.

They all sat down at the table. At the one end was Dante's seat, with Farrugia at the other. To Farrugia's right, Paola, and to his left sat Alessandro, which left Gennaro and Bianca to sit to the left and right of Dante. Dishes were set and waiting. For the moment, Gennaro was in the kitchen with Bianca as his assistant in preparing and plating.

Gennaro had arrived not long after Bianca's return, because there was pasta to prepare for the first course. Gennaro had demonstrated and explained to her the ancient tradition of mothers transmitting to their daughters the art of pasta-making, the intricacies of pasta forms and signatures in the creation, much like the way Persian women would make beautiful rugs at their looms and sign their names into the weave of the fabric. Gennaro explained that, just like grammar and syntax, each region had its own pasta form. For her part, Bianca would've been happy to get store-brought, pre-cooked pasta, but Gennaro had insisted that Farrugia's pasta would have no egg. And besides, he said, the northerners overcook their pasta and it is too heavy on the stomach. This is why he had asked her to buy *grano duro* wheat. Hardy and eggless pasta.

Gennaro created *ditali*, a short pasta, and since Paola was from Bergamo he thought to create something Calabrese and something Lombard so she would not feel so out of sorts with the food this afternoon. *Pasta e patate*, his solution, was *ditali* with a creamy potato and pancetta sauce. This was to be followed with the antipasti of dry toasts with a fresh tomato and garlic topping, *friselle con pomodoro crudo*, and whatever Alessandro and his girlfriend brought for dessert.

Alessandro, uncertain of the courses, brought red and white wines. Paola came with a box of sponge cakes, little yellow domes dusted with sugar and topped with tiny chocolate birds, a traditional dessert from Bergamo, she said.

The meal had started out well. Flattery came after the introductions and everyone took to their seats. The conversation started after the pasta was served, after the round of *complimenti* to the chef.

Paola started the conversation. "Alessandro tells me that you, Dante, and you, Gennaro, worked on the Roma Underground scandal with his professor, Renato Moretti from the University of Salerno. Impressive."

While Dante deferred to Gennaro, Farrugia and Bianca ate silently, observing Paola and each other.

"Like any investigation, it was a collaborative effort," Gennaro said, "and Bianca here did some excellent research."

"And you, Commissario? Did you have a role?"

"Please, we're eating as friends. Call me Isidore, or Farrugia at least if you're not comfortable with the informality. As to your question, I was tangential to the investigation. Merely an auxiliary."

Paola smiled. "But you're hardly tangential now with the Lele investigation."

"I don't think we should talk about the Palmisano case while we eat," Alessandro said. "The matter is still upsetting."

Bianca moved to the kitchen but kept an ear cocked to the conversation. Dante asked, "You know some of the details then?"

"I know some from Paola, yes," Alessandro answered.

Dante smiled.

Bianca returned with the *friselle*. Those last words made her feel she had gone to the wrong class and hadn't done the reading. "I'd like to know some of the details, if nobody minds, or I can wait until we are done eating." Bianca sat down, looking around the table. Gennaro looked down into his wine for a sip and then at Farrugia.

Farrugia tried to be encouraging. "If the hostess doesn't mind, then you should by all means, Paola. It's possible in reviewing the facts we might have some insights."

With no hint of embarrassment, Paola described the location, the car, the positioning of the body and the unfortunate implication of indiscretion and indignity.

"Any evidence that someone was with him?" Bianca asked. Farrugia caught her eye with a look she couldn't decipher.

Paola shook her head.

"Did he have a cell phone on his person?" Dante asked.

Gennaro and Farrugia looked at each other. It was a we-hadn't-thought-of-that look.

"He did, yes," Paola said, "but that's not my specialty. I only do ballistics."

"And there was no evidence of a shooting?" Bianca asked.

Paola shook her head again. "I had an easy day, right, Isidore? I had nothing to do at the scene since there were no firearms involved. Palmisano would never carry a weapon. We know he was against personal possession of firearms. Unlike American celebrities or politicians, he never used bodyguards. My colleagues did most of the work until the coroner came to collect the body."

Alessandro, like all boyfriends, felt the need to provide some defense, since Paola was receiving such intense attention. "Paola is one of the few women ballistics experts in Lombardy."

Gennaro lifted his glass. "Congratulations. That's progress."

"Not many ballistics experts, or not many women ballistics experts?" Farrugia asked.

Paola sipped her wine. "I'm the only woman, but the Ballistics Department is quite small, and it depends on the police station. I'm the regional expert, although there are some local experts."

"Impressive," Farrugia said.

They talked for some time about the elections and speculated on what would have been had Palmisano lived. Gennaro excused himself to start the coffee and plate the bird-like desserts.

Paola said to Bianca, "You speak Italian well."

"Thank you."

"My parents and my late grandparents spoke the dialect, Bergamese, which can sound quite harsh. I had to unlearn the accent and keep it at home with my parents. I worry it creeps in now and then. It's not like we have difficulty understanding each other in Lombardy."

"I understand you just fine," Bianca answered.

"May I ask how you helped in the Roma investigation? Alessandro was not clear. I know you're an American, so I know you couldn't be law enforcement. Are you a consultant of some sort?"

Gennaro and Farrugia awaited Bianca's answer.

"Something like that. I'm competent, shall we say, in computer forensics, and I've been told that I possess a natural aptitude at research."

"I see," Paola said with that lovely smile.

Farrugia gave her a subtle nod, pleased with her answer. Nice.

After coffee, after dessert, after idle chitchat, not work-related, Alessandro and Paola left.

The four remained. They switched to English.

"Completely slipped my mind not to ask or verify about a cell phone," Gennaro said.

"How stupid of me! Who the hell doesn't have a cell phone these days?"

"Calm down," Farrugia said. "I missed it too. The fault is with me. You don't think about cell phones because you hate yours. Palmisano's cell phone should be in the manifest of the crime scene if he had it with him when he died. I think that is the least of my problems."

Gennaro shifted back in his chair, offended. "Your problem? Excuse me. I was the one with my ass up in the air to Farese and Perego before they decided to pick you as lead investigator. And what is this about I don't think about cell phones? Are you implying I'm a fossil because I'm about to retire?"

Bianca's hand rushed out to pat Gennaro's hand in an effort to calm him down. "I think what Isidò is trying to say is that he is trying to figure out Paola."

"You mean whether she's the leak in Ballistics," Dante said. "She just said that there are few experts, and she was the only woman in the region. Am I right, Isidò?"

"That's part of it, Dante. That's part of it. I'd like to know why the local expert wasn't there. We were in Senna Lodigiana and it would've been easy enough to send a ballistics expert from Lodi. Gennaro and I had driven over fifty kilometers. Lodi is twenty kilometers. Paola had come all that way from Bergamo, assuming she got the call in the morning."

Bianca leaned across the table, her finger pushing a crumb from the *friselle* next to a small square of tomato. "Unless someone wanted a woman there for future publicity. The only ballistics expert, a woman, on the scene makes it a high profile case."

"It already is a high-profile case," Dante said. "The man was on his way to becoming prime minister."

"No need to sound upset," she said, "but what I don't get is why she stayed at the scene if there was no need for her."

"What do you think, Isidò?"

"I'm perplexed, but she did leave after I apologized to her," he said, and explained the apology. "So she didn't exactly stay at the scene. I guess you can say that she was following protocol in leaving after the lead investigator dismissed her. That would be me. But she was on the scene until I arrived, so no one is sure about what she saw. She knew about the cell phone, but yet she never mentioned the porno magazines, did she?"

"Porno magazines?" Bianca said.

Farrugia explained them, described the various genres, and where the CSU expert found them.

Dante and Bianca were silent, as was Gennaro.

Farrugia said, "Either she didn't see them or know about them, or thought nothing of them, if she did. You know, just another guy and his porn. A gay man's sexuality might not be something she understands too well since she is straight, and for all we know she has no direct knowledge of gay men except for the typical stereotype and—"

"Typical stereotype?" Bianca asked.

"Dresses well, literate . . . metrosexual," Farrugia said.

Gennaro smiled and added, "The type who would take yoga?"

Farrugia gave him a withering look.

"And?" Dante asked.

Farrugia said, "She wouldn't say a thing about his pornography, given his state—the man already had his pants down and, well, you know, *in flagrante delicto*."

"There's another consideration," Bianca said. "You said that the magazines were in the trunk of the car?"

Farrugia nodded.

"She might've not made the connection that a man would need the magazines to . . ."

"What?" Dante asked.

Farrugia snapped his fingers. Gennaro glared at the habit.

"Don't be so simple-headed, Dante. If Paola didn't know, Bianca is suggesting why she might not have mentioned it. What Bianca is saying is that women are more evolved than us. They most often use their imagination, whereas we need the visual."

"Must be all that yoga," Gennaro mumbled and kicked back the last of his wine.

Dante looked at Bianca. She smiled at him and batted her eyelashes up and down.

"Paola wouldn't make the connection that a man would get out of the car, get his magazines, return to the front seat, and do his business," Farrugia said, "but in this case we know Palmisano didn't do that because there were no footprints."

Bianca sipped more wine. "Was there any evidence that somebody gave him a blowjob?"

Dante gave her a shocked look.

"What? Are you a prude? Would you prefer that I say *oral sex?*"

"No. There were no fingerprints on the passenger side to suggest some-one entered the car from that side. No palm print on the car seat and—"

"The damn palm print," Gennaro said.

Farrugia ignored him. "Nothing in the backseat either. If anyone was there the car was wiped clean, but still no footprints on either side or around the car, other than the honeymooner hikers who found the body. And the magazines seem planted. None of this suggests Paola was the leak about the Gévelots."

Bianca was smiling again. "Then again nobody knows that yet. Ragonese hasn't done his eulogy yet."

"That asshole," Gennaro commented.

Bianca cleared her throat. "We wait and see. The magazines are a com-pelling discrepancy. You still have others to interview, and the coroner owes you a report. As for Paola . . . we know Alessandro doesn't have a good record with women. Remember our Hungarian sex kitten in Rome?"

She heard grunts of agreement.

"What are your thoughts about Paola?" Farrugia asked. "You're right. I do have more factors to weigh in before I make any conclusions. I'd like to know what is on his cell phone and why Lodi didn't send a bal-listics expert. In fact, I'm wondering why it was our CSU team and not Lodi or some joint enterprise that processed the scene. Shit. I hadn't thought of that, either."

"My thoughts?" Bianca said. "Let's say Paola is involved. Speculation. She is the perfect media image. Attractive and accomplished—only woman ballistics expert from Milan, lives in Bergamo, split in half between the Lega Nord and coalition Democrats, and we don't know to which half her politics belong. But if she were involved—she was at the scene long enough to know how people were thinking and in what direction the case is going."

After Gennaro and Farrugia left, as Bianca and Dante prepared for bed, Dante said, "I wanted to ask you something."

"Can it wait? I'm tired of thinking."

He rolled over to his side, head on the pillow. "I'm not a prude."

She smiled as she changed into her négligée. She got into their bed and turned him onto his back. The wine had made her feel good, and it was a nice change to engage the boys in a police procedural, unlike her Brooks case.

"I was just teasing you, Dante, I know you're not a prude." She started to kiss him and then straddled him, kissing the side of his neck. She was warm; the duvet was pulled up. She continued kissing him but he was stiff, and not in the way she had hoped.

"What's wrong?"

"Are you happy with me?"

"Yes, very much. I know we have our differences, but that's normal. I'm very happy with you."

"Happy sexually?"

She smiled and resumed kissing. "Let me prove it."

She was shocked when his hands pushed her shoulders up and he asked, "Am I your bitch?"

18

Perego arranged for a miracle on their day off. Farrugia now had his own office.

Perego had left him a voicemail on his cell earlier. After listening to it, Farrugia walked down to the end of the hall. The path was familiar; he knew of only one office this way. There, he found a brand new desk, the latest office supplies, a properly configured computer system, wires neatly stowed and out of sight, a beautiful flat-screen, a wireless keyboard and mouse, even a coffee mug.

There were the expected glitches.

The phone lines were not discrete, Farrugia disliked computers, and last but not least, he was to share the office space. The office was halved, not unlike the baby brought before Solomon.

"Morning," Farrugia said to his office mate.

"Morning, Commissario Farrugia," Gennaro replied.

"What is all this?"

Gennaro shrugged. "You know management: do more with less. That's your desk, you know, the new one."

"I'm sorry Gennaro. I didn't know."

The office secretary, whom neither of them had met other than the brief introduction, walked in, said his hellos, and handed each of them a piece of paper.

"What's this?" Farrugia asked.

The nameless man said, "Yearly job description. Direct from Central Administration."

Gennaro tossed the paper onto his desk. "We haven't been here a year."

"Mere formality. All of us have to write our job descriptions once a year. Quality-improvement initiative."

"Our job description?" Farrugia asked.

The man nodded, smiled, and left the office.

Farrugia turned around and faced Gennaro for guidance. "There's that phrase again—'mere formality.' I'm a civil servant and my description is on file. Had you ever heard of anything like his before?"

Gennaro shrugged. "No. Just look at it as their asking you to build your own coffin. Forgotten, but not remembered."

Farrugia stood there puzzled until the phone at Gennaro's desk rang. Farrugia took off his jacket and dropped into a seat. Nice chair. St. Ambrose was kind.

"Hello? I'm sorry for the confusion . . . No, I'm not . . . I'm sorry that I don't sound like Commissario Farrugia, but I appreciate the compliment. We're sharing the same phone line for the time being. Who is this?"

Farrugia came over when Gennaro beckoned. Gennaro scribbled on the notepad, "Dr. Primo Foà," and while Gennaro's pen was poised for the next fact, Farrugia parsed what he knew. Uncommon name, Jewish, and minus the accent it reminded him of Vittorio Foa crossed with Primo Levi. Gennaro's pen wrote and underlined, "coroner."

Gennaro continued as the intermediary. "'Heart attack,' you say?" Gennaro looked up at Farrugia. This was a surprise and not a surprise. "What? I'm both impressed and surprised that the tox report came back so quickly. I always thought that took weeks," Gennaro said into the receiver and wrote on the notepad, "Viagra OD."

Farrugia read and his eyebrows lifted. He had not expected that.

"Yes, doctor. I can understand why the tox report was expedited . . . Thank you for calling our office, Doctor Foà. I will convey all of this to Commissario Farrugia, and it goes without saying that this information must remain confidential until a formal announcement is made about the deceased. We can't let the media speculate . . . I appreciate that you understand. It's a sensitive case, yes . . . I agree with you: solid facts and a solid presentation are essential. Again, thank you, Doctor. Have a good day."

Farrugia tapped the pad. "So he took Viagra, overdid it, and had a fatal heart attack."

Gennaro was quiet a moment. "Palmisano had no script for Viagra."

"He could have easily ordered it on the web under a fake name. Politicians are often worried about the public perception of their health problems, especially virility. So they'll get their drugs, like Viagra, through a friend. It's a ghost script. Off the books."

Gennaro was shaking his head, looking glum.

"No? Tell me."

Gennaro threw down the pen and ran his hands over his face. "The doctor just told me that for a man like Lele, Viagra would've been con-traindicated since he had a mild heart condition. The heart condition might be public knowledge. I'll check, but the doctor said it was a mild case of angina and Lele took nitro. I'll check the scene manifest to see if he had nitro pills on him. Cardiac patients will usually carry them. Very easy to overlook."

Farrugia returned to his desk. "And the Viagra would've kill him?"

"If he took the nitro, and then the Viagra, he'd have sudden drop of blood pressure and the rest," Gennaro whistled and used his hand to illustrate descent, "is downhill from there. The doctor found traces of nitro under his tongue and the toxicology report showed a ridiculous dose of Viagra in his system. That explains his . . . you know what at the scene."

Farrugia's desk phone rang. The ring tone sounded different.

"Interoffice call," Gennaro said

Farrugia picked it up.

"Commissario, this is Internal Affairs. We need to arrange a follow-up meeting as soon as possible."

"Yes, I see."

"How soon would you be available?"

"I'll let you know. Thank you. Bye."

Gennaro watched Farrugia put down the receiver.

"That was awfully quick," Gennaro said.

"That was IA. I'll let Perego know. He said that he'll take care of them for me. I should go and tell him. I'm still not buying the heart attack. Why would he take that much Viagra? Was he afraid of disappointing himself?"

"Are you sexually excited by someone holding a gun to your head?"

"Not as a rule. What are you . . . oh."

"Exactly. If someone were trying to force him to take the Viagra, it'd make for an embarrassing situation. Plausible?"

"Yes. While I visit Perego, please see whether the nitro was in the manifest and I want to start on that cell phone of his—and I know that we need to interview his party members on the night of."

"Yes, Commissario Farrugia," Gennaro said.

"Please, don't bust my balls."

Farrugia's cell phone rang. Unexpected.

"Yes." Farrugia listened.

It was one of those calls that made Farrugia switch the phone to the other ear and talk in a lower register.

"I'll meet with you, of course. I understand. We both need to be private about this meeting. I agree. Neither of us needs the attention. How does this sound? I belong to an exclusive gym and have some guest passes. Our privacy is guaranteed there. We can meet at, say, five thirty p.m., do a yoga class, talk, and have dinner somewhere." He listened some more. "Wonderful. The gym is on Via Falcone, meters away from the Piazza Duomo. You can't miss it. See you then." He clicked the cell phone closed.

Gennaro was staring at him. "We're on a case and I'm doing errands for you—nitro, cell phone, manifest this and manifest that, ballistics team—and you're making a date for yoga?"

Farrugia wasn't amused. "That was Arnaldo Litrico. You know the name?"

Gennaro's eyebrows perked up. "Lele's partner."

19

All arguments, like narratives, start *in medias res*. For Bianca and Dante, the word *bitch* was the end of the previous chapter.

"You were reading my papers," Bianca shouted, stalking away from him.

"Paper. It had fallen out. I picked it up and I read it. I returned it. I saw the others. Couldn't help myself."

She spun around. "You read it and the others and now you're asking me what they mean."

"Well . . . yes. If it didn't mean anything, you wouldn't be so upset."

"I'm upset because you read my notes."

Fine. He could play this, too. "Yeah, I'm upset that you didn't share any of it with me. You were keeping a secret from me."

"There were no results, Dante. There wasn't anything to share."

"Still you hid it from me. I mean something is better than nothing. Farrugia and Gennaro could use help and you know that."

She was defiant, staring at him. "Think I'm stupid not to know they need help?"

"I didn't call you stupid. You know me better than that."

"Thought I knew you. Thought you knew better than to snoop and when to mind your own business."

"'Mind my own business'? How can you say that after what those two have done for you?"

She started walking away, which was one of his peeves, as she well knew. "Don't remind me what they've done for me, Dante. I'm tired of hearing it."

"Maybe you do need reminding. Maybe you need to be reminded and get out of your own head. You've been living with Rendition and with Loki for too long. You have friends and you have me. You trust us, but you go outside for help? You're not the only one who—"

She walked right up to him. "'Inside my own head?' What? I'm a self-centered bitch?"

"Stop it! I didn't call you any of those things."

She imitated his voice. "'I didn't call you any of those things.' No, you didn't, Dante, but you implied it. You're calling me a bitch. It demeans me."

"Demeans you? I see; it's all about you." He threw his hands up. "Meanwhile, Farrugia has most of the country thinking he killed three people."

"Blame Ragonese for that, not me."

Dante lowered his voice, approximating calm. "You're right. Ragonese is an idiot—a real *stronzo*. I'm all for journalistic freedom, but only if there are standards, and that piece of shit has no standards. But that doesn't change Farrugia's predicament, and we shouldn't sit idle and watch him get fucked and see his career get ruined."

Hands on her hips—not a good sign. "You sure you didn't mean *stronza,* as I'm the piece of shit. Of course, I know Farrugia is in trouble."

"Stop making it about you. You sound like a typical Ameri—I'm sorry, I'm sorry I said that. It's about Farrugia . . . but you know what? Let's make this about you, because none of this would have happened if you hadn't taken Farrugia along."

She glared at Dante. "I didn't take Farrugia along. He invited himself."

Dante shrugged. "Case in point."

"What the fuck is that supposed to mean?"

"You didn't invite him. Farrugia brought it all on himself, and you'd be in a body bag now if he hadn't. But hey, it's not about you."

"Screw you. So I am a bitch?"

Dante stood there in silence. He could hear his heart beating in his fingertips with his arms crossed, completing the circuit of adrenaline.

"Say something, Dante. Just say something."

"Just saying . . ."

She walked around him. "Just saying . . . what, Dante?"

"In my experience, a bitch doesn't know she's a bitch."

She stared at him and did the one thing that defeats all men: she started crying.

Bianca started with an indefinable sound that led to a crack then a heave and a biblical wail. "It's not about me or Farrugia. It's about Charlie, bleeding next to the trash and what he said to me before he ran off to his death, and how I'm so helpless, and Loki said, 'STAY AWAY,' and I thought I could solve it, fix it for Charlie, for Farrugia and now, for you, and I can't. Oh, Dante, I can't."

"I'm sorry." Dante took her into his arms. "We can do this. I don't know how, but we will."

He heard the sniffles and didn't think about his shirt.

Milan is a city built on water, on the land between the Ticino and Adda rivers, a city that grew over the centuries in near-perfect Giottoesque circles, which gave it mystery, a city that was exactly on the 45th parallel, halfway between the North Pole and the Equator, with the Duomo as the center of centers. In one of the many ancient alleys that Druids had built around the Duomo, on his cell phone, Farrugia found himself in the bull's-eye of a perfect mess.

"Yes, I talked to Perego" Farrugia said. "He bought time with IA, which was a surprise. Any luck with the list of things."

"Lele did have a pill fob for his nitro pills," Gennaro said. "Rather than keep it around his neck, like most patients, he preferred to keep it in his pocket or in his suit jacket. It might have been a matter of vanity, since it would've shown up in photographs around his neck."

"That certainly makes sense. Any script for Viagra?"

"None that I could find. You can broach that with Litrico."

"I will. I didn't think we'd find a script, though. Doesn't mean that

Arnaldo or their circle of friends didn't share the enhancer. How about the ballistics team?"

Gennaro laughed. "I like that, 'enhancer,' I'll pass it on to Silvio. As for the ballistics team, Lodi does have one, and like us, they also have a CSU team. Lodi's CSU has a woman—checked out of curiosity. I have no answer as to why they didn't respond to the scene or why this couldn't have been a joint investigation. An argument could be made about territory, but I'd think that once Lodi realized the potential notoriety of the case they would've clamored over it."

"There's still time for that, Gennaro. There's always time. We still have to interview the party members Lele met with that night and—"

Farrugia could hear a rustling of papers. Gennaro said, "Got the list in my hand and we have appointments, starting at one thousand hours."

"You've been busy."

"Farrugia?"

"Yes."

"You should be on your way to yoga."

"I am."

"Isidò?"

"Does Arnaldo know that his Lele is dead?"

After their fight, Dante was making coffee for the two of them—her style, using the Bodlum French-press. He was waiting to push the plunger down. Bianca was in the workroom, pad of paper out for notes, and waiting for him to join her. Instant messenger conference. This would be new for him.

He had made the call to let Gennaro know that he'd be in later in the morning the next day. Gennaro said something about him and Farrugia interviewing Lele's party acquaintances north of Milan.

"Make it late afternoon," he had said. Dante had not expected this largesse.

"We can all reconvene and discuss status and strategy," Gennaro had added. "Alessandro can pick up some of the follow-through on Farrugia's list."

Dante was afraid to ask about Farrugia's list. And when he had inquired about Farrugia, the answer was something like, "Think he is doing yoga tonight. He says it eases his mind, helps him sleep. Tomorrow afternoon."

Dante finally pushed the plunger, poured, and took the coffee mugs into the room.

"Thanks." She took the initial sip, set down her mug. "Did you tell them you might be late tomorrow?"

"I did. Rather late now as it is, so I know I'll need a nap later." He looked at his watch, confirming that it was late, delaying the start of this strange conference. "So are you sure the time difference is no problem?"

"I doubt it. In the past I never had issues. It's not like I know where Loki is located."

He sipped. "Ever try to locate her?" He had never asked Bianca a direct question about her former employer, Rendition, before.

She sipped, examined the screen. "Yep. Can't tell you how many times I've tried and always ended up with nothing. Loki scrambles ISP numbers and GPS satellite feeds."

"It's scary that someone can do that. Who has that kind of access?"

"People you don't want to meet or know."

The IM ping sounded and they both saw the androgynous avatar. Dante said nothing about Bianca's avatar.

"How does this work?" Dante asked. "Just ask her outright, right?" He realized that he said something like Silvio.

"Sssh," she said as she typed out her comment. "Doesn't work that way, Dante. You don't just ask an explicit question. It's not how the game is played."

"This is a game? You've got to be kidding. What did you type?" He looked at the screen.

"If Adastra is the way to pain, so is AIDS."

"I don't get it," Dante said.

"I'm starting the thread, and from there the logic will reveal itself. Why don't you just watch and—"

She was interrupted by Loki's ping and response.

Loki wrote. "Still the same. STAY AWAY." Not encouraging.

While Dante watched, Bianca's personality and demeanor began to transform. Her hands curled, ready to speed-type, and her eyes narrowed to re-read the letters and tease out any nuance there might be in the words on the screen.

"Can't stay away & not about 2 bec/challenge. Stakes ↑ now," she wrote.

Loki responded with, "CB↓ RP↓ & IF on way."

Dante leaned forward again to try and understand, and Bianca translated, "Charlie Brooks dead, Palmisano is dead, and Isidore Farrugia is on his way."

Wait. Was Farrugia's life in danger?

Bianca hammered back, "Anthropomorphic = human characteristics."

"Isn't it more important to find out who's trying to kill Farrugia?" Dante said.

"Not part of the rules, Dante. Be patient and watch, please."

Loki typed out. "Peek at sw?"

Bianca typed out, "M1 sw = weapons launch."

Pause.

Dante asked, "What is she doing?"

"Either about to give me another clue or tell me something. Look!" She pointed at the windowpane. "Loki is typing, and since it is taking Loki longer than usual, I'll bet Loki will tell me something."

Dante sipped his coffee. "You keep saying *Loki*. I haven't heard you once say *he* or *she*."

"That's only because I don't know. Loki is back. It's a statement."

Dante looked at the screen. "AIDS = acquisition, like the virus, Acquired . . ."

"Looks like a clue," he said.

Bianca's finger was tapping the side of the keyboard. She was thinking. He looked at the finger. Odd choice. Wedding finger.

"Your coffee is getting cold. So it's a statement, huh?"

"I'm thinking, Dante. The tank's software, if we assume it's like traditional weapons systems, should be about launching the weapons, unless—"

"Unless what?"

She said to him, "Unless the sw is, like she said, like AIDS . . . acquisition . . . acquiring . . . acquired . . . the software is about acquiring the target," and typed to Loki, "Target?"

Dante shifted in his chair. "Jet fighter pilots lock on a target and they have those—" He waved his hands in front of his face—"Special helmets where they can see targets three hundred and sixty degrees like they were human flies. Once they see, that is, they acquire the target with their eyes, the software follows their eye movements and the software launches the weapons. Fail-safe."

Her hands were resting on the keyboard. "Jet-fighter pilots do that, don't they? I bet you helicopters can, too. But I don't get the connection—they're airborne, whereas a tank is terrestrial. A tank's target wouldn't move that quickly. They wouldn't need to be instantly responsive."

Loki was pinging her with a sound file of Sinatra's "Where are you?"

Bianca typed. "Cute. Dislike Frank. Acquisition?"

Loki typed back. "Tautology: Acquisition & Anthropomorphic."

"What the hell does that mean?" Bianca asked.

Dante read it again. "Different words to say the same thing. Circular logic."

"I know what tautology means, Dante. Loki is telling me that the answer has been given, but I must not be seeing it, even though it's in front of me."

"I'm just saying Loki is telling you that acquisition is anthropomorphic."

She stared at him. "You know, when you use 'just saying,' it makes you sound adolescent." She faced the screen, glanced over at the Nordic avatar, watching it change from man to woman and back.

"Got it!" she yelled and pulled Dante in to kiss him. His coffee spilled.

"What?"

"The weapons system on the Adastra tank doesn't acquire objects to destroy. It acquires humans to destroy."

"Huh?"

Bianca typed, "Anthro sw = 4 human targets @ close 25¢."

Dante's eyes squinted.

"Anthropomorphic Intelligent Design is software designed to acquire and kill human targets in close-quarters."

"Good. Now can you translate your translation? Weapons are meant to kill people. What difference does it make whether it is close or long-distance?"

"There is a difference. Think about this: a tank kills from a distance and it's safe, but it's a different situation up close. Blind spots—a tank has blind spots all around it. Think of the American war films with tanks and tell me, what do you see? You always have a patrol on either side of the tank."

He thought of *Patton*. She was right. "And?"

"An infantry patrol protects the tank's blind spots—on both sides of the tank. Design a software to protect those blind spots and you save lives and you save money on ammunition."

"Save money?"

"Tanks use sabots. They're far more expensive than bullets. Somehow this software detects humans around it and the machine guns from the cupolas are configured to eliminate the targets."

Dante sat up. "I've no idea what the hell a sabot is, but I do know what a cupola is, and I'm not liking what comes to mind from your description. But here's the question I have . . . She's making that noise again."

Bianca turned in her chair, ignoring the screen, and faced Dante. "What is it?"

"How does the software differentiate an enemy from a friend?"

"Good question," Bianca said.

Dante leaned in to read the screen.

Loki had typed. "DA = there."

"Does that mean what I think it means?"

"Yeah. Loki knows you're here."

Farrugia consulted his watch. Early.

The Piazza Duomo was, as always, busy with traffic. A time-lapsed montage would show smart and snappy ladies on their way to shop at La Rinascente and the Excelsior on the northern side, towards Corso Vittorio Emanuele; executives in business suits and with attaché cases would be seen dashing from the Metro exits to the banking quarter on the other side of the Galleria; and hip teenagers would flock in packs to Via Torino as the photographers fed pigeons, snapped mementos, and hawked them to tourists. Arab and Asian immigrants would be chatting on the Duomo steps while the sun went through the rose window on the façade and warmed a specific tile of the zodiac on the floor inside each month.

Farrugia walked over to the museum where Mussolini gave Fascist speeches. Where now he learned to do downward dog and turn himself into a tree for the sake of lowering his blood pressure.

Arnaldo Litrico was meters ahead, his yoga mat bag slung over his shoulder, surveying Via Falcone. The face and physique bore all the genetic hallmarks that would destine anyone possessed of them to a career in any one of the fashion houses. Litrico was lean, tall, in charcoal slacks, a white shirt under a mild-purple sweater and leather jacket. The overall dark silhouette complemented the dark hair, matching stubble, but not the intense eyes. Litrico was one of those people who actually looked better than he photographed.

They recognized each other.

"I see you're acquainted with yoga," Farrugia said. "Let's walk."

"It helps me relax. Peace of mind."

Farrugia couldn't agree more, but said nothing as he pointed to the door of the club, and opened it for him.

"Thank you."

After Farrugia gave the blank guest pass to Litrico to present to the club's concierge, Litrico signed both the register and the guest pass and put down a contact number in the register. Farrugia noted the different name and suspected that the number was equally false. Good for Litrico, smart, and less of a headache with IA for Farrugia, if they tailed him. They went to the elevator.

The doors closed.

"Been in Milan long?" Farrugia asked.

"Not long. I've never been a fan of the city. Never quite grew on me."

"Does Lele like Milan?"

Litrico smiled. "He learned to tolerate it. I think Milan grew on *him*, but home is where you grow up. You miss Reggio?"

Farrugia noted Litrico's use of the past tense. The thought of missing Calabria went through his mental sieve next.

"Home is never the same when you start living life," he said.

The door opened, and Farrugia's hand held it for his guest. Litrico suggested that they talk before the yoga class. Farrugia directed them to the food area. They found a table. Ordered nothing.

"How did you find my number?" Farrugia asked.

"The gay mafia. We're everywhere."

Farrugia liked the humor and laughed. "I was just curious, but that's the least of my worries."

"I know. I saw all of Ragonese's shows. Not that I wanted to, but he's an unavoidable plague these days. You know he's launching a one-hour show to review your career, from your mother's death to your work with the anti-mafia projects with Falcone and Borsellino and the Maxi-Trials?"

Farrugia was not amused. "So I keep hearing. I don't plan to watch it. I'm afraid I'll hurt myself, either from laughing or punching the screen. I have no great love for the media, particularly with how my name is now associated with Via Manzoni and the bullets."

Litrico nodded. "I had to learn to deal with the media because of Lele. He's a politician and it's in his blood, like a sailor and the sea, to know how to roll with the ups and downs, the false storms and the idle moments. It didn't come naturally to me. Still doesn't."

"You seem to have done well," Farrugia said. "I saw the picture that Ragonese plastered of the two of you with your friends. I assume by now—and the picture was dated a few years ago—you've become acclimated to the paparazzi and the media. Magazines have dubbed you two 'The First Couple.'"

Litrico laughed. "Ah, The First Couple. I've heard that one. I'm better now, but it wasn't always that way."

"I don't understand."

"The day that Ragonese put that photograph on display was the day Lele and I had had a huge fight. Eh . . . huge disagreement. I was incensed that the bastards wouldn't allow us to enjoy our vacation. Lele calmed me down. He has that calming voice."

Farrugia nodded, offered a smile. "Anyway, Lele assured me that the people who were trying to humiliate him, paint him as some degenerate, sex-obsessed maniac, would learn that kind of media strategy would backfire on them, because people are more progressive, more tolerant. That the holier-than-thou bullshit doesn't work. It backfired on Berlusconi."

Farrugia smiled. "I remember Berlusconi trying that with 'Nichi' Vendola. It did backfire, but I don't know whether it was because people were progressive. Then again, I wouldn't know. Nobody would've ever thought your Catania would be receptive to gays. Italy is still the only Western European nation that doesn't recognize the gay life and gay partnerships."

Litrico was laughing.

"Did I say something . . . ?"

"'Recognize the gay life.' The gay life is no different from the straight one, Farrugia. Now the reason I called you is because I'm worried about Lele. I know my gut, and I sense that something is wrong. I tried calling him on his cell and no answer. Tried numerous times. I've always understood that he's busy, but Lele has always called me at night before going to bed, wherever he is."

Farrugia sat forward, hands clasped. "Why approach me? You have Lele's counsel, his secretary and—"

"I don't trust them."

"Yet you trust me?"

"I do, and not because you're a cop."

"Why me then?" Farrugia asked, his hands to his chest.

"It's something Lele said to me once."

"About the people who wanted to humiliate him?"

"No, not them. Political candidates come and go. It was something else. He told me that the guy who is getting screwed over the most is probably the most honest man in the lot and has nothing to lose. He's the man who holds the truth whether he knows it or not. Lele told me this day would come."

Farrugia asked. "What day is that?"

"When he'd get close enough to being prime minister to be seen as a credible candidate, when he'd start talking policy, talking about a policy critical of those in the upper balcony. He said that the multinationals would reach out with their tentacles and harm him."

Farrugia listened, not liking the word "tentacles," since it apparently now applied to more than mafia. "And you think Lele is in danger?"

"I think it's beyond that."

Farrugia tried not to look shocked. "What makes you say that?"

"I listen to my intuition. All of Lele's advisors wanted him to rescind his tough stance on Vicenza and Sardinia. At first they thought it was just a good sound byte but that he'd back off once he got more percentage points in popularity. But when Lele met with the Americans and corporate representatives, he—What is it?"

Farrugia's hand had gone up. "But I thought all that about Vicenza and Sardinia was NATO-driven with U.N. approval?"

"Of course, it is. But you know those two organizations are like multi-national corporations, and the U.S. leads the way through the front door with its military, and with the U.S. military come the contractors. Sub-contractors to the U.S. military are not held accountable to the same standard of the law. Who the hell do you think was going to build those radar installations? I'll tell you: the Americans and their defense-industry companies and sub-contractors."

Farrugia's face darkened. He understood the implications of Lele's legislation that would define terrorism, terrorist, and terrorist act. "Who were these interested companies and sub-contractors that were looking at Sardinia?"

Litrico seemed exasperated. "It's more like who *wasn't* interested, Farrugia. In Lele's mind it wasn't about the balance of terror but the danger of dividing the spoils. He saw Sardinia as the spoils." He calmed down and looked around to see whether anyone was listening. They were still alone. "Lele mentioned a lot of names, but he said it wasn't the radar that gave him the most concern, it was . . ."

"Who?"

"Some company named Adastra. They were insistent. They had powerful lobbyists in Washington. Adastra was, he said, a company with a list of sub-contractors as long as our arms. Lele said that Adastra was salivating over Sardinia."

Farrugia's face contorted. "Sardinia is mountainous. What's appealing about mountains?"

"Lele told me that Adastra was enthusiastic about testing their helicopters, like the ones they gave the *Guardia di Finanza* at cost."

"At cost? I didn't know that."

"*At cost* was their way of getting in good with our politicians. Every hand gets greased. As for the company—after the U.S. involvement in Iraq and Afghanistan, Adastra was anxious to test out their next project in the mountains of Sardinia, but Lele said it wasn't helicopters. It was tanks, and he thought they were trying something new with drones."

"Tanks and drones?"

"We should get into the locker room and change for yoga."

"We should," Farrugia said automatically. Tanks and drones . . .

"And Farrugia?"

"Yes?"

"Then . . . perhaps you'll tell me what happened to Lele?"

20

Litrico's head hung down, doubtless from shock. He ignored the large water bottle next to him in the small café at the gym after the shower, after Noelle's yin yoga class.

"So that's how he died?"

"Forgive me for not having told you earlier," Farrugia said. "I didn't want to cause you pain. But I'd rather you hear it from me first, for decency's sake, than from the media. It is only a matter of time before they grab hold of the story. I swear to you that I've told you everything that I know to date, from the crime scene to what the coroner said."

"Thank you," Litrico said. "I'm not angry with you. You should know that I'm not surprised this has happened, but I'd never expected . . . for it to be this way." The man was a model of stoicism.

"I wish I could say I understand, but that would dishonor you and Lele."

"I appreciate your empathy, Farrugia."

"Why don't you just call me Isidore, or if you prefer, Isidò?"

"Thank you."

"I need to ask you about the Viagra and nitroglycerine. Did Lele have frequent attacks of angina?"

Litrico shook his head.

"I know that exercise and stress can trigger angina. Sex qualifies as physical activity, so you do understand why I ask, don't you?"

"I do. Lele was in good health. He knew his limits. The nitro was medically necessary, a precaution, you understand."

Farrugia accepted the answer. "He kept those pills on a fob. And he had a script?"

"He did—in his pocket, for the fob, because he didn't want people to know. He had a script through one of those online pharmacies, but no script for Viagra. He didn't need it."

"Even for fun, for recreational purposes? Did he experiment? From the picture I saw on Ragonese's show, it looked as if you two were social. Friends lend an aspirin and . . . you know."

Litrico shook his head.

"Even poppers? I know some gay—"

"Never. And before you ask me I'll also tell you that Lele was not into cruising, into anonymous sex. Healthy libido, yes, but he was absolutely terrified of STDs, especially AIDS. We both remember the late eighties and early nineties, when the gay community had to deal with death and discrimination. You know he was Catholic?"

Farrugia was silent. He did not like the arc to his thinking.

"Isidò?"

"Yes?"

"What is your next step in the investigation?"

Farrugia knew it was police business, not to be shared with civilians, but he answered. "Routine interviews. I have to establish the timeline. This is a high-profile case, so everything will be scrutinized."

"I see. You have to interview the advisors he was with the night he died."

"Advisors? I was told that they were party members," Farrugia said, unsure of the distinction. "Any particular individuals I should pay attention to?"

"This group was Lele's northern advisors. If you mean as suspects? I don't trust any of them."

Just great, a pit of vipers to pick a suspect from.

Litrico could sense the conclusion. "I trusted Lele, yes, but I don't trust them. I told him daily that he shouldn't either. He laughed at me. Told me, 'par for the course in politics.' My last conversation with him was as he was driving to Lodi."

"Politicians are a necessary evil. No offense to Lele, and for the company he kept professionally, but any particular reason why you didn't trust his advisors?"

"Besides their pedigrees?"

"Not sure I understand what you mean."

"The L&S is a coalition party. Coalitions are always about negotiations, about *quid pro quo*. 'I do this and you do that.' Some of the politicians who came into Lele's party are like the mafia *pentiti*. They confess their sins, seek amnesty and rehabilitation for past indiscretions, and claim their allegiance to the new party, but they continue old habits and owe old favors. Lele knew that."

Wonderful. Everyone was a suspect. Favors to *whom* and for *what* was another issue. He thought of his next question and how he would best put it to Litrico.

"In Lele's car, I mentioned that there was pornography, but I didn't specify the genre."

Litrico gestured his confusion. "I don't understand. What's complicated about porn?"

"I need to ask for certainty. Was Lele interested in twinks, or bears? You know—as a fantasy or out of curiosity?"

Litrico almost giggled and covered his mouth. "I'm sorry. I didn't mean to laugh, Isidò, but that's ridiculous. Lele was repulsed by twinks because he felt it was borderline child molestation. He liked grown men. And, as far as bears and cubs are concerned, he appreciated fit men, and leather did nothing for his libido. I hate to disillusion you, but Lele was very plain vanilla."

"Plain vanilla?"

"Routine, ordinary, lights-on, as far as sex goes. His idea of variety was to use his other hand."

"Use his other hand?"

"His left. Lele was right-handed, like the majority of people. He always used his left hand. That was his idea of novelty."

"Ah, yes, the 'majority of people,'" Farrugia smiled as he repeated the phrase.

"Anything else?"

"Will you be okay?"

"I'll have to pretend I'm surprised when I'm given the news and stay out of Ragonese's way. But I'll be okay, Isidore."

"Do Lele's advisors know that you're in Milan?"

"I imagine they do. If they don't, somebody'll let them know."

"Ragonese?"

"Does it matter? And thank you for the yoga class. I should get going."

"Dinner?"

"No, thanks. I don't have much of an appetite."

Farrugia's empathy understood. Tell a man his loved one is dead and ask him out to dinner. Just like a politician, like a snake—neither creature knows how to blink.

Farrugia looked at his left hand. Lele was posed using his right.

Gennaro would not be pleased in the morning.

21

Farrugia spoke into his cell while Gennaro drove.

"Litrico, this is Farrugia. I wanted to thank you for last night. I'm not good at this sort of thing and voicemail seems impersonal, so I'll try you later. You have my number if you wish to call me. I hope we can see each other again. Talk soon."

Gennaro was on the A1 out of Milan to Lodi, through farmland as flat as a dinner plate, broken only by the occasional, lonely stand of trees and the power lines marching across the background. Farrugia took a pastry and resisted the urge to tease Gennaro about take-out for breakfast, or that it seemed so American: two cops together with high-powered coffee, sharing obscenely sweet pastries, and on their way to question socially-connected suspects.

Then he thought of Litrico's shocked stoicism, and the urge to tease went away.

Farrugia looked at the list in his lap. A real pantheon of politicians.

Gennaro had pulled a list from the web, their affiliation, and their key staff members and, under L&S, he check-marked the five individuals with whom Lele had been scheduled to meet that fateful night. All men. Two of them were L&S purists while one was a convert from another party—one of Litrico's *pentiti*—while another was a moderate; and the last one was a venerable ancient who, like the three colors on the flag, had had a sumptuous career, starting with the more liberal Communists, then the Christian Democrats, the slightly left of right Republicans, and finally, the L&S. A man for all seasons.

As for the complete list of politicians for the election, Litrico had been right; it was a rogues' gallery of *pentiti*, with names both he and Gennaro—and most of Italy, for that matter—had seen or heard of for more than two decades now. The most senior members on this list had come of political age around the time Moro was kidnapped and murdered. Late seventies. They had weathered their own party politics and purges, investigations, economic rises and falls, international crises, and numerous changes in American and EU policies. And they all survived the scandals.

Gladio and Propaganda Due. Tangentopoli. SISMI-Telecom. Berlusconi. Cinziagate.

"Care to tell me what Litrico said last night?" Gennaro asked.

Farrugia was still reviewing the list. "Before or after yoga?"

"I stopped teasing you about the yoga. What did Arnaldo Litrico have to say?"

"I wasn't teasing you. We had two separate conversations, *before* and *after* yoga."

"Fine. Tell me about before."

Farrugia explained to Gennaro about Adastra and the significance of Sardinia. The tanks and Lele's intuition about drones.

"Lele had some serious balls," Gennaro said. "That anti-terrorist legislation of his is something only the left would've dreamt of, but Lele was about to make it a reality. He won't now, unless the L&S can salvage their party. Nobody would've thought of taking a stance like he did with NATO and the U.N., especially with the Americans and their companies in the background."

"Times are changing," Farrugia said. "Lele had come along at the right time and place. After Italy became a convenient scapegoat for the debt crisis, Lele made his move. He was a very shrewd man. He knew the debt had started in America and where from: private debt. It was from that situation he leveraged support redefining *terrorist*."

Traffic was smooth. Gennaro was making good time. They would make it in time for the appointment. Gennaro was processing the conversation before yoga. If he was angry about the possibility of Sardinia becoming used as a private playground he kept it to himself.

"After yoga?"

Farrugia winced. "I told him what we saw. Litrico knows that Lele is dead. He knows we're going out to Lodi to do these interviews."

"Shit, Farrugia, you shouldn't have told him what we saw. That could compromise the investigation. There's a good chance this case will be analyzed and studied for decades, and we don't need the attention. You're in no position—What's with this tsk-tsk and that smile of yours?"

Farrugia had done his finger-wagging and tsk-tsk, accompanied with a smug shit-eating grin. "I did not tell him what I thought about what we had seen."

Gennaro glared at him from the driver's side. Twice.

"You know if you say that fast enough, you might just sound like Tweety Bird. Don't get too clever, Isidore Farrugia, because we're both houseguests. This is Milan. You still have IA and we both have Farese and Perego, and Ragonese just finished a one-hour special about you last night."

"I was too busy to watch. What did that idiot have to say about me?"

"He was poetic about Falcone and Borsellino, and he recapped the Buscetta testimony. He dilated on the vendetta killings, which he, of course, used as a pretext to do a flashback."

Farrugia made a face. "Flashback to what? Is this a noir film?"

"A flashback to you as a young man and—"

Farrugia sat up straight in the passenger seat. "What are you saying?"

"Ragonese went on to give a history of San Luca and its own mafia wars, you know, the 'Ndrangheta. He explained that you found your mother dead and he was suggesting her death had not only inspired your ambition to destroy the mafia, but that it had also unhinged you."

"Unhinged me? He's suggesting I'm mentally unstable. The bastard!"

"It was all done through suggestion and implication, Isidò. Look at the positive side."

"There is a positive side?"

"People will interpret that as admirable. You might be unorthodox and—"

"And what did he have to say about the men who killed my mother?"

"He was neutral. A surprise, I know. Ragonese let it out that you killed them, without getting into details, but you know people'll be sympathetic. She was your mother, after all. Now, what did Litrico say after yoga."

Farrugia explained the angina, the Viagra, and the left hand.

"Left hand?" Gennaro said. "Hmm, I never would've thought of that."

"You should try it sometime."

"Very funny. But it's odd, don't you think?"

"I know."

"Did you tell him?"

"I didn't tell him we found him using his right hand. I'd never thought about it. After all, the majority of people are right-handed. For that matter, so was Lele."

They continued the drive. The sky had gotten darker and a light mist had started to fall. The GPS purred with announcements of kilometers gone by and kilometers to go in a soothing female voice. Gennaro told Farrugia that Dante would be joining them at the office later in the afternoon. They both agreed that they should reconvene and compare notes with Alessandro, Bianca, and Dante. Farrugia suggested that they should include Litrico but exclude Paola and demand a blood oath from Alessandro that he would not under any circumstance disclose the conversation to her. Gennaro balked at the Litrico suggestion, but Farrugia persuaded him that only Litrico had genuine insight into the L&S characters they were about to meet and interview; and the man also knew Lele's mind and motivations.

They found a Lodi police car blocking the long driveway to the house. Farrugia began to suspect they never should have informed the party members ahead of time that they would be meeting with them. Both men got out of their car and identified themselves to the officer who stepped out of his car into the misting rain. They exchanged terse pleasantries.

"I've been instructed not to allow you onto the premises," the officer said. He was a young man who looked as if he had been on the force for about three years. He was just doing his job. Farrugia was not interested in trying to intimidate him, but he did want answers.

"By whose authority?" he asked.

"Lodi Chief of Police, Commissario. This is our interview."

"What? *Your* interview?" Gennaro screamed, surprising the young man.

Farrugia stepped closer to the man. "But Milan processed the crime scene."

"I understand that, Commissario, but my orders are not to let you on the property."

"I appreciate that you're following orders," he said, "but this is our case and those are our interviews. Did they teach you about chain of evidence?"

"My orders, Commissario."

"Isidò?"

"Not now," Farrugia said, his head indicating that another officer was about to approach them. An older man closed the other car's door, adjusted his jacket, looked up at the sky, confirming the obvious rain, and starting walking to them.

"Your partner or your superior?" Farrugia asked the young officer.

"Superior."

"Thank you."

"Gentlemen," the man said, giving his name, but didn't bother to hear their names or shake their hands. It was clear that he knew them.

Farrugia got to the point. "Lodi is poaching our case?"

"Your case? I don't think so, Commissario Farrugia. It was decided that it's in the best interest of objectivity that this case be handed over to Lodi. Given the attention you're receiving in the media, who is to say that the police department wouldn't be criticized? The man died here, so the investigation stays here. Jurisdiction."

"Police department criticized? As far as everyone is concerned this is a natural causes case, but I'll guess you'll never know differently, since you stole the case. Do you want the man's body, too? It's in Milan."

The man stepped forward but kept his distance. "Do you have any reason to think that this case is not natural causes? Because if you do, I suggest that you speak with the lead investigator, but he has left and is in Lodi."

"Really."

"The interviews were completed this morning."

Farrugia looked at his watch. "We made our appointment at ten a.m., and you mean to tell me that five men were already interviewed and their statements taken and you've called it a day. Commendably quick work."

The other officer said nothing for a moment. "The L&S party members are very busy men and we accommodated their schedule."

"You know this is bullshit!" Gennaro shouted. "We don't even get to sit in on the interviews as observers?"

The man shrugged, called to his subordinate, instructing him to return to the car. "If you have issues or want to make a complaint, then please talk to your superior. I think his name is Perego. Oh, and I forgot—"

"What?" Farrugia said with a venomous sputter. The rain was falling harder.

"You should e-mail or fax over your notes to Lodi at your convenience."

Gennaro was already in the driver's seat when Farrugia got into the car, slammed the door, and looked at his partner. "What? You're going to tell me that your day is getting better?"

"No. I was thinking," Gennaro answered.

"What? That Farese and Perego have screwed us again? I'm thinking the same thing."

Gennaro put the car in reverse, did the K-turn, increased the speed of the wiper blades. "I'm thinking this must be what it's like to use the left hand."

Farrugia opened up his cell phone to call Perego.

The drive back was solemn, with the rain as musical accompaniment. Farrugia was sour. Gennaro was thinking of his retirement in Campania. He was thinking that he could get a nice, modest apartment, revisit scenic places, enjoy the lemons of Sorrento, the music of Rossini, forget Rome, forget Milan, and spend his days re-reading Croce, trying his hand at the dense prose of Eco, and reminiscing while watching Totò on television.

But, like Christ's return, that all seemed like future time, indeterminably delayed. He had forgotten: the Apocalypse had to come first.

The speed of the elevator and Farrugia's repeated pressing of the floor button was not helping matters.

"Isidò, pressing the damn button is not going to get us there any sooner. I know you are angry."

"I'm not angry, Gennaro. I'm furious."

"I know you are but maybe all of this is a blessing. This whole case stank from the start. Let Lodi take the glory, and when the news breaks, people will think about that instead of you."

Farrugia said nothing as the overhead light chimed. With no stops on the way up, this ride was looking like an express lift to their floor.

The doors opened and the usual crowd was gathered around the television.

"Not this shit again," Gennaro said. "What will Ragonese have for us today?"

Gennaro wondered, until he saw numerous wet faces, heard men sniffling and saw the stone faces of Farese and Perego.

22

"Once again I report to you, my countrymen, that today is a day of mourning. Raffaele Palmisano is dead. All I can tell you is what the Lodi authorities told me this morning: Mr. Palmisano was found dead in his car two days ago, after meeting with his colleagues from the L&S. They met here." The camera panned down the long driveway that Farrugia and Gennaro had been barred from travelling up. "Now, I ask the same question that has surely passed through your mind just as you heard this terrible news, 'Two days ago?' I'm told that Lele *was not* reported missing by either his L&S colleagues or by his partner. It was assumed, I guess, that with our future leader's busy schedules he had decided to rest before he resumed campaigning, but that is not what had happened."

In one corner, Silvio was translating for Farese. Someone yelled out, "Tell us what happened, you fool." Silvio translated that as well. Gennaro was consoled by the solitary fact that the circumstances of his death in his car were truly known to only a handful of people in the room.

Someone increased the volume on the television.

"No, my friends, that is not what happened. Lele is dead. While not all the facts are in, what is known is that Lele died near here. What is known is that the Milanese police were first sent to investigate the scene before jurisdiction was handed over to Lodi Police. Nothing suggests foul play, God forbid, but what'll disturb you most is whom Milan had sent out here to investigate the scene of death. It will surprise—it may even shock and offend some viewers—but Milan sent none other than Commissario Farrugia, our questionable hero from Via Manzoni."

Ragonese shook his head. The rain made him affectionately miserable.

"Of all the resources in Milan, they send him. I ask, why him? Why blemish the record of a good man with one we doubt? I ask you, why Milan first and Lodi second? Is Milan better than Lodi? I was reassured this morning that Lodi has reclaimed their jurisdiction and that we will have answers from them. Until then, I'm at a loss for words. We have lost a great man. It was only recently that Lele sat across from me during an interview." As Ragonese spoke a tear rolled down his cheek and the faces behind him looked somber. "So I turn our viewers over to my colleagues at the studio, who'll replay footage from that last interview and provide a précis of Lele's political career until we learn more information. I'm told that the Free Channel has composed a touching tune in honor of Lele Palmisano. It is called 'The Candidate from Catania,' so until then I encourage you—whether you supported Lele or not—to honor his memory. Thank you."

Someone clicked the television off as Silvio concluded his translation of Ragonese's elegy in rapid English. Farrugia whispered to Perego and pointed to his office at the end of the hall.

Perego closed the door. The office was claustrophobic enough for its natural inhabitants, Farrugia and Gennaro, but it now included Farese and Silvio.

Perego was the first to speak. "Before you say a word, Farrugia, I need to explain about Lodi."

"Please do. It was a pleasant ride. I had thought the rain just added atmosphere, like a horror film, before Gennaro and I realized that you, Farese, and the Lodi Police Department were pissing on us." Silvio looked mortified. "Please, Silvio, don't mistranslate me. I want Farese to know that I include him in the festivities."

"Watch your tone, Farrugia," Perego said. "I'm still your superior."

"Are you? Because if you were indeed my superior I'd think you would have backed me up, or provided me the courtesy of a phone call to tell me that I was about to be fucked by Lodi. I have had this case from the day you gave it to me after having dumped DiBello. The least you could've done was warned us. We were humiliated. We stood in the rain to be reminded that we were to hand over all our files to Lodi. So which one of you two—you or Farese—is going to tell me to cooperate and hand over everything? Should it be by e-mail or would you like Gennaro and me to box it all up and drive it out to Lodi? I'm just curious."

Silvio was yammering away to catch Farese up with Farrugia's anger. Gennaro pulled over Farrugia's chair, then his own, tapped the seat of Farrugia's, encouraging him to sit down while he sat down in his own chair. Farrugia sat and Gennaro crossed his arms and his one leg over and stared at Perego.

"You have something to say, Gennaro?"

"Not a word, Perego. I think my partner has put it all nicely."

"So you have nothing to add? I mean we should all get our feelings out in the open, while we can."

Gennaro pointed to Silvio. "Getting all of this?" The translator nodded. Gennaro smiled. "Good. I want to make sure Signore U.S. Attorney Michael Farese understands everything. You were about to explain to us about Lodi, Perego."

"They pulled rank. They went over my head."

Gennaro pushed Farrugia, about to stand up in a fit of anger, back into his chair. "This is Milan! They're Lodi. Milan is the capital of the region, and what are they? A city next to the Adda . . . and Silvio?"

Silvio swallowed hard, faced Farrugia.

"Please let Signore Farese know that the Adda is a river."

"Calm down, Gennaro," Perego said. "Like I said, this came from above me, from the Lodi chief of police himself, who is taking the view that Lodi has jurisdiction and that we should back off, hand over our files, let things simmer down and then we'll call it a joint investigation in due time. For now, I suggest we all calm down, especially you, Farrugia. I agree, it is bullshit but it's politics."

"Fine," Gennaro said, "it's political. Just remember that people have long memories. Farrugia and I are just simple *terroni* and we try our best to eat the polenta served up here. Now, who is sending the e-mail that'll hand over all our work?"

Perego looked at Farese and understood Farese's look as a decision.

"We've decided on no e-mail," Perego said. "We can bullshit them and tell them that the reports are in several departments, which is not too far from the truth. Dr. Foà has been tight-lipped, and I do trust him not to leak the cause of death. We know Ballistics isn't involved in this as they were in the Via Manzoni fiasco. So, as far as anyone here is concerned, the toxicology report isn't official, and that should buy us time. I'll tell them that copies of the reports are forthcoming, but that we need to photocopy them. "

"I'm hearing that *we* again. Photocopy the reports?" Gennaro asked. "Will you also tell them that the old timer needs to type up his notes? Even I use the computer and even I know everything these days is electronic. You expect them to accept paper?"

"Yes, I do. We have to stall them. Silvio can photocopy."

"Me?" Silvio said.

Perego smiled. "You're in the inner circle, and nobody else but these two, and Allegretti and Monotti, are allowed near the files. Photocopy them and by all means do it as fast as you can."

"Fast as I can, sir?" Silvio said.

Perego said, "You do understand sarcasm, don't you, Silvio?"

"Sarcasm?"

Farrugia laughed. "Congratulations, Silvio. Even in Milan, you're a secretary."

Dante knocked on the door, stuck his head in. "Ragonese is back on the television and it's not looking good."

They all exited.

Silvio was translating to Farese although Farese heard Ragonese's name and didn't need any explanation.

"This is your Giancarlo again. My head is spinning with another revelation. First this morning there was news of Lele and now this—"

"Get on with it, you windbag," someone yelled. Farese didn't ask for commentary.

". . . only moments ago I received a communiqué from Gruppo 9. G9 is once again holding us in their thrall. I hold here in my hand their statement. I will read it to you."

> *Today is a day that all of Italy should mark in the history books. Let there be no revisionism this time, for the proud people of Italy should know that they've been saved from a degenerate leader, a future tyrant, through the death of Lele Palmisano. We should not mourn a despot. Our great republic shall not be blighted with his existence, his memory, or his decadent ideology. And we have in our possession his partner Arnaldo Litrico—*

"What?" Gennaro yelled.

> *—we will make our demands known through the next Free Channel newscast. We've instructed the Free Channel to read out to viewers a web address where all of Italy can see that Arnaldo Litrico, our prisoner, is alive and well. Furthermore, in good faith, viewers will discover that G9 are freedom fighters and that this web page will make it clear the depravity and deception behind which the police have hidden one dark secret. The police deceived you about Via Manzoni and they've deceived you again with Commissario Isidore Farrugia. Go to the web and find out what else Signore Farrugia hides from the people.*

Gennaro's eyes went to Farrugia, who was radiating ominous calm. "And that is all they have written," Ragonese said. "My colleagues have just signaled to me that the web address spoken of is appearing on the bottom of your screens. Thank you."

Several people in the office scribbled down the address from the scrolling banner, after Ragonese put down his microphone and walked off.

The volume was muted while Silvio finished translating for Farese, as several others ran to their desks to access the web. One coworker read out the URL to another who typed in the address. The team gathered around the monitor. Perego asked the man to increase the volume on his computer's media settings.

It didn't sound good for Litrico.

It didn't look good for Farrugia.

A battered man appeared on the screen.

A crappy handheld camera was filming Litrico under even crappier lighting, inducing motion sickness before the footage steadied. Some loud sounds, then a muffled sound, a prodding voice, and some incoherent instructions were heard.

Farrugia knew this film clip would be analyzed down to the pixel. Litrico's stay in Milan and all his interactions, from sunrise to sunset, would be on a storyboard in a matter of hours. Specialists would evaluate his clothes down to the pulled thread and see whether a mote of dust or an accidental burr might betray his secret location. Financial data would be retrieved and scrubbed. The specifics as to how the Free Channel received the communiqué, this file, and the URL were already undergoing computer forensics. A timeline would be established.

Litrico held up a newspaper—standard operating procedure for proof of life. The *Corriere della Sera*. Today's date—with which they knew G9 had snagged him recently. When the camera zoomed out, Litrico was nervous, his eyes blinking rapidly, and he was pleading for instructions. He was told to shut up. His left hand kept touching his face.

A gloved hand appeared next to the man's head. A cell phone. A gloved finger pressed the button. But Farrugia knew what was coming. Damn.

Litrico, this is Farrugia. I wanted to thank you for last night. I'm not good at this sort of thing and voicemail seems impersonal so I'll try you later. You have my number if you wish to call me. I hope we can see each other again. Talk soon.

Damn, damn, damn.

23

The team was working on reports, trying their best within the confines of the office space not to get in each other's way or on each other's nerves, when the secretary appeared again.

"What can I do for you?" Gennaro asked. Alessandro, Dante, and Farrugia turned their heads to the young man standing there and smiling, cheerful and effervescent in that artificial mannerism common to both Human Resources and airline staff. Silvio was outside the door in the hallway.

"Just a reminder, gentlemen, that I need your job descriptions soon."

Farrugia walked over to the man. "You realize that we're working on a kidnapping?"

"I know, but the job descriptions are very important."

"Please leave us alone. We'll get the job descriptions to you when we're ready. Right now, we don't want another Moro Affair on our hands."

Silvio was at the door. He cleared his throat to get Farrugia's attention.

"What is it, Silvio? I thought you were photocopying."

"May I come in and talk to the team since I'm in the inner circle?"

"Time is of the essence, Silvio," Farrugia said with praying hands.

"It won't take long."

"Come in, if you must."

Silvio entered and closed the door behind him. Faces looked up at him and quick "hullos" were heard. Everyone spoke English because Silvio, although Italian, was now an official translator and insisted on English. He was a student of English back in Rome, where he saw English as a means for career advancement out of his dead-end role of "secretary." Gennaro looked over at Farrugia for an explanation. Farrugia shrugged his shoulders and moved around Dante to get to his desk.

"What can we do for you, Silvio?" Gennaro asked. Alessandro and Dante were reviewing preliminary forensics on the film from the audiovisual and computer specialists.

"I was reproducing the electronic files on the emulator and I became engaged to a discrepancy," Silvio said in his usual serious tone.

Gennaro continued reading one of the financial traces on Litrico. "That's nice, Silvio." Gennaro circled a line on the page in front of him.

"You don't understand, Mr. DiBello, that this is a perturbing vexation."

"A perturbing what? And please, call me Gennaro."

"Thank you. Thank you. It's an honor. As I said perturbing because I think she is not who she says she was."

"Who is she?" Farrugia asked.

"That's exactly what I'm saying, Commissario. Who is she?"

"Isidò," Gennaro said, "please let the man call you Isidore. It may lessen your misery."

"Fine. Silvio, you may call me Isidore, but now tell me what the hell you mean before I kick you out of this office without opening the door first."

"Thank you. Thank you. It's an honor. As I was saying . . . I'm reading the statement from the witnesses."

Alessandro asked, "Why were you reading?"

"What else am I to do, Mr. Monotti, while the emulator is emulating? Time is on my hands." Silvio tapped his wristwatch.

"It's Sandro, and don't tell me it's an honor because I already know it is. What's bothering you? And what witnesses are you talking about?"

"I was reading the statements taken from the hikers where Lele was found. God rest his soul."

"Go ahead," Gennaro said.

"They say that they were in the vicinity early that morning. They are honeymooners, right? I was thinking that they were in the area because the road is under reconstruction and they might've wanted to frisk each other, as they are newlyweds in love, but this is what I found exotic—"

"You mean *strange?*" Dante asked.

"No. I mean *exotic*. More beyond strange. They explain to the first officers that they are Americans. There you have it."

"Nobody told us they were Americans," Farrugia said. "We were just told that they were hikers staying at a local bed-and-breakfast, and honeymooners."

Gennaro ignored Farrugia. He looked at Silvio. "I'm not sure I understand you—not that I ever thought I did—but we knew they were newlyweds and they were hiking. So what? We figured that to save themselves embarrassment they'd lied about why they were on the closed-off path. But American newlyweds would want to frisk each other as much as Italians. I don't understand your point, Silvio."

Silvio waved the statement around in the air. "They're not Americans. Nobody said they were Americans because they gave their statements in Italian. And the statement mostly comes from her. I've been reading the transcript of the video recording the police made of the interview. He stayed quiet while she did all the talking. That could mean that he will have a good marriage because he lets her speak and—"

Farrugia snapped the copy of the transcript out of Silvio's hands.

No translator was ever mentioned or that they were Americans because they gave their statement in Italian. He read off a few lines of the statement. Straight-forward Italian. Simple, but to the point.

He was missing something. "What else, Silvio?"

Silvio was dramatic with his hands, like a conductor who was coaxing his orchestra to a finale. "Their Italian is too Italian. Nobody speaks that good. No American."

Alessandro said, "They could've had a good teacher. Studied for years."

"Yes, yes, but habit is always in the mind. When we learn another language we always remember our mother. You reflect your mother on the other tongue. For example, I learned English but I pronounce my

English vowels like an Italian, because I will always be an Italian no matter what. And when I see an English word I have to arrest myself before I make a pronunciatory crime. The two hardest things an American must learn in Italian is how to pronounce double consonants, and that the person is in the verb. Obvious, isn't it?"

They looked at Silvio.

"Look at her verbs."

The team read the statement and looked at Silvio like school children learning how to factor an equation. Lost.

"We put our person in the verb, whereas an American remembers their mother and uses subject pronouns." More confused looks. Silvio pointed to the pages. "Our verb endings indicate mood, number, person, tense, and, in some cases, gender, but an American would say, 'I like, he likes, she likes, it likes.'"

Dante picked up the paper, read it, and handed it back to Silvio. "So she spoke very good Italian. Like Sandro said, it's possible she had a good teacher. Are you saying that even with good instruction, somehow your first language and its grammatical logic should show up?"

"That was what I was saying. An American speaks redundantese because of their *madrelingua*. They'll communicate and be understood, but only a native would say *riuscire* for 'to be able,' 'to succeed,' while a beginner uses *io posso* for 'I can' at every turn. And look here—she uses the negative perfectly, and she doesn't sound like a grammar book. She puts in fillers—" Silvio pointed to words that were the English equivalents to *like* and *you know* in Italian. "No matter how many years you study nobody can teach when and where to use fillers in another language. Mother always wins. In her statement she says that she's twenty-eight years old. Impossible, that she is an American. She's an Italian. "

Dante asked, "But what if she grew up in a bilingual home in the United States?"

"The laws of probabilities are against her."

Alessandro asked, "Why?"

"Most Italians who went to America came from the south. Many of them were not educated or spoke standard Italian. They spoke their local dialect." Silvio pointed at the paper. "The children would speak the language of their antecessors. She doesn't speak with a trace of the old *paisà* who immigrated to the United States. She speaks standard. Not a word of dialect. Not one."

"Mother always wins, huh?" Dante said.

"She wins. Always."

Farrugia asked, "Have you told anyone about this?"

Silvio shook his head vigorously.

"Good, Silvio. Please keep this within the team. You've given us some valuable insight. Do you have any other thoughts about this case?"

"One other thing," Silvio said. "Lele met with his party members. He is from Catania and these are his northern cousins, so to speak, and I was wondering . . ."

Farrugia put his arm around Silvio. "What were you wondering, Silvio?"

"Every family fights, right? This party, the L&S, is like a mixed marriage, north and south, left and right, middle, Communist, Democrat . . . they must fight, and I wonder if when they fight, like all family do, if they fight fair, out in the open, or behind closed doors. Somebody could have called Lele a *cattocomunista* and somebody in the family has to disapprove, right? It has been an honor, but I must return to the emulation process."

The door closed. For whatever reason, the team continued speaking in English.

"I think I understood what he said about the hikers," Dante said, "but that last bit I'm a little unsure."

Farrugia, hands in his pockets like Lino, said, "He's saying we'll never know what happened at that family reunion between Lele and his northern L&S members. Sandro? I want you to start researching what we know about this honeymoon couple."

"Why me?"

"Because a woman is involved. Women motivate you. Gennaro . . . about Lele's cell?"

An office colleague knocked on their door.

Gennaro spoke for the group. "Please, don't tell me. Ragonese?"

"No, sir. It's the web site. It's been updated. You have the URL?"

"I do. Thank you."

Gennaro pulled his keyboard over and typed in the URL as the group gathered around the monitor. The previous film footage of Litrico was gone, and a blank, black space was loading. Internet traffic was bogging down the feed.

Gennaro picked up the phone and called Computer Forensics. "Where the hell did the Litrico footage go?" Pause. "What do you mean it disappeared? A loud upset voice came out over the line. "Just tell me that we have a copy along with the rest of Italy. What? Good." Another pause. "I'm waiting for the feed to come in on my screen. What? Yeah, I'm listening." Another pause. "Thanks. Bye."

"And?"

Gennaro lapsed into English since his nerves were upset. "They have a copy. The footage just disappeared like that. Forensics said the video had been uploaded from a cyber-café in Milan. Time on the computer was paid for in cash and probably with a fake ID."

"Film footage from a café?" Dante asked in English.

"They're working on it, but all they said was that it was a woman in sunglasses and a leather jacket with some weird ruffles. Possibly a wig. All strictly preliminary . . . but I'm sure we'll know more about her, from head to heels. Knowing the computer team, we'll know the color of her nails and underwear."

But something had triggered an alarm for Farrugia. "Ruffles on a leather jacket?"

Sandro interrupted, "You mean 'head to toe' not 'head to heels.'"

"You want to join Silvio at the emulator?"

Dante pointed at the screen. The feed was downloading.

The Laura Pausini song "E ritorno da te" was playing, and the pictures were streaming. It was a time-lapsed series of pictures, cued to the love-soaked lyrics. It was a serious face, a laughing face, a concerned and empathetic face.

It was Farrugia sitting opposite Litrico.

Damn no longer covered it.

24

Farrugia was deep in thought as Dante drove to Via Melchiorre Gioia.

"You're thinking IA took those pictures?"

"I don't know anything anymore, Dante."

"I thought with the IA agent in the yoga class and—"

"Please don't be offended, Dante, but shut up so I can think. I need to think."

Farrugia returned to the vitreous depths of his imagination, clouded over, it seemed to him, by cataracts of assumptions. His eyes and his mind were certainly getting dull. He had not thought to ask whether Lele had a cell phone. He had not thought to ask for any details about the hiking couple. He had assumed that Lele was in the masturbatory majority with his right hand around his . . . and he had left that voicemail.

Had someone filmed him, or did the fitness club have video surveillance that someone else had lifted and exploited? Was there more to come—perhaps of Litrico and of him wearing towels on their way to the shower area, or perhaps of Litrico and him in one of those suggestive yoga poses. Or better yet, in seemingly post-orgasmic bliss in shavasana?

Then there was the "woman in sunglasses and a leather jacket with some weird ruffles." Someone else knew that he had been there at Via Manzoni, and if they knew about his having being there, then they had to know about Bianca. Or perhaps they hadn't expected Bianca or him, and intended only to follow Charlie Brooks, but got surprised and had improvised on the scene, absorbing the loss of two of their team. He had assumed that the two men following Charlie wanted to kill him. Perhaps he had to see that as a false assumption now, too. Perhaps they simply wanted to intimidate him, retrieve the jump key. Perhaps they had planned to kidnap him and put fear down his spine, teach him a lesson. These men had to have known about his blog. Shut that down first and then kill him? No, Farrugia, had they wanted to kill him they would've done so from the onset.

As the columns of algae formed in front of his eyes and cast shadows, he tried to swim through more of his thoughts, to search for the sunlight as he once did when he swam out as a young man into the clear-blue waters from the beach of Scalea. He'd descend like one of the pearl divers, hold his breath for as long as he could, and look up at the surface from below, where he would watch the sunlight invade the water above like the Sybarites and pirates. But the light from heaven always failed to pierce the ancient waters. He was safe to observe everything because he was young and didn't believe he'd ever grow old. He'd hold his breath in until his lungs were near bursting and then he'd swim up, up, swim higher, higher, until he was almost out of air. He would then burst through the surface like Neptune enraged by some offense.

"Isidò?"

"What?"

"We're here. We're at the apartment."

Gennaro was in the kitchen with Bianca. He was cooking. She was grateful for that.

Spaghetti aglio, olio e peperoncino. The pungent garlic pervaded the air. It was a common dish for a fast meal. Each household had its version of quick cooking. Gennaro was keeping the garlic in the dish. He used *pepe rosso*, a mild red pepper, and added fresh parsley for color. It was a dish that demanded more salt than usual in the pasta water, and he was pairing the meal with a light red wine with less tannin to avoid aggravating the heat already in the dish.

No cheese for the pasta and no Paola for Alessandro. Sworn to secrecy.

They sat and Gennaro served the pasta. They'd eat while they talked to make use of their time together. For Farrugia and especially for Litrico, time was the devourer of all things.

Tempus edax rerum.

She'd seen the videos—Dante had called her with the URL almost before Ragonese had finished giving it. Now Farrugia summarized the conversation with Litrico. The legislation. Not trusting the L&S top members. Sardinia. Tanks and Lele's thoughts about drones. Bianca learned about Silvio's brilliant observation, and then about the Lodi takeover of the interviews and the request for all the Lele files. She learned that Perego had assigned the photocopying to Silvio, who was told to take his time. Nobody was certain whether, filtered through Silvio's mind, he would have understood that delay was intended, but seeing as Silvio was reading the reports as he copied them, it seemed logical that his assignment would get done when it got done.

"Where's Farese in all of this?" Bianca asked.

Gennaro twirled his pasta. "Congealed to Perego's side like a Siamese twin."

"He went over to the embassy to talk with the Brooks family," Alessandro said. "I guess to keep them updated."

Gennaro poured the wine. "I can't imagine what he is telling the family. It's been one perpetual distraction after another. First, their son is murdered and Farrugia is the hero. Then Farrugia is the anti-hero. Lele is dead. Litrico is kidnapped. Farrugia is gay. That was meant as a joke, Isidò."

Farrugia ate with concentration.

Dante said, "He's been thinking."

"I don't blame him for brooding," Gennaro said, "like he did the last time, now that that film is circulating with 'E ritorno da te' providing a prophetic insult."

Farrugia continued his silence. They all fell silent for a brief moment.

Then Farrugia spoke. "I don't see IA's motivation. They plant someone in my yoga class and then post a video of me with Litrico? It makes no sense."

"It could've been just surveillance," Alessandro said, "and somebody else took it. They might've not known Litrico would be kidnapped."

"Did you see your friend in the yoga class?" Gennaro asked.

"The IA mole wasn't there. All this time I was thinking Brooks and Lele—and now Litrico—that they were all apples and orange . . . two different cases, until I heard Litrico speak about the tanks and Sardinia and I heard Lele's position on the matter. That is too coincidental. Adastra and Lele . . . Lele and tanks . . . but what I don't get is, why kidnap Litrico?"

Alessandro put down his wine glass. "Is it possible Litrico knew something about the tanks and didn't tell you? Something that Lele also knew?"

"That would imply that Lele was silenced," Gennaro said, "but we still can't even prove that he was murdered. It certainly is suggestive: the porn magazines look staged, and Lele was propped up with his right hand. No pun intended. Litrico said he used his left when he . . . well, you know. Forgive me, Bianca."

"Gennaro, I was the one who asked if he'd gotten a blowjob."

Farrugia snapped his fingers.

Gennaro said, "Must you do that? It really annoys me."

"Alessandro?" Farrugia asked, "anything on the honeymooners?"

"Not much. They paid for the bed and breakfast with cash. The proprietor had taken down the number of their license plates. It's his policy since he has limited parking. The plates turned out to be a rental. Again, paid in cash."

Bianca asked, "If they were Americans, what about passports?"

"The proprietor had recorded the numbers. Standard procedure. I went to Farese to see if he could expedite the research, but I had to leave him a voicemail. That's how I found out he had left for the embassy."

Gennaro pushed his plate away. "Never thought going into this that there might be a connection between Brooks's murder and Lele's death. I still don't get why Litrico was kidnapped, but—"

"I don't know about the Farrugia and Litrico video, but I think I might have an idea as to why Litrico was kidnapped," Bianca said.

"Why?" Gennaro and Alessandro asked, seconds apart.

"I think Alessandro touched on the idea when he wondered whether or not Litrico knew more about the tanks than he told Farrugia. All of you assumed that Lele was against the tanks because Adastra wanted to use Sardinia as their playpen—and I think they do—but that's only a part of the reason why the tanks were so important to Lele. While Lele was against NATO and American business pillaging Vicenza and Sardinia, Litrico suggested a connection between tanks and drones. I think Lele knew more about the tanks, and Litrico's kidnappers want to know if he knows more about the tanks."

"The anti-terrorism legislation?" Alessandro asked.

Gennaro didn't sip his wine. "What could be so special about a tank?"

"Not just *a* tank. *These* tanks that Lele had been so concerned about are special. Very special."

Dante said, "Are you going to tell them?"

"Tell us about what, Bianca?" Farrugia asked.

"These tanks use special software that protects them."

"How?" Gennaro asked.

"The software somehow identifies the enemy near the tank." She explained a tank's blind spots and why two columns of an infantry patrol were necessary.

There was silence until Alessandro asked, "How does the software separate . . . I mean differentiate a friendly soldier from an enemy soldier?"

Dante hit the table. "I had said the same thing."

"Litrico said that Lele suspected drones were involved," Farrugia said. "The U.S. used them in the wars in Afghanistan and Iraq, right? Is it possible that the software in the tanks talks to drones, or the drones talk to the tank and that is how the enemy soldiers are identified?"

Bianca's eyes widened. If Lele was right then drones would mean Adastra was creating a key weapon system.

Gennaro looked at Dante. "So you knew about this, too?"

More silence until Farrugia asked Bianca, "And Adastra makes this software?"

Alessandro got up and took the wine bottle to pour more wine. "Lele was against the tanks, knew about the software, and he told Litrico in confidence. They're a couple, I get that much. The kidnappers want to know what he knows. That must mean Adastra was behind the kidnapping."

"And the Brooks murder," Gennaro added.

Alessandro continued. "They kill the kid because he uncovered the secret software? They kill him to protect intellectual property? Okay, I can see that, but I thought this kid had stolen a picture of the tank. How did you find out about the software? Was there some kind of file that you overlooked, Bianca?"

Dante was looking at her.

Farrugia also poured himself some wine. "Here is what I think: Charlie took a picture of the tank's schematic, somebody else knew, and this somebody wanted to scare him. They shut off his blog and that didn't work. They decided to get physical. Things escalated when they saw Bianca and me, the kid ran, and they killed him."

Alessandro shook his head. "Do you think Brooks was killed when they realized he and Bianca were going to meet? They had to know all along that he and Bianca were conversing."

"I know I left no trail behind," Bianca said. "Nobody knew that I was talking to him."

Farrugia put his elbows on the table. "If Bianca is right, it would support my escalation theory. They follow him. They want to scare him, rough him up perhaps, but they kill him when they see Bianca and me. They didn't want to take any chances about what he might have said to Bianca, which means she is in danger. All they saw him do was kiss her and run. We assumed that they knew nothing about a jump key."

Gennaro turned to Bianca. "Dante was asking you if you were going to tell us something. Tell us what?"

"I told you. About the software and what it can do." Sip of wine. "That kind of software is illegal to make in the U.S. and it's against the Geneva Convention."

"My dear, the Geneva Convention also says you can't kill someone," Gennaro said. "It says shoot, if you must, to disable someone. Shoot the enemy in the legs so it takes more men to take a wounded man off the field of battle. The Convention is just a symbolic excuse for human stupidity. What else do you know?"

"I told you what I know, Gennaro."

Farrugia walked over and put his chair next to hers. "I think you're asking the wrong question, Gennaro. I think the question is not 'what else do you know?' but 'how did you find out what you know?' The last time we talked we knew about Adastra but all this talk about smart software is new information, isn't it Bianca?"

She hated the pressure, hated Farrugia's warm, dark-eyed stare, and his gentle manner. She had enough trouble committing to Dante, and now she was being asked to commit to them all, to create ties that anchored her down, made her less her own person, opened her to their anger, their expectations.

And she hated most that they were right. She owed them this.

She told them about Loki.

Alessandro was numb, and Dante sat against the wall in silence and waited. Farrugia was emotionless.

Gennaro was screaming. "After all the hell that organization put you through, why would you contact one of their people? You came to Rome to get away from Rendition. You went to Boston and spent most of your time looking over your shoulder because of Rendition. I'll overlook the fact you almost got killed. I'll overlook the fact that—"

"I've already said all of this to her," Dante said.

Gennaro pointed his finger at Dante. "You're no better. You knew and didn't tell us. The two of you are like an adulterous couple." Gennaro pointed to Alessandro and Farrugia, "We're your friends."

Bianca's voice cracked. "I didn't think . . . I didn't think the cases were related."

Gennaro stood up. "Not related? I need to get some air. I'll be on the balcony. If it's high enough I might just throw myself over." Gennaro left the room.

Farrugia stared at her.

"Say something, Isidò," she said. "Dante's yelled at me, Gennaro's yelled at me. How about you, Alessandro? You have something to say?"

"Nothing."

"Farrugia?"

He held up his hands in speechless surrender.

They heard the balcony door slide open. Gennaro was back in the room.

"That was quick," Dante said.

Gennaro glared at him, then pulled up his chair next to Bianca. "I'm disappointed in you, Bianca. I wish I could convey to you how disappointed, but we've come this far, and unless anyone has a better idea I suggest we contact this Locust person."

Bianca wiped away a tear. "It's Loki. Not Locust."

"You can't be serious?" Farrugia said.

"You have a better idea, Isidò? This Loki person contacted you in Rome and got you to Boston because Bianca was in danger."

"That's different, Gennaro. I didn't know it was Loki. All I knew at the time was a file came across my desk, and I put two and two together that there was an assassin after her."

"That's my point. Self-interest or not, this Loki cared enough about Bianca to do that, and was smart enough that you didn't even know you were being used. All I'm saying is we're committed this far, so why not find out what else Loki knows? We can't be any more fucked than we are, right?" Farrugia gave Gennaro a look. "Okay, I shouldn't tempt the Fates, but we've got nothing to lose."

Absolute silence.

Gennaro added, "We all have to be in agreement about this."

"I'm in," said Dante.

Alessandro raised his hand.

Everyone looked at Farrugia.

"There is one thing I have wanted to mention," he said. "When Bianca was there that day at Via Manzoni, she was wearing a nice leather jacket—an Alessandra Colombo with a ruffle fringe. The woman who paid at the café to upload 'E ritorno da te' was wearing a very similar jacket, which means that she was there at Via Manzoni. Somebody else knows about Bianca. So, yes, I'm in."

Gennaro clapped his hands and rubbed them together. "Excellent. I want to meet this mysterious Loki."

Bianca got up. "Make coffee. Bring chairs into the workroom."

Alessandro checked his watch. "Doesn't Loki sleep?"

"Loki never sleeps."

Farrugia said, "I'm certain that Litrico isn't asleep."

25

He stood at the stove, waiting for the blue flame with the same solemnity as when he was a boy in church waiting to receive the Eucharist, oblivious to time, hearing the sacred liturgy in his ears. It was, even then, all repetition and ritual, all words, as he'd stare up at the ceiling with corrupt cherubs from past centuries looking down and judging him. And here in the kitchen now he was waiting, staring at the stark white stovetop, peeking with impatience under the steel lid, strumming his fingers on the whiteness, noticing the lattice of black grates. And instead of an eternal god in his ears, a deity in the smallest of hidden acts for the faithful child, he smelled the welcoming scent of adulthood filling the air; the pitch-black caffè was ready.

"Gennaro!" one of them yelled for him to join them in the workroom.

"Coming."

"We've got your chair."

As he entered the workroom with the tray of demitasse cups, he said, "You know there are ants in the kitchen."

And in that chair reserved for him, Gennaro sat down. Before him, instead of a neorealist film on television, there was a computer screen, Bianca at the controls, like one of those sci-fi characters. Gennaro felt his age. He missed the days when a voice on the phone sufficed.

"If she is online she'll respond," Bianca said.

"Nice avatar, although kind of kinky." Alessandro pointed at her avatar, a photograph taken of the bottom half of her face, white teeth clenching the open manacle of a pair of stainless-steel handcuffs, lips done in black lip-gloss, and her hair combed while it was wet. She was wearing a narrow leather band around her neck with small pointed studs.

"Thanks," she answered, as everyone took a demitasse from the serving tray and finished off the shot of caffeine with a fast tilting back of the head.

"She's on," Bianca announced, her fingers ready at the keyboard.

"Now, they'll play Q and A," Dante explained as if he was a museum docent and Bianca was a living display. "There are no direct questions, but rather a logical sequence to uncover the answer."

Gennaro sighed. Impatience.

Alessandro said, "We have to see if Loki has an idea why Brooks was killed. We've been stumped as to why they shut off his blog before they killed him, rather than just kill him and then end the blog and—"

"Sandro," Farrugia said, "the kid is dead. Litrico is not, at least as far as we know. Let's save a life first and then worry about Brooks."

"Sssh," Bianca said. "I'm thinking."

Then the words scrolled across the chat window. "How R U darling?"

Dante laughed. "Tell her I said 'hi.'"

"Please, Dante. This isn't cyber fantasy time."

Gennaro spoke up from behind Bianca. "Ask if she knows about Lele."

"That's good," Bianca said and typed, "Know RP?"

"Of course. Candidate from Catania."

"AL?" Bianca typed. It took a moment for Gennaro to recognize Litrico's initials.

"Y," Loki answered. Yes, apparently.

"We think RP knew AIDS & told AL & G9 wants 2 know what he knows."

Gennaro squinted at this and asked Alessandro, "What the hell does that say?"

"We think Raffaele Palmisano knew Anthropomorphic Intelligent Design Software and told Arnaldo Litrico, and Gruppo 9 wants to know what AL knows."

"Quite obvious."

"'System' not 'software,' Sandro, because the tank and the software are an integrated unit," Bianca said as she typed, "No proof on CB that he knew of sw, knew of tank and FS = 0 on sw design & intent."

Gennaro stared at the screen as Alessandro translated. "She is telling Loki that she thinks Charlie Brooks knew about the tank, but not about the software and that the software functional specification says nothing about what the software is supposed to do."

"You can decipher all that?"

"Ask her how the software is supposed to tell the difference between your soldier and theirs?" Dante asked. Alessandro seconded that thought.

Farrugia yelled, "What about AL? Look at me! I'm talking gibberish like these three . . . Arnaldo Litrico? What about Litrico? The man we're trying to save!"

Loki's avatar blinked.

Bianca wrote, "There?"

"Adsum . . ." Latin for *I'm present*. "We there?"

"We?" Bianca read. "Shit, she knows."

"What? Knows what?" Dante said.

"She knows that it's more than just you and me talking to her."

"Lie to her and just tell her you and DA, like the last time," he said.

"I can't do that, Dante. If I violate Loki's trust then it's all over."

Gennaro sighed. "Now I've seen and heard everything. She's talking to Rendition and to a person she's never met and she's worried about trust? Meanwhile, we've dealt with spies and assassins and now terrorists, and she's worried about trust through a computer screen. And to think, people stopped believing in God."

"What are you going to tell Loki?" Farrugia asked.

"The only thing I can. The truth," Bianca said and keyed, "AM, DA, GD, and IF."

Alessandro leaned over and said, "Me, Dante, you, and Farrugia."

"I think I figured that out, Sandro, but thank you."

"Sorry."

Loki typed. "Whole Scooby gang? Not good. Told U STAY AWAY from this."

Farrugia moved in now to look at the screen. "'From this?' Ask her from whom? Adastra or G9?"

Bianca typed it. Long pause.

"There?" Bianca typed.

Loki typed. "Can't say. Adastra or Gruppo."

They all read the screen and Bianca typed, "Can't say, won't say, or don't know?"

Pause.

Loki responded, "This all started with a picture, right?"

Bianca typed, "A tank. Y."

Loki answered with a smiling emoticon, and added, "Differentiation between friendly and enemy is done w/thermal analysis & biometrics. Complicated algorithms but possible & sw ≠ w/tank but integrated in electronics overhead out in the field."

"Electronics overhead," Gennaro read out loud.

Alessandro said, "Think she meant overhead electronics?"

Bianca's fingers rested on the keyboard.

"What is it?" Dante asked her.

"Electronics overhead . . . overhead electronics. This thing uses drones."

Farrugia yelled, "What about Litrico?"

Bianca translated. "Loki is saying the way that the software differentiates between a good guy and bad guy is through some kind of complicated recognition system, but the interesting thing is, Loki says it's not in the tank but with—"

"Who gives a damn?" Farrugia yelled. "The kid is dead. What about Litrico? Worry about this afterwards!"

Bianca typed, "OK . . . All started w pic, but 'Can't say'?"

Loki typed back, "I'll give U a pic & some words & U guess answer?"

"What is Loki saying now?" Farrugia asked.

"Let's play a game," Alessandro said.

Farrugia started cursing in dialect, invoking demons and devils.

An image of a sword appeared.

Bianca typed, "Sword."

The word. A German one appeared on the screen. *"Schwert."*

Alessandro said in Italian, *"Spada."* Weapon again.

Then another word, a French one, appeared on the screen. *"Glaive."*

Alessandro said in Italian, *"Brando?"* Blade?

Gennaro took hold of the keyboard. "I just type, right?"

"Yes, but Loki doesn't know much Italian," Bianca said.

Gennaro looked for the key. "If I'm right, it won't matter."

He pecked out in slow-but-determined fashion his answer, while Farrugia yelled at him, "You playing this game, too, Gennaro?"

Gennaro replied, "Isidò, now is not the time, but if I'm right you can curse heaven and hell for all of us, because if I'm correct, then we are all truly dancing with the devil."

He finished typing and hit the return key, and all of them saw the phrase that he had typed.

"Strategia della tensione . . . Gladio."

Farrugia looked at the screen and then back at Gennaro with alarm. Dante turned pale.

Bianca said, "I don't get it. Somebody explain this to me."

"Strategy of tension. And *Gladio* is plain old Italian for *sword.*"

"I know the Italian, but what the hell does it all mean and what does it have to do with a sword?" She looked to Gennaro and then to Farrugia and was about to say something when the IM pinged and they all looked at the screen.

"Correct. STAY AWAY."

26

They exited en masse from the elevator with the doors opening out to an enraged Perego screaming, "I want to know how this is possible! Do all of you understand me? I want somebody to tell me how the hell this happened." A collection of mortified faces straight out of a Bosch painting stared at Perego, and then at them behind Perego.

Perego, with his reddened face in sharp contrast to his open-collared white shirt, eyed them when he spun around in his nice Bikkembergs shoes. The team stared back, disoriented, like fathers who had just been told their newborn was indeed ugly.

The office behind Perego scattered with the welcome distraction that their arrival provided. The only sounds, aside from the closing of the doors behind them, the chime of the descending elevator, some keyboards clacking, a few phones not allowed beyond one ring so as not to enrage Perego further, was the thumping bass of Silvio's foot kicking the copier machine behind glass.

Perego rushed up to Dante. "You've got five minutes before they come up this elevator. And you," Perego added, in the direction of Farrugia, "get the hell out of here so you're not seen."

"IA?" Farrugia asked.

"I wish. At least I can tell them to screw off. Two witnesses from Via Manzoni are coming in."

"What witnesses from Manzoni?" Alessandro asked. "Statements have been taken. Is it somebody new or somebody coming in to modify his or her statement?"

Perego looked them over, suspicious; then he blinked and calmed down, knowing that he owed them a coherent explanation. "The video—and I don't mean the one of Farrugia and Litrico, but another one and—," holding up his hand to stem any interruptions, "—before you ask what video, I'll tell you. Somebody posted another one and it has gone viral. This video is the one we had of the cyber café, the one in which the female suspect, possibly one of the hikers, was purchasing time on the computer to post the Farrugia and Litrico video."

"How the hell did that get on the web?" Farrugia barked.

"Good question," Perego screamed back. "I thought I had Ballistics putting a hole in my head, but now I've got to look at my forensic teams. I've got another leak." Computers and Audio-Visual were in deep shit. "I don't even know where to start and I've got the Lodi office screaming at me and the Commissioner and . . ."

Gennaro was surprised that he actually felt pity. "Calm down, Lino. Maybe it wasn't forensics. Any chance that simpleton of humanity, Ragonese, got hold of it?"

Perego was looking around for a weapon, for a clue. "I don't know. I want Farrugia to go check out the café and get out of here. Allegretti, you talk to one of the two witnesses."

"Two? Why are they coming here?" Dante asked. "Why not the local police station?"

"They called the help line at Ragonese's Channel and—"

"So Ragonese *is* behind this?" Gennaro said. Farrugia stepped in closer to listen to the conversation.

"Not as far as we can tell. The Free Channel denies knowing a thing about this video."

"Of course they will deny it," Alessandro said, "but you know that Ragonese will have it on the news, and he'll identify this woman as a G9 member before we know a damn thing about her. And the next thing you know we'll have an Italian Patty Hearst."

Gennaro was impressed—and from their looks, Farrugia and Perego were as well. Alessandro knew who Patty Hearst was. Who would have guessed?

"What?" Alessandro said, shoulders up in shock from the look they gave him.

Silvio could be heard cursing.

"You said 'two witnesses,'" Farrugia said. "Who are they?"

"Two college kids. I don't know if they knew Brooks, attended classes with him, or what, but they said when they were at Bar Gadda they had seen a woman. They said 'an attractive woman' who was wearing 'a leather jacket like the one the woman on the video wore.' They said they hadn't thought about Manzoni until they saw that jacket in the viral clip. I read their statement. Not much. They mention a woman but no jacket. I'm guessing because of all the commotion that day. Now, Farrugia, get the hell out of here."

"Why do I have to leave?"

"Because the last thing I need is to hear from an attorney that the sight of you intimidated a witness's statement. Go, screw, and go see what you can find out at the café. Allegretti interviews one kid in his office and DiBello can take the other kid. DiBello?"

"Yes."

"Either use a free room or take whatever measures you need to so your kid doesn't see any evidence that you share a room with Farrugia. If that is too much, then hand the kid over to Monotti—but Monotti, make sure you don't use the same room as Allegretti. Witnesses must be separated from each other for their statements, got it?"

"Why me?" Alessandro asked.

"Because I said so."

Perego stalked away. Farrugia located the stairwell and moved as the elevator's light lit up with each rising floor.

Dante said to both Alessandro and Gennaro standing there, "Thank God I don't keep a picture of her on my desk."

"Alessandro," Gennaro said, "I find it very convenient that this leaked video of a woman in our friend's jacket gave these witnesses an excuse to come forward."

Alessandro nodded. "I'll bear that in mind."

Silvio's cursing was now settling into desperate half Italian and half English pleas, but his foot provided the tempo to his lover's lament.

The cyber-café was on Via Torino, and Farrugia understood immediately why the mystery woman picked this place of all places in Milan to prance into and be seen as she uploaded the Romeo-and-Romeo video. The street had all the teenage fashion stores, a Footlocker, and a McDonald's—which carried tonier connotations in Milan than it did in Boston. It was impossible not to be seen in this place. The café was not a dark dungeon for gaming teens or basement conspirators, or some cheap bodega with one computer in the back next to bags of rice. The floor plan was bright, split between a ground level with cubicles and open desks, immaculate surfaces, and an upper gallery that resembled a walkway for prison guards. A person could be observed from several angles. There was no glare from the screens, or from the overhead lights, and any camera from any corner of the room or any webcam at the computer stations had that reach-into-the-screen-with-Skype clarity. She knew what she was doing when she had walked into this place.

Farrugia was having second thoughts. He could be seen as clearly as she was, and if he walked into this place, the metaverse would start speculating about his motivations for chasing some mystery lady in leather. Fortunately the Free Channel van pulling up in front of the cyber-café made the decision for him. He turned and walked away. The new sunglasses were worth the investment.

He decided. Call Bianca and discuss Loki.

Gladio.

He was interested in what Silvio had called "the person in the verb." Farrugia wanted to know the gender, number, and the person or persons who determined when the sword was unsheathed and whom it would cut next.

27

Gennaro put on his double-breasted light coat, a timeless and classic style, crossed over his light scarf, a summer print with some beige and white with broad squares of black and red, and then he buttoned it up.

He saw Alessandro and Alessandro saw him.

"Where you going, Chief?"

"I didn't get much sleep last night. Do me a favor and interview the kid when he arrives."

"Yeah, sure, Chief. Get some sleep and don't worry about Perego."

"Sandro?"

"Yeah, Chief."

"I was impressed you knew who Patty Hearst was when we were talking to Perego. How did you . . . ?"

"A John Waters film."

"John Waters?"

"He's a quirky American filmmaker."

"Oh." Gennaro paused, adjusting his coat in the shoulders with a shrug. "Thanks for doing the interview for me."

Gennaro walked over to the elevator, seeing Silvio, who saw him in a moment of respite between foot and emulator. Gennaro waved and Silvio waved back.

He heard the elevator chimes. Two young men exited.

Gennaro entered, found the button for the bottom floor and pressed it.

Strategia della tensione was written on her notepad, sitting in silence and awaiting contemplation. The font on the screen was as elegant as cut crystal.

She read and repeated it, admiring the poetry in the phrase, thinking how it could be written on the page with near Aldine beauty or, perhaps, typed out on the screen in a Robert Slimbach font, perhaps in Arno Pro.

She poured herself more caffè. She would have preferred to sleep, could feel the heaviness in her eyelids, but she was too wired from the Loki exchange to even think about it. The computer was on and she felt the usual urge to research, to dabble, and get a better handle on the *strategy* and the *tension*.

Divide and conquer was the nearest equivalent to a stratagem in the Anglo world of politics. *Bait and switch* might be the equivalent in retail commerce. But in Italy, *strategia della tensione* was a legitimate descendent of *imperium*, with a twist: there was a new instructor teaching statecraft to seasoned actors and, as with any drama, the audience, the people, were the ones who paid.

She selected a web page, sipped, read, sipped again and read about Gladio.

The objective was precise: overtake any regularly elected Communist government in Europe. The tool was crude: coup d'état. And the strategy: discredit the Left with disinformation. And the tension? Convince the general population that left-wing terrorists would attack at any moment. And do it by actually staging a terrorist attack.

Gladio recruited its members from former Fascist or neo-Fascist groups, law enforcement agencies, and the military. Units were established in Austria and France, which explained Loki's German and French words. The symbol, the Roman sword, the *gladius*, was a Fascist symbol, and not the metonym for the gladiators seen in the Hollywood sand-and-sandal films, with the actors wearing wristband watches.

Text ringtone went off. Farrugia? It seemed that he wanted to meet with her later, but yoga first. If it helped the man to sleep . . . maybe she should try it herself. But she returned to her research.

Drive the civilian population to elect candidates other than the

Communists and fund all the other parties. Jump in bed with anybody but a Communist. She clicked another hyperlink, another rabbit hole, and she read about the CP candidate Enrico Berlinguer and the numerous permutations of the Communist Party. Italy's misfortune in post-war Europe was to be the only country with the largest concentration of Communist candidates until 1993, when the Communist Party fragmented into multiple mini-parties.

Back to the surface for some air.

Gladio had infested the Italian infrastructure throughout the sixties, seventies, and eighties, including law enforcement, the political parties, and some terrorist groups.

Always look for the money because money never lies.

Bianca knew how difficult it was to do financial forensics. Adastra might be easier, but with Litrico's kidnapping, time was critical. There was the added complication: in Italy, money flowed like a river to Rome and drained into the Vatican. Or it flowed north to Milan to drain into hundreds of banks around the Piazza Scala.

No small irony that it was Fascist Mussolini who made the Vatican a sovereign state. First post-modern state. Giordano Bruno Guerri titled it perfectly with his book *Gli Italiani sotto la Chiesa. Italians under the Church.* The Vatican Bank, the IOR, is technically a foreign bank in a foreign territory. It does not respond to the IMF, the World Bank, the U.N., or anyone else.

An Italian politician in the Years of Lead walked with a three-headed dog: Gladio, the Vatican, and the Mafia. The question was who walked whom and how taut was the leash between the politician and the guardian of hells.

Almost no Italian politician escaped Vatican dictates. God and his representatives on earth were impossible to avoid. Business with the Vatican was inevitable, and where God asked for faith, his legates asked for some form of obedience. The ring must be kissed.

Consider Berlusconi: he bowed to the Pope and kissed his ring the morning after a night with underage escorts. The exchange? He promoted very strict laws on bioethics and other sensitive issues, and in exchange the Church closed an eye (if not both) to his indiscretions. What wasn't negotiable? *Valori non negoziabili.*

Bianca considered that somewhere between Gladio and the mafia there had to be some connection. Gennaro implied as much.

A phrase on the web page in front of her captured her attention.

It was from Licio Gelli, former Fascist, Italian financier, grand master of Propaganda 2, another Masonic cabal, and a master architect of tension after the 1969 Piazza Fontana bombing. "The doors of all bank vaults open to the right."

Right as in universal truth, right as in the political right, and right as in class interest, to use a Communist phrase. But the chill she felt was when she thought, might makes right. That was the American mind-set, from the post-war through the Cold War, but the USSR was gone, shattered like a bottle of vodka.

Bianca thought of Silvio and one of their literary discussions. It was a tangent, she knew, but she couldn't help but recall that Silvio was reading an academic essay when they last talked in Rome. The essay was entitled "We are all German Romantics." Jacques Darras from the Université d'Amien was the scholar's name.

The thought she had now, with the Cold War dead: We are all Americans.

The text ring tone went off. Farrugia again?

No, it was Gennaro in need of coffee and conversation.

Noelle's voice was pleasant, even when she pronounced the Sanskrit for the pose. Everything else was pleasant Italian in her modest and broad northern vowels. She always pronounced the asanas in the Sanskrit manner, with just a hint of her Italian left in it.

Sucirandhrasana. Threading-the-needle pose. "Basic pose," she said, "for loosening the arms, shoulders, upper back, and neck." Farrugia was on his mat listening to her cueing him.

The cyber-café and the Free Channel van were not an option. Returning to the office where two university students were being interviewed, the ones who had been on Via Manzoni the day Brooks was killed—the day they had thought they might hit on Bianca, and the day they had seen him either crossing the street or rushing past them after two suspects—was not an option. The yoga studio at the fitness club was a pleasant alternative, a sanctuary with Noelle as his guardian priestess.

Farrugia was on his hands and knees. She called the pose "table," but any man, heterosexual or otherwise, would call it *alla pecorina*—doing it sheep-style. An American would say doggy-style. It still felt passive.

"Slide your right hand between your left hand and left knee," she said. "Slide that arm all the way out to the left so the right shoulder and the side of your head rest comfortably on the floor. Inhale and reach with the left hand up towards the ceiling."

Farrugia felt his muscles stretching but not without resisting. At least nothing was cracking.

"Inhale and explore that stretch," she said in a soothing tone. "Find your place, find your deepest stretch, then stay there and reach out through the fingers."

Reach out for what? Farrugia had no place here in Milan and certainly not in Calabria. It was then he realized with his ear to the ground that he was alone in the world, getting older, and that there was nobody to be there for him when the day came when he could no longer go to the store for minor items, should he be frail or fall sick. He had no children to call and no wife, not even a girlfriend. Farrugia realized all he had was the job.

"Breathe and hold for six breaths. Hold, and find your place."

Inexplicably, Farrugia found his eyes were filling with wetness. Not from fear, but with sadness that his life was nothing more in symbolic terms than masculine authority: his badge and his weapon. A modern cave man, without the club or spear.

"Now, go to child's pose. *Balasana*. Breathe and let your lower back smile as we prepare for the other side. When you're ready, go into downward dog. *Adho Mukha Svanasana*."

Ridiculous, he thought, "let your lower back smile." But he'd smile if Noelle were to talk to him. Funny. He was a grown man with his ass up in the air, and as he got older, he became more and more a shy boy, afraid of speaking to a beautiful woman whose voice he found erotic. Now, back to sheep-style pose. Farrugia was shocked. He found himself mumbling the Sanskrit, *Bidalasana* or Cat Pose.

Noelle reversed her instruction for the other side, the left arm and shoulder.

Farrugia was breathing and holding, finding his stretch, closing his eyes and thinking of *strategia della tensione* and the Years of Lead, his anti-mafia cases and the occasional shadowy types who would muscle in on his cases, giving scumbags he had collared immunity in the interests of the state, or clemency as gratitude for past patriotic services. All bullshit.

With his eyes closed, he found himself smiling because the stretching was working. He was finding the spot, finding the place, the somatic location, and his mind was directing positive energy to that knot between his shoulders. His mind had placed the thread through the needle. His mind was the eye, his thought the thread, and his body was the needle.

He felt good until he opened his eyes.

There, two mats back, was his not-so-secret IA admirer.

Gennaro took off his coat and placed his scarf on top of it. Bianca had started the coffee. He walked into the kitchen where she was at the stove, waiting for God in their coffee. He smiled with understanding. They were both tired.

"You still have that problem with ants. The cinnamon isn't working."

Bianca looked at the burnt-orange residue on the floor. They were both silent.

"Have you thought about hiring an exterminator?"

"I'd rather not resort to killing them. I'm hoping that they'll just go away. Dante said cinnamon was a natural remedy, a deterrent."

Gennaro shook his head. "If only people were as non-violent to the least of God's creatures." He smiled. "Meet you in the workroom."

"Gennaro?"

"You want to talk about the strategy of tension?"

"How'd you know?"

"You look like a man who hasn't been to confession in decades."

He smiled again. "What do the Americans say? Takes one to know one. I'll meet you in the workroom."

She offered him coffee. They sat in the other room.

"We should discuss this in English," he told her.

"But *strategia della tensione*—why not in Italian?"

"Because it's an American affair. I can see from the computer that you've been researching. Tell me what you've learned."

Gennaro sipped some coffee. It was strong and bracing like Lombard weather. Manzoni was right: *Quel cielo di Lombardia, così bello—quando è bello . . .* "The sky of Lombardy, so beautiful—when it is beautiful." This conversation, however, was about remembering a dark sky.

"Where should I start?" Bianca asked.

"Go back to the major terrorist acts. Start there."

"Which one? There's Piazza Fontana, the Peteano massacre, and the Bologna massacre."

"Fontana . . . 1969, since it's when Gladio and the strategy came into public consciousness. You've heard the expression 'false flag' in your readings on Gladio?"

"Yes. It's a tactic to have the public look in the wrong direction. A diversion."

Gennaro offered a weak lift of his lips for a smile. "Give me your analysis of Fontana from the top."

"We could just talk about Marco Giordana's movie, *Romanzo di Una Strage*."

"No. Everyone is talking about it. I'm happy it took three Donatello Awards. Stick with words on a page, like we did then."

"December 12, 1969 at 4:37 p.m. a bomb went off at a Milanese bank not far from the Duomo. Anarchists were blamed, and Giuseppe Pinelli, leader of the Anarchist Black Cross, died in police custody and—"

"Lost consciousness and fell out of a window," Gennaro said. "Supposedly. Continue."

"A police officer was charged, later murdered."

"The false flag? The police officer's name was Luigi Calabresi. The Leftists blamed Calabresi for Pinelli's death, but it has been demonstrated that Pinelli had nothing to do with Piazza Fontana."

"Right," Bianca said. "The far-left group of workers and intellectuals, the *Lotta Continua*, killed Calabresi. Supposedly. There were several false flags, since the anarchists were first blamed and then some far-right groups had their share of accusations lodged against them and—"

"The far-right group, the *Ordine Nuovo*, was neo-Fascist. Remember, Gladio recruited from the Fascists. In the end, the consensus was that the far-right was responsible for the whole thing and received funding from the Americans. And several of the principles in the Fontana massacre had ties to ranking members in the Italian government. Stefano Delle Chiaie, for example, was a friend of Licio Gelli and was implicated in another Gladioesque operation in South America. See how disinformation becomes disorientating?"

"I do, believe me." Bianca stopped to think of it all. She said, "There were plenty of acquittals and finger-pointing at multiple secret agencies: Algerians; the CIA; and, in a complete turnaround, the Israelis were saying that the Palestinians hadn't done it."

Gennaro listened with patience. His face hadn't registered one twitch of surprise, the face of an Italian who accepted his nation's history.

"You've done well, Bianca," he said. "The key to the lock is that Gladio took extreme measures to prevent a viable Communist government in Italy; and I think that you can now see why someone like Lele would've been a destabilizing element in Europe if he had become prime minister. But you missed one critical element."

"I did?"

"The psychological one, the emotional cost of living in the Years of Lead."

"Give me an example," she said.

Gennaro looked at her with cool detachment. "The evening news used to open every night with the names of those who had been killed or injured by terrorists. The question was not, '*Have* they hit today?' but rather, '*Whom* and *where* have they hit today?'"

Gennaro paused and swallowed hard. He was silent for at least a minute. He passed his left forearm across his eyes. A rogue tear.

Bianca sipped some of her coffee. "The question I have is: Is there any connection between you and Gladio?"

Gennaro put his elbows on his knees, for conversational emphasis. "The year when all these horrors about Gladio duplicity started coming out was 1990. In retrospect, Fontana was the emblem. Soon after, in 1992, the bribery scandals, Tangentopoli, came out in the papers. And then Borsellino and Falcone were assassinated. Prime Ministers Andreotti and Cossiga didn't even bother to deny their roles within Gladio. In fact, Cossiga was proud of it. There were calls for impeachment and—"

Bianca held her demitasse up. "I know all that. We were talking about you."

"I had no direct role with Gladio, but it had infiltrated law enforcement. Think about what I was doing in 1990. I was working with Falcone and Borsellino trying to clean out the sewers. The problem with any sewer is that you always find rats, and some rats you have to let go. What I'm trying to say is that almost anyone, including me, who worked the anti-mafia cases inevitably came up against Gladio whether they were aware of it or not."

Bianca's face registered slight confusion.

Gennaro stood up, stretched his legs. "During the war, the U.S. government approached mafiosi and asked for their help in fighting the Communists. Lucky Luciano practically guaranteed the U.S. government that the Bay of Naples would be Communist-free. The one thing that bound the U.S. and the mafia was capital. Both worked on private enterprise. A Communist was their natural enemy."

"But the USSR is long dead, Gennaro."

"That didn't stop mafiosi from using their get-out-of-jail-free card. I guess there is some honor in keeping promises. As for the politicians—why dismantle something that works? Why give up fifty years of control when puppets can do the bidding and guarantee your hegemony?" he asked with a nuanced turn of his head.

"So Lele pushes NATO and U.S. interests back onto their heels. I get that. But the Communist Party isn't what it was."

"It never was . . . you understand that to an Italian, a Communist doesn't have the same image as it does to an American. An Italian is likely to think of the old Communist mayor in his hometown who ran the municipality well, who implemented a free public kindergarten and built housing for the working classes. He wasn't Boris or Vlad, ready to launch nuclear missiles."

"And after 1990 . . . people knew about Gladio. What then?"

"*Segreto di Pulcinella*," he said. "A secret everybody knows but nobody talks about. It's like the gay person in your family that everybody knows is gay, but doesn't discuss because it's bad manners. I wish for a better analogy. It's like saying that the head of the state's secret agency is a civil servant with clean hands. Gladio was justified as a necessary evil, and our politicians went along with the terrorizing of the Italian people for decades."

"And now it's happening again? The G9? Are they the false-flag?"

"I believe in the Socratic method. What do you think?"

"That's more the psychoanalysis method than the Socratic. It all seems cynical. Want some more coffee?"

"Please. Cynical was Moro meeting with Kissinger and being told to 'behave or else,' and cynical was hearing that Kissinger and Licio Gelli were nominated for Nobel Prizes."

They paused for coffee.

"Okay, the G9 are the false flag for killing Brooks," Bianca said, "but I'm not seeing a connection between them and Lele. I can see Lele's anti-terrorist legislation being the true concern because—"

"Because only a Communist or a Socialist or someone on the far-left would think of corporations as terrorists. Corporations wouldn't be very happy."

Bianca smiled. "You like to interrupt me, but you haven't answered my question about you and Gladio. About them and the mafia."

"You know my earlier anti-mafia work with Falcone was focused on the mafia in Naples."

"I know. You're an expert on the Camorra."

"You're flattering me. Nonetheless, I made my reputation when I was about Sandro's age in 1980, almost thirty, so you can do your math and figure out that I was just a kid when Fontana happened. In 1980 there was a terrible earthquake in Irpinia, east of Naples. The relief funding went straight into the hands of the Camorra."

"And Gladio?"

Gennaro sat back in the chair. "As we've been discussing, Gladio concerned itself with Communism. The South, where I come from, is traditionally conservative, Calabria and Sicily in particular, but organized crime is connected to virtually anyone who counts in the south—"

"My turn to interrupt . . . because money binds and forgives enemies."

"Exactly."

"And what about Gladio and you?"

"You're persistent. I saw many of my Camorra cases evaporate because the suspects, former Fascists, were given special rights, or were acquitted outright. That was where I saw Gladio, as did Borsellino and Falcone; but Paolo and Giovanni were geniuses at getting charges to stick. They were the pioneers. I was an apprentice."

"Borsellino and Falcone," Bianca repeated. "I don't see any link between Lele and G9."

"Just wait. Have patience, Bianca. It's coming."

"Far as the public knows, Lele died of a heart attack. Not exactly terrorizing the populous."

"It's all following a script. First you drum up sympathy for the man, stir up more sympathy now that his lover has been kidnapped, but in the end it'll come out that he was jerking off and Lele will be discredited. The G9 will be blamed for the kidnapping, and that's when the Italian people will run right into the lap of the law-and-order candidates. It all goes back to the northern candidates needing the South for an upcoming election."

"Well, it did seem staged. Lele used the wrong hand?"

"My opinion? He used the wrong hand as a signal to Litrico to keep his mouth shut, because only a lover would know that kind of detail."

"What was that about the North and South?"

"The South has become perfect for a law-and-order candidate," Gennaro said. "Kill their favorite son and have them scream for justice. The candidate who shows up close to election time with a law-and-order plan and swears for Gruppo blood is the Messiah."

"And business is back to usual for Adastra?"

He stared and said nothing. His eyes focused on her face.

"What?" she said.

"You doubt it? For a person who worked for Rendition you should know better. That's why I was upset that you had contacted this Loki person. I encouraged talking to Loki to confirm my suspicions."

"Did Loki confirm your suspicions?"

"She knew about the software, didn't she? She led you to Gladio with a picture of the sword. The typical American doesn't know about Gladio. I might not know this Loki personally, but I can tell you that Rendition is nothing but a small choir of castrati compared to Gladio. You forget that Italy gave the world opera. Do you know Beppe Severgnini's comment about opera?"

"What did he say?" Bianca asked.

"'We can always tell when the fat lady is about to sing.' I should get my coat."

"Cold, huh? You really dislike the North and the weather in Milan."

He stopped before leaving the room; his face was serious. "I can give you a thousand reasons why I feel uncomfortable in Milan, the least of which is the weather. I can bitch about the people and the grayness of the architecture and how industrial the city looks to me, and I can talk about how long the North has screwed the South, from the way the history books are written to how the South was fucked over in the *Cassa del Mezzogiorno* scheme. But you can guess that the real reason of my discomfort is also ironic."

Gennaro could see in Bianca's face that *Cassa del Mezzogiorno* was alien to her.

"A funding mechanism in the fifties and sixties to industrialize the South. But what happened was that northern companies created fake subsidiaries in the South, got the subsidies, then closed down and laid off the people as soon as they had the money. So at the end of the day it was a diversion of public money to the northern businesses. The irony is that southerners migrated north after the new jobs and gave the mafia new opportunities."

"And the irony?"

Gennaro laughed. "Dante got Hell all wrong. It should've been a northern city with circles of ice, cold ice. It's ironic that Dante was a Florentine. You should get your things."

"My things?"

"Yes. You don't think with the cyber-café video the G9 doesn't know about you? That *they* don't know about you? You're not safe. Take what you need. You've had practice disappearing on short notice before. I'm getting my coat now."

Shit. He was right. She should have seen that.

She started closing down the windows on the computer, but paused to look at an image on a journalist's web page. It was a mock image done to remind the viewer of the Communist hammer and sickle, but the graphic designer, in keeping with the same red and that slight yellowish hue, offered instead of the hammer and sickle, another design: the hammer and anvil.

Bianca first thought of William Blake's tiger poem because it had lines about the hammer and anvil, but then reflexively she thought of an Italian idiom that didn't have a word-for-word equivalent in English. She closed the window and powered down the computer.

Essere tra l'incudine e il martello.

Between the anvil and the hammer. Or the near equivalent in English, between a rock and a hard place.

She had her old bag packed with a change of clothes, a book, her sunglasses and toiletries, cash, disposable cell phones, and SIM cards. All she had to do was grab it. She had her laptop and computer peripherals. Gennaro was waiting. She put down more cinnamon. Damn ants.

"Ready?" he asked.

She nodded.

"I've parked in the underground parking structure. Dante mentioned to me once about some concourse between this apartment complex and the parking structure?"

She realized Gennaro had switched to Italian. Bianca was so accustomed to the language, she didn't even notice at first. Apparently this escape was a more Italian endeavor.

She explained that the concourse was an underground path for tenants during winter and any kind of inclement weather. "We can use it without going outside."

"Good. You use the concourse. I go outside. See you soon."

They separated. Gennaro walked outside the apartment complex, stood like an idiot pretending to fumble for his keys before he continued to walk. He'd even stopped to check his beloved cell phone, look around the neighborhood some, while his ear confirmed that there were no voice-mail messages. He could have walked the subterranean connection with her, but he wanted people to see him leaving. With any luck, they would assume without thinking that Bianca had stayed behind.

Stall for time. Stall for her. Stall the idiots he was certain were watching him.

In the underground parking structure, he saw her and tapped the button on his key chain. His car yelped; the lights blinked on then off.

"I'll let Dante know. I'll drop you off. It won't be as nice as your apartment, but it'll do." He handed her a key.

"What's this?"

"Your place is a hotel about two blocks north. Wear sunglasses when you get out of the car. The key has the name of the hotel and room number. The room is registered under another name. You'll be safe." He gave her the false name.

"And you?"

"Text me later on this cell phone number. It's new. Disposable. Here, take down the number and give it back to me. I'll let you know about all of us meeting later."

She memorized the cell's number. She refrained from asking any questions about it, but he obviously had taken lessons from her.

"Should I sit in front or in the back seat?"

"Neither. Get in the trunk. You can't be seen in my car above ground."

"You're joking?" she asked as he lifted the trunk's hinge.

"There's a blanket for you. Get in."

Silence. She looked at him. This must be *trust*.

She got in.

Once inside the dark space she got herself comfortable. She was tired and tried not to think.

The hand that wielded a sword could also wield a hammer.

Whatever was on the anvil received the blow.

28

Dante was the happier of the two. Alessandro was simply relieved and it showed; he was sharpening a Nava pencil when Perego knocked and entered their office.

"You two interview those college kids?"

"We have," they answered in near unison.

"And?"

"Should I or should you tell him?" Dante asked Alessandro, whose answer was to push another Nava into the electronic chipper.

"No two witnesses ever see the same car accident," Dante said.

"Figures," Perego said, "I was afraid of that. One blessing, I guess, is that it's less for Farrugia to worry about. The curse, I suspect, is that it does nothing for him with IA and more with Ragonese."

"Ragonese? What now?" Alessandro asked.

"The Free Channel has a van out on the street in front of our building. He's on the television in less than five minutes. Go look, if it's of any interest to you," Perego said on his way out.

It was a cliché, the two young witnesses had nothing of substance to say—nothing that would help either a defense or prosecuting attorney. A woman was a woman, and unless she was found with the telltale leather jacket, their interviews amounted to nothing. And the statements were obtained in two separate rooms.

After "brown leather" for the jacket, the rest of the details diverged. She had black hair. She had dark brown with some red in it. She was *this* height. She was *that* height. She had *these* sunglasses, she had *those* sunglasses, and so on. One said tulle material and the other said lace. A man might not give a damn about frills and fringe on a jacket, but an attorney and any woman in a future jury would, because they'd know the difference between tulle fabric and lace. They'd be screwed if one of the judges were a woman.

Gennaro exited the elevator, unbuttoned his coat, and walked to his office.

"Chief is back," Alessandro said.

"I wonder whether he has heard from Farrugia."

"Farrugia is probably in a yoga class. Have you spoken to Bianca?"

"No."

"Called her?"

"Tried, but she hasn't returned my calls."

The sound of the pencil sharpener again and then Alessandro singing, "Sounds like somebody is in trouble."

Farrugia followed his yoga partner out and waited for the right moment to have a talk.

The man hadn't expected to be seized and spun around with such violence or have his spine collide with his parked car as Farrugia pressed him backwards into the metal with no place to move and with nothing except a carrier bag cushioning his flesh against his own automobile. The intense face in front of him was the complete opposite of the one that emanated spiritual bliss in the yoga class.

"Isidore Farrugia?"

"Commissario Farrugia to you. What's your rank?"

"Rank?"

"Yes, rank. What are you in IA?"

"IA?"

Farrugia leaned into the man more. This dumb-and-innocent act wasn't going to work. Farrugia had too many years and dealt with too many criminals, from the sleaze-types who dealt heroin to the polite contract killers who hid their sociopathy under nice suits, to accept this amateur hour.

"You think I'm Internal Affairs," the man said. "I'm not. I'm not IA!"

"What?"

"I'm not IA."

Farrugia relaxed his grip on the man, though still suspicious. He was thinking *Ahimsa* in Noelle's nice Sanskrit voice when he saw the crumpled yoga-mat bag. Nonviolence. Not IA.

"Who are you?"

"Claudio Ferrero. I'm a journalist with *La Stampa*. My identification is in my jacket, if you'll let me get it out for you."

"*La Stampa* is in Turin. What are you doing in Milan?"

Now released from Farrugia's grip, the man rearranged his jacket. He reached into his jacket pocket while Farrugia waited with beckoning fingers.

"*Professionista o pubblicista?*" Farrugia asked, distinguishing a professional journalist from a contributing writer.

The man handed Farrugia his driver's license and a weathered document from the *Ordine dei Giornalisti,* which was about as relevant to some in the modern world as the guild system. The man was who he said he was.

Farrugia handed him back his documents. "Journalist, eh?"

"Investigative journalist."

Farrugia's laugh was more of a sarcastic snort. "Is there any other kind?"

"Yeah, there's Giancarlo Ragonese."

The statement won Farrugia over to this Ferrero's side. But the name annihilated all the benefits of Farrugia's yoga class.

"On this overcast day I stand outside one of Milan's offices of the Guardia di Finanza. We all recognize their cars." The camera panned to a gray car with yellow pinstripes and returned to a close-up of Ragonese's face with full beard. "You ask, 'Why the Guardia di Finanza, Giancarlo?' and I'll answer you because, my fellow countrymen, you ought to know that our authorities continue to deceive us. In this building, Comissario

Isidore Farrugia and his cohorts sit behind their desks, at their looms, and weave their deceits."

"What the hell is he talking about?" said a voice in the office crowd.

"Pure rhetoric," another voice said. "Let the donkey speak."

"Yes, you have heard me. Lies. I'll explain. This morning we began at the cyber-café to learn what we could about the mystery woman in the leather jacket we had all seen on our computers. All of you have seen the brief video clip."

The Free Channel inserted a small box in the corner of the screen and replayed it.

"Just like Patty Hearst, huh?" Perego asked Alessandro with a nudge.

The box disappeared and Ragonese continued.

"We discovered from the computer experts at the café this morning that this woman came and went, uploaded the film from one of their computers, paying for computer time in cash. And all my viewers say, 'So what, Giancarlo? We know this,' but there's more. These computer experts have told me that the film of this Lady in Leather was not given to the police, but taken. You heard me right. Taken."

"What the hell is he babbling about?" someone said. "We got the film after it was uploaded. It's in public domain."

"Ssh."

"I was informed in no uncertain terms and shown forensic documents from the café's own geek squad that their system was hacked into and a copy of the footage was taken, and that all their computer systems were scoured. They've traced this electronic violation to this building, and the film is in Guardia di Finanza custody along with other digital files. The police must do their job, but how much is too much? Why are such aggressive measures taken when a young man's killers are at large?"

"How the hell did this happen?" Perego screamed.

The room went silent. Silvio came out of the copy-machine office, paper in hand. He stood to next to Gennaro.

Ragonese was looking up at the building behind him on the screen while Perego ranted, "That bearded lizard is downstairs on our doorstep and if I had a—"

"That's exactly the response he wants you to have, Lino," Gennaro said.

Silvio handed Gennaro the paper and walked away. Lele's death certificate.

Ragonese continued speaking into the camera. "In light of the Brooks tragedy, this seems like a misallocation of resources. In light of the additional loss of a promising politician, Lele Palmisano, we are trying to celebrate a man's life. The pot has been stirred."

"You stir shit," someone yelled.

"As you know, the Free Channel will run our own special on the American politician Harvey Milk, and we'll have a roundtable discussion about homosexuality in politics, from ancient Greece to modern times. While we try to celebrate Lele's life, we are besieged with discrepancies such as this nonsense at the café. What does this woman have to do with Commissario Farrugia and Litrico? Does any of this have a thing to do with Lele's death? I ask these questions because when I look at that police car behind me, I don't see gray and yellow paint. I see lead. I see cowardice."

29

Bianca never would of thought that she would be able to sleep in the trunk of a car, but she did. Not an experience she'd wished to repeat, but she understood Gennaro's rationale in relocating her here.

Here was a modest hotel not far from Cadorna, a railway station. The amphitheatre of Mediolanum was close by as well. The room amenities were nice, but the one she cared the most about was the high-speed connection to cyberspace.

She had reflected on her conversation with Gennaro, and it left her embarrassed. She was analytical, thorough, and historical, while Gennaro, good Gennaro, was patient. The conversation was not a dialogue; it was a symbolic encounter between two cultures. While she was hardly a consumerist American and he was not an overblown parody of a southern Italian, the discussion was like the waters off of Cape Point in South Africa, where the Atlantic and Indian oceans meet: mutual understanding, but different currents running through them.

Gennaro had not seen her presentation as mere chronology and facts, as she had. He was hearing the biography of a nation. She could see why someone like Giulio Andreotti could be called *Divus Iulius*, after the divine Caesar, but Gennaro, like every Italian, understood the significance of a Caesar in Rome and not abroad. When Bianca saw that journalist's page, she thought hammer absent the sickle—thought Communism. Gennaro might've looked at the same image of the anvil and the hammer and interpreted it differently: the American hammer and the Italian anvil.

Computer screen up, powered up, connected to the web.

It was time to return to Via Manzoni.

In the feed that Bianca found, the woman in the cyber-café wore a jacket similar to her own, because she had seen her meet with Charlie. She was there. So now Bianca had to find her.

Bianca hacked into the traffic surveillance archives. IA was right. Farrugia had been sitting in his car for what seemed an interminable time before he got out and crossed the street. IA was right to be suspicious. The feed was crap and of limited use, although damning for Farrugia. Trying for something more proximal to Charlie and her at Bar Gadda, she stopped and started the surveillance film like a junior editor. It didn't have to be pretty. It just had to yield a clue. If police departments across the world could snap a picture of someone running a red light with a stupid grin on their face, she would find her mystery girl in leather.

Too many parked cars. But other than Farrugia in his own, nobody appeared to be hanging out in their vehicles.

She had to be moving or standing still. Farrugia had underestimated the surveillance cameras, but it had been a traffic feed that drew IA's attention. She wondered whether Farrugia had equally underestimated the shop cameras. "Cheap shit and limited," he had said. Bianca eliminated shop cameras distant from Bar Gadda. Her girl would not have seen her or Charlie, or her leather jacket, so well. She eliminated the shops that would interest only men. She saw only two shops that might interest a woman: one for high-end lingerie and the other for shoes. Bianca prioritized shoes over lingerie. She doubted that any self-respecting anarchist would put contemplating the boudoir on a higher plane than duty; and besides, lingerie was for special occasions and something women wore for men.

Shoes first because women dress for other women. A woman in a revolutionary group was likely to be overly competitive, regardless of gender, but especially competitive with other women. Shoes were perfect. Bianca zoomed in on a figure. Pixels distorted. She zoomed out. Too many shadows and a profile, but the height looked about right; body shape looked right. She wished she had another screen but she didn't.

She closed the window and started burrowing into Guardia di

Finanza electronic files to find the witness statement on Lele's death. The firewalls were a little trickier than usual. Something was up. She took that as her cue to limit her time because someone had become suspicious about external access. She had to find what she needed before she tripped the firewall.

The files were predictable and organized by date. No password. She had the names of the female hiker and her husband.

Closing that window, she opened up another and stared at a command line. Government directory files.

Time to look for the passport.

The names were aliases. Not a surprise. Time to try mystery girl's passport number at Linate and Malpensa over the last four weeks. Nothing. Last six weeks, last eight weeks . . . nothing. Fake. This person had been in Milan for months or years. She thought, *sleeper*, possibly multiple identities, pays in cash; the rental car and B&B are a wash. She was definitely somebody's agent.

Bianca didn't bother with the male. She knew they were a team.

She paced the room as if in a prison cell. Back and forth on her feet and ideas in her head. Her next step had to be intuitive, not rational; something somebody was not likely to think or connect between Charlie and Lele.

Random thoughts careened around in her head. First thought, that journalist's riff on stock Communist imagery with the hammer and anvil online. Then it was an American covert agency using the *gladius*, the Roman sword, as their symbol for a decades-long operation. And oddly enough, the last thought, Ragonese's last oration that alluded to Cicero and damning Farrugia as Catiline in public.

Intuitive.

Cicero led her to Lucretius and another Italian journalist, Luigi Barzini because both had said the same thing: Italians were not interested in straight lines. They were interested in curves, whether it was in their architecture or thinking.

Gennaro's comment "it's an American affair" sunk in. He meant Gladio, while the rest—P2, Ambrosiano, et cetera—were interconnected and interference. The Roman sword reminded her that the *gladius* as a weapon was double-edged and tapered for stabbing. It was a brutal weapon that cut both ways. The person who picked the symbol understood psychological warfare. The intent was nonviolent violence, like using cinnamon on the ants in her kitchen. The reality was when you needed to call the exterminator. That's when it became terrorism.

Charlie was exterminated. So was Lele. Litrico was still up for grabs.

The intuitive step was to do what all cops do: follow a hunch. Gennaro was right; Lele's anti-terrorism was the true concern, but to see how the sword cut the other way she had to follow her instinct.

She returned to the keyboard and started researching not the American company, Adastra, or the latest American foreign-policy agreement with Italy, or trade, or even the American embassy. Bianca was interested in one American, U.S. Attorney Michael Farese.

A hunch.

"So you're investigating me," Farrugia asked from the man's passenger seat.

"Not exactly. You turned out to be an unexpected blip on the screen."

"A blip? That's comforting. So who are you investigating?" Farrugia tried to not feel insulted, but he understood how the unexpected cropped up in an investigation.

"It's *what* I'm investigating, not whom." Claudio took the turn onto Via Meravigli, squeezing past one of the orange-and-white trams tourists praised as quaint and natives cursed as slow. They had decided on a short ride to get to know each other.

"Thank you for the nuanced pronoun, but answer the question, please."

"Not sure I want to. Am I breaking any laws if I don't?"

"No, just wasting my time," Farrugia said. "It's clear we don't trust each other, so this is hopeless."

"How about we build trust? You tell me something about Via Manzoni and I'll tell you something. Between us and us only."

"How do I know I can trust you?"

"You don't. But I can tell you, I'm no Ragonese and *La Stampa* is known for quality journalism."

Farrugia stared out the window. He was correct about his employer. This quid-pro-quo was childish and very foolish, though. "Since you suggested it, you go first."

"Fair enough. This investigation is on my own time. I'm using vacation time to be here in Milan. I'm looking into an American company, a defense contractor."

Farrugia's eyes narrowed. The world was not that small, and this was too coincidental. He needed to tread carefully.

"Heard what I said? Your turn."

"Adastra," Farrugia said.

"Yeah, how'd you know?"

"Because you're asking about Via Manzoni, because you're asking about Charlie Brooks. You're unbelievable . . . you're just another journalist. Pull over and let me get out."

"Calm down," Claudio said. "Please. I got interested in Adastra because of Charlie Brooks, yes. He had a blog and I followed it as a lurker, but it was taken down and Charlie got scared."

"Scared? Scared of the people who shut down his blog? Scared of his employer?"

Claudio gripped the wheel. "I'm not sure they're different. I contacted Charlie offline. I wouldn't have put him on the spot online by commenting on his blog. I think it spooked him that I'd found him, and he must've figured if I could find him they could find him just as easily. I can see the logic of shutting down his blog, but not murder. And if they wanted to kill him, then why did they even bother with shutting off his blog?"

"Okay, go on. You want me to trust you? Keep talking, and take it slowly with the driving," Farrugia said.

"Nobody knows this—and I mean nobody knows this—but Charlie was onto something at Adastra. All he told me was that it was a tank."

"A tank?"

"I don't know a damn thing more about this tank, but it's odd because Adastra does helicopters and avionics. No tanks. Charlie told me this tank was special, but he wouldn't tell me what it was that was special about it. All I know is it started out innocently."

"What started out innocently?"

Claudio's voice had settled into a calm, revealing rhythm, the quid-pro-quo forgotten. A natural storyteller. "Charlie was an intern and splitting his work-day between law and economics at Adastra. It seems like he made a good impression and he had the lay of the land. I remember him telling me that because I didn't understand that expression, lay of the land."

"He had free reign," Farrugia said.

"Huh?"

"It seems that he had made a good impression. He had access and knew where to look for things."

"Yeah, he had the lay of the land, and that was when Charlie said he'd discovered this tank, except he didn't know it was a secret project. He just thought it was an idea. He was excited about the tank because of his father and—"

"His father?"

Claudio blended neatly into traffic around the circle at Largo Cairoli, looking over at Farrugia. "His father was in the American tank division. I think when Charlie had seen this tank he wanted to impress his father. He started researching it and found out . . . whatever it was that got him killed."

"Impress his father? When was the last time you two had communicated?"

"A few days before he was killed."

"What did he have to say?"

"Not much. He said he was scared, but he was planning to meet someone who he said could help him expose Adastra."

"And what made Charlie think he could trust this person?" Farrugia was curious. He had his own trust issues with Bianca, after all.

"I don't know. He did tell me he thought it was a woman though. I became interested in you because you were the last person to see Charlie alive, but then when I saw the woman on the video clip in the café, I was wondering whether she was the same woman he was supposed to meet. I have no idea."

The car slowed down and Claudio pulled into a parking space. They had done a long trip in a circle, more or less. The gym was down the street.

"Or you're wondering whether she was the one who'd set him up to be killed?"

"If she's that person," Claudio said.

"What makes you say that?"

"She certainly isn't doing you any favors."

Farrugia gave him a weird look, as if he had a stitch in his side. It was either that knot between his shoulders or the spear into his side.

They exchanged cards.

Claudio was happy to have Farrugia's number and Farrugia was happy not to have divulged too much. He kept thinking of *building trust* as *threading the needle*.

30

Farrugia returned to the office. Gennaro didn't say a word.

"I've been calling Bianca and no answer. Have you had any luck?" Farrugia asked.

"She's busy."

"Should I be worried, Gennaro?"

Gennaro smiled. "Yes. I texted her, and we'll meet up soon."

"I heard about Ragonese on the way into the building."

"Did yoga help?"

Farrugia was surprised by the interest. "Yes, it was a good class. Thank you for asking. Has she said anything?"

Gennaro didn't look up from the paper on his desk.

"Gennaro?"

He looked up.

"What did she say?"

"She's working on a project, and she's narrowing her focus to a sharp point."

"Really? That's what she said?"

"In so many words. Would you like me to quote her? She said to me in Italian, '*Ho messo troppa carne al fuoco.*'" Farrugia translated it into English in his head: I put too much meat on the fire. He said, "Should I be worrying now or later?"

Alessandro had his feet up on the desk, twirling a pencil. He saw Dante entering with a stack of file folders.

The door closed. "What's on your mind, Sandro?"

"I was thinking about the other night. I was too young during the

Years of Lead to have understood what was going on, but I remember as a kid my relatives discussing it. So when I saw Gennaro type out that phrase and saw the graphic on the screen I got nervous because I remembered the fear and sadness on my parents' faces."

"It was a difficult and very confusing period of time," Dante said, sorting out the stack. "It's hard to keep track of, but everything turned out to be connected, although it took time to sort it all out. It was very messy."

"How'd you think Gennaro knew about you-know-who?"

"He used to work mafia cases."

Alessandro nodded.

"Think of it as a good story," Dante said. "You need suspense and tension. How do you create that? You create misdirection by having a set of logic that leads people to the wrong conclusion, when, in fact, the same set of logic leads to the truth. It's all in the perception and interpretation."

Sandro mused with his pencil. "Sounds like what the Americans call 'government-conspiracy theory.'"

Dante thought about it for a second. "Yeah, just like we are having this entire conversation without saying Gladio or *strategia della tensione*. We might as well be talking about the Devil. As for government-conspiracy theory—I guess it is, but there's a difference, Sandro. In America people think, 'Oh my, they could never have done something like that!' whereas here, we know they can and they did."

Sandro put his feet down. "Uh-oh."

"What is it?"

"It's Perego at the elevator. I think IA just walked in."

Gennaro ignored the voice from the elevator and headed into the copier room, remembering, "Silvio's English Spoken Here."

"You gave me this," he said, holding up Lele's death certificate, "but do you also have the death certificates for the two Manzoni assassins?

I'm looking to see whether there are any supplemental notes."

"I do have them and there are supplementals indeed," Silvio said, sorting through the stack. "Here they are."

"You've made copies?" Gennaro asked and Silvio nodded. "And Lele's certificate—it's been copied also?"

"Yes. I'm retaining the reproduced reproductions."

"Thanks, Silvio."

As Gennaro returned in the direction from which he had come, he heard Perego. "Gennaro, please come here." He walked towards the inevitable introduction with a fake smile on his face while Perego did the formulaic, "I'd like you to meet Ettore Brambilla from the Ministry of Internal Affairs," and Gennaro heard himself introduced to Farrugia's presumed nemesis.

"Nice to meet you," he said. "It's a pleasure."

"Your reputation precedes you, DiBello. You've done remarkable work in the past."

This was code for "you're a dinosaur headed for the tar pit, and Godspeed."

"I've read your reports to the late Magistrate Falcone on the Totaro case," Brambilla said.

Gennaro smiled and remained quiet. The Totaro Case was the one that had gotten his wife murdered and him transferred to Rome. Fake smile, show of teeth, and keeping a clamp on his unholy thoughts.

Cue for Perego who said, "DiBello shares his office with Commissario Farrugia while he is with us in Milan."

Nods and more official smiles. Only the Gestapo click of the heels was missing.

Gennaro excused himself. He had work to do.

Gennaro entered the office and closed the door and said, "IA" to Farrugia.

"He can come in if he wants, but I don't have to talk to him. No union rep. What have you got there?"

"Files on the two Gévelot assassins. I have an idea, Farrugia."

"Wonderful. You've made them French."

"For all we know, they were. Go out into the hallway and close the door behind you, Isidò. I need to make a call, and I don't want Perego and your friend to overhear my conversation. They're less likely to talk to you out in the hallway, and if they want a conference you can invoke your right to have a union rep present."

Farrugia collected his jacket and made a face. "Kicked out of the office I don't have."

Gennaro took out one of his cell phones and dialed the number after Farrugia closed the door. "Doctor Foà? DiBello here. Yes, we've talked before. Same person. Do you have a minute?"

The genial Foà remained a man of culture and good manners.

"I've got a question for you, Doctor. Yes, I know the number appears different on your phone. I'm not in the office and I'm using my cell. You can say inspiration inspired me." Gennaro realized Silvio was creeping into his Italian. "I was wondering about these two Manzoni killers. I see that you did the autopsies. The report is in front of me."

The good doctor recalled doing the autopsy and that he had never seen such a thing: murder-suicide between contract-killers.

"I thought it was procedure to fingerprint and run the prints through the databases. I didn't see any, or references to matches."

Gennaro listened to Foà explain that the two men had no matches or unique identifiers.

"Just wanted to confirm what I'd read. Thank you, Doctor."

Gennaro looked up and then around. The door was closed. He opened the desk drawer and rummaged for that relic of yesteryear: whiteout.

It did the trick on the *allegati*, one of the supplemental pages to the file on one of the Manzoni killers. Gennaro had the good fortune that this page was a blend of typing and handwritten notes. Now it was time to hunt for that other relic: a typewriter. He folded up the piece of paper and tucked it into his jacket.

Farrugia returned, all smiles.

Gennaro asked, "How did it go?"

"Very pleasant. We said hellos, but that was it. He was here to see Perego."

Gennaro said, "Excellent," and was out the door on his quest to create one word on his piece of paper.

Then he was off to Silvio's emporium with the new word.

Silvio would reproduce the paper production and include its renovated renovation.

31

Another one?

Gennaro had just texted her about a time and a place for the next meeting. She knew Gennaro eschewed modern technology, but maybe it was true that converts sang the loudest in the choir, and Gennaro had become one of the excellent ones with his cell phone.

Bianca looked down at the little screen of gray with the Mecha font. "F wants 2 talk 2 U. He'll call soon."

So Gennaro had learned textspeak. *Mirabile dictu.*

The phone vibrated in her hand. Not now. "Farrugia?"

"I need a favor."

"Now's not the time, Isidò. I'm in the middle of research."

"I need you to check out a name for me. Claudio Ferrero. He's a journalist with *La Stampa* from—"

"Why can't you do that? You're a cop. I think you guys have computers now."

"I wish it were that easy, but everything in and out of this building is under surveillance. You name it and it's covered and tracked."

"Including this phone call, you idiot, if you just called me on your phone."

"I'm using Gennaro's cell phone. One of them, that is—you know he's carrying two cells now. You know how much he loves cell phones."

"I don't have time for this. I'll be tossing this cell after this conversation. Why are you so concerned with this journalist?"

"I need to know if I can trust him."

"You know what, Isidò? I have things to do. I'll see you later. As for trusting—I think you have to figure out on your own whom you can trust. I did and it involved sleeping in the trunk of a car. Bye."

Farrugia stared at the phone.

"What's the matter?" Gennaro asked from his desk.

"She said something about trust and the trunk of a car before she hung up on me."

"Oh." Gennaro paused. "I guess she's upset about that."

Michael Farese.

She was reviewing the biographical details. Mom and Dad were second-generation Italians whose families had come from Conza della Campania. Gennaro would approve: not too far north—about forty kilometers north of Naples. Grandfather had changed the name Ferrese to Farese.

Education looked standard for an old-school Italian-American. His parents must have had certain ideas for their Michael. Parochial school was Catholic. High school was also Catholic, but college was a respectable state school. She guessed that the working-class kid's flair for journalism hadn't gotten him those scholarships from the Vatican to offset the cost for an undergraduate degree in journalism with a minor concentration in international relations.

Law school came after a stint working the docks with Dad. Uncle was killed; collateral damage in a mafia contract killing. This must be the spur to his interest in organized crime.

Farese, while slumming in the DA's Office, built up a solid conviction rate and a low, very low, rate of overturns in the Court of Appeals. He moved up in the rank-and-file lawyers in the state's attorney general's office, where he started making a name for himself in the organized-crime unit.

This is where the journalism paid off. The man could write. She could vouch for his charisma. Farese's legal briefs and journal articles had earned him a reputation for eloquence and as a passionate hard-liner against mafiosi and corporate white-collar criminals. Farese was a

Falcone fan, and his convictions showcased the late magistrate's influence. He knew how to compel made men into betraying the Omertà, the mafia code of silence. Farese was the priest to the *pentiti*.

At the U.S. Department of Justice, he continued onward and upward. The Boston fiasco was nothing more than a lump in the rug, which included one dead witness and a substantial body count.

His background in international relations came into play when he arrived in Rome for the Roma Underground scandal. That was when they had first met. Farese had started publishing articles on the international structure of organized crime, the multinational tentacles of numerous mafias: Calabrian, Neapolitan, Sicilian, and the Russians. Was Farese another ambitious Rudy Giuliani, who had also worked with Falcone in the late eighties?

Seemed logical, but what didn't seem logical was her seeing that Farese had traveled to the Netherlands and Sweden. Russian mafia connection?

Bianca took a break. The hotel's Keurig coffee machine made her think of the old-fashioned juicers, because she had to pull down a handle to make her coffee. Decent coffee but it was not the same as her moka on the stovetop.

Sweden in 1986 and the Netherlands in 2002.

While sipping her coffee she opened up the news portal in Torino and started reading articles by Farrugia's new friend, Claudio Ferrero. Not bad. Bilingual journalist, so she selected one of his pieces in English. Very in-depth analysis, a cultured man, although she saw a few infelicities in his English that even a hard-line Italian editor would miss. Interesting use of prepositions: correct to the Italian mind, but offbeat in English usage, although the sense of the passage was never compromised. She saw that either Claudio or the editor disliked using dashes. She took another sip of coffee and saw something interesting.

Claudio had written an article on the recent history of reformist politics. She read it.

Olof Palme, Swedish politician, and Pim Fortuyn, a Dutch politician.

Both were Social Democrats. Both had run on reformist platforms: Palme was a Socialist seeking better controls on businesses in Sweden while Fortuyn, dismissed as the Dutch Jörg Haider for his controversial views on immigration, multiculturalism, and Islam, was a former Communist and Social Democrat with liberal views on same-sex marriage and euthanasia. Lele was a political hybrid of these two men.

Both Palme and Fortuyn had been assassinated.

1986 and 2002.

Gennaro walked into the office of Alessandro and Dante.

"Hi, Boss."

"Hi, Chief."

"Morning to you both. Are both of you free or dinner tonight? I was thinking of calling a team meeting. Farrugia said he's bringing a friend."

Dante asked, "Is this friend of his somebody we can trust?"

"Farrugia says so."

"Can I bring Paola?" Alessandro asked.

"Isn't it short notice?"

"But I'm meeting her for lunch. I can ask. She's driving down from Bergamo."

"Lunch and then dinner? You'll look needy to the woman, Sandro. You should know better." Gennaro tapped Alessandro's shoulder. "But while I'm here I wanted to ask your opinion about these documents. Tell me what you think of them when you get a chance and we can discuss them tonight. This one here is Lele's death certificate and the other one is a page from the supplemental notes on one of the assassins at Via Manzoni. Look them over and tell me what you think."

Gennaro handed him the papers.

"What am I looking for, Chief?" Alessandro asked.

"I don't know, and that's why I'm giving it to you. You know, fresh eyes see truths in plain sight."

"Okay, Chief, I'll try. And Paola? Do I really seem needy?"

"Maybe just a little. Besides, I'm not sure whether Bianca wants another woman there tonight."

Alessandro put the papers in his jacket. "What's that supposed to mean? I never had any reason to believe Bianca disliked Paola."

"I didn't say that she did, but you know women better than I do, Sandro. You don't put two of them together without having the inevitable complications. Gotta go; I'll text the two of you about the time and place." Gennaro closed the door behind him.

Alessandro looked over at Dante. "Text us? He sounds like a teenager now. Was that Silvio or Gennaro DiBello speaking Italian? And what was that he was saying about my girlfriend and Bianca?"

"I think he was saying that there'll be no Paola for you tonight."

Bianca was frustrated. The instinct with Farese had to be right; there had to be something to her comparison of Lele with those other two politicians. Two violent deaths and one from natural causes. Bianca closed her eyes and welcomed associative logic, random thoughts, and caffeinated inspiration.

She repeated *strategia della tensione* and meditated on *strategia*. There was Don Matteo's *La strategia dello scorpione*, which made her think of Nero Wolfe in a cassock. And there was Bertolucci's *Strategia del ragno*, which made her think of a Borges story, Calvino's first novel, and then Dante's explanation of *tensione* to her before they fell asleep. He had distilled it as a metaphor for narrative strategy.

Misdirection . . . perception and interpretation.

Bianca knew she didn't have time to analyze the Palme and Fortuyn assassinations for false flags, but she knew Farese's appearance was not mere formality.

She could look at any money trail Farese might have left behind, but her preliminary search had uncovered no such trail. All DoJ and some State Department funding. But money always talked, and Farese's money was saying "U.S. government." But there was no obvious connection between him and Adastra.

Money talked but . . . perception and interpretation were the trickier parts. Bianca had learned that in the Robert Strand case. She had also learned at Rendition that money warns. An educated Italian like Claudio Ferrero would say money comes from the Latin *monere*, to warn. The word came from the honking of the geese at the Temple of Juno on the *Campidoglio*, the Capitoline Hill. The geese would warn the Romans of invaders.

And Dante, a fan of Eco's semiotics, would add that the world is full of warnings, if we were initiated into reading the mysteries of the signs around us. He had shown her this to be the case with medieval architecture in Rome. No saint is ever portrayed without a monster.

Moneo, monere, monui, monitus.

She had looked: the money trail that funded G9—nothing. Her quick perusal of Lele's finances showed the same: nothing. What monies she did find in both cases had come from so many sources, blatant or hidden and mutating, that it would put her enemy Lorenzo Bevilacqua, architect of the Roma Underground scandal, to shame; and she didn't have the time to look into it any further.

There was not enough time to research finances while Litrico was captive somewhere. No word about him or from him was disconcerting. No demands yet. Nothing with Litrico resembled the kidnapped Aldo Moro, who would write cryptic letters to the outside world before his final sleep in the trunk of a car. Not one word from Litrico.

She had trusted Gennaro when she got into the trunk. Now she had to take another non-intuitive leap, and trust again.

Time to contact Loki.

32

Bianca tapped the desk as she watched her avatar, waiting for Loki. Sandro had said it was sexy. She had designed her avatar years ago. Maybe it was time for a new incarnation.

Loki's avatar began as numbers for a corporate tax form 10ki, which looked approximately like "Loki" on the screen. Even Loki had changed in the time they'd known each other. The Loki avatar had blinked, danced a stripper's routine around the red *R* of Rendition, and, more recently, changed genders.

Bianca's avatar had become as passé as a chef plating a dish with towers of food and sprigs of parsley. She was like an Ovidian character resisting metamorphosis.

Loki came online.

"R U there?" Bianca typed.

"Will not discuss AA," and by that Loki meant Adastra.

"No need 2 bring out ur tanks or update ur sw."

Loki's avatar was morphing genders. And nationalities. Nordic.

Loki typed: "Shoot."

"Time = crucial. Farese."

"Y." Why?

"Connection?"

"Told U, no AA discussion." The avatar made a nasty Nordic face.

"Not asking that. Connection 2 RP?"

Loki's avatar blinked. Bianca said to the screen, "I can't believe I'm looking at an avatar's body language for clues."

"Want 2 play a game?"

Bianca sighed and repeated, "Time = critical." Seconds later Loki's avatar took up the entire screen and the eyes blinked at her. This time

Loki was a woman, complete with blinking green eyes and undeniable cleavage. The avatar minimized and Bianca saw in the windowpane that Loki was typing.

"Does the archangel go into battle against the dragon singing a song?"

Bianca stared at the line. She typed, "Michael = archangel?" Bianca saw more typing at the bottom of the windowpane. The reply came out like a series of stock quotes.

"There once was a team on a boat that sailed the northern sea. They always rowed together. Though they fight & fight, it's all 4 show because of the gold. The world is their ocean. The Frenchman takes Africa. The Brit drinks tea, his cousin drinks coffee; but both do the laundry together. Italians & Arabs around the pond fight in public but love each other behind closed doors. The ship is a boat with many flags but there is no pirate. The ship = a ship bec there is water."

Bianca typed, "WTF?"

Was this some exaggerated limerick about a rowing club of leprechauns in search of a pot of gold at the end of the rainbow?

Loki's avatar's eyes blinked, changing the color of its eyes.

Bianca repeated, "WTF?"

Loki responded, "Sorry, darling. Truth must B earned. Start w ur angel. +1."

Bianca read +1 to mean that she was correct: Michael Farese was an archangel. Each of the archangels had a responsibility. Gabriel blew the trumpet to signal the Apocalypse. Michael led the angelic cavalry against the serpent, Satan.

She typed, "Archangel = warrior." This was a reasonable start since Michael had led an army of lawyers against the mafia. No idea about a song.

"Guess again." Loki's avatar was rolling dice.

Fuck.

Loki was typing again. "What's the sign of where you live?"

"Milan? Lombard red-on-white Crusaders' Cross."

"Too modern."

"Modern? 12th century ≠ modern."

"Testy. Think Celtic & don't cheat & use the web." Loki's avatar was tsking her.

Bitch.

Bianca swore that Milan's symbol was the Lombard Cross because the Lombard League had used it on their shields against the Emperor Barbarossa.

Loki typed, "Something old, something new, something borrowed, something . . ."

Then it came to her. She and Dante had seen it in Varese. Loki was alluding to the blue dragon. Celts had founded Milan, and their symbol was a dragon with a child in its mouth. It was easy to mistake it for a serpent because it had no legs, but Dante had told her it had ears. Serpents don't have ears. The half-devoured child was some Celtic birth-and-rebirth myth.

Bianca typed, "Milan = dragon. *Biscione.*"

She included the Italian word for a type of snake. The cross and snake was the symbol seen on Alfa Romeo cars. The Padanians call it *El dragh bloeu*, or The Blue Dragon, an ancient Lombard symbol.

"Pass on that *biscotti*." Emoticon.

"Ha ha & singing song?"

"Sad dragon w RP dead. Isn't a song just another way 2 cry?"

Bianca refrained from typing another WTF, so she read the line again . . . and again. The only noise she knew regarding angels was a melodic harp and Gabriel's trumpet, but that was at the end times, and Loki had just implied that Milan was not Satan.

Bianca typed, "Angels sing 2 God."

"False concept. They don't sing. We have 1 angel. The rest? War cry."

"Angels have a war cry?"

"They cry = Hebrew. Mikha'el."

So Farese was leading a battle charge of some kind in Milan, city of the dragon.

Bianca typed, "Is MF the antichrist? Is Milan the antichrist? Is the antichrist in Milan?"

"Think in symbols."

Bianca thought and then typed out: "Milan = blue dragon. Not mafia case. 0 Antichrist?"

Loki typed back: "What is the symbol for Michael?"

Bianca had wished that Dante had initiated her into the reading of signs and symbols, or that she had had more catechism classes. Or read more Eco. Long pause. She had no idea.

"IDK" for I don't know.

"Balance scales 2 weigh human souls."

"Y Milan? Is it because RP was here?"

"Can't answer. Milan = start of all fads from the thigh 2 heel."

Bianca smiled. "Milan = fashion center/intellectual center 4 the Italian leg. Don't 4get heel 2 toe, or the leg will kick U in the a$$."

Loki's now-male avatar magnified and winked an eye at her. Guy humor.

Bianca typed, "What army?"

"Think of boat before U think tank."

"What boat?"

Pause. A string of Loki statements filled up Bianca's screen.

"Boat & northern sea. World = ocean.

"All show. Row 4 gold.

"French & Africa. Brits & cousins do dirty laundry.

"Italians & Arabs around the pond. Fight & love.

"Flags. 1 ship. 0 pirates."

The windowpane indicated that Loki was still typing.

"There are no pirates but there is a balance scale."

Pause.

"Mikha'el = Hebrew = Who is like God?"

Last pause.

"Who owns the scales?"

Loki went offline.

Bianca hadn't had time to type it again, but she still thought it. *What the fuck?*

33

Gennaro had picked the restaurant, a small but reputable trattoria, known for its quiet environment, business clientele, and moderate prices, and because he had wanted to try the *Cima di Rape*, broccoli rabe with hot pepper and garlic, their *Tagliata Trevisana*, a fillet steak, done rare, sliced and served on a hot plate with grilled Trevisana leaves; and he picked it because the Via Generale Gustavo Fara was not a dangerous distance for Bianca.

Bianca arrived first. A hug and two kisses later she asked, in Italian, which they continued to speak, "Where are Alessandro and Dante? They usually are inseparable."

"I don't know. I need a drink and so do you." Gennaro raised his hand for the waiter.

"It's not like you to drink, Gennaro."

"I'm retiring soon and I ought to break some habits. How are the accommodations?"

"Pleasant. I locked up my computer in storage at the railroad station."

They settled on an aperitivo, a *negroni*, with a plate of olives. A Florentine drink in origin, Campari with sweet vermouth, meant to stimulate the appetite. It was a drink with a kick to it, though neither of them would admit to the warming buzz in their heads. They'd smile more at each other nonetheless. The group had not had a meal out in a long time.

"Here comes Farrugia and his friend. I wonder whether they met in yoga. He said we can trust him," Gennaro said before standing up to accept Claudio Ferrero. Bianca said *La Stampa* in a soft voice as she stood up with him to participate in the introductions.

"I've read some of your articles in English, Mr. Ferrero. Incisive journalism."

"Investigative, Ms. Nerini. Since you read me in English and I rarely have the occasion to practice my spoken English, I'd prefer that we talk in that language, if nobody minds?"

"Sure," she said. "English it is."

"Is that okay with you, Mr. DiBello, and how about you, Isidò?"

Farrugia agreed, and as he took his seat next to his old friend, Gennaro said, "Isidò?"

To which Farrugia answered, "We're friends."

"Fast friends, I see."

Bianca said to Claudio, "We're waiting on two others."

"Three," Gennaro said. "Paola, Alessandro's girlfriend, is also joining us."

"Why is Paola coming?" Bianca asked.

Claudio folded his napkin and took an olive. "You disapprove of her?"

Gennaro watched Bianca as she answered. "I have my concerns. Paola is a ballistics expert from Bergamo."

Claudio found it amusing. "That would make a good ditty, 'The Ballistics Expert from Bergamo.'"

Gennaro folded his hands over. "We already have the journalist who has given us 'The Candidate from Catania.'" Gennaro smiled. Claudio didn't.

"Oh, I see. Have she and your friend Alessandro been dating since the time of the Manzoni incident? She must be the one who analyzed the bullets. That fact must not sit well with Isidore." They said nothing as the man kept talking. "I think I see why Ms. Nerini disapproves. Perhaps, she's protective of Alessandro. Is Paola trustworthy?"

Gennaro and Bianca contemplated each other. Just then Dante appeared.

"I'm sorry I'm late. Something has come up."

Farrugia made the introductions to Claudio.

"Where's Sandro?" Gennaro asked, to which Dante mumbled

something about Sandro and Paolo running late. The waiter was told to wait a few more minutes but not before serving a round of aperitivi.

Gennaro asked Claudio, "You're investigating the Manzoni case?"

Claudio said that he was and explained everything he had told Farrugia about Brooks. Gennaro glanced over on occasion at Bianca. Enough so that Claudio noticed Bianca was the matriarch of the table.

"What is it?" he asked.

Gennaro blinked at Bianca. "It's your decision, Bianca."

Claudio asked again, "What does that mean, 'Your decision'?"

"It means I know something and Gennaro is letting me decide whether I should trust you or not." She explained to Claudio about Adastra, the tank, and the anti-personnel software probably used by drones in communication with tanks.

"Wow," Claudio said. "I'd just thought the kid wanted to brag to his father about a cool tank his company was working on."

"He might've. He might've not known about the software until later. I suspect that was when he became more active with his blog."

Dante asked, "The thing that has bothered all of us is his blog. It was shut down, and then he was killed. Shouldn't it have been the reverse?"

"Unless it was a warning and he didn't listen," Claudio said.

"I thought that too," Farrugia said, "but I think it became a matter of escalation—that the persuasion had veered off course. Shut the blog off. Kid persists. Go scare the kid. Intimidate him, you know. He arranges his meeting with Bianca. They see me. Things got out of hand. Boom! The kid is dead. The assassin murder-suicide in the alley is something I can't quite explain, other than they didn't want to be taken in."

"Did they see Bianca?" Claudio asked.

Bianca nodded. "I was wearing a unique leather jacket." Her description of the Alessandra Colombo jacket brought the conversation to a momentary stop.

Claudio said, "We can assume then that others were there and that they saw her, since we have the cyber café film."

Dante looked down at his watch. "Where's Alessandro? I'm getting hungry." The consensus was growing but their stomachs decided: five more minutes.

"It's possible that it did escalate, as Farrugia suggested," Claudio said. "That supports the notion that the killers might have tried as long as they could to avoid killing Brooks because of his father. But that assumes that his father was involved."

Bianca said, "Because he's a veteran of the First Cavalry Division? That implies respect."

"That, too, but I was thinking he might be a consultant to Adastra. Can't prove it, but a man of his experience would be a perfect consultant. He drove tanks for twenty-plus years for the U.S. Army."

Shocked faces all around. How had they missed this?

Claudio repeated, "I can't prove it yet. It would take research and access to files I don't have now that Charlie is dead."

Farrugia and Gennaro turned quickly to Bianca.

"I didn't have time to look," she said. "Too many contractors and subcontractors, and then Lele got killed and Litrico was kidnapped. Damn! First, you guys didn't think to check Lele's cell phone, and Ballistics leaks the damn Gévelots. I won't even mention Lodi."

Claudio touched Bianca's hand. "Hold on. Lele was killed?"

Gennaro tilted back the last of his *negroni*. "Viagra overdose. Suspicious. Lele had a mild heart condition. Viagra would've been contraindicated. Farrugia is convinced that it was all staged, and the rest of us aren't disagreeing." He explained the left versus right hand. "Farrugia and I have concluded that the hikers at the scene had to have had some kind of involvement, either with staging the crime scene or killing him. Personally, I think the woman hiker and the one seen in the cyber café are one and the same. She saw Bianca at Bar Gadda and now she's trying to draw Bianca out."

"Shit," Claudio said.

"Shit is right," Bianca said. "I can't believe I screwed up and didn't follow through. Brooks as a consultant—why didn't I think of that?"

Farrugia cleared his throat. "What if Charlie had started out wanting to brag about the tank to his father because his father was, as you said, a career man, but Charlie didn't know that his father was a consultant. It's very likely that his father was paid out of some slush fund, Bianca, so don't blame yourself and—"

"Where are you going with this?" Gennaro asked.

"I think I know," Claudio said.

The group waited for Claudio's explanation.

"Charlie Jr. finds out Charlie Sr. is involved. The kid was on both the economics analysis team and the ethics committee, so it becomes a matter of principle to Charlie—maybe more so than family loyalty. Charlie Sr. is thinking the Army comes first. Son confronts father somehow. They argue. Charlie Jr. decides the way to deal with this is to start a blog, and then he finds about the software and—"

"Except Dad knew about the software and that Charlie would eventually find it," Bianca said. "Somebody tells Dad, 'Shut your kid up. This is a courtesy warning.' Shutting the blog down was step one. Next step was—"

"Doesn't matter," Farrugia said and they turned to him. "It all adds up that Charlie Sr. had his own son killed, or knew that his son would get killed."

Gennaro looked glum, "That's fucked. Pardon my English."

"Speaking of fucked," Bianca said. "Here comes Alessandro."

Another round of introductions and Alessandro introduced Paola. Alessandro was looking rather knackered and Paola was glowing. Bianca was not amused.

"I'm really sorry we were late. Traffic was difficult."

Farrugia asked, "In Milan or from Bergamo?"

Gennaro smiled.

Food became the great intermediary. Bianca and Farrugia started with a *saluni* of vegetables and chose seafood pasta for their main dish. They both liked the clams and mussels. Claudio ordered a hearty *Cinghiale alla Maremma*, wild boar with polenta. Dante decided on the traditional Milanese breaded veal, *cotoletta alla Milanese*. Alessandro and Paola each ordered another traditional Milanese dish, rice with saffron, *risotto alla Milanese*.

There was Chianti. Plenty of it before the desserts: *tiramisu* and *torta della Nonna*.

Paola excused herself to use the bathroom. In her absence, Alessandro said, "Sorry I was late. What did I miss?"

Bianca answered in English, "Nothing much. Claudio here is a journalist and he was explaining his work to us before you and Paola arrived.

Paola made her way back to her seat.

Bianca turned to Claudio. "I read your article in English about reformist politicians. You discussed events in the Netherlands and Sweden."

Gennaro wasn't sure what she was talking about, but he leaned back and let her talk. He knew it would become clear. Paola and Alessandro were flirting at the other end of the table, but he sensed they were listening and that Alessandro wanted to make good for his absence, even though Paola enjoyed her game of distracting him.

"Events?" Pause. "Oh, that article. I wrote that a long time ago. Yes, disturbing events. I agree."

"I think there is a connection between those two events and a recent one. Politics being what they are . . ."

Gennaro asked, "And what makes you think that?"

"A little elf pointed it out to me."

Claudio said in Italian, "I thought it was little birds who whispered words of English into the ears."

Farrugia called over the waiter and ordered Sambuca for the table. Gennaro was happy that it didn't involve snapping fingers.

"Don't forget *con la mosca*."

She was alluding to their old habit of having Sambuca with three coffee beans inside each glass, representing health, happiness, and prosperity. *Mosca* is Italian for "fly." But for her, the beans symbolized something else. She was reminding him and Farrugia that it was the coffee beans that had led them to the discovery of others listening to their conversation clandestinely in Rome.

"I don't think we really should," Alessandro said. "Paola has to drive back to Bergamo."

"You're leaving?" Gennaro said.

"No, he isn't," Paola said. "I know he should stay with his friends. I'll just ask that you allow him to walk me to my car, and I promise I'll send him right back. Thank you for a wonderful evening." The couple headed to the door.

"Quiet woman," Claudio said. "Hardly said a word all evening."

"She's been listening, though," Bianca said. "Besides, I don't think talking is her forte, but I'm sure she knows Alessandro and bullets very well."

Dante said, "Healthy appetite on her. You were right, Gennaro."

Bianca replied, "I wonder why. Right about what?"

"That inviting Paola to dinner was a good idea," Gennaro said smoothly. "Now, what is this mysterious talk about events?"

Bianca answered. "Let's wait for Alessandro."

Alessandro returned minutes later.

The waiter arrived with the Sambuca, including one for Alessandro. Farrugia teased him about the lipstick on his lips.

They all moved closer to each other as Claudio explained the events. He gave a summary profile of each politician, Palme and Fortuyn, their biographical particulars and their intellectual dispositions, before providing them with an objective presentation of their political platforms. He described their assassinations and the aftermath, the repercussions in both Sweden and the Netherlands, respectively.

When he was done, Farrugia was the first to speak. "The two of them, give or take, sound exactly like Lele—except, of course, Lele was very assertive about redefining terrorist legislation."

"There's a remarkable similarity," Gennaro said.

"Especially when you throw in a disturbing coincidence," Bianca said.

"This is what your elf told you?" Gennaro said.

"That's right. After each incident, 1986, then 2002, and now with Lele, U.S. Attorney Farese showed up. I looked over his publications and there was nothing to show for his time after these appearances."

Claudio asked, "No papers on terrorism? Mafia?"

"Nothing."

"Then what was he doing?" Farrugia asked and then snapped his fingers. "Sorry, Gennaro. Silvio said Farese was spending more of his time over at the Embassy. They speak English there, but he wouldn't need Silvio to talk to the Brooks family. Good thing Silvio has his project."

"How is Silvio?" Bianca asked.

Gennaro said, "Emulating the paperwork on the Manzoni case."

Claudio was confused.

"It would take some explaining. Drink all you want and Silvio still wouldn't make sense."

"Poor Silvio," Bianca said, "How is his English?"

Gennaro explained the insight Silvio had given them about the hikers and the woman's too-perfect Italian. Claudio laughed and laughed, but conceded that Silvio was a genius, intentional or not.

Dante, enjoying his Sambuca, asked, "And I assume that your little elf was as brilliant and as helpful, Bianca?"

Claudio asked, "What is he talking about? What elf? Who is this elf? What ever happened to *the little bird told me?*"

Gennaro ordered another Sambuca. They all decided on a second round of *Sambuca con la mosca.*

"I can't reveal my source, Claudio," Bianca said. "You can understand that."

"I understand, but did the elf say something helpful?"

Bianca was silent until she noticed Farrugia waiting. Farrugia dumped more energy into waiting than anyone Gennaro knew. "More like provocative. It's a riddle."

The drinks arrived.

"Isn't it always?" Gennaro said.

Bianca unfolded a piece of paper. She had written out the full riddle and then the one-liners that Loki had given her. The paper started with Gennaro who passed it to Farrugia. Dante received it, read it, and handed it to Claudio. The journalist held onto the paper the longest. Bianca discussed her answers: a blue dragon and the angelic war cry. Claudio focused on the one-liners.

Farrugia asked Claudio, "Do you have any idea what all that means? It reads like Nostradamus to me."

Dante got up and found a chair and moved it closer to Claudio so they could share the paper. "All hidden knowledge is a matter of initiation. Answers are in the act of reading."

Alessandro laughed. "Dante, this isn't allegory or medieval architecture."

"I wasn't thinking medieval architecture. Think Collodi."

"The author of *Pinocchio*?" Farrugia asked.

Dante said. "I've read a recent article that suggests Collodi had been initiated into an esoteric society, and that Pinocchio was his metaphoric rendition of the initiation ceremony. The scholar also suggested Apuleius's *The Golden Ass* inspired Collodi."

Gennaro looked at him. "Please don't use that word."

"What word?"

Bianca said, "Rendition."

Alessandro blurted out, "Collodi? What has any of this got to do with Lele?"

"Cosa Nostra has an initiation ritual," Farrugia said. "All secret societies do. I'm thinking with this North-South coalition that Lele had going with the L&S that there might've been an initiation ceremony or some kind of secret something. It'd explain why he was disgraced—found the way he was and . . . I don't know, but it might make sense if someone in his party had him killed. Had Lele betrayed them? Or had it come to a power struggle?"

Silence.

Alessandro was the first to speak. "I wonder if Gladio had a secret initiation."

Claudio turned pale as Dante explained his thesis, "If we take Pinocchio as the story of a path to awareness, we understand why Pinocchio can see that the Blue Fairy is dead: because now he is aware. She was always dead from the start of the story, but Pinocchio couldn't see that. And after he realizes this fact, he will be able to see her again, though he knows she is dead. After the initiation, boy to man, or whatever the path of awareness, one sees the world differently."

Gennaro said, "I Corinthians 13.11."

Bianca said, "This is not the Disney version I knew."

"I still don't see the connection to Lele," Gennaro said. "What does it mean?"

"It means that there was dissension in the L&S Party, but we wouldn't know that because we weren't allowed to interview the party members with Lele the night he died," Farrugia said.

Claudio's eyes squinted. "Why not? Who stopped you?"

"Lodi—the Lodi Police. They claimed jurisdiction," Gennaro said. "It's bullshit."

"No it isn't," Claudio said. "It's not bullshit if law enforcement is protecting Lele's assassins and giving them enough time to escape."

Dante's chair made an uncomfortable grating sound before he leaned back in it, his hands clasped behind his head like a military prisoner. They stared at him.

"Gladio infiltrated law enforcement," Dante said.

Gennaro added, "Law enforcement infiltrated anarchist groups to destabilize the political scene."

Claudio held up the paper. "I think our answer is here. At least, some part of it is."

They all moved in closer as Claudio put the paper in the center of the table for them to read Loki's clues.

There once was a team on a boat that sailed the northern sea. They always rowed together. Though they fight & fight—it's all 4 show because of the gold. The world is their ocean. The Frenchman takes Africa. The Brit drinks tea, his cousin drinks coffee; but both do the laundry together. Italians & Arabs around the pond fight in public but love each other behind closed doors. The ship is a boat with many flags but there is no pirate. The ship = a ship bec there is water.

"Still reads like gibberish to me," Gennaro said.

"It's a journey story," Dante said. "Think of Homer. All the passengers have unique roles, and nationalities are named, but what these heroes present to their world is not what they are but what they seem to be and—"

Bianca clapped her hands. "A false-flag. Each nationality has a flag."

"Or a particular deception," Alessandro said.

"'World is their ocean,'" Claudio said. "I had expected 'the world is their oyster.'"

Alessandro said, "I think the disturbing part is 'there is no pirate.' That reinforces that everything is an illusion."

Gennaro said, "Alessandro?"

"Yes, Chief."

"You're a genius."

"I am?"

They all looked at Gennaro.

"Don't you get it? *Strategia della tensione.*"

Silence. Absolute stillness.

"And Farese?" Bianca asked.

Claudio answered. "He's a part of it. He's an angel of death. He showed up after two assassinations, and he is here now. He helps right the balance. You said so yourself that he has the balancing scales as a symbol."

"I thought Michael was a militant archangel?" said Farrugia. "I'm confused."

"I'm confused also," Alessandro said. "Scales of justice, right? He's a lawyer."

But Gennaro was feeling like his mind was finally starting to work. "That's not it."

"It's not?" Bianca asked.

"Only an old Catholic like me would remember this," Gennaro said. "Michael is militant, yes, but he wasn't always. It is like a revised history book. Michael's first role was as a healer."

"A healer?" Alessandro asked, looking around the table.

"Pope Gregory the Great said that St. Michael ended the plague in Italy when he saw him sheath a flaming sword. Farese keeps the peace. He balances out the tension amongst the members. Part of the strategy is to keep the populace under terror, but the other part is to prevent the members from devouring each other."

Dante asked, "But who does Farese work for?"

Gennaro shrugged. "Probably the next Andreotti."

Farrugia was still staring at the paper. He would not argue with what Gennaro said, but there was something more. "It doesn't matter. All the passengers are committed to the same goal, just like Gladio was intent on preventing Communism from taking hold in Italy. We have to look at the passengers."

"French," Claudio said.

Gennaro answered. "The French had colonies in Africa, and many of the Gladio members fled to France, were given amnesty, and never extradited."

"Brits and . . . I don't get this part. Who are their cousins? The Germans? The languages are similar."

Bianca took the paper. "Not the Germans. The Americans. 'Two nations separated by a common language.'"

Farrugia nodded. "The laundry has to be done. The Americans and Brits do the dirty work. They do the killing, like our supposed hikers who spoke perfect Italian. Cynical."

Gennaro sighed. "Not as cynical as the Italians and Arabs. We dislike them in public but share the bed with them at night. Think of the Italians and the Libyans and the Palestinians and all those other nice guys around the Mediterranean pond."

"So they have the ocean, huh?" Alessandro asked.

"That's where Lele came in."

Everyone looked at Claudio.

He read, "'Team on a boat that sailed the northern sea.' It almost sounds like that Annie Lennox song, 'Sweet Dreams,' but I assure you it is a nightmare. On one level, your elf was alluding to an assassination team, but I think we have to look at it from another level."

"A second level?" Alessandro asked, and Claudio nodded.

Farrugia took the paper. He read and his eyes met with Claudio's over the edge of the paper. "Thinking what I'm thinking?"

"Yes."

"Care to elaborate?" Dante asked.

Farrugia answered. "Lele proposed legislation that threatened corporations, and he was adamant about Adastra in Sardinia. This 'northern sea' . . ."

"What?" Bianca asked.

"Another corporation. Or at least a multinational."

Gennaro shook his head. "I'm not understanding you, Isidò."

Claudio started. "North Atlantic . . ."

Farrugia finished it. "Treaty Organization. NATO."

Silence.

"Gennaro?"

"Yes, Bianca?"

She pulled out a book and put it on the table in front of him. "Please give this to Silvio for me. We used to talk literature. I think he'd enjoy these stories."

Farrugia looked over at the English edition. Herman Melville. *Bartleby the Scrivener and Other Works.*

34

"Boss?"

"Yes, Dante."

"I know there were a lot of distractions last night with Claudio and Paola there, but you didn't discuss the paperwork you gave to Alessandro. Did you forget?"

"I know, and I didn't forget." Not seeing Alessandro behind the desk, Gennaro picked up one of the Nava pencils and smiled at Dante, taking the pencil with him.

"Boss?"

"Yes."

"I didn't want to say it last night, but I was thinking . . . do you trust Claudio?"

"What does Bianca think?"

"She has a good feeling about him, which I find odd. It's not in her character to trust."

"People can change, Dante. It's rare, true, but they can." Gennaro once again turned to make his way back to his own office.

"Boss?"

He stopped. "Yes, Dante."

Dante looked over at his partner's desk, then back to Gennaro, and said, "I'm worried about him. I can crack all the jokes I want about blanks and bullets with our ballistics expert from Bergamo or about the lead in Alessandro's pencil, but I'm worried that Sandro will get hurt. You know him and women."

"You're a good friend, Dante, but trust Sandro to be Sandro. I've got to go."

"Bianca says, 'Please don't forget to give Silvio his book.'"

Farrugia was in early, at his desk, engrossed in a magazine. He mumbled his morning greeting as soon as Gennaro had entered the office, but he didn't look up, which disturbed Gennaro.

The magazine was a yoga journal of some sort that Gennaro had seen at the kiosk numerous times. The covers were almost always done in bright colors, usually yellows and oranges with a splash of a vibrant blue on occasion, and almost always with an attractive female in some kind of pose that was half erotic, half spiritually cosmic. Gennaro feared disturbing Farrugia's concentration. The magazine's cover was facing Gennaro. It was one of those dual-language editions; Italian if read one way, in English when flipped over and read from the back.

"Milan's Man Does Yoga" was the feature article in English—Gennaro could make it out even with the title upside down.

"Did you know that most human beings do not breathe properly?" Farrugia said.

"My relationship with oxygen is just fine, Isidò, but thank you for your concern. It is when I stop breathing that I should worry. Any thoughts on suspects within the L&S?"

"To be honest, no. I've looked at the profiles of the members who had been with Lele the night he died, and it's anybody's guess."

"Why do you say that?"

Farrugia put down his magazine. He fanned out the paperwork like a deck of cards and said, "Take your pick."

"We don't have time for games, my friend. Half the Italian police force is looking for Litrico, and nobody is making a fuss about Lodi blocking our interviews. There are no leads with the G9 on Brooks. Not even one crank call."

"I know."

"Need I mention that I wasn't too comforted with your friend Claudio's suggestion that Lodi police might've bought time for the suspects to get away? Just what we need—politicians in some kind of internal feud, and the police are in their beds to turn off the night-light. Our trail on the hikers gets colder with each day. The café video seems like a dead-end. What have you got?"

"Luca Parietti was there. He's a long-standing Piedmontese politician with strong feelings about the Northern League, since he remembers when Piedmont was lost to the Northern League by a narrow margin."

"I know the name. Next?"

"Nino Remigi was there. He's a conservative who has weathered the scandals in the Lombard regional government."

Gennaro waved his hand.

"Speroni: very straight-by-the-book politician, a Catholic who never misses Mass, but he won't kiss the Pope's ring in public."

"Clever, but De Gasperi did that with the Pope first. Next."

"Let's see," Farrugia shuffled some papers on his desk. "Ignacio Cuccoli. He's a character who had membership in just about every party until he joined the L&S."

"That's four men. We were supposed to interview five men. Remember?"

"I remember. I was saving the best for last, Gennaro."

"Who?"

"Not a man, but a woman."

Gennaro said, "I thought that the house belonged to Mamo Campanelli."

"Massimo Campanelli, yes, but guess what?"

"If I want games, I'll go to Loki, Isidò. Feed me and don't let me starve in my own office."

"He wasn't there."

"Mamo wasn't there? What do you mean he wasn't there? It's his house."

"He was in the hospital. Respiratory illness. I verified it, but his wife was there."

"Gaspara Campanelli?" Gennaro knew the name, as did all of Italy. She was a politician for years before she stepped down to raise her children. Her husband continued in politics. "Mamo" was a typical Lombard Calvinist Catholic, who helped build up the economic prosperity of Lombardy. As for Gaspara, now that her children were grown up, there were rumors she might succeed her husband, since his health was less than ideal.

"Gennaro? Are you listening to me?"

"Yes. I'm sorry. I was thinking. What is it?"

Farrugia said, "It's possible she was more than a hostess, since there has been talk of her returning to the political scene. We've all seen her on television speaking about how important the family is and how wonderful it is to be a mother."

"I've heard those rumors, and I've gotten sick of the non-stop infomercials. Reminds me of how the Fascists used to talk about the family unit. So we have nothing?"

"Nothing. No interview transcripts from Lodi either, not that I think they'd help us. They're probably carefully scripted, and everyone knows the roles they play. Perego has been doing a good job of stalling them. They get passive-aggressive. Without interviews we have nothing, although, knowing how politicians talk and can drag anything out, we'll *never* have anything."

There was a knock at the door.

Ragonese.

Gennaro looked at his wristwatch. "That was faster than I'd expected."

Bianca set up her workspace the morning after collecting her things from out of the rail station's storage locker. She and Dante had spent the night discussing Claudio. Dante had spent the initial part of their time together assuring her that she had not been sloppy with her research, since she was still berating herself for not having thought of Brooks Sr. as a consultant. Dante had reminded her that Claudio had no proof to back up his speculation, but they agreed that it all fit nicely.

This was her domain, her element: financial forensics. Her objective: Charles Brooks Sr.

She had already acquired the biographical details and had a sense for the psychological profile of a career military man. God, country, and, usually, Republican, with the built-in rhetoric that Democrats cut defense budgets because they lack spines and testicles. Too soft on the jealous enemies of the American way of life.

Campaign contributions confirmed that assumption. Tax forms seemed to show that Senior was an income-declaring, tax-paying, law-abiding Virginian. Membership with the gun lobby was a no-brainer. One credit and one debit card each for husband and wife; credit cards were always paid in full monthly, if they were used at all. Bianca was finding this boring. Too plain; the only thing missing was "missionary is mandatory."

She looked at the tax forms she hacked out of the IRS system. Her review of the tax preparer didn't reveal a thing, until she mined the relationship between the tax preparer and Charles Brooks Sr. It hadn't made her nose tickle at first. It did now.

Senior knew Tax Preparer through their church.

Brooks Sr. was Catholic. The man was involved in his community, like millions of dutiful Americans. She read that he led a catechism class, found a few online articles that spoke of the man as a warrior for God, citing his Army past, that he had now come home to retire and tend to his passions: his faith and history. Had the article been written in Latin, he would've sounded like Cincinnatus who had come home to yoke his farm animals and till his fields and wait for a quiet death.

Brooks was an amateur scholar of mechanized cavalry. Compelling.

She had almost ignored the homepage for his catechism class. Beaming young faces of pure minds ready to receive the teachings of Holy Mother Church, and ready for their vaccinations against the temptations of the world. Bianca was about to click out of the page until she saw the logo. It was the perfect chiasmus.

War and Knowledge. Knowledge and War.

The samurai called it *Bunburyodo*. Brooks Sr. used the same image as the samurai: a sword resting on a book.

Giancarlo Ragonese's stupid head and wild beard was in front of the camera. The office had crowded around the screen. Again.

Only Silvio was absent from the spectacle. Gennaro saw him reading while the copier was clicking and spitting out the collated pages with metronomic numbness. Poor Silvio. The tragedy of bureaucracy. To think how many trees had been felled for Lodi, yet despite all those copies Silvio had made, there were no leads on Lele's death.

The machine jammed. The collator of the emulator coughed and made an obscene sound. Gennaro turned his head away. Silvio returned to his kicking and using profanities in his adopted language.

"This is your Giancarlo, and I come to you today with disturbing revelations for our Republic. We have been lied to and misled once again."

Someone spiked the volume for the television.

Ragonese held up papers in his hand. "These were given to me by a reliable source. And if any authority were to ask me to reveal my source in court, I'd have my own questions. I will importune them in the name of our Republic to show me their stainless morality. Like Diogenes, I will say unto them, 'Show me an honest man. Otherwise get out of my sunlight.' Yes, I'm angry. These are the days of anger, my friends. I'm angry because we are looking for light and we have been given nothing but shadows and more darkness. I—"

"What a windbag!" someone said.

"Ssh."

Perego, hands on his hips, was like a cowboy. The man's face was already pink and growing darker.

"Two papers here concern the deaths of Charles Brooks, the American student, murdered mafiosi-style, and Lele Palmisano, the meteoric candidate from Catania. As to the young man killed days ago on Via Manzoni, I have a copy of an official memorandum with numerous authors. I'll refrain from commenting on the sloppiness of the paper with its half-typed and frequent scrawls because what draws my attention is—"

"What does it say, you idiot?"

"Ssh!" Perego again.

"Remember the Gévelot bullets? Remember our two dead assassins? I quote another famous man, 'those evil-doers.' This document says 'Yes' inside the box for 'Match found.' Please get the camera up close for our viewers."

Every head in the room craned forward as if the paper were right in front of them while the camera zoomed in.

"'Match for what, Giancarlo?' 'Yes' means there was a match for a fingerprint from one of the killers. Now, I ask you, if the police to whom we entrust our safety and well-being have found a match, then it stands to reason they know the name of the young man's killer, but what is that?" Ragonese cupped his ear. "I hear nothing. We heard nothing. Have we regressed to the day when we had mafia killings and knew names, but did not speak names because we were afraid? Are we afraid to name names? Has it come to this that our trusted officials withhold information without explanation? What will they say to the Brooks family at the American Embassy? Can Milan tell his mother, 'We don't know who killed your son'?"

"What about Lele, you insufferable piece of—"

"Ssh!"

"And Lele? This document I hold is his death certificate. We've been misled, my countrymen. We've been misled by a half-truth. Our leaders are like Sybil in the cave. You get an answer only if you ask the right question in the correct way. Here it says in layman's terms that Lele died of a heart attack. 'But we knew this, Giancarlo,' you say to me, but I'll read to you from the document. This document, unlike the other one, has but one author. It says, 'Cardiac failure related to the overabundant presence of Sildenafil citrate.' In plain speech, my countrymen, an overdose of Viagra, and 'secondary contributory factor is autoerotic misadventure.'"

Ragonese shook his head in disgust. "I'm simply speechless. The image I'll leave to you. All I can say is that Diogenes did not find his honest man. I'm not hopeful I'll find one among our excellent ones in Milan. Diogenes disproved Plato's definition of Man as a 'featherless biped' by plucking a chicken and delivering it to the Academy. The philosophers redefined Man. Our leaders redefine Man and they redefine leadership."

Redefine man? Was Ragonese now baiting feminists? Or gays?

"I'm not as clever as Diogenes, but I can agree with him that we can look at bones—at the bones of our dead political ideals—and remain incapable of discerning *free* from *slave*. But as citizens, as voters, I implore you not to accept or to condone the chickens amongst us who think they are men. This is Giancarlo Ragonese for the Free Channel."

Even before the screen turned black, Perego, red-faced, was screaming, "I want that coroner on my phone. Foà—that son of a bitch!"

Everyone fled except for Gennaro, who stood there smiling. He checked his watch.

The elevator chimed and out walked Alessandro. "Hi, Chief."

"Sandro. I've got a question for you."

"Yes, Chief."

"Enjoying Bergamo?"

"It was the traffic, Chief. I swear—What's this . . . why are you handing me one of my pencils?"

"You might want to stab yourself with it later."

35

Alessandro entered the office to find Dante reading.

"How is it that you can be reading when Ragonese has just lit up Milan?"

Dante didn't look up from his book. "Ragonese is an ass."

"Beside the point, Dante. Silvio is reading; you're reading. Now isn't the time."

Dante turned a page. "You seem to have time for Bergamo."

Alessandro sat down and his chair let out air like a fart without the methane. They stared at each other until the only other sound was that of Alessandro jamming Gennaro's pencil back into the holder.

"Let me have it," Alessandro said. "I heard about Ragonese's documentation."

"What? I have no idea what you're talking about. I've been reading."

"You argue this way with Bianca?"

"I'm reading, Sandro. Just because your balls are sore doesn't mean you should be busting mine."

Alessandro stared at him. A moment passed. "What are you reading?"

"Umberto Eco."

"Before lunch? Are you trying to kill the appetite? Which essay?"

"The one he wrote after 'Power of Falsehood.' It is about *dietrologia* and our culture."

Alessandro smirked. "So Eco is into the study of things behind things. Enjoy yourself."

"Eco is always about how to read. He isn't *doing* dietrologia. He's not a conspiracy nut."

Gennaro entered the office. Dante returned to his reading, after he mumbled his hullo in a listless manner. Gennaro looked at Alessandro for an explanation.

"Eco and behindology. The study of things behind things. It must be his Jesuit education."

"Eco says medieval scholars knew the world was round. Dante Alighieri had to have known that the world was round. He entered Hell at one end and saw stars from the bottom of Mount Purgatory."

Alessandro, affecting a child's annoying whine, said, "Eco says . . . Eco says."

"Enough, children," Gennaro said. "Alessandro?"

"Yes, Chief?"

"You sound like a bird and no better than Ragonese. And you, Dante?"

"Yes, Boss?"

"Make better use of your head and change the view. If you're looking for an insight into signs and symbols, then do what my wife always said."

"Sorry, Chief."

"Me, too," Alessandro said. "What did she say, Boss?"

Gennaro was silent a moment. "One day while she was sewing, I'd asked how the hell she managed to sew without sticking herself with the needle." Gennaro paused again. "She said, 'Everyone worries about the needle when they should trust the thread.'"

Alessandro looked at Dante, who seemed as puzzled as he was.

"You two kiss and make up, then get back to work." Gennaro headed for the door.

Before Gennaro made his exit, Dante called out a question to him. "Did you need something from us?"

"Forget it."

"Where are you off to, Chief?" Alessandro asked.

"To apologize to Dr. Foà. Oh, and Sandro?"

"Yeah."

"Keep the pencil in the office."

"Yes, Chief."

With that Gennaro opened the door, walked out, and closed the door behind him.

Dante asked, "Where did *that* come from, Sandro?"

Bianca was enjoying the scent of the money trail. Laundered money has a unique odor. It was a very clever scheme. Brooks Sr. tithed to his local church. A military man didn't make much; Mrs. Brooks didn't come from money, but every year ten percent of their household income went to the church, which in turn sent the money off to the Vatican. She had thought the local church would absorb the tithe to offset their operational costs, but this was not the case. It went across the pond. In fact, it went to one specific Vatican bank.

To a branch in Milan and a bookstore in Milan, and it looked like the parish church was ordering books. Why would a church in the United States be ordering books in Italy? At Brooks Sr.'s request. Odd.

While Brooks Sr. taught catechism, he was also giving both information and motivational sessions. This is a very common practice with career military men who returned to civilian life. The business-types, always in search of jargon, ate it up.

Bianca saw "information" and "motivational" as code for recruiting and consulting. The local church provided the perfect front. All of this reminded her of the small modest plaque she once saw in Boston. Actually, it was in Brookline, outside of Boston, where John F. Kennedy had been born. She had discovered the plaque on a street away from Coolidge Corner, on Harvard Street, where the first generation of OSS intelligence officers—who later transmuted into the CIA—had started to assemble statecraft. Nice plaque next to a school. They had used a front, too.

Bianca started cross-referencing. Tax deductions for meetings and travel expenses have to be itemized. The IRS never has enough time, staffing, or computing power to look for trends or inconsistencies until they zero in on a target. But she had her target.

Scrolling down she saw consistent names on bi-weekly information and motivational sessions. One of these names was likely to be an alias. Time to funnel the names through a sieve. She highlighted the most likely name for a copy and paste.

No address or contact phone number. She cross-referenced the name with the parish school. There were some children with the same last name, since it was a common-enough last name, but the fathers were a mixed lot. Some of the men were divorced, one was dead, another was now single, and others were long-time married. Not exactly what she was looking for. All of them had a variety of employers. Again, not what she was looking for in her profile of a connection between Brooks and Italy, with the church as mere conduit: the front, a go-between. She was not out to prove the church was involved. She needed a point-person.

She hacked into the parish's secretary's computer. Child's play—what parish secretary was going to know what she was handling? She was probably one of many good-hearted souls who volunteer their time for the parish. File, type, answer phones, and keep a schedule—simple tasks for that future salvation. The secretary was likely some retired lady one minute and a high school kid with piercings and an attitude the next—an imperfect chain of competent subterfuge. She found scans of the attendance sheets for Brooks Sr.'s sessions. Each attendee got a book from the bookstore in Milan.

Scroll. Scroll. Click and open. Click and close. She saw the same names.

She stopped. One name. The same last name, but her mouse's arrow looked at the employer's column on this attendance sheet. This certain somebody wrote "AA."

Bianca smiled. She knew. She was confident.

Nobody would question AA because Alcoholics Anonymous used a quasi-religious, successful 12-step program that did not conflict with Catholicism. Bianca knew the name was an alias, but it belonged to someone who showed up consistently for Brooks Sr.'s information and motivation sessions. The next step for her was to correlate dates and transaction. This was the handler, the go-between. AA was not Alcoholics Anonymous.

AA was Ad Astra. Adastra.

36

"Let me explain," Gennaro said to him.

Perego sat behind his desk. He looked as if ready to attack Gennaro, the only thing holding him back was the stacks of papers on his desk. He looked like a soldier in a foxhole, about to go over the top. But all Perego had for a weapon was that lean Lombard face of his and a mastiff's stare.

One false move and it would be all over for Gennaro.

"Please do explain, because I just gave the last of my mind and my reputation to Dr. Foà. I've got bullets leaking, and now I've got death certificates and a supplemental page in the hands of that jackass journalist. Giancarlo Ragonese the Milanese Jackal, is what he is."

Gennaro waited for Perego to wind down, waited until the stare returned and he had an opportunity to ask a question of his own. "What does Farese have to say about all of this?"

Perego leaned back in his chair. "What do you care what Farese thinks?"

"Call me curious. What did Dr. Foà have to say?"

The mastiff's stare showed a twitch, the tilt of the head was missing. "At first he acted outraged, but he didn't sound like a typical bureaucrat."

"How so?"

"I don't get you, DiBello. I call you into my office and you're asking me questions." Another hard Perego stare. "But to answer your question, I meant that Foà didn't sound like a typical jerk because he didn't blame someone else or offer some bullshit excuse. He actually answered his phone. When he heard who I was, after he'd told me off, he said I should go talk to you. That's why you are here."

"He said *that*?"

"He did, so now that we've established the screenplay, please cut to the scene where I realize all is not what it seems. Or is it?"

"Is it?"

The mastiff stare returned, this time with a bobbing pen. "Don't try my patience, DiBello. Explain."

"You knew that we had a leak. I found a way to identify the leak. Hear the expression 'two birds with one stone'?"

"Yes," Perego answered. "I thought it was 'kill two birds with one stone.'"

"It is, but I have something different in mind."

"You do?"

"I do. This time the bird kills itself."

The mastiff stare softened a bit. "I'm listening."

They saw the building from across the street. Correct address.

"This is it?" Claudio asked.

"Are you sure?" Dante asked.

"This is the address Bianca gave Gennaro," said Farrugia. "So how long do we sit and stare at it?"

Dante swung the car door open.

"Easy with the door, will ya," Farrugia said. "I almost got killed at Via Manzoni, so please, I don't need the damn rental agency penalizing me for damages."

"Sorry, Isidò. It's just that I'm pissed off at Bianca. She didn't tell me."

Bianca could call him mid-day and convey her enthusiasm for the new Abercrombie & Fitch on Corso Giacomo Matteotti, the only one in continental Europe. But when it came to something serious, she told Gennaro first instead of him.

"When did she tell Gennaro?" Claudio asked.

"An hour or so ago. She texted him on his cell—not his normal one, but his other one."

"He has *two* cell phones? Isn't one enough?"

Both Dante and Farrugia eyed each other after Claudio had said it. Dante did find it funny. "It'd take too long to explain his love for cell phones, but yes, Gennaro has two. We're happy when he uses one."

"What exactly are we looking for here?" Claudio was like a kid with never-ending questions. At least Farrugia was used to interrogations. "I don't know," he said. "Gennaro didn't explain much. He said that Biancahad found someconnection between Brooks Sr. and this bookstore. All I got was, 'Check it out.'"

Dante studied the façade. *Razionalismo italiano.* Italian rationalist architecture, but this place seemed like a poor man's knock-off of a Gruppo 7 design, because it looked so out of place, as if it belonged outside of Milan. The place could pass for an imitation of the *Guardia di Finanza's* museum in Como, the *Casa del Fascio.*

Across the street stood the framework, like any other Milanese department store, and it was a store, but where the square glass should welcome in the light there were blinds blocking it out, denying anyone on the sidewalk a view of what was inside. The sign said Bookstore. English-language books only,like the American Bookshop in front of the Castello Sforzesco. Slow-walking American tourists were seen at opposite ends of the street, like gunfighters about to meet in the middle for the confrontation, except this was a conflict in stereotypes of floral patterns, massive tree-trunk legs, distended bellies against the hyper-fit sleek physiques on the prowl in monochromatic Armani.

"You two should go in," Farrugia said.

"Why won't you join us?" Claudio asked.

"I think he's concerned that somebody will recognize him," Dante said. "Someone from Via Manzzoni."

"He can't hide forever," Claudio answered.

"No, I can't, but my gut tells me that Bianca would want me to time my entrances better. You two go ahead and just try to remember the smallest detail. It might make a difference."

"Your gut, huh?" Claudio said.

Farrugia returned to his car, while Claudio and Dante crossed the street.

For Dante, the inside of the bookstore was like an Eco essay on American and Italian culture, with on one side of the room, America, and the love-hate response on the other. There was Mickey Mouse, or Topolino as he was known in Italian, on one side, and Toffolino the human on the other; Felix the Cat and Fritz the Cat, Walt Disney and Robert Crumb; a picture of John Waters, the director, with Leslie Van Houten, Manson Family member, and the poster of Che Guevara. The last pairing was Bush with Berlusconi for America and a vintage poster of Uncle Sam's "I Want You" for Italy.

"May I help you?" asked a young man in Italian, about mid-thirties, with scruffy graduate stubble, a distressed American university T-shirt, toned arms, and khaki slacks. No blinding white sneakers, but a nice pair of Bikkembergs. Claudio seemed to approve of the shoes with the casual American look.

"I'm looking for a book in English," Dante asked.

"The title, please?" the bookseller said.

"*Throwing the Last Molotov*, but I'm not aware who realized the anthology of essays," Dante said in Italian.

Claudio gave Dante an odd look after the young man turned away with his "Follow me, please," also in Italian.

The bookseller guided them to the Politics shelf. He walked with a librarian's confidence. His eyes traveled left to right across the shelves, fingers fanning the spines. He excused himself on the pretense that he needed to use the computer to look up the title.

With the man out of earshot, Claudio said in a soft voice, "Why the verb *realizzare* for a book? This isn't a video store."

"Ssh. I was thinking of the manual *Anarchist's Cookbook*, but don't worry."

"Why not?"

"The book I want doesn't exist. He's coming back now."

The man with the perfect smile returned with diplomatic regret. "I'm sorry but we don't seem to carry that title."

"Thank you. My friend and I will browse around," Dante said, and Claudio smiled. The man did a slight bow, turned and walked away, leaving them in front of Cesare Battisti's prison memoir.

"This place doesn't see much business, does it?" Claudio said.

"Blame the internet. Small booksellers are getting hammered." Dante thumbed through a book. "Rather unfortunate."

Claudio focused on the picture of the two Mr. Bs, Bush and Berlusconi, in tuxedos,wine glasses up and heads tilted inward like Siamese twins. "Why do I get the impression something is very wrong about this place?"

Dante noticed that the masonry between the bookcases was stippled, as if something had been removed. "Because I think there is."

Dante decided he would purchase a book. Claudio walked with him, but a few steps away from where he had pulled the book from its shelf,Dante stopped and grabbed Claudio's arm. "Do you smell something?"

Claudio sniffed. "Potpourri? No . . . wait, it smells like cinnamon."

Dante paid for the book andthanked the man for his assistance. Outside, he started walking up and down the street in hurried bursts, looking for a spot where he could cross the street and beat the traffic.

Dante was first in the car. Front seat. He placedhis new bookon the floor.He slammed the car door and the look on his face stopped Farrugia from saying a word.

Claudio was in back. He mumbled something sarcastic about the car's ample space and stuck his head between Dante and Farrugia, over the armrest. "What the hell is wrong with you, Dante?"

"I've got a bad feeling about this place."

"I'd said the same thing, remember?" Claudio said.

Farrugia eyed them both and asked Dante, "Calm down and take your time. What was it?"

Dante looked out the window and said with his finger wagging at the place across the street. "That bookseller is what's wrong."

"The place was bizarre, but aside from the décor it is a bookstore."

"Not that. Remember Silvio's comment about the mother tongue? His Italian was too good. The way he dressed said American, but the shoes said Italian. He wasn't the least bit confused that I had said 'realized' about a book, and another thing—that wall bothered me."

Farrugia looked over to Claudio and then asked Dante, "What wall?"

Dante explained to Farrugia about the stippling, how the wall was poorly resurfaced.

"A lot of the buildings in that style used to have mosaics," Farrugia said, "but after the Fascists lost power the architects had the mosaics ripped out."

And then the final piece fell into place. "The apartment! Via Melchiorre Gioia now!"

Farrugia turned the engine over. "But Bianca isn't there, Dante."

"Gioia! Drive, Isidò."

Claudio fell back into the backseat as Farrugia injected the car into traffic and participated in a profane exchange with another driver.

Farrugia's eyes looked for his next move: right turn from the left lane. A stream of horns replied to his sudden maneuver. More curses. Claudio rolled to the other side of the car with his own choice profanity.

"Will you please explain to me why . . . why Melchiorre Gioia?"

"Cinnamon."

"Cinnamon?" Claudio asked.

Dante answered, "I hope I have ants."

37

The air in the apartment smelled of Christmas. The lighting was dim; the blinds were pulled shut. The first cop on the scene always got that coppery taste of a 9-volt battery in his mouth, and he responded to it with the unclipping of a leather cinch and metal.

So by the time the door swung slowly in an arc from partial to full entry, Farrugia had his gun out. His hand, big and dark on Dante's chest, and his eyes narrowed at Claudio, were his way of saying to them, "Let me go in first."

The apartment had been given a terrible once-over. This was not a delicate, rhapsodic rearrangement of particulars. This was not as if someone had wanted to prove that it could be done like some messy note from a mafia boss to a witness demanding "Don't testify," in no uncertain terms. That kind of search was neater than this.

Everything had been moved, relocated, left in disarray. Books had been yanked off the shelves and thrown to the floor. Some of the books had been left lying face-down, pulled from the bookcase by their binding, their boards splayed out liked wings, spines shaken as if the unwanted reader had been trying to shake words off the pages, hoping that a secret insert would fall out. There was debris everywhere, but there were some spots left untrammeled, where the visitor might have stood, thinking what to do next, perhaps stumped in his, her, or their guessing game, perplexed in their quest. All Farrugia, Dante, and Claudio knew was that someone had come looking for something. Looking hard.

"All clear." Farrugia holstered his weapon and motioned to them that they could come in.

Dante walked quickly through the rooms to visit those sentimental objects whose placement only he knew. Claudio and Farrugia, not knowing the apartment, stood by the door, not wanting to aggravate the misery. When Dante returned they convened in the kitchen.

The lowered blinds made any natural light seem sullen, almost bruised, brutal, as it washed over the kitchen cabinets, the counter, and the floor. Farrugia tilted the blinds to let in honest light.

Enraged, frustrated, the *guest* had hurled the plastic container of bulk cinnamon that Bianca had left on the counter to the kitchen floor. Its contents had flown in every direction from the point of impact.

Claudio and Farrugia stood there in respectful silence. Dante, also silent, had turned on his DeLonghi to prepare espresso. He asked them whether they wanted any. It was late in the morning, and nobody drank espresso this late, but Claudio and Farrugia nodded. Dante pulled out saucers and demitasses.

The tiles were stark as bone and the splash of spice offered the best clue at the scene. Like a bloody footprint, the criminal had walked through the cinnamon.

A partial footprint. Pumps? All three recognized a shape of the sole and a heel that the intruder had left behind.

And out from that swath walked one resilient, defiant witness.

An ant.

"Of course she isn't in the apartment, Isidò," Gennaro said into his primary cell phone, as he watched the crowd in the office gathering for another storm in front of the television screen.

"You're not listening. I said she's not at the hotel."

"What do you mean she isn't at the hotel? I registered her under a different name. Use your brains . . . you think I would've been that stupid?" Gennaro saw the television screen changing faces as someone clicked through the channels.

"Not as stupid as you apparently think I am. Dante and I took Claudio back to the hotel and straight to their room. A maid said that the *signora* had left the day before. Dante calculated it had to have been after he had left. He was angry that she had said nothing to him."

"I can imagine. So Claudio is with you now?"

Farrugia said something, but Gennaro lowered his phone. Perego had walked in and taken his place in front of the television, and not alone. Farese was with him.

"Yes, I heard you," he said quickly. "I don't know what to tell you about Bianca. She had sent me a text on the other phone. That was the last I had heard from her. That was how I gave you the address for the bookstore. Look, I've got to go. Something tells me that you and Dante should come to the office. Bring Claudio if you want; and maybe you should listen to the radio on your way over. Bye."

Farrugia said something but Gennaro had terminated the call.

Free Channel. Giancarlo had his microphone. No papers were in his hand this time, thank God. Gennaro found a place in the office crowd as a spectator. He and Perego exchanged looks while Silvio sidled up to Farese, ready to translate.

Had Giancarlo been a redhead, Gennaro would've called him the Iscariot of newscasters, but since the man was a brunette he'd settle for bearded raven, bearer of bad news.

"It is I, your Giancarlo, with good news and bad news. We have received communication from the G9. They have Arnaldo Litrico and in a moment we will broadcast the footage given to us. This footage arrived this morning at the Free Channel. We are mystified as to who delivered it. Our security cameras show only the image that we are now broadcasting to your screens."

The screen displayed a man walking into the main lobby of the Free Channel studio. He was wearing a dark rain poncho, hood pulled up and over his head. Dark sunglasses and gloves. The time-lapsed film showed him walking in and leaving a small package on the counter and then leaving. He didn't appear to have spoken to the desk officer. The security man had said something to him and then started to move out from behind the counter when he had received no response, but the mysterious courier had hopped onto his bike and pedaled away. The tape was played again and again with the agonizing slowness of the Zapruder film and revealing just as much: nothing but speculation. The cameraman cued back to Ragonese.

"The good news is that Litrico appears to be healthy, given his circumstances. The bad news is, for those of you old enough to remember the Aldo Moro kidnapping, the footage is eerie. Please watch. I will return shortly."

The image of Litrico, before the audio clicked up, looked like a palimpsest of Moro in captivity. Litrico was wearing an open-necked shirt, his hair unkempt. He seemed tired but not exhausted. He had been allowed the dignity of a morning shave. The room itself was as dark as a northern-renaissance painting, forcing everyone to wonder about the lighting. There was no mistaking the iconography. Litrico was in a cage. Claustrophobic ambience and just the right amount of shadows, just enough to see him and something else: a large-faced clock on the pockmarked wall behind him. The hands of the clock were stopped at 10:25.

The world remembers Armistice, the end of the First Great War, at eleven o'clock. The Americans remember the collapse of the first tower of 9/11 at 9:59 a.m. And on August 2 at 10:25 a.m., Italy remembers the Bologna train station massacre.

Litrico, like Moro, denied mistreatment. He told the camera that no authority should negotiate with his captors whom he called "desperate cowards."

"I will not write letters. I will not plead for my life. Whatever happens to me, it is my wish that I not be interpreted as some martyr. I am not Moro. I am not Pasolini. I am simply an Italian. Whether you dislike my homosexuality, whether you dislike the platform of Raffaele

Palmisano and the *Libertà e Solidarietà Party*, I ask that you remember I am an Italian. Not a *terrone* or *polentone*. I could be you. I am you. And make no mistake in thinking these *revolutionaries* are romantic or heroic figures. They are misguided. Lele would not have wanted this. He was against violence. This affair is not written nor preordained. It is not. You are the author, and if there is to be any slogan then let it be *ninety-nine and one percent*."

Ragonese reappeared on the screen. Silvio was explaining to Farese that *terrone* was a derogatory word for southern Italians and *polentone* was a derogatory word for northern Italians—the equivalents of redneck and polenta-eater.

"There you have it, my fellow countrymen. There were no demands for money or calls for liberation of comrades-in-arms. Nothing. The Free Channel has handed this film over to the authorities, but not before we did our own preliminary analysis. The camera and audio were amateurish, as you saw. There were no background noises that could give us any clue as to the location. We know that the police have had roadblocks and checked cars, trains, and abandoned buildings without much success. All we see here is this brave man sitting in a cage with a clock behind him; all we see is poor lighting that illuminated time, a scarred wall, and all we have heard is a voice that reminds us that, differences aside, he is an Italian and we are Italians, one Italy once again at the mercy of terrorists. I commend his courage and his call for unity. Ninety-nine percent of us live in fear but it takes only one percent to inspire us and remind us of our freedom, our power as a people. Thank you."

The room was silent except for the lone voice of Silvio translating.

38

Bianca ignored Gennaro's text.

She was busy at the keyboard, downloading and storing the financial exchanges between Adastra and Brooks Sr. The defense conglomerate had paid Brooks "consulting fees" through a subcontractor and a slush fund. Brooks Sr. had been using his local church as a front for meetings with an Adastra representative. Did the ancient law of sanctuary protect business conducted on sacred ground? Probably not.

Brooks was reimbursed for his travels to the field, where he drove tanks. Bianca's research showed no travel for Brooks Sr. outside the United States. Was he given another identity and passport? She couldn't even prove how much he knew about the software, but Charlie did have status reports indicating targets had been "successfully eliminated." Unfortunately, there were no descriptions of the targets, anthropomorphic or otherwise.

Brooks Sr. used some of his earnings in a gesture to his faith, first donating to his local church and then to *the* Church. The local church sent its monies to Rome. That much she had already known. What she hadn't known was another piece to the puzzle. She had traced Ad Astra's payments to Brooks Sr. back to its origin: Italy. Adastra S.r.l., with the S.r.l. designating a foreign parent company with a subsidiary in Italy. *Società a responsabilità limitata* meant limited liability is required. How limited, she wondered.

She revisited her earlier thought. Money flows like a river to Rome and drains into the Vatican, or it flows north to Milan.

Now, how did Farese fit into all of this?

Farrugia exited the elevator with Dante and Claudio.

He saw the unexpected faces of Farese, Perego, and Ettore Brambilla from the Ministry of Internal Affairs engaged in an argument. Silvio was the unfortunate foot soldier stuck between that triumvirate, unarmed and with no words in either language to save him. It seemed, from the little that Farrugia heard, that Perego had been trying to move this argument to an office, but Brambilla and Farese were refusing the intimacy of a smaller room for their public squabble. Brambilla, in particular, was already on a different page of another complaint while the office staff around them pretended not to hear the three men.

Perego noticed Farrugia standing with Dante and Claudio outside the elevator. The elevator chime seemed to announce Farrugia's foray into the fight.

"Where the hell have you been, Farrugia?" Perego screamed.

"Investigating a lead."

"What lead?" Perego yelled at Farrugia while Brambilla yelled at Perego, "I thought he was restricted to desk duty." Brambilla then said to Farrugia, "We need to talk."

"Not without my union rep."

"What have you got?" Farese asked.

"Not sure," Farrugia answered in English. Silvio, hand on his head, was tired and grateful for a pause.

Perego yanked down his tie. "What do you mean you're not sure?"

Brambilla turned to Perego and screamed, "I want an explanation! First, we have the Gévelots, and now a disgraced detective investigating a hot case."

"Ballistics is not my responsibility," Perego screamed back.

"Then there is Ragonese with a death certificate and a fingerprint. Second leak. How do you explain that, Perego?"

"Talk to Dr. Foà."

"I tried. The man won't pick up the phone."

"And that is supposed to be my problem? You're with the Ministry. Go visit him. Foà is the coroner. He shouldn't be hard to find. He is the only one in his office who's still breathing."

Brambilla grabbed Perego, which put an end to translation as Farese and Silvio tried to separate the two. Gennaro walked up to the scene next to Farrugia and watched the show for a moment.

Then he whistled a loud, piercing sound in the office. Everyone stopped moving.

"Thank you," Gennaro said. "Now listen. We have one dead political candidate and one kidnapped victim. One *live* victim, you understand. The three of you can kill each other on your own time. Commissario Farrugia said he was not sure, but he has a clue. Commissario?"

"I heard what Ragonese said over the radio on the drive over. I need to see that film footage."

Someone in the office said, "It's been uploaded. Over here, Commissario."

"Please retrieve it and play it full-screen on your computer," Farrugia said.

Perego and Brambilla mumbled apologies and they joined Farese with the others gathering around the man's desk as the video started to play. Litrico was speaking.

"Freeze it there!" Farrugia said.

"What is it, Isidò? The clock?" Gennaro said. "That's for Bologna."

"Not the clock. Dante? Claudio? Come here and tell me what you think of this."

People made way for the two men. Farrugia instructed the man to slide the footage back a few seconds and then resume play. Claudio and Dante watched.

"Notice anything?" Farrugia asked.

Dante's finger pointed at the wall on the screen. "That's the wall. That's the wall I was telling you about."

Farrugia awaited Claudio's opinion.

Claudio squinted. "It's certainly consistent."

Perego stepped forward and leaned down to the screen. Brambilla did the same as the film was backed up and played in slow-motion.

"I don't understand," commented Perego.

"I do," Farrugia said.

"What do you need?" Perego asked.

"Question me later, and that includes you," he said to Brambilla who held up his hands. No resistance. "I need the Rapid-Response Team, and get me the CSU investigator from Lele's scene here as soon as possible."

"Why?" Farese asked.

"Questions later." Perego picked up a phone. "We do as the Commissario says."

Brambilla asked, "What about Lodi?"

Hand over receiver, Perego said, "We're in Milan. Fuck Lodi."

Silvio asked Farese, "Would you like me to translate that?"

Farese chose the door. He slammed it behind him.

39

"A hunch?" Perego asked. "All you have is a hunch?"

"A hunch," answered Farrugia.

"And what about you?" Perego asked Gennaro, but included Alessandro, Claudio, and Dante, who were standing behind Farrugia just as the Apostles should have stood behind Christ when he was before Pilate.

No answer from Gennaro.

"A cop's hunch, huh?" Perego pulled his tie-knot loose and studied Farrugia. "You realize if I call this in and you're wrong, Farrugia, that we're all looking at reprimands. You're already in the sling with Internal Affairs. After Ragonese gets done with us he'll be made *Cavaliere* and if we're lucky we'll be translating Silvio's English into Italian."

Claudio cleared his throat. "If I may . . ."

"What?"

"With all due respect, sir, Dante and I were inside the bookstore. Joke all you want about Silvio, but the man's insight was absolutely spot-on."

"So you know about that . . . what exactly do you mean?"

Dante interjected with a quick summary about Silvio's linguistic theory about madrelingua, the implausibility that an American could speak flawless, colloquial Italian. "In some way, a non-native speaker would have tripped up somewhere along the way and given, in this case, *herself*, away."

"And you think you have found the male half of this tourist team?" Perego asked.

"We have only the woman's statement from the scene," Claudio said. "We know she had a companion there, but we have no statement from the other party because she had done all the talking."

With his tie loosened, Perego hunched over and planted his fists onto the desk, ready to snarl at Claudio if he made some fatal mistake. But Claudio explained how Dante had asked for the book as if it were a film, the peculiar wall, the disconcerting potpourri scent, without interruption. Perego appeared as if he wanted to throttle him.

"You want me to order in a tactical team based on the bookseller not having blinked at Dante's use of *realizzare,* or because the place smells like a granny's bathroom? Are you all out of your minds?" That question he had directed at Farrugia's followers. To Claudio, Perego said, "Maybe you should join Silvio and photocopy records."

"It's not just the wall and the cinnamon," Claudio answered.

"Well, what else, then?"

"The décor."

"I see. The décor?"

Claudio ignored the sneer in Perego's question. "The place was a mishmash of American kitsch. Mickey Mouse and Fritz the Cat, Manson and Che Guevara, and an Uncle Sam poster."

Perego went behind his desk and kicked his chair back, too angry to sit down. "This isn't an American crime show and some bullshit excuse of probable cause where some judge miraculously signs a search warrant before the next commercial. Is this how you do work in Turin?"

"No, sir, we're quite thorough there."

"I went and read some of your pieces. Good stuff, Mr. Ferrero, but we need more than bad taste in artwork and good use of language."

"Then how about this," said Claudio. "You design the place with absolutely perfect symmetry of left and right politics, anarchic and conservative, from post-World War II to the present day, and then you top it all off with a picture of the two Mr. Bs."

Perego glanced at Dante. "What the hell is he talking about?"

"There was a framed picture of George Bush and Silvio Berlusconi," said Dante.

"Two politicians and potpourri. Fantastic!"

Farrugia waved Claudio and Dante back from Perego's desk. Gennaro stood there with his hands clasped behind his back.

Farrugia said in a low enough voice for quiet diplomacy to Perego, "Imagine a bookstore used as a front for an organization that claims to be anarchist but turns out to be receiving funding from some ultra-conservative sources. That funding could be coming from concerned citizens here at home, right or wrong, or it could be coming from very deep pockets abroad. So I ask you, how is it a bookstore that sells political literature only in English stays in business? Do tourists come to Milan to be politically informed? Before you tell us to go and run a financial analysis to corroborate our suspicions and claims, may I remind you we have a kidnap victim at stake here? Not quite Aldo Moro, but . . ."

Perego went eyeball to eyeball with Farrugia. "You're right, Litrico is not Moro, but . . ."

"That's where you're wrong. Litrico is exactly like Moro in one respect, and that is—" He waved his finger at Perego. "Nobody seems to be in a hurry to rescue him. You want that on your conscience?"

Perego picked up the telephone.

The ATPI—*Antiterrorismo Pronto Impiego*, the *Guardia di Finanza*'s counter-terrorist unit—met with Farrugia not far from the bookstore to coordinate the plan.

"What do we do about the bookseller?" Dante asked Farrugia.

"Claudio will call him, order a book and ask for him to deliver it to his office—we've set up a dummy office a few blocks away. When the man shows up we'll take him. That'll prevent him from signaling anyone back there to harm Litrico. We don't know how many are in back with him."

"Okay, that gets the bookseller out of the way, but what if the bookstore has an alarm system or some kind of surveillance system where somebody can know we are coming in?"

Farrugia was examining a map, marking with his finger where Claudio would be stationed, the distance, and calculating the time it might take the bookseller to travel on his bike.

"The team has experts on that, Dante. They're watching the store now and we have to trust them to do their work. We can talk tactics all we want, but these men are professionals. Leave the logistics to them."

An officer came into the van and handed Farrugia a Kevlar jacket. The call had been made. Now they were waiting for the communication that the bookseller had left the store. A squelch and then some broad Lombard vowels announced that the man was pedaling away on his bicycle. The counter-terrorism team synchronized their watches. With the bicycle out of sight, the team and Farrugia poured out of the nondescript vans and scurried in formation across the street like a cloud of dark locusts.

A series of nods confirmed that the alarm and video systems were now frozen, so whoever might be observing the surveillance screens would see nothing but a looped interval of fixed images. Better to be safe than sorry. Once inside, the ATPI team did a thermal scan of the pockmarked wall.

The scan revealed two figures, one seated and one standing nearby. Hand signals conveyed the count.

Farrugia had asked earlier if there was some other, nonviolent way to overtake the captor and rescue Litrico. Pipe in knockout gas, he suggested. But the ATPI team leader said gas affected people differently, not unlike a visit to the dentist. The bad guy might get suspicious, kill the hostage and make a run for it. Farrugia knew the time for tactics was over. He had to trust someone else to drive the operation.

The counter-terrorist response team looked like humanoid insects. They were wearing fireproof gear, ceramic armor plating, and masks with large dark eyes from American sci-fi movies. Except these had anti-flash lenses, and the humans wrapped in all that exoskeleton breathed through a respirator, while underneath the headgear they heard and communicated with each through a special mic and headset. Each one of them was synchronized with the others to ensure lethal precision. The scan said that this was a small kill-zone with very little margin for error. They carried 9mm pistols, perfect for close-quarter combat.

In came a small cannon, called the Harvey Wall Banger for reasons Farrugia couldn't discern. The team would breach the wall with a water-filled plastic projectile. Farrugia could feel his body heat coming up through his scalp. He felt his heartbeat in his armpits and against the Kevlar.

It was a ten-minute bike ride to Claudio's fake office. Another team would overtake the bookseller there; without incident, he hoped.

A hand in black gauntlet went up, fingers extended for a countdown.

Masked eyes waited. The last finger dropped. They fired the cannon. The team burst through the shattered masonry and the dusty mortar. White dust curled in the air like smoke, almost obscene against the lights from the helmets moving forward in formation.

Farrugia was following in after the man in front of him, his hand on the man's shoulder.

Up ahead he saw a woman start to stand, her arm coming up with a gun in her hand. She was pointing it at a recumbent Litrico, who was locked inside a cage. In that instant, Farrugia knew there would be no cease and desist warning.

Two shots were fired—one to her chest and one to her head.

In the perfunctory aftermath, after the chorus of calm voices saying "clear" and "check," Farrugia surveyed the narrow kill zone.

The clock on the wall, frozen to Bologna time, 1969, provoked his own instinct to check his watch. He saw the seconds racing on. He had forgotten to push the button once the rescue had ended. His watch was inaccurate, but he estimated that the operation from van doors to now had ticked in at less than three minutes.

Litrico was weak, disoriented, and whisked away like a child to an ambulance.

A team member had announced to the rest of them that the bookseller had been taken alive.

Farrugia nodded in numbness. He heard a metallic and plastic sound. The dead woman was being zipped up in a blue-black body bag.

The last thing of her that Farrugia saw was the flash of a white ankle and the flat wedge of a black pump.

Bianca chewed on her fingernail. She loathed the habit, but she was anxious while her query ran. The only thing Farese had in common with Brooks Sr. was that they were both Catholic, which amounted to nothing, really. Farese did not tithe, belonged to no Catholic organizations and, other than the time she had met him in Rome, had never been to that city, and while he was in Rome, had never visited the Vatican or walked into St. Peter's.

Her query involved comparing dates and transactions between Brooks Sr.'s monies received and transferred between Milan and Rome, as well as Adastra consulting fees, cross-referenced with Farese's financial history in the same time period. It was a time-consuming query, with possible combinations increasing geometrically with the number of accounts involved. Two cups of coffee later, she still was not seeing any results. She was thinking of aborting the query and exploring her other theory: his political aspirations, seeing whether he was seeking or planning to seek office. Every political candidate must deal with special interest groups and make trade-offs to get funding. He had started off Democrat and then switched to Republican.

The hourglass turned over and over on her screen, the sands of digital time emptying and filling.

The IM screen popped up.

"U need 2 stop."

"Y?" Bianca typed.

"Dead end. Ur dead end."

"Farese?"

Loki's avatar went full-screen as a female version of the Norse trickster, eyes blinking, with nice gloves on the hands. Bianca watched the avatar pull off one glove and throw it down. Interesting, a completely pissed off 3-D avatar.

"Forget Farese," Loki answered, and the avatar wagged its finger *no-no*.

Bianca typed with intensity. "Farese: No tie 2 Sr.; no tie 2 AA, but there has to be an F-connection: Palme & Fortuyn, 86 & 02, & now RP."

"Drop it," Loki responded, her avatar minimizing and turning male.

"& Sr.'s symbol, the sword & book?"

"Merely a symbol. Subject to conjecture. Untraceable 2 Farese or AA."

Bianca thought about it. Loki was right about that, but she had financials between Brooks and Adastra. She saw in the windowpane that Loki was typing. She waited.

"Want advice? . . . as a friend . . . personal advice?"

Bianca typed, "Why do U care?"

"I do but this is a matter of—"

"What? National security? U know that—"

"Trust. U need 2 trust me on this." And with that Loki's avatar's eyebrows arched. It was a plea.

"What do I do?" Bianca replied.

"Give me what you have & get a good night's sleep. Check hd in AM & take it 2 GdF." Loki's answer instructed her to hand over her work, trust her, retrieve the results in the morning from the computer's harddrive and go to the *Guardia di Finanza's* office.

"Hint of some kind, please."

Loki's avatar winked and across the screen appeared, "99 & 1 percent."

Loki disappeared, ending their chat. Bianca picked up the phone.

She didn't call Gennaro or Farrugia this time.

She called Dante.

40

Dante knew the smells in the office from experience: chlorine and sweets. The one by itself meant swimming, nothing more, nothing less, but adding in the other meant melancholia. Alessandro was depressed.

When Alessandro wanted to think, when he really wanted to stretch his mind, he did not evolve—he regressed and sought water. In Rome he had done thousands of laps in the Piscina delle Rose over the years. Milan had proven somewhat frustrating until the Caimi swimming pool was rescued from blight and decay. Every now and then Alessandro went off to the Porta Romana quarter to think, and he swam and swam under the chlorinated blue water with his tall, thin body, swimming trunks, goggles strapped to his blonde head over his green eyes. He swam until his mind had become clear as water and he had forgotten his troubles, forgotten that he had been born in the hills of Tuscany and had returned to the sea.

Sandro was at the desk eating one of those living breakfasts from Parco Sempione. He had evolved this morning, all right, from water to land, from piscina pleasure to modern mammal in the office, behind the desk, drowning his brain with sugar.

"What is bothering you, Sandro?"

"Nothing."

It would be Paola. "I understand if you don't want to talk about it, but I'm here if you do."

Alessandro crumpled up the wax paper. "I broke up with Paola," he said with his mouth full.

"I'm sorry to hear that. I know it is a cliché, but you'll recover with time."

Alessandro threw the paper at the trashcan. It bounced off the side and rolled into the middle of the office. "I was excited this time. I just didn't realize I couldn't trust her. I showed her Lele's death certificate and the *allegati* on one of the assassins because I thought I could get her opinion. Gennaro had asked me my opinion, and I was at a loss."

He walked over and picked up the missed ball of wax paper. "I was confused that nobody had thought to pursue the fingerprint match. The form said it right there that there was a match, but I guess with all the commotion . . . I shared it with her, talked to her about it, and the next thing I know a copy of both documents is with Giancarlo Ragonese. I have no luck with women. None. First in Rome and now here."

"Sometimes what you think is bad might actually save you from something worse."

"Something worse? I'm sure Gennaro doesn't trust me now. If word gets out that I—"

"You're worrying too much. Gennaro wouldn't jeopardize your career."

Alessandro shrugged. "How about you and Bianca? Do you trust each other?"

Dante wanted to answer, "I trust her," but there was a knock on the door.

The man from Receivables jutted his head through the opened door.

Alessandro yelled, "Ah, don't tell me it's Ragonese again."

"No. It's Silvio."

"Silvio?" Dante said. "What's wrong with Silvio?"

Receivables answered, "I don't know. I think he is losing his mind."

"What do you mean 'losing his mind'?" Alessandro asked. "I thought he was with Farese this morning at the Embassy. What is Silvio doing?"

"He just keeps saying, '*Preferisco non*' over and over again. In English."

Dante and Alessandro got up and exited their office. By the time they were halfway down the hallway Gennaro was behind them asking, "Is it a medical emergency or is it Ragonese again?"

Alessandro answered, "Silvio is losing his mind."

"Oh," Gennaro answered.

A crowd had gathered around Silvio's desk, a temporary desk Perego had assigned to him since it had been thought that Silvio would not be spending as much time in the office if he were to be acting as Farese's personal interpreter. But with Farese at the Embassy most of the time, where he needed no translator, and the request from Lodi for copies of the Lele reports, which Perego had delegated to him, it had been assumed that Silvio had cracked, somewhere between the latest emulator malfunction and translating Italian into his approximation of English.

Silvio sat as stoic as Marcus Aurelius in his chair, behind his desk, hands folded like an altar boy. His attire betrayed no mental destitution. The shirt was beautifully ironed. The tie matched his suit, and his hair was combed. Silvio looked like Silvio. Except more serene.

In front of him, however, was the enraged Human Resources representative. The office gathered around to watch these two engaged in verbal combat. The HR rep, not knowing a word of English, had been screaming in Italian, while Silvio had been answering in simple English, simple coherent English.

The HR representative asked in Italian, "What do you mean you didn't fill out the job description?"

"I prefer not to."

"Why? Is there something wrong with the form?" the HR rep asked.

"I prefer not to."

"Everybody has to fill out the form. It's policy!"

"I prefer not to."

"Give me one good reason why you shouldn't fill out the form?"

"I prefer not to."

The Human Resources representative surveyed the crowd for an explanation, for some assistance. He surveyed others, then to Alessandro, Dante, and Gennaro. Farrugia had just arrived and had caught only the exchange between HR and Silvio. "What is happening?" he whispered to Dante.

Before Dante could even shrug, the HR rep said in desperate Italian, "You're his friends. You worked with him in Rome. Talk some sense into him."

The crowd parted for Perego. "What is the meaning of all this?"

Perego stared at Silvio, who continued to keep his hands folded, the same serene expression on his face, and then at the HR rep, papers in hand, and pink-faced.

"He won't fill out the form," the HR rep said.

"What form?" Perego asked.

"Job description form, the one from Central Administration."

Perego turned to Silvio and asked, "Silvio, why won't you fill out the form?"

"I prefer not to."

Perego said to the HR rep, "Are those the other descriptions?"

"Yes, sir. All of them are there except his and yours."

Perego thumbed through all the forms, glanced over a few of them. He walked over to the shredder, inserted the papers in and watched them sink down into the mechanical teeth, and turned off the machine when it was finished.

The mortified HR rep asked Perego, "Don't tell me you've gone crazy like him?"

"Him? He's the wisest man in the room. I'm going back to my office. Anything else?"

"But why?" the HR rep asked. "You shredded all of them. Why? Tell me why?"

Perego answered, "I prefer not to," and walked away.

"Excuse me," said one of the office men to Farrugia, holding a box. "Yes."

"I have this box for you. One of the leads from API had this sent over. They said they found it at the crime scene and thought you would be interested."

Gennaro saw the box. "The *Antiterrorismo Pronto Impiego* sent this?"

"Yes."

"What is it?" Farrugia asked.

"Books," the man said as Gennaro took the box and thanked him.

Gennaro held the box while Farrugia pried the lid off.

"What is it?"

"Books, like the man said, Gennaro, but wait . . ."

"What is it?"

"It's a shipping invoice to some church in the United States. Virginia. Addressed to . . . Charles Brooks, Sr."

Bianca checked her computer in the morning. The computer's hard drive had a zipped file that was categorized into two folders, AA and F. Adastra and Farese. She opened up the Adastra file folder. Numerous spreadsheets, formatted with Germanic thoroughness: all the cells in each of the sheets had comments and the workbooks were hyperlinked to other sheets and workbooks, which in turn were linked to each other within the file directory.

The beauty of numbers is that they do not lie. Money does not lie.

Each section, whether it was Adastra or Farese, was an auditor's dream. No matter where an auditor started in these files, everything was logical and inter-connected. The hyper-reality of a corrupt financial enterprise was often self-referential, confusing, and tautological. Loki had recreated a logical universe of dollars and euros, routing numbers and pathways from the United States to Italy, with stops along the way in offshore accounts and banking houses throughout Europe and Asia. Adastra was a multinational virus like the mafia, with tentacles everywhere and in everything. Like a tobacco company, Adastra diversified across numerous industries, from household goods to real estate to owning multiple-media channels.

Lele had seen the future: a corporation without borders, without laws in place to check its growth. Lele had anticipated the multinational corporation as terrorist, and not just for its development of a tank that used specialized software to identify and kill enemy soldiers on the field.

As she examined the files, she saw how Loki had attenuated her own work, integrated it with new data and packaged it into a coherent presentation. Bianca took out two jumpkeys, duplicated Adastra to one and Farese to the other. She labeled the Farese jumpkey with an *F*. The other key she did not label.

After she checked out of the hotel, she'd find herself a nice high-end cyber-café, print out a copy of the Adastra files, and have it bound for the *Guardia di Finanza*. She had spoken to Dante about a time to meet for lunch with the team, but only after she had apologized for not having told him that she had checked into another hotel the night after they had met Paola.

Bianca had explained her suspicions and that she did not want to risk the G9 visiting her. She had predicted somebody would visit the apartment.

She had told him. "That's a no-brainer."

He had agreed. In fact, he had been very understanding.

Three things bothered her, though, about the files from Loki. The connection between Adastra and Gruppo 9, Farese's role, and the unexpected and most peculiar observation of all: while numbers are a universal language, the comments in the Adastra file directory were in Italian.

Comments in the Farese file directory . . . in English.

41

Alessandro, Dante, Gennaro, and Farrugia had put on their jackets and were waiting for the elevator when Perego came over and asked them, "Where are all of you going?"

Gennaro spoke for the group, "We were thinking of grabbing lunch. There is an exquisite restaurant over at—"

"Sorry to kill your appetite, but you're going to a meeting with me. In fact, all of you are coming to a meeting with me." Perego appeared as if he had no interest in lunch.

Dante sputtered. "But—"

"I don't want to hear 'I prefer not to' from you. I prefer not to myself, but this meeting is with the regional commissioner, Farese, IA, and I'm sure that God Himself will be there, too. That reminds me, somebody tell Silvio that his services will be required."

"The Commissioner?" Gennaro said.

"What about my union rep?" Farrugia asked.

"Forget your union rep, Farrugia," Perego said.

"You seem worried, Lino," Gennaro said.

"I am. The Commissioner is best heard and not seen, and when he wants to see you it is not a good omen. You thought you had it bad getting transferred from Rome to here? We might all be sharing an office in Portugal, with the Belgians organizing the office move, the Germans paying for our relocation, and our salary coming from Greece, while the HR Policy Manual remains Double Dutch. I need to get my jacket."

"But I was supposed to meet my girlfriend for lunch."

"You live nearby. Call her. Bring her along. I don't care."

Good thing Bianca understood punctuality. She was waiting in the lobby with a large bound document in a sturdy plastic bag. Dante whispered into her ear what Gennaro had told him about the box that Farrugia had received before they all went into Perego's car.

It was a quiet ride except for one brief exchange between Bianca and Silvio.

"Thank you for the book, Signora. It was wonderful."

"I'm glad. Have you found a story that you like the best?"

Silvio answered. "Bartleby. I comprehend his incomprehension."

Aldo Giurlani—the Commissioner and not the writer—was a man to be feared. He spoke little. He was an avowed atheist who did not afford those in his presence the consolation of a crucifix on the wall, although they might have wished for God's presence. He had a disconcerting habit of letting those in front of him speak at length. It might easily be mistaken for politeness, until the hapless victims realized he would eviscerate them with their own words. Giurlani was a Florentine with a Sicilian's unforgiving memory, a dangerous combination.

Farese met them in the antechamber to Giurlani's office. When Perego suggested that Bianca wait outside, Farese said he did not mind her presence. And when Perego insisted that she had no official capacity to be present, Farese insisted and reminded Perego that she had helped in the Roma Underground scandal. Bianca had asked Farese and Perego to introduce her as a secretary and say nothing more. Dante seemed confused. When Perego tried one last time, she interrupted him, handed him her bag, just as Giurlani's secretary came out and said the Commissioner was ready to see them. She led, and the men followed.

They stood before Giurlani. To one side of the room was Ettore Brambilla from the Ministry of Internal Affairs with Farrugia's interrogator, the head of Ballistics, the CSU Team Lead from the Lele scene, the Lodi Police Chief, and a lawyer from the Free Channel.

This group came over and introduced themselves to the Guardia di

Finanza team while Giurlani watched all of them. Bianca was introduced to all of these men as a secretary. She stood to the far left in front of Giurlani's desk.

His eyes went from left to right, from the Finanza staff to the mixed bunch of everyone else. "Good, we all know each other now. As for me, you know my name and I'll assume you know my reputation. I am a man of evidence and I'm searching for an explanation. Let me recite the evidence. I have a young American from a reputable family murdered in an alleyway. I have a respectable inspector on a vacation that just happens to be there. The ballistics report mentions bullets that remind the nation of a murder from over thirty years ago. I have the media declaring the inspector a hero one moment and a coward the next. I have the inspector's statement that he did not discharge his weapon. I'm not a ballistics expert, but even I can discern a 9mm bullet fired by a Beretta *Raffica* from a Gévelot."

Giurlani was moving some file folders as he spoke. Not a word was said from the other side of the table, except for Silvio murmuring to Farese. Giurlani scanned his visitors, this time from the right side of the desk to the left.

"I have an esteemed politician found dead in a car, an autopsy report that says 'misadventure,' and statements from American hikers taken down in Italian by the CSU. Excellent." A file folder landed with a slapping sound.

"I have supplemental notes related to the autopsies on the two Manzoni assassins, which the media somehow said had a fingerprint match, but had been neglected. Excellent for our reputation." Another file folder hit the desk.

"I have a bookseller under arrest. I have his confession. He says that he and his girlfriend were members of Gruppo 9. I have the CSU Team Lead's identification of her from her post-mortem as one of the hikers. Her boyfriend, the bookseller, is the other hiker. Things are improving. The boyfriend's confession goes a long way to explaining the politician's death. They were paid to make it look scandalous, but he won't say by whom, how much, or when."

Giurlani held up the document containing the confession and set it aside. "He gave us names, places of G9 meetings, and so forth and so on. We can have endless hours of fun arresting G9 members. All well and good, don't you think? He is just what this country needs—another *penitente.*"

Giurlani plopped down another file folder.

"I have requests from Internal Affairs as to why Commissario Farrugia was on vacation, why he was at Bar Gadda on Via Manzoni, why he was at the bookstore, and, most recently, why the bookseller's girlfriend, a G9 member, was killed outright and not taken alive. I have never seen such a use of the interrogative and yet no answers. But, I have her autopsy report. For the life of me I don't understand why cinnamon was found on the soles of her shoes." The man set aside the autopsy report.

"These are the facts I have," he said, pointing to all the files. "Now I'd like them explained. And please think before you talk, because I have little patience today."

Silvio finished translating for Farese. The room was silent again. Nobody uttered a word. Some of the men searched for patterns in the rug while others hoped that someone would break the silence.

"Signora?" Giurlani asked in polite Italian.

"Yes, Commissioner Giurlani," she answered in Italian.

"It is my experience—and this is years of experience—that the secretary usually knows everything. Also, as I learned in dealing with the mafia, the person who shows up at the meeting unannounced and unknown to almost everyone else in the room is usually the one who knows everything. It seems to me that you are likely to know twice what the men in this room know, and three times more than me. Perhaps you have an explanation that will enlighten me. Please tell me if you know something."

Bianca had arrived at the clichéd point of no return. She knew what she had to do and that her Italian was about to be put to the test. She understood Silvio in a new way, respected the journey he had made from Italian to English, since she had been doing the reverse since her arrival in Italy. A spy had once said that you have two souls when you learn another language. Well, in English, she was Alabaster Black. In Italian she was Bianca Nerini.

In Italian they'd say, "Into the wolf's mouth." *In bocca al lupo*. The response is not polite: *Crepi il lupo!* May the wolf croak!

She swallowed. *Here goes it.*

She glanced at the Commissioner and explained Brooks Jr.'s having worked for Adastra and how he had discovered the tank. How he had initially thought he could impress his father, a tank veteran, with information and a schematic of the tank, and how the young man might have discovered the special anti-personnel software.

"And you have proof of this?" Giurlani asked.

"I have the schematic and documents from Brooks Jr."

"How did you obtain these documents?"

"He slipped them into my pocket when I met with him. Commissario Farrugia was my backup."

Brambilla stepped forward to say something, but Giurlani raised his hand. "You'll have your turn. Wait. Mind your manners and let the lady finish. Now, you were saying that Farrugia was your backup. Were you conducting an investigation then?"

"It didn't start out that way. I'm just a secretary, a mere consultant, you know, and I took the call from this distressed young man. Since Commissario Farrugia and I had worked in Rome, I felt comfortable asking him for his assistance. It evolved into an undercover investigation."

Dante was stunned. He had known that Bianca's Italian was good, more than just passable, but he was seeing her command of the language in a new light now. He was impressed and he was proud.

Giurlani asked Perego, "Is this true?"

Perego glimpsed at Bianca and then to Farrugia, who was looking down at the rug.

Giurlani asked again, "Is this true?"

Perego cleared his throat. "Yes, Commissioner. It became a secret operation, as she said."

Giurlani moved in his chair. "Unfortunately, things had gone awry. Signora, what else came of your investigation?"

Bianca explained the financial forensics that tied Brooks Sr. to Adastra and that Adastra had been laundering money through Milanese and Vatican banks. She added that Adastra had been funding the G9 and that Adastra had received cash infusions from some of the wealthiest Italians in the country, from their companies, and had made contributions to all the political parties, including the L&S.

"The wealthiest in the country?" Giurlani asked.

"The top one percent."

"And have you any proof of this?"

"Mr. Perego has the detailed reports with all the financial data. I can provide you with an electronic copy of those reports."

Giurlani motioned for Perego to come forward. Perego moved forward with the bag rustling. He reached into the bag and hoisted the bound volume onto Giurlani's desk.

Giurlani contemplated the height of the pages. He said to Bianca, "You have any idea what this report will do?"

Bianca paused. "Thin out the one percent, I would imagine."

Giurlani offered what was rarely associated with him: a smile. "Even if a percentage of that one percent ever saw the inside of a courtroom, this country would see another summer of suicides. I'm impressed with this undercover work. The assassins?"

Bianca answered, "G9."

Giurlani's hand toyed with his lips. "Hmm, I'd think those two would have been rather sophisticated for small fries like the G9. Any foreign involvement?"

Bianca looked over at Farese. "No. There was none."

"American investors in Adastra?"

Bianca turned her head back to Giurlani. "Yes."

"American one percent, perhaps?"

"Perhaps."

Giurlani moved the mammoth volume to one side of his desk. He folded his hands and looked at the two groups. "I'll assume that the Ballistics Department was a little overzealous. Any objections from Ballistics?"

A voice said, "None."

"Good," Giurlani said. "Now to the matter of Raffaele Palmisano; I would like for the Signora to rest her voice and let one of the men talk. Someone care to explain to me why I don't have leads, any suspects, in Lele's death?"

Gennaro stepped forward but Giurlani raised his hand. Gennaro stepped back in line. Giurlani had pulled a file folder from the stack and read the documentation in front of him.

"Since Internal Affairs was so kind as to interrogate Commissario Farrugia with enthusiasm," he said, "I'd like for them to explain why the Lodi Police Department refused DiBello and Farrugia access to L&S party members."

The Lodi Police Chief stepped forward, "I object, Commissioner."

"On what grounds?"

"Your implications. We were not obstructing justice. It was a matter of territory."

Giurlani smiled again. "Territory? But Milan had the Palmisano case before you. They hadn't had the names of the L&S members at the time to conduct interviews or even establish their timeline. Why object?"

The Lodi chief, not accustomed to being in any kind of hot seat, was turning red. "It was an upsetting experience. We were trying to respect the wishes of the Campanelli family who had hosted the L&S get-together, Commissioner."

"Don't you mean The Last Supper?"

The police chief's face blossomed red as a rose. "Milan had already botched it up."

"Botched what? They were doing their job. Somebody in Ballistics had leaked the information to the Free Channel. How is that Milan's fault? Furthermore, why didn't you at least extend the courtesy of sharing the investigation?"

The police chief stared off at space. "We were respecting the privacy of the Campanelli family. Her husband is quite ill and—"

Giurlani dropped the deadly courtesy for the first time since they'd entered the room. "Bullshit! Her husband was in the hospital and she was home hosting a party. How concerned was she? A man is dead. These guests stayed overnight in her house. You tell me her husband was sick, and yet the entire country knows she is seeding the ground for a political comeback."

There was a long pause.

"Tell you what I think," Giurlani said, the politeness back in place. "And I'll say this as mere speculation. I hope there is no fiscal connection between Gaspara Campanelli and your department, or with you personally. No donations, no public-relations garbage. But I'll let Brambilla assess that situation for me. I look forward to their report exonerating you. Assuming it does. Understood?"

"Yes, Commissioner."

Giurlani opened a file folder. "Lele and the death certificate. I would not dare to dispute Dr. Primo Foà. Besides, the G9 bookseller confessed to staging the post-mortem scene. The confession says they'd compelled the man to masturbate after they had force-fed him Viagra. I would like to know where his nitroglycerine pills were, since Foà cites a heart condition and the manifest says there were no pills in the container. I'd hate to think they are with Signora Campanelli's husband, but that is pure fantasy, isn't it? Mr. Palmisano was, in essence, murdered. A fine scandal if it were to get into the media, which brings me to our beloved orator, Giancarlo Ragonese, and his television show. How did Ragonese get the death certificate and the fingerprint match mentioned on one of the assassins?"

Everyone in the room gazed at the lawyer from the Free Channel.

He answered, without a moment's hesitation, "Journalistic privilege."

Giurlani stared at the man, paused, "'Journalistic privilege,' eh? I'll indulge you and say that Giancarlo Ragonese is one of the finest journalists of our generation, but strangely that answer doesn't satisfy me. Please try again."

"A reliable source within police ranks."

"Wonderful. Could you please be more specific?"

The lawyer said, "Guardia di Finanza."

Giurlani turned his head to Perego. "Your thoughts?"

Gennaro stepped forward. "I can explain."

"No, let me," Alessandro said, stepping forward with his hand across Gennaro's chest, signaling that Gennaro should step back.

"You have something to say?" Giurlani asked.

"I do. I was told about the bullets. I was also given a copy of the autopsy report and fingerprint match, and asked for my opinion. I shared them with my girlfriend. She leaked the information to the Free Channel. I take full responsibility."

Giurlani studied Alessandro and asked, politely, "Is this girlfriend within the Guardia di Finanza?"

"No. She is a ballistics expert from Bergamo. Ex-girlfriend, Commissioner."

"That certainly explains both of our leaks. I don't know what you were thinking or whether you were thinking at all, Mr. Monotti, but at least you're the first one in this menagerie who has owned up to his actions."

"May I say something, Commissioner?" Gennaro said.

"You don't have to, Gennaro," Alessandro said.

"But I do, Sandro. Commissioner? I did give the papers to Mr.

Monotti, but I had already suspected there was a leak, and that it was with Ballistics, so I copied Lele's document as is, but altered the one on the assassin. There was no fingerprint match. I'm sure that when you find the original amongst all those files on your desk you'll see there was no match."

Giurlani, who knew where everything was on his desk, located the file, pulled the piece of paper out and handed it to the Free Channel lawyer. "Your beloved Ragonese accepted documents without corroboration. You do know the laws concerning libel and slander?"

The lawyer handed the paper back.

The police chief stepped forward. "I have a complaint."

"Do you now?" Giurlani asked.

"I received the copies from the Guardia di Finanza, and they are worthless. How will my department proceed with our investigation?"

"Worthless? How?" Giurlani asked.

"It's practically a box of empty paper. Their secretary is useless."

Giurlani's eyebrows went up, and he nodded at Bianca. "I doubt that this Signora is incompetent, sir. If anyone is—"

Silvio broke from his translating but stayed in English, presumably from momentum. "She did nothing wrong! The emulator preferred not to emulate."

The room went silent.

The police chief asked, "What did he say? What does that mean?"

"Don't you even understand a little bit of English?" Giurlani glanced at the man. "He said the copier wasn't working right."

He closed a file folder and told them they were all excused, except Bianca. The men left and Bianca asked for Farese to wait for her outside in the hallway.

"Signora?"

"Yes?"

"I know all the names in the Guardia di Finanza except yours." Giurlani put his hand out. "Never mind. I wanted to thank you."

"For what?"

"You've accomplished more than I have in my entire career. A woman like you should be the one sitting in this office."

42

Farese was waiting for Bianca outside in the hallway with Silvio. She asked Silvio for a few moments alone with the U.S. Attorney, since this conversation would be in English.

"That was impressive what you did in there," Farese said.

"You mean my telling only half of the story?"

"I don't know what you mean?"

"Numbers tell the truth, but not if you don't have all the numbers. Giurlani's report doesn't talk about your part in the equation."

"Care to elaborate?" he said with a studied politeness Giurlani would have found familiar.

"The Giurlani report doesn't talk about how Adastra is one of the primary funding sources for your future political career. You plan to run on the Republican ticket. I won't ask for what office since we both know that. The report doesn't connect Adastra U.S. with Adastra S.r.l., but there is enough with Adastra Italia and the G9 to keep the judicial system busy. The report doesn't point to any interference between the U.S. government and L&S and the G9, but we know better. The report also leaves those two assassins as the great mystery because anyone with half a brain will know they weren't G9. But we know that, don't we, Michael?"

Farese paused. "You know, even if I weren't running for office this would've probably happened."

She smiled. "Idealism always gets you killed, in romance and in the real world."

Farese said nothing at first. Then, "What do you want?"

Bianca pulled the jump key out of her pocket. "Giurlani's jump key is different from this one. This one is labeled *F*, and we both know why.

You find a way for Adastra to kill that project of theirs, and by that I mean kill their software. I couldn't give a damn about the tank. I don't care how you do it, but do it."

Farese smiled, "And if I don't?"

"You know what'll happen, Michael. Don't be naïve."

"I'm a lawyer, Alabaster. Part of the game is to see the play in motion."

She studied his face. "It's been a long time since anyone called me by my real name. Since you need for me to spell it out for you, I will. If you don't stop Adastra's software, what is on this jumpkey will go viral, and that other one percent, the one in the United States, will not be very happy, and you won't be on any posters for any political office. If that doesn't work, then a box of books from a certain bookstore in Milan to a certain church in Virginia could be made public. For now, it's tucked away somewhere safe."

Farese's eyes examined the floor. "Cost of doing business. Fair enough. How do I know we can trust each other?"

She smiled, "You don't. Trust is irrational, a leap of faith."

"You know that Charlie Brooks Sr. will never be indicted."

"I know that, but I also know that even if the press sees only one-tenth of Giurlani's report, Mr. Brooks Sr. will never step foot in Italy again, even if the Pope invited him to a private mass."

"You have a point. You know someone might construe you as patriotic, since you protected your government."

"It's not patriotism. I'm practical. I know that nobody can stop the U.S. government when it comes to money or maintaining power. *Strategia della tensione.*"

"I'll assume you'll say that Lele taught you that."

"No, Michael. I learned that long ago. You just reinforced what I already knew. I did learn some crucial details along the way."

"I should go. Silvio is waiting for me." Farese started to walk away from her.

"Oh, Michael."

"Yes?"

Bianca walked the few short steps over to him. "One last thing. I want to meet Mrs. Brooks before she leaves the Embassy. Just her. I have no use for her husband."

43

Back at the office, the elevator ride was quiet. At the office level, Perego held the door open for Bianca. He asked for a word alone with her.

"Yes?" she asked.

"Thank you. I don't know how you did all that, and it's probably best that I didn't know. I'm just worried about one thing. What if Giurlani or anyone in that office tries to research you?"

"Just as in Rome, they'll see that I'm listed as a consultant. They'll find I get paid just like everybody else." She knew there was an untraceable money trail to a bank in Rome, untraceable because she never touched the money. No profit, no connection to services rendered.

Perego thanked her again and went to his office.

Dante whistled as the team retired to Gennaro and Farrugia's office. Claudio had been waiting in the office for Farrugia. Bianca had joined them.

Everyone was settled into chairs. Claudio was apprised of all that happened at Giurlani's office, the exchanges, with Alessandro mimicking Giurlani's voice and how he had shot down the Lodi police chief and then the Free Channel lawyer.

Dante said, "I couldn't believe that Giurlani knew what Silvio meant by emulator." They laughed.

Gennaro asked Bianca, "What about you and Farese? You two have a talk?"

"We did. Nothing important."

"Bianca?" Claudio asked. "Do you have that paper from the other night? The one that had the riddle."

"I'm sorry, Claudio. I don't. Why?"

"I thought we had solved that," Alessandro said.

Claudio said, "Yeah, you're right. It's probably nothing."

Bianca was smiling, "Don't be like that, Claudio. We were all talking English that night, so was it something that you didn't understand, but were afraid to ask about? C'mon, tell us."

"She's right," Dante said. "Don't be embarrassed. She corrects my English all the time. Hey, it's the only way you're going to learn, right?"

Farrugia joined the fun. "You can always ask Silvio to translate for you."

Claudio got up and closed the door and returned to his seat. He leaned forward and clasped his hands together, rubbed them and said, "You guys told me how Silvio talked about *madrelingua* and the hikers and all that . . . well, I got to thinking about my own confusion. I kept asking 'Why an elf?' and 'I thought little birds told secrets' and why *ocean* and not *oyster* because the riddle said the 'world is their ocean,' and I kept thinking it should be 'world is our oyster' and . . ."

Alessandro asked, "And what?"

"I don't know. I'm being silly, but I was thinking that maybe this elf is Italian."

Dante said, "I prefer not to," and the boys in the room started laughing. Everyone except Bianca. She took in the laughter but time stood still for her because all she could think was that all the notes in the Giurlani spreadsheets were in Italian. Perfect, too perfect, Italian. The Farese file directory was in English, and when had she first met Loki?

Rome.

She thought of the red *R*. She thought, Rendition. She thought, *tentacles.*

44

Farrugia rested on his mat, the lights dimmed overhead. His blanket was pulled up; his shoulder blades were spreading. Relaxation. He could finally enjoy a vacation. Perego had called Rome and explained the "undercover work," and since his manager had already been hearing about Farrugia in the press and hoping for the worst, he had no choice but to concede that the time Farrugia had spent in Milan since his arrival there had been for work. Therefore, his real vacation should start now. Effective immediately.

Litrico had joined him for the yoga class. Claudio was next to Litrico. Farrugia could not find a spot for all of them to be together.

"*Shavasana*. Final relaxation," Noelle said in her calming voice. "Relax and let it all go. Let your body feel rejuvenated, feel refreshed." She walked softly around the room, narrating the conclusion to the class. "You have given yourself a gift, call it what you wish, but it is yours. *Namaste*. Absolute peace and release."

Farrugia's eyes squinted as he watched her pass by, refusing to deny that he liked what he saw: dark, luxuriant curls, a petite ballerina's body, a nice nose, and since she had walked past him in previous classes he had come to admire her feet. And he had thought that feet were the least attractive part of the human body.

"Go deep into your breath and let your fears and worries disappear. Give yourself permission to release and forget this afternoon, this morning, yesterday, and the past. Allow only this moment. Open yourself up to this present moment," she said, and Farrugia found himself smiling. He could forgive some weight. His own. He could accept imperfection. He might even enjoy Milan and get around to planning Gennaro's retirement party. Gennaro retired in a few months. Farrugia was determined to make sure that Gennaro received a great party.

Farrugia sat up; the class sat up, one by one. There was always some-one who fell asleep in corpse pose. Farrugia thought it was funny the first time, but now he understood. The class faced Noelle, and Farrugia felt alive, refreshed and rejuvenated, just as she said, and everyone chanted "Om" three times. It was the cosmic syllable of creation and Farrugia absorbed the vibratory power of the mantra in his trunk, on his tongue, through his teeth, and out his lips.

"Om."

The class began to dissolve, with people rolling up their mats, fold-ing over their blankets, collecting props and straps, and returning all of them to the storage rooms at the side of the studio. Mats were dropped into vertical pigeonholes. Blocks were shelved and blankets stacked. Straps were placed in a pile. Farrugia had put his props away and, seeing that Litrico had been kind enough to take his own and Claudio's over, he decided to walk over and talk to him.

"Claudio?"

"Yes, Isidò."

"I was wondering whether you were free tonight for dinner."

Claudio hesitated. "Oh, I'm sorry but I've already made other plans. Litrico had asked me out."

"He has?"

"I contacted him and we talked. It was rocky at first, but I told him I admired Lele. We talked and I offered to help him with planning the funeral and the memorial services. I mentioned yoga, and when he real-ized that I know you he relaxed and I guess that was a good sign."

"Oh, I understand. Maybe some other time then?"

Litrico returned, and Farrugia watched the two of them head for the clear glass doors hand in hand.

Farrugia heard a voice from behind him. "They make a nice couple, don't they?"

It was Noelle. "I guess they do, don't they?"

"Are you friends with them? Are you . . . ?"

"No. No. Not that there is anything wrong with . . . I just didn't know that Claudio was—"

Noelle smiled. "I thought it was obvious."

"I'm Isidore Farrugia."

"I know. You're *the* Commissario Isidore Farrugia."

He blushed.

"I haven't eaten so if you . . ."

Ah, Isidò, that gut instinct is good this time. That hair, her eyes, and that voice . . . ah, you're still young.

The team sat in Gennaro and Farrugia's office. Mid-morning break. Silvio participated in the banter.

He was even speaking Italian again, taking a break after all his interpreting work with Farese. Everyone found it odd hearing him in Italian after so long.

Dante threw a paper airplane, and Farrugia accepted advice from Alessandro about women, since he had said he had a second date planned with Noelle.

"Milanese women are different," Alessandro was saying. "What the hell, Dante?" He picked Dante's paper airplane out of his hair.

"Stay away from Bergamo," Gennaro said. They all burst out laughing.

Just then Perego walked in. The room became quiet.

"What? Why so quiet? I'm not an undertaker and I'm sure as hell not Pinolo. I'm just here to drop something off for Gennaro."

"What is it that I can do for you, Lino?"

"Not for me," Perego said. "From Giurlani."

They all stopped laughing.

"I guess he must have heard that you were retiring, Gennaro, because he sent me these papers. Here." Perego handed Gennaro the envelope.

"What is it, Chief?" Alessandro asked.

"Internal Affairs?" Farrugia asked.

Gennaro shook his head and kept reading.

"What is it, Boss?" Dante asked.

"I don't know whether that is what you wanted before you retired, but the decision is yours," Perego said. "I'll support you either way, Gennaro. Your choice."

"Thank you, Lino."

Just as Perego was about to leave he said, "Have you heard?"

"What?" Alessandro asked.

"Ragonese is reporting the weather now, and Gaspara Campanelli is head of the L&S. She's running on a law-and-order platform. Tough as nails, and the polls are up, north and south."

Nobody laughed. They watched Perego leave the room.

"What is it, Gennaro?" Farrugia asked.

"Giurlani is asking whether I'd consider transferring to do a special investigation for him. My decision."

Alessandro threw the pencil across his desk. "Aw, mother of God, another transfer. Unbelievable."

"Calm down, Sandro. It's my choice, and Giurlani says here in this letter that I can take the whole team with me if I like, and that even includes Silvio."

"Where to, Boss?" Dante asked.

Gennaro put the paper on the desk, realizing how life came full circle. "Naples. The Totaro family. Camorra."

The room became quiet. Ominously quiet.

"What will you do?" Silvio asked. "Will we stay or go?"

45

The American Embassy was on Via Principe Amedeo. Ironic and appropriate, she thought, since Amedeo is Italian for "lover of God," and America certainly does love God, the Old Testament version. Giò Ponti designed the Montecatini Building, where the State Department conducted diplomatic business. The building overlooked the Piazza Stati Uniti d'America in downtown Milan.

She was waiting for Farese. Her cell rang. She checked the caller ID; it was Dante.

Farese was walking towards her.

"I don't have time, Dante," she said, but then a second later really heard his question. "What do you mean 'how do I feel about Naples?' I've got to go." She closed the lid of the phone.

"She's inside," Farese said. "You have about ten minutes."

"Thanks."

Mrs. Brooks was seated in a chair staring vacantly out the window. An elegant woman, she was past fifty, unafraid to grow her hair below the shoulders, dark blonde hair that still held a curl and some vitality. She had maintained a nice figure and wore next to no makeup except some modest lipstick and eyeliner. Her eyes betrayed her state of mind.

"Mrs. Brooks?"

"I'm so sorry. I didn't hear you come in. You are?"

"Bianca."

"You speak English. I'm relieved," Mrs. Brooks said, inviting Bianca to sit down.

"I won't take up too much of your time."

"Please stay. I feel like a prisoner here. I don't know the language, and my husband is in perpetual meetings. I assume the meetings are about what happened to our son and . . . I'm sorry to ramble and speak only about myself. Do you work here?"

"No, I don't. I'm sorry for your loss."

Mrs. Brooks smiled and looked down into her hands. Bianca saw a crumpled tissue in them.

"I don't understand why I'm not allowed into these meetings. I've been a military wife for over twenty years. Nobody can tell me a thing about what happened to my boy, and I'm frustrated. I gave birth. I'm not a flower."

Bianca moved her chair so that she was sitting right across from Mrs. Brooks.

"What exactly is your role?" Mrs. Brooks said. "Were you sent to occupy my time? Did my husband send for you?"

"No, Mrs. Brooks. I wasn't sent. I'm an analyst."

"That mean you're CIA?"

Bianca shook her head. Not quite.

"Some other agency?" Mrs. Brooks asked.

"You can say that, but that's not important."

"But you know something about my son's death."

Bianca nodded. She could see the woman's eyes well.

"Did he suffer?"

Bianca shook her head.

"What can you tell me?" Mrs. Brooks said, sniffling and holding back, her eyes trying to be stoical. But the hand holding the tissue trembled.

"I was the last person Charlie saw before he was killed. He trusted me. I didn't know what was going to happen, Mrs. Brooks. You won't hear about me in the news or find me mentioned in any reports. I don't exist."

Bianca saw the woman's hand shaking, and Bianca didn't know why, but she placed her hand over the mother's hand and felt the woman place her other hand on top of hers, also trembling. Empathy.

Bianca paused, looking at their hands together. "Charlie trusted me.

He said something to me before he was killed."

"What did he say?"

"Tell Mom I love her and tell Dad I'm sorry."

The mother's hands tightened as they held Bianca's and, as the woman leaned over, Bianca felt tears fall onto her hands.

Afterword

Four Decades of Threads and Needle

By Claudio Ferrara
Journalist, Author, and Translator
Milan

That morning I hadn't understood at first why Signora Ines, the head-mistress, had rushed into our classroom right in the middle of our les-sons with a terrified look on her face. She'd run to our teacher, Signorina Carmen, and whispered something into her ear.

The bright smile of our *maestra* grew dimmer and dimmer while the headmistress kept whispering. While Signora Ines headed back for the door, she rose from her seat and moved from behind her desk to stand in front of it. She addressed us in the quietest tone possible and announced that school was over for the day. She asked whether we had someone waiting for us at home; most of us raised our hands. She divided us into small groups near the door, then into smaller groups by destination and instructed us to hurry home, to keep to the walls along our way and under no circumstance stop or, worse, speak to any adult who was a stranger.

While I was taking my coat off the hook in the corridor, I noticed that Signora Ines was repeating the process in each and every classroom. In a few minutes, the wide Fascist-style hall of the old school building, and then the street, would be teeming with noisy swarms of primary-school pupils—the boys in their black smocks with white collars, the girls in their white blouses; those who had no one at home and all the younger children waited in the schoolyard under the watchful eye of the teachers.

My best buddy from school also happened to live in the same neighborhood where I lived, so we formed our own small group of two. I remember the two of us laughing and joking while we walked our way back home. While all that caution on the part of the headmistress and the teachers *had* struck me as suspicious, it had not unduly; after all, we were two ten-year-olds who had been given a day off on a sunny spring morning, which, under other circumstances, would have been a cause for celebration.

As I looked around on the streets, though, I started realizing that *everybody* seemed to have taken the day off that morning. Weird.

When I arrived home soon after—I lived in a small town—I found my mother sitting in front of the TV. This was very unusual too: turning on the telly before five p.m. was strictly prohibited in my family. And, in any case, the State network RAI—the *only* TV network back then, for that matter—had very little to broadcast during the day.

She too looked sad and concerned. She was watching a special edition of the news. The man on the screen was saying that the Red Brigades, the infamous group of extreme-left terrorists, had kidnapped Aldo Moro, the president of the ruling Christian Democrat party and one of the few beloved politicians in the country. The four policemen of his escort had all been shot dead.

It was March 16, 1978.

In that very moment I finally understood why Signora Ines had had such a look of terror on her face.

Everybody thought the country was on the brink of a civil war, and would continue to think so for the next fifty-five days, until Moro's lifeless body was found in the trunk of a red Renault 4, which had managed to secret itself, by some mysterious means, into the super-patrolled center of Rome in an alley exactly halfway between the respective headquarters of the country's two biggest political parties: the Christian Democratic Party and the Communist Party.

This is what it was like being a child in Italy during the *Anni di Piombo*, the Years of Lead, the bloody trail that blows into existence with a bomb killing seventeen and injuring eighty-eight at Milan's Piazza Fontana on December 12, 1969 and starts fading out of it in 1981 with the blitz that frees U.S. General James L. Dozier from his captors; again the Red Brigades. The year 1984 has come to be considered the official end of the *Anni di Piombo*.

Still cannot figure it out?

Imagine that for fifteen years you sat down to watch the evening news, and every evening you saw the same visual, a person jumping out of the World Trade Center towers, but each evening a different person jumping out to his or her death.

Imagine that, day in and day out.

Every day on the television and in the newspapers, there appears a new name.

Rinse and repeat on the retina.

For an American reader the analogy I just drew to 9/11 is a powerful and upsetting one, but for us Italians it is an approximation of what it was like living during those years, where shock was not limited to one day, but sustained over time. The corrosive and cumulative assault of images of mangled bodies, smoky ruins, assassinations and bombings so shocked the national psyche that, once over, the *Anni di Piombo* would remain a taboo topic for many years.

This is exactly the atmosphere I felt plunged back into when I started reading *Threading the Needle*, with an additional twist from the pervasive presence of the Ragonese-style omnipresent and intrusive media in contemporary society.

"What would I think, what would I *feel*, if a killing like that of Palmisano happened in real life—in *today's* Italy?" I started asking myself while reading.

"I would feel anger and fear," I answered. And, most of all, I would probably think that the *Strategia della Tensione*, the Strategy of Tension, was back.

This is an all too familiar concept for any Italian my age, old enough to remember those lists of the dead on the evening news: the theory that a hidden agenda *stayed behind* apparently spontaneous bursts of terrorism (we'll see in a moment why I put the phrase in italics) with the aim of forcing people to support stricter and stricter law-and-order legislation and even an authoritarian coup, if need be—an agenda that had not been written by those toting the guns—and not necessarily in Italy.

I remember how frustrating it was, years later, trying to explain it to my foreign friends and being frowned upon in response as if I were some kind of conspiracy-theory freak, or as if the Years of Lead had been a sort of Italian specialty, like lasagna or risotto, and, as such, were of no concern to them.

Yet much evidence has been uncovered since then, indeed so much that the Strategy of Tension has been proven to be no conspiracy theory. And very much an imported product.

October 24, 1990: Prime Minister Giulio Andreotti publicly acknowledged on national television the existence of *Gladio*, the Italian branch of a secretive NATO organization called *Stay Behind*.

Shortly after, many others followed. The NATO countries of Denmark, Germany, Greece, the Netherlands, Norway, Portugal, and even the UK all admitted that they had their own Gladios. The non-NATO countries of Austria, Cyprus, Finland, Spain, Sweden, and Switzerland would admit the same.

Stay Behind had initially been conceived after WWII as a rapid-deployment force aimed at starting a guerrilla-style resistance movement in the event of a Soviet invasion of Western Europe. However, all through the McCarthy Era, at the height of the Cold War after the Cuban missile crisis, and right down to the Reagan-Thatcher *Evil Empire* anti-Commie frenzy, it had thrived and evolved into something different.

As demonstrated in the seminal works of Daniele Ganser, *NATO's Secret Armies: Operation Gladio and Terrorism in Western Europe*, and Richard Cottrell, *Gladio, NATO's Dagger at the Heart of Europe*, Stay Behind had rapidly become a secret policy committee—a sort of Western Stasi—in charge of taming any internal menace threatening the capitalist status quo, by any means necessary. Including the cunning manipulation of existing terrorist groups and the creation of synthetic ones, a tactic known as a False Flag operation, or closing an eye on the preparation of genuine terrorist attacks while having them monitored all the way, the Let-it-happen tactic.

It was anything goes for the sake of fighting Communism: from recruiting neo-Nazis and neo-Fascists to colluding with the mafias, to dealing drugs and weapons back and forth through a surprisingly permeable Iron Curtain.

Sporting the biggest Communist party in the Western world, Italy would soon become the favorite playground for these Men in Black—just much more sinister than Will Smith and Tommy Lee Jones.

For us Italians, Andreotti's disclosure was no disclosure, really.

We might not have known the name Gladio before, but it was understood that corrupt government agencies—*servizi deviati*, in Italian—had lent more than one hand to the terrorists, with the support of a foreign power. Add that it was clear to everybody that Italy was a de facto U.S. protectorate and you can fill in the blanks yourself.

I understand that here is where the American mind and the European mind diverge. Consciously or unconsciously, most Americans think, "they couldn't, they wouldn't," whereas a European would think, "they not only could and would, but actually *did*."

Therefore, it is even more to Gabriel Valjan's credit that with *Threading the Needle* he, as an American, was nonetheless capable of unusual insight into the *Misteri Italiani*, the Italian Mysteries, without taking any prejudicial standpoint, one way or the other, or putting the blame on anyone, but rather inviting readers to judge for themselves.

Threading the Needle is set in my hometown of Milan and this made it more emotional to me. This authorial decision is further evidence of Valjan's insight into the complexity of Italian culture, for Milan is a cosmopolitan city. A workaholic melting-pot; people from all corners of the country; foreigners, and all the Italian contradictions, from the North-South divide to the clash between tradition and strong family values on one side, and the globalized society on the other. Ever since the country's unification in 1870, known as il Risorgimento in Italian, Milan has been the home to all the major changes in Italy. Fascism was founded here in 1922 and it ended here in 1945; Mussolini was hanged, upside down, in Piazzale Loreto; the Strategy of Tension started here with Piazza Fontana in 1969, and it is here that the tidal wave of the "Clean Hands" or Mani pulite operation swept away the corrupt traditional parties in 1992 to end the First Republic and witness the rise of "the Berlusconi phenomenon."

Unlike most Americans, who look in puzzled stupor at a certain European intolerance towards alleged American arrogance, Valjan tries to understand the European reasons by putting more recent episodes of such arrogance into the context of this scenario.

This is the case with the so-called *Cermis Incident* of 1998, which he weaves into the plot: a reckless U.S. Marine Corps pilot and his navigator jolly-riding their Prowlers too low to the ground severed a cable line and caused a cable-car cabin to fall to the ground. Twenty people of different European nationalities plunged over two hundred feet to their deaths. Italian investigators had to concede jurisdiction to the U.S. military and the pilots were acquitted after a rushed mock trial in the U.S.

The images of the Marines walking out of the court as free men and smiling were a slap in the face to the victims' families.

With the tearing down of the Berlin Wall in 1989, Communism was dead, one could say. Gladio was now history.

Maybe. But . . . Why destroy what works?

This is the doubt that Valjan casts in the brilliant plot of *Threading the Needle*, the question he asks every reader to answer according to his or her own conscience and understanding.

When the anti-mafia judges Giovanni Falcone and Paolo Borsellino were killed one shortly after the other in 1992, they were investigating the murky relations between top Mafiosi and prominent politicians. Their assassinations demonstrated that those relationships, which had once been justified in the name of the fight against Communism, were still in place after the Red Threat had become only a memory.

Threading the needle is to trust the thread, and the skillful hand, and not to fear that the needle will stab the finger. Following the thread, however, is not easy. Threading requires skill and instinct, the up-and-down, back-and-forth, and over-and-under of logic.

Cui bono? is the question that helps us thread the needle through the fabric of history. To whose benefit? The question the author asks us to answer before the bodies of Lele Palmisano—a living contradiction:

openly gay, a Communist and a Catholic, and from macho, traditional southern Italy—and of Charlie Brooks, a young American student, maybe too curious, maybe too clever.

In doing so, he metaphorically provokes us to ask ourselves the same question in relation to all those real-life political killings for which a culprit—often conveniently alone and insane, a *useful idiot*—was found suspiciously too soon. From JFK's assassination to 9/11, from Pim Fortuyn in the Netherlands to Olof Palme in Sweden and the more recent Utøya Island slaughter in Norway.

Rewind.

Go back to that sunny March morning now.

And ask yourself: *Cui bono?* To whose benefit?

The Moro killing is considered the turning point in the history of Italian left-wing terrorism. Until then, the Red Brigades had enjoyed a certain degree of support from the working classes in the big industrial cities of northern Italy. Kidnapping and killing a politician who was respected by one and all, no matter what the political affiliation, backfired against the *Brigatisti* and marked the beginning of their end.

Why such an inappropriate choice?

If they were powerful enough to reach the president of the ruling party, why not aim at a much less beloved figure, such as Giulio Andreotti himself, nicknamed *Beelzebub*, among other names?

And why later would the hardcore among the *Brigatisti* call Moro's kidnappers *traitors* during the trial?

Maybe Moro's faults had not been against the proletariat, after all.

Moro was the man who had been stubbornly seeking an agreement between his own Christian Democrat party and the Communist party, the great heresy known as *Compromesso Storico*, the Historical Compromise, even though Nixon's messenger, Henry Kissinger, himself had warned him that he would "pay dearly for it," as Malcolm Moore reported in his March 11, 2008 article in London's *The Telegraph*, "U.S. Envoy Admits Role in Aldo Moro Killing," and also cited in Arthur E. Rowse's "Gladio: The Secret U.S. War to Subvert Italian Democracy," *Covert Action Quarterly* (Washington DC: Summer 1994).

Moro was also the man whose moral suasion, back in that December 1969, had prevented the president of the Republic from declaring a state of emergency and paving the way to a neo-Fascist *golpe*.

Investigative journalist Mino Pecorelli exposed in coded language the key persons involved in the Moro kidnapping and killing, and their political motivations. He had also mysteriously acquired Moro's letters written in captivity and published them. Pecorelli's barbed missives suggested that Moro's location had been known all along and that inaction had been deliberate. Moro had to die because Italy could not become Communist. Pecorelli's code had been explicit enough to get him killed: he was gunned down in his car in Rome in 1979.

Cui bono?

Today, just as then, those with power who wish to advance a political agenda must shape public sentiment, compel public cooperation. Unfortunately, it is much easier to do all of this through violent means, because it is impossible to unite everyone through reason alone; easier to fabricate belief through disorientation and fear, through mythology; and when the enemy is vanquished it is time to create another enemy. A mechanism is in place. The means justify the end and—the end justifies the means.

This afterword has traced a disturbing parallel between the Italian Years of Lead and 9/11. In both cases one can believe either the official truth or the numerous conspiracy theories or something in between. However, the idea that utilizing terrorism to coerce cooperation with authoritarian law and order is, to some, a heavy but acceptable price to pay, keeps uncomfortably lingering over our heads after we finish reading *Threading the Needle*.

No court will say a government orders assassinations, although some Italian courts did try to do so, as in the Abu Omar case. But when the enemy is defeated and the complex apparatus is still turning its gears, still has its offices and dutiful workers, then it is either time to close shop or invent a new boogeyman.

April 2013, Year of Italian Culture in the United States

Post Scriptum
Shortly after finishing this Afterword, I heard the sad news about what happened at the Boston Marathon. I had wanted to end my short essay with a hint that, in these times of a global economy, financial terrorism is the more probable scenario than traditional outbursts of violence, and that the current sovereign debt crisis in Europe is the first example of a strategy of financial tension. However, destiny would seem to have decided otherwise. Three innocent persons, including an eight-year-old, lost their lives, and 170 were seriously injured in an act that bears all the hallmarks of a typical strategy of tension scheme: people hit at random, no claims from known terrorist groups, mysterious individuals spotted while running away from the crime scene, and not from places where you would expect a bomber to be fleeing from. The path to truth about April 2013 in Boston will be a long and difficult one, as the authorities sift through and examine in the minutest detail all the evidence, both physical and photographic. And, whatever the outcome, it is another demonstration that one does not destroy what works.

Turning to Stone

The Fourth Installment of the Roma Series
2014 Release

1

"We should go, Alessandro," Gennaro said.

"Just a minute, Boss. I'm waiting to see what the financial analysts have to say."

"We can listen to the news in the car."

"I know, but why wait when we can get the forecast now."

Alessandro, standing near the office's flat-screen television, clicker in hand, spiked the volume. Gennaro DiBello resigned himself to staring out of the high-rise window, overlooking the Bay of Naples. He saw a U.S. destroyer in the distance en route to Bagnoli.

Dante was putting his papers away before leaving for lunch. He put the stack into his desk drawer, locked it, and began the ritual of backing up his electronic files to a jump key and powering down his monitor. Living with Bianca was showing in his daily work habits. Silvio was at his desk, in his own world, with his own mound of paperwork, his Italian-English dictionary closed but ready.

"Here they are," Alessandro pointed the remote at the screen and stepped up the volume again. He was a defiant kid who had to get the last word, Gennaro thought.

Gennaro saw their boss, Pio Piersanti, approaching. "Incoming."

"What is it?" Alessandro said and, seeing Piersanti through the glass, shut off the television.

"What's the word, DiBello?" asked the man entering the room.

"The word is nothing."

"Monotti," Piersanti gestured toward Alessandro, "turn that back on. I want to see what they have to say."

The television came back on. A scrolling marquee on the bottom of the screen repeated Moody's judgment: Downgrade on Italian bonds.

Piersanti's face soured. "Shit. There goes the bond auction tomorrow." He turned from the screen to Gennaro and said, "Shouldn't you be on your way to meet with Giurlani, DiBello?"

"I am. We are. I'm waiting for them."

"Late lunch," Piersanti said, confirming the time on his wristwatch.

"Yes, and then we're back here to give our reports to you and Giurlani."

"Excellent. Giurlani has a lot of faith in you and your group here. He pulled some serious strings to get your team transferred from Milan to Naples, including Isidore Farrugia. The Brooks murder was a PR nightmare. I don't know how he did it."

"I thought the answer was simple: Aldo Giurlani is the regional commissioner, and when Milan talks, Naples and Rome listen. If you'll excuse me, we should get going."

"I won't delay you. You and this crew of yours have healthy appetites so please don't kill me on the expense report. My boss might think I'm in bed with the System." System was local slang for the Camorra, the infamous Naples crime syndicate.

Pio Piersanti, Gennaro's new boss, was a decent man, with an alliterative and triplet of holy names. Unlike Pinolo, Gennaro's former boss in Rome, he wasn't a penny-pincher or a ball-breaker.

"Dottore?" It was Enzo, the mail clerk.

"Something for me?"

"Yes. I have a package. You'll have to sign for it."

"What is it?"

"Books in English. All the same title and author," the young man answered.

Gennaro's name and address were typed out. No name in the sender space. All rather peculiar, Gennaro mumbled. He hadn't forgotten the heightened security measures. The postmark was days old because the Neapolitan Guardia di Finanza Security downstairs used canine units for sniffing out suspicious parcels for chemicals and explosives. Security was not victim to Italy's latest austerity measures.

Gennaro signed and handed over the clipboard. Enzo left and Alessandro, Dante, and Silvio gathered around him as he examined the contents. The enclosed books were rubber-banded together. Five copies.

"What is it, Chief? Looks like a thin volume. Poetry?"

"You're just like a kid, Sandro. You know that?"

Dante looked at the cardboard mailer and noticed the postmark. "Better for a package to be late than have someone go to pieces. Literally. Security probably dusted this for prints."

"C'mon, Boss. What is the title?" Alessandro pestered.

"*The Man of Smoke*. Aldo Palazzeschi, a dead writer," Gennaro answered.

"Why five copies, Chief? And why in English?" Alessandro asked.

"How the hell should I know?" Gennaro said, as his eyebrows lifted. "There are four of us here. One for each of us, I guess, but that leaves one extra copy."

Dante took his copy and then another. They all looked at him.

"One for Bianca since she is part of the team. Now, let's go meet the Commissioner for lunch. The elevator is waiting. Shall we?"

Alessandro said to Gennaro when the bell chimed, "Palazzeschi was the pen name for Aldo Giurlani."

"I know, Sandro. He was an anti-Fascist."

Commissioner Aldo Giurlani, who had worked with them in Milan, had insisted on meeting the group in the city center for lunch. A public place was best, he had said, but had kept his travel itinerary secret. All

Gennaro knew was the name of the restaurant, the appointed hour, and that the commissioner was arriving by car with a modest security detail. The commissioner, who had been receiving death threats, was fast becoming a worthy successor of Paolo Borsellino and Giovanni Falcone for his innovative strategies against organized crime.

Gennaro, at the wheel, was suddenly stalled in a stagnant sea of cars on Via San Biagio. They heard them in the distance, but could not see any emergency vehicles in the side-view mirror. *Nee-nah. Nee-nah.*

"What the hell is going on?" Alessandro said in the backseat.

"No idea," Gennaro answered, peering in his side view mirror.

People were running on foot between cars, around them, like water around rocks. The flood of flesh was fleeing like hordes of humanity in a science-fiction film. Gennaro gripped the wheel, seeking some escape with his small Fiat Punto. He had navigated the construction site around the Greek and Roman ruins, passed remnants of colonial rule, ignored the Fascist architecture of Banca di Napoli on Via Toledo. Yet there he sat, stranded, adrift, among motionless cars, surrounded by people on foot. As he surveyed the congestion as far as the eye could see, he realized he could get out of his Punto, walk over to the Banca Commerciale Italiana, visit the Caravaggio on the second floor, light a votive, before any car began to move again.

Sandro's finger tapped his shoulder. "There's a lollipop." One of the carabinieri, a blue-suited policeman with a Stop-and-Go paddle, had come out to direct traffic.

As the policeman's torso neared his window, Gennaro rolled the window down and showed his identification, asking for an explanation. There was the intimation of smoke in the summer air, Gennaro could smell it. The policeman held up his lollipop and peered down and surveyed the group inside the car. The policeman tipped his hat.

"There's been a car bombing in the Spanish Quarter on Via San Gregorio Armeno."

"Camorra?"

The officer shrugged. "Perhaps. I can use my whistle to move you to the curb."

"We're supposed to meet someone for lunch."

"I'm afraid that you're not going anywhere, unless you can fly. I will direct you to the side of the road. Park there and call your party on your cell phone. You will be at least half an hour late. They still have to cordon off the scene."

"Shit," Gennaro said. He slapped the steering wheel hard. He decided to admit defeat. He said to the cop, "That'll do, thank you."

After several loud whistle blows and slow, painful cuts of the wheel and hostile stares from other drivers, Gennaro managed to squeeze his Punto near the curb. His parallel parking would have failed a driver's exam. Giurlani was going to be pissed off, but what could he do?

"Let's get out and see what we can of the scene," he told his passengers. Dante exited from the passenger side, Alessandro and Silvio maneuvered out of the backseat. Once he was on the sidewalk, Gennaro flipped open the cell phone and speed-dialed Giurlani. Without saying a word they started walking uphill in the direction of the acrid stench until they saw wisps of black and grey smoke.

"No luck getting through to Giurlani?" Dante asked.

"I'm trying, but he's not picking up."

Dante's own cell phone began to ring. He fished it out of his jacket pocket. "Pronto . . . Isidò? Where are you?" Dante stood still and the rest waited for him to say something. Dante cupped the receiver. "Farrugia heard about the car bombing. He's at the restaurant. I'll tell him that we'll be late." A few words later Dante closed his phone.

They traversed the cobblestones together. Farrugia had been working undercover to track the Camorra's trade in steroids and recreational drugs. Narcotics work was where he had started his career until he became an anti-mafia expert. Illicit drugs in Naples were yet another hothouse of endless euros for the System.

"It smells nasty," Alessandro said, squinting his eyes and coughing.

"Burnt rubber and melting plastic are the worst," Dante said, while Gennaro tried Giurlani again on his cell phone. Dante noticed but didn't say a word.

"No answer," Gennaro said, snapping the cell phone shut.

The stench and smoke worsened as they crested the hill. They saw the car and several policemen across the street. Firemen had yet to arrive. The car and its contents were nothing now but crackling flames and twisted steel. The top of the car had been sheared off at a jagged angle. A torso in what was the driver's seat was still visible, smoldering, as well as the shape of an arm and a hand faithful to the wheel. The passenger in the backseat was nothing more than a charcoal stump of charred flesh. Gennaro thought of the late Vonnegut, *Slaughterhouse Five*, and fried jumbo grasshoppers.

Alessandro, flashing his badge, called over to one of the cops, who began walking toward them. "What happened?" Alessandro asked.

"Witnesses said the car was coming down the street when three motor-cyclists ambushed it. One motorcyclist came out in front to block the car. The driver jammed on his brakes. Two gunmen with Kalashnikovs on the other motorcycles sprayed the car while the one in front took out a bazooka or an RPG and fired it into the car."

The young policeman pointed to the ejected shell casings and shat-tered glass on the stony street.

"A bazooka, an RPG?" Alessandro asked. "I wouldn't expect wit-nesses to know the difference between a bazooka and a rocket-propelled grenade." Alessandro wiped his tearing eyes. "Did any of the witnesses have anything to say about the gunmen or the victims?"

"Not really. The motorcyclists wore helmets, visors down. Three men were in the car. We'll know more once we trace the plates."

"Camorristi with AK-47s. Typical," Dante said.

Gennaro, like the rest of them, looked at the license plate. Milan.

Dante said, "Maybe you should call Giurlani again, Chief?"

"That won't be necessary."

"Why not?"

"Still have that book?"

"It's in the car. Why?"

"Because the books were a message." Gennaro stared at the car wreck. His eyes seemed distant and immune to the smoke.

Alessandro looked over at Dante for an explanation. "What is he talking about?"

Gennaro answered. "Aldo Palazzeschi was a pen name. You said so yourself, Sandro."

"For Aldo Giurlani, why?"

Gennaro nudged his chin at the wreckage. "Dante's book might be in my car, but Giurlani is in that one."

Alessandro looked confused, even alarmed, as his head moved between Gennaro and the violent scene. He stared at Gennaro for an explanation.

"That's the message. Our Commissioner Giurlani is now a man of smoke."

Gennaro started his descent back to his car.

Nee-nah. Nee-nah. The sirens had arrived.

Acknowledgements

My gratitude for:

Dean Hunt, with his vigiliant pen, who proofed again and again.

Line-editor Dave King, for his love of Bach and Catarella.

Claudio Ferrara, my Virgil, through the dark woods of Italian history.

Sherry Foley, whose watchful eyes read the draft and saved me from myself.

Deb Well, another critical pair of eyes and ears on dialog and plotting.

James Logan and Jessica Kristie at Winter Goose, who continue to believe in me.

Caitlyn DiPompo, for her encouraging words and for reading what I write.

Rachel Anderson, publicist extraordinaire.

My readers at Dana: Georgina Morales Hampe, Karen Brousseau, Marty McClellan, and Margaret Taggart.

About the Author

Ronan Bennett short-listed Gabriel Valjan for the *2010 Fish Short Story Prize* for his Boston noir, "Back in the Day." Gabriel's short stories and some of his poetry continue to appear in literary journals and online magazines. He recently won first prize in *ZOUCH* Magazine's inaugural Lit Bit Contest. He lives in New England but has traveled extensively, receiving his undergraduate education in California and completing graduate school in England.

CPSIA information can be obtained at www.ICGtesting.com
Printed in the USA
LVOW06s2341161113

361608LV00004B/729/P